A-zou: A Woman Living in Interesting Times

Additional books by author:

Firehouse Fraternity Oral History Series:
Volume I: Becoming a Firefighter
Volume II: Life Between Alarms
Volume III: Equipment
Volume IV: Responding
Volume V: Riots to Renaissance
Volume VI: Changing the NFD

The Newark Riots: A View from the Firehouse

An Eerie Silence: An Oral History of Newark
Firefighters at the WTC

Hervey's Boys: New Jersey's First Chinese Community
1870-1886 (And What Happened After That)

Fiction:
The Firebox Stalker
The Hand Life Dealt you

Children's Fiction:
A Hundred Battles (YA)
A Broken Glass (YA)
Balancing Act (Middle Grade)

A-zou: A Woman Living in Interesting Times

Neal Stoffers

Springfield and Hunterdon Publishing
Copyright 2019
www.newarkfireoralhistory.com

First Printing: 2019

ISBN 978-1-970034-24-0

Springfield and Hunterdon Publishing
East Brunswick, NJ 08816

Chapter One

A sudden jolt shook Victoria Phaff awake. Flights across the Pacific were rarely peaceful. How many times had she flown from New Jersey to Taiwan? A month had been spent visiting her mother's family there every summer since her birth. That would make this the twenty-fourth visit to the island Mama had once called home, although this was the second flight of the year. The first had been spent visiting. Now they were going to say a final farewell to A-zou. Her great-grandmother had slipped from this life peacefully after ninety-six interesting years of living. The curse, "May you live in interesting times" came to mind. A-zou had certainly done that.

Vicki roused herself and glanced at the small screen imbedded in the back of the seat she was facing. The glowing green on black map indicated they were about two hours from Taipei. Another bit of turbulence reminded her to look to her right. If ever there was a white knuckled flyer, it was Wei Jia-yi. A quick look revealed Mama sitting nervously staring at a movie on her screen, obviously no longer enjoying it. It always surprised people when she told them her mother hated flying. Thirty years before she had earned her living as an airline stewardess. A smile crossed Vicki's face remembering a teenage outburst when she laughed at her mother's fear. That little bit of artistry had cost her a week of socializing with her friends. Her father had explained afterwards that Mama had been on a Korean Airlines flight the day before the Soviets had shot down Flight 07. Even though the Soviet Union was no more, the former stewardess could not shake thoughts of disaster from her mind. In contrast, Dad was sleeping in the seat beyond Mama. Ed Phaff slept through anything. A talent he inherited from his father who was known to sleep through air raids when he served in Europe during the Second World War.

She straightened herself and reached for the cookie left over from dinner. Experience told her breakfast would be coming around shortly, but she needed to munch on something while reviewing her predicament. A jumble of contradictory emotions pulsed through her mind as she bit off a piece of the almond cookie. She was saddened by the passing of A-zou, yet her great-grandmother's death opened up possibilities that had not existed before their last trip back. Somehow, Vicki had the feeling that the old girl had outwitted the system one last time. The whites and grays of the plane's interior were soothing to the eye while the dull roar of an aluminum fuselage pushing through the atmosphere provided a steady background hum for her thoughts.

She and A-zou had shared an unusual relationship based exclusively on visual cues and tender touches. A-zou had spoken only Taiwanese. Vicki spoke English and Mandarin. There could be no quiet sharing of stories from another time, no private little secrets between the two of them. Instead her great-grandmother had given unconditional love mixed with beaming pride. Vicki had spent her entire life basking in it and would sorely miss it, but A-zou had given her one last gift before she left. A gift that could change the course of her life and lead to happiness or to despair, she would know which before returning to the States.

The auburn haired woman stretched a little as she gathered her thoughts. Thank God they now flew in deluxe class instead of the economy seating of her youth. Deluxe gave her room to extend her legs freely. They were one of her most attractive features thanks to her love of dance. The extra leg room would normally have made sleeping easy. In that way she was daddy's girl, but not this trip. It had been a day and a half since she had anything resembling quality sleep. They had been in transit for twenty-two exhausting hours, but sleep still eluded her.

Mama noticed her daughter was awake. She took off her headset and asked, "You cannot sleep?"

"I have a lot on my mind," Vicki sighed before asking the one woman who might be able to answer the questions haunting her. "Do you think Zhi-mei *A-yi* will be there?"

"*A-yi?*" her mother replied. "What did A-hong say?"

"He wasn't sure. They were having a lot of mother-son conversations, but not about A-zou."

"I wouldn't expect them to discuss A-zou. But I think it would be un-filial and ungrateful of her if she did not attend."

"Do you think she will speak with me?"

Mama hesitated for a moment, as if trying to soften the blow. "No, I do not think she wants to talk with you and I don't think you should force yourself on her. You are no longer the cute little cousin who helped her son study English. She thinks you have become the biggest threat to her happiness."

The stewardesses were beginning to serve breakfast, so Vicki quietly accepted her mother's words. It was not as if the pronouncement was a surprise. She shared the assessment. How had this conundrum developed? Accompanying Mama on her visit the past summer had only been an excuse to get some distance from the last of a long line of failed relationships. Chill out in Taiwan, figuratively speaking considering the heat of a Taiwanese summer, and ask A-zou some genealogy questions. That had been the planned method of forgetting about Roger. She could remember her mother's disapproval and warnings as if it were yesterday.

****

"So, what did you not like about Roger?" The question caught Vicki by surprise. Not the bluntness of it, that was a given. It was the fact that her mother had mentioned a boyfriend by name. Usually she did not attempt to remember or even pronounce the name of her date, but Mama seemed to really like Roger. They were standing in front of the stuffed brown bear at Anchorage International Airport waiting for their continuation flight to Taipei. Announcements for flights echoed in the background as tired travelers quietly sat waiting, resigned to their fate. The first seven hours of their trip had been uneventful. It was the next nine hours in the air that would be most grueling. Not because of the flight. The challenge would be Mama's question. Vicki had been anticipating it for the past month. Her mother's tone said the conversation was not going to be pleasant.

Looking away from the bear, Vicki saw the sun dip below the horizon. In a few minutes it would reappear, beginning a new day in a land of the midnight sun. How should she answer her mother's query? The truth would surely produce a flurry of impatient, annoying, and unanswerable questions. Experience had taught her the truth had a nasty way of coming out at the most inopportune times, so she sighed and plunged in.

"Roger had issues."

"Issues? What kind of issues?" her mother snapped. "An engineering honors student with so many job offers, tall, handsome, respectful, what more could you ask for?"

Vicki paused a moment, not wanting to blurt out something that would come back to bite her. "Our personalities were not in sync." Her mother's facial expression instantly changed from quizzical to disapproving.

"What does this mean, 'not in sync'?" she shot back.

"We weren't on the same page," Vicki answered defensively, instantly realizing Mama would not understand that idiom any more than the last one. "There was no real connection between us. He's a great guy, but not what I'm looking for."

Mama was becoming more agitated with each response from her daughter. Vicki was trying with everything she had to avoid using the explanation she had used so many times before. "He's not an A-hong." How had her cousin become the gold standard upon which all of her relationships were judged? It had been cute until he had come to study at Rutgers. Then their relationship had evolved and the turnover rate of her boyfriends had picked up. The significance of that change had not been lost on her parents. Her mother had suddenly become hypercritical of her dating habits. Now Mama's laser sharp focus was aimed at the one subject Vicki was trying to exorcise from her consciousness. There was little in the terminal at this time of night to provide a distraction. Most of the shops were closed. Calls for flights produced some movement among the passengers seated around them, but not enough to draw Mama's attention.

"Not what you are looking for?" was the exasperated response. "You have to sharpen your eyes. You cannot have what you are looking for. Do not ruin your life searching for someone who does not exist. There is only one of each of us, only one A-hong. He is your cousin. You cannot change that, so you have to change how you measure men. Roger was a perfect fit."

Vicki felt anger rising inside her. How could her mother be so insensitive? The pain of breaking with Roger was still too fresh. He may have been a perfect fit for Mama, but she was not the one who would have to live with him. She was oblivious to the incessant arguments and his need to control. He had treated her like an engineering problem that could be solved with a standard formula. He had never spoken to her heart, had never really shared his inner most self. The man had started out with such promise, only to turn into a two dimensional mind that could not break free of the world he knew. He was a nice guy with whom to share a drink, but not one with whom to share your life. There would be no challenging her mind with deep philosophical discussions from Roger. If it could not be resolved with some sort of algorithm, he was lost. After a prolonged inner battle, she had admitted to the obvious and ended the affair. A-hong had nothing to do with it.

"Mama, I think we should end this discussion," swallowing her anger. "There was more wrong with that relationship than you realize." The call for their flight gave them both an excuse to drop the subject. They began making their way to the boarding gate. There was no further exchange until they were airborne.

After her mother had settled in and calmed down, Vicki tried to change the subject.

"Will A-zou be able to handle my questions?" she asked cautiously.

"Able to? Of course," her mother chuckled. "Willing to? I don't know. There were so many topics that were hushed up when I was growing up, so many things left unsaid."

Vicki had heard this before, but she was hopeful since all she wanted were the names of A-zou's parents and grandparents. Anything else would be gravy. Her worry was not great-grandma's willingness to speak. Would her health allow her to answer the questions? Mama had said A-zou's strength was waning. Fleeing the memory of Roger was only one reason she was returning to Taiwan. She could not shake the feeling that this would be her last chance to say goodbye. Liver disease was slowly consuming A-zou.

They settled into the routine of an international flight. Stewardesses came around with bags of peanuts, customs forms, and glasses of water. The seatbelt light went off. People pulled their tablets out of the seat arms and began filling out the forms. Neither she nor Mama had anything to declare. What could you possibly bring to a dying ninety-five year old woman other than love? Vicki felt the greatest gift she could give A-zou was the knowledge that her family tree would be preserved. If a genealogy of her mother's family even existed, it did not include any females. In androcentric Taiwan, only males had a place on the family tree. After taking a course in genealogy, Vicki had traced the Phaff family back to the 17th century. Granted a distant cousin of her father's had done much of the heavy lifting, but she had spent quite a bit of time pouring through old records to fill in the gaps. It was time consuming and in the end very rewarding. The final result was a feeling of connection with the past. It was one thing to read about the Civil War, but another when she found out her paternal great-great grandfather had fought at Petersburg. The challenges of working on her mother's side where enticing, although she would need help. Did records even exist from the Imperial period? Did the Japanese keep records from the colonial period? Most importantly, would her relatives be willing to talk about it? Her mother had always been reluctant. Whenever Vicki had asked Mama had put her off, saying it was a boring story and then changed the subject.

Even though they had already had one spat, Vicki felt the need to push her mother for more information. If she asked the right questions, A-zou might be willing to share more of her story, but she needed more information to formulate those questions.

"Mama, what do you know about A-zou?"

"About A-zou? Not very much," was the answer. "I was not allowed to ask questions. It was always 'hush', do not talk about such things. I have overheard conversations, but did not understand all that was said."

"Didn't understand?" Vicki puzzled.

"Yes, some are childhood memories, others are from when I was older, but I was not part of the conversation," she recalled. "As soon as they realized I was in the room, the conversation ended."

Vicki remembered a few times when conversations between A-ma and A-zou had come to an abrupt end as soon as Mama had stepped into a room. She did not remember the tone of those discussions as being pleasant. What could they be hiding?

"Can you tell me what you know about A-zou's life?" she asked tentatively.

"I guess you are old enough now," Mama sighed.

"Old enough?" Vicki thought. What could have possibly happened that would require censorship?

"I know that my grandfather died while my mother was young," she began. "The story told to me was he died of pneumonia, but I am not sure that is true. He and A-zou had a candy shop. They were supposed to have developed a prize winning treat. After he died she ran the store, which was remarkable at that time. Since A-zou only had daughters, she raised A-ma as if she were a son. Probably, she was hoping A-ma would take care of her when she grew old." She paused for a moment as if she were collecting her thoughts. This gave Vicki a chance to ask a question.

"Was her marriage arranged?"

"I'm sure it was, but that was never spoken about," Mama answered quietly. "A-ma's marriage was arranged. I know that. She worked in a bank and A-gong's father came in, saw her, and asked a matchmaker to arrange it."

This was new to Vicki. Her mother had never spoken about her grandfather. He had died when she was a toddler. The cause of his death was never explained. Mama was not the only one who was "hushed" after asking the wrong question.

"What do you remember about your father?" she asked trying to follow the flow of the conversation, but with a bad feeling in her gut. She watched her mother instantly shut down.

"I thought we were talking about A-zou," Mama chided. "We have a long flight. Why don't you sleep a little? We can talk later."

They never did.

Chapter Two

The hotel van pulled off Zhongshan North Road and began to climb the hill toward the Grand Hotel. Vicki was exhausted and frustrated. A little voice had told her not to go there when she asked about her grandfather. She might be old enough to hear A-zou's story, but the subject of A-gong was still taboo. The van slowly climbed the hill. A wide set of white marble stairs with carvings of dragons marched up the incline on their left. A rarely used tree covered walkway leading up from the street ascended on the right. She remembered playing "stoop ball" on the marble stairs as a child. Bouncing a rubber ball off a grand marble "stoop" seemed natural at the time. It was not until she grew a little older that she realized most tourists used the stairs as a photo op, primarily because of what rose up beyond them.

Beyond the stairs a tall set of arches covered with red, green, and gold designs from the Imperial period stood guardian over a walkway. These provided the foreground for what was claimed to be the only hotel in the world designed as a Chinese Imperial palace. Huge red pillars reached up twelve stories to a golden colored pagoda like roof. Balconies for the hotel rooms filled in the space between the pillars. The red, green, and gold designs of the arches were replicated on the balconies and walls of the main building. A canopy similar in design to the roof so many stories above it protected the entrance to the lobby. This rested on less substantial but equally impressive pillars. A dozen large flags of the Republic of China stood guard on the left of arriving taxis, vans, and limousines, flapping vigorously in a continuous breeze while doormen waited for guests to alight.

The van pulled under the canopy, revealing floor to ceiling glass windows that allowed a view of the largest hotel lobby in the world. As soon as the van rolled to a halt, the doormen, garbed in tan uniforms with hats, jackets, and white gloves sprang into action. When they saw who occupied the van, large smiles creased their faces. These men were like family. They had watched Vicki grow up.

"Ah, little Vicki!" David called out in accented English. "Long time no see!" His name tag displayed his English name above his Chinese name. She had always thought David was appropriate since his Chinese name was De Wei. She had called him uncle since she could talk.

"Shushu, zhende hao jiu bu jian," she replied in Mandarin. It had been more than a year since she had been here after all. The men swarming over the van quickly switched to Taiwanese to greet her mother as they snatched up their luggage. The two women grabbed their purses and staggered through the hot, humid air and the opened ornate glass doors into the welcomed coolness of the lobby.

Large red pillars marched in pairs toward a white marble staircase, forming a natural corridor that was lined with display cases. The floors were covered with huge, plush, deep red oriental rugs. Greetings were shouted as they walked to the front desk. A stranger might mistake their notoriety for fame, but it was simply friendship. Over the years her mother had given advice and comfort or just a simple compliment to so many of the people who worked here. The Taiwanese had long memories for kindness.

They strolled toward the staircase at the far end of the lobby. The same thick rugs that covered the lobby floor caressed each stair. On the wall at the top of the first flight of the staircase was a large bronze sculpture depicting a scene from the classic book *Shi Ji* by Si-Ma Qian. The staircase divided in two at this landing, branching off to the left and right leading to a mezzanine level. A coffee shop, open 24/7 for the international patrons who arrived at any time of the day, was located here. She had gone here once as a child with her dad and ordered a grill cheese sandwich. Dad had thought it was cute. Mama was not happy. Each of the floors above the mezzanine was decorated in the style of a different imperial dynasty, although only academics and China specialists could appreciate it.

Chairs and tables were placed strategically throughout the lobby, allowing for quiet conversation in comfort. She often wondered how many business deals had been sealed here. They turned to the right before the stairs and marched to the front desk. A long carved marble counter provided ample room for the discrete conversations sometimes necessary at an international hotel. No discretion was possible or attempted when Wei Jia-yi returned.

"Ah, yo!" the senior woman at check-in shouted in Mandarin, "I've been waiting for you."

Her mother responded with equal enthusiasm, quickly switching to Taiwanese leaving Vicki out of the conversation. Ten years before, this would have upset her. Why speak Taiwanese when everyone speaks Mandarin? She had since learned that it was comforting for Mama to speak her mother tongue, so Vicki accepted it. She went to collapse in one of the nearby seats, resigned to a long incomprehensible conversation, when she heard her name called.

"Sue!" she said a little too loudly. "What are you doing here?"

Her cousin Wei Su-hui was walking toward her from the direction of the ladies room under the staircase. Vicki rarely used Su-hui's Chinese name, instead shortening it to Sue when they spoke English and in Taiwan they usually preferred the semi-privacy that language gave them. In America they reversed it, speaking Mandarin, although she still did not use Su-hui's given name. Instead, following Chinese tradition, Vicki addressed her younger cousin as *meimei.*

"Vicki," Sue laughed. "I was hoping Joe might be with you."

If Sue were American, Vicki would have thrown a bear hug around her. It was so good to see her, but when in China do as the Chinese do. Instead of a hug, she reached out and held both her cousins hands, an exhausted but very genuine smile on her face.

"Joe?" she teased. "Still crazy for my cousin?"

"He said he was going to try and fly with you," was the defensive reply.

"First, he had too much to do before the trip," Vicki explained. "But even if dad could have shaken him loss, there wasn't room on the plane for all three of us. He'll be here tomorrow."

"Tomorrow?" the word was laced with disappointment. "Oh well, but you must be exhausted. Let's sit and talk while your mother checks in."

They sank into two chairs with a small table between them. Dropping their purses on the table, they leaned toward each other.

"So, what happened with Roger?" Sue asked.

"Oh, bad subject," Vicki sighed. "Mama jumped all over me. I have unrealistic expectations. Roger was perfect. Well, Roger may be a math and science whiz, but he didn't have a clue about how to talk to a lady."

Sue laughed when she heard this. She had never met him, but Joe had. Vicki knew Joe's opinion and it was not positive. It was obvious her cousins had discussed her love life and agreed with her choice. That was reassuring after the little tiff with Mama.

"And how are things with Joe?" Vicki probed.

"You know how long term relationships go," Sue answered with a coy smile.

"Long term?" Vicki laughed. "Why long term? Because you've known him so long? I wouldn't call it a relationship until after he graduated."

"Well that's two years," Sue shot back. "Compared to some women I know, that's very long term."

"Ouch," Vicki complained. "That hurt."

"Sorry," Sue apologized." I couldn't resist. You left yourself wide open."

"I'm tired. Hey, quick change of subject. How is A-zou really doing? Sometimes my mother gets dramatic."

"A-zou? "Sue replied. "Not well. Her liver is failing. Is that why your mom came now?"

"Yes, she thinks this may be the last chance we'll get to see her."

"My father agrees," Sue sighed. "He doesn't think she will make it to the new year."

If that proved to be true, then they were here to say good-bye. This gave her even more impetus to push her genealogy project forward. She wondered, could Sue help?

"What do you know about A-zou?" she asked on a lark. Maybe her uncle was more open about the subject than his sister.

Sue grew quiet for a moment before confessing, "Not much at all. Whenever I asked my father, he would just chuckle and say she was a mystery. A-ma would only snap at me if I asked. So I gave up. A-zou never volunteered anything. Why do you ask?"

Vicki exhaled slowly in frustration. Parents and grandparents were supposed to encourage children to ask questions about their family history. Why did her family seem so closed mouth?

"I want to ask A-zou about her family, her parents and grandparents. Trace the family back as far as I can," she explained. Then a thought crossed her mind that might solve any language problems without involving her mother. "Sue, how good is your Taiwanese?"

Her cousin laughed. "My English is way better, *Laoshi*. Taiwanese is kind of limited to simple everyday conversational, shopping vocabulary and of course scolding."

Vicki accepted Sue calling her "teacher". After so many summers tutoring her and A-hong, the title seemed appropriate. They both laughed at the last category of Taiwanese mentioned. She could also scold in fluent Taiwanese, although she did not always know the true meaning of what she said. It did not sound like Sue would be able to fill the language gap.

"I was just trying to figure out a way to distance my mother from my little project," she said. "I'm not so sure I can rely on her to give an accurate translation if A-zou decides to share more than just names."

"Why don't you ask A-hong?" Sue suggested. "He spends a lot of time with her now and his parents made sure his Taiwanese was good."

The expression on Sue's face told Vicki her cousin realized her suggestion had hit a raw nerve. "Your mother would have a problem with A-hong, wouldn't she?" she asked in a contrite tone.

"No, she would never have a problem with A-hong," Vicki reassured her. "After everything he has done for A-zou, Mama considers him a hero. Her problem is with me." This was followed by an exasperated laugh. They sat quietly for a moment. The sound of Mama's conversation floated across the lobby. Vicki took the short break in their talk to glance around, noting the changes. Her father had informed her that the government no longer subsidized the hotel, which was owned by high placed people and used by any foreign dignitaries. After a fire had occurred during a roof renovation, there had been a heated debate in the National Legislature and the Grand had been cut free to compete on the open market. Space was at a premium and had to be used to generate revenue. A coffee shop now occupied one corner of the lobby. Beyond the coffee shop was a dining hall that hosted the best breakfast buffet in Taipei. Then there were the display cases nestled between the pillars that lined the route guests walked to reach the front desk.

"Do you have a problem with A-hong?" Sue asked gingerly, breaking the silence.

"Yes, he's my cousin," Vicki laughed wryly before realizing what she said. "Oh, God, I don't believe I said that."

Sue was in the midst of one of those soundless laughing episodes, her hand covering a wide open mouth as she doubled over and gripped her stomach. Vicki was sure that stomach was going to ache when she calmed down. Great, she thought, now I'm the entertainment for the day.

"If you tell anyone I said that," Vicki growled under her breath after noticing that their conversation was beginning to draw attention. "I'll kill you." Then she began laughing in spite of herself.

Sue calmed down and caught her breathe before reassuring Vicki. "Your secret is safe with me," she said. "Although I don't know how much of a secret it is."

Vicki's laughter changed to a nervous chuckle. "What do you mean by that?" Was Sue's meaning the same as her comprehension? She would be mortified if the entire family in Taiwan was aware she used A-hong as a litmus test for all her dates. What if they shared her mother's point of view? Did they all think she was looking for a clone of her cousin? What if they thought she was trying to attract A-hong? The idea of simply staying in her hotel room until their return flight crossed her mind after that thought.

"It's easy to see you are looking for someone like A-hong," Sue chuckled. "Not many like him in Taiwan. Maybe you can find an ABC in New Jersey."

"An ABC in Jersey," Vicki muttered. There was no shortage of that breed of men, but they tended to be one dimensional, all-American types. She had not met one yet who could hold their own in a conversation beyond the subject they studied in college. Engineers and accountants spoke numbers; English and philosophy majors spoke words; but none were bilingual. At least Sue did not appear to share her mother's opinion that A-hong was unique and so required her to quickly change her psyche and adjust her taste in men.

"I don't limit my choices to just American Born Chinese," Vicki bragged. "I break hearts indiscriminately."

Sue smiled before responding. "I know you too well, *jie-jie*. That sounded so much like – What would you call it? – false bravado. Are you over Roger yet or does it still hurt to talk about it?"

Vicki knew Sue would not be fooled. She reached over and touched her cousin's hand. "Thanks for noticing. No, I'm not quite over it yet. It takes a little time before the disappointment becomes a dull blade. Right now it's still sharp."

"I'm available when you need to talk," was the quiet response "Now how can I help you with your project?" Before Vicki could answer, Mama called her.

"Got to go," she said to Sue. "A shower and a little sleep await me upstairs."

"Okay, I have to get to work. What are your plans for later?"

"I'm sure my mother has obligatory visits lined up. Don't know when we can see A-zou," Vicki sighed. "That will take a trip to Ping-dong."

"No it won't," Sue informed her. "I should have told you sooner. My father wanted her to get the best care possible. She's in Taipei."

"She's in Taipei?" Vicki whispered in relief. "That makes things much easier." With that the young women stood up and walked to the front desk counter. Vicki knew she would have to answer a barrage of questions from the staff as they fussed over her return. It did not bother her. So many of them had watched her grow up; it was expected that they would want an update. She had a few questions for them as well. The second sentence of the Confucian Analects crossed her mind, "Is it wonderful when friends come from afar?" She was coming from a further distance than Confucius would have ever expected. Roger never could get the concept.

Chapter Three

The noise from the street market one floor below imposed itself on Vicki through the open aluminum framed windows of her grandmother's narrow balcony. She was balancing on one foot with her hand leaning on the white washed concrete wall for added support while removing her shoes. Her purse rested on the floor next to her. The last rays of a fading sunset streamed through the wall of windows above her hand. These entered the apartment through the opaque glass panels that formed part of the wall opposite the windows. This arrangement made A-ma's living room cozy during the winter months. Unfortunately it was summer, which meant oppressive heat unless the air-conditioning was on. An unlikely happenstance since A-zou did not like air-conditioning. Thank God Mama had insisted on coming tonight when the temperature was somewhere below sweltering.

A familiar pungent odor drifted in through the window screens as she slid a foot into awaiting slippers. The smell of *chou doufu* was part of her childhood memories. Stinky tofu, who could resist a meal with such a name? It was one of the few dishes her father refused to eat. She had tried it with him once after much persuasion from her mother. Never again. Mama was unhappy about it, but it remained one of those acquired tastes that Vicki had never acquired. A vendor on the street below must be preparing the delicacy for the crowd of shoppers hurrying to pick up the makings for dinner.

The voices of her mother and A-ma came through the open doorway. They were speaking quietly in Taiwanese. A-zou's voice joined in, coming from an open bedroom door which let out onto the balcony. She did not sound pleased. With the racket from the street market, could A-zou have been sleeping? Before Vicki could attempt an answer to her own question, A-ma said something that included her name. This softened A-zou's tone. Vicki could hear the sound of her getting up from the bed.

Completing the switch from street shoes to home footwear, she stood up straight and took in her surroundings, searching for change. Access to the rest of A-ma's L shaped balcony remained blocked by a mustard yellow Whirlpool washer. The odd shaped small red tiles of the balcony floor were a little duller from wear. Not surprising since this narrow walkway was the equivalent of a laundry room for A-ma. She had no clothes dryer, so laundry day included many treks from the washer through her apartment and out onto the balcony on the other side of the mustard yellow blockage. There, bamboo poles hung on wires which descended from the ceiling. The poles supported hangers that draped the wet clothes in the humid air. Below the hanging clothes, plastic boxes containing assorted household items that had passed their days of usefulness stood waiting for sorting and discard. Nothing had really changed here since she was a little girl.

Feeling comforted by the simple and familiar Vicki retrieved her purse and stepped through the open sliding aluminum and glass doors onto the black marble floor of the living room. Mama and A-ma moved into the back of the room. Vicki could hear A-zou's shuffle from the same direction. Grasping the back of a chair, the elderly woman slowly made her way into the room, switching for support from the chair to the large ornate table which rested under the family altar hanging on the rear wall. The strain was visible on her face, but as soon as she saw Vicki a broad smile masked her efforts.

"A-zou," Vicki said cheerfully. *"Gua ai li."* It was one of the few Taiwanese phrases she knew and also some of the first words her mother had taught her, "I love you". This elicited the usual response from her great-grandmother. Vicki did not understand the words, but knew their meaning. "So American, we Chinese don't have to say such things, it is understood."

It was all part of a ritual that had been in place since Vicki could speak, another small act that gave comfort. A-zou's protest was obligatory. Her happy chuckle was heartfelt, although illness made it weak. A-ma moved to help her mother reach a seat, but A-zou impatiently waved her off, too proud to accept help unless needed. After reaching the chair normally used by A-ma for watching television, A-zou dropped down breathing heavily. Watching this struggle tore at Vicki's heart. Her great-grandmother had always been so full of energy. Now she was thin and frail, as if a huge spider had drawn the life from her. The decision to accompany Mama had been the right one.

Her mother had informed Vicki on the taxi ride from the hotel that A-zou had only reluctantly agreed to talk about her parents. To her it was comical that anyone would want to know about a woman's maiden family. Disappointed but not discouraged, Vicki was resigned to obtaining the names of A-zou's parents and grandparents. These would give her a thread to the past. If she could somehow coax a family story or two out of A-zou, it would be like weaving a tapestry. From all she had heard over the past few days, that would be unlikely.

Vicki sat on the couch, took a note pad out of her purse, and placed both on the table in front of her. Mama and A-ma drew up dark, carved wooden chairs from the table. A-zou was suddenly the focus of the room and Vicki was sure she was enjoying it.

A-zou said something to Mama who turned to Vicki and asked, "So what do you want to know?"

This caused Vicki to stutter step. She had not expected to just begin. A-zou usually commented on her appearance, asked about her studies, and inquired about any young men in her life. It took a moment to get her mind in gear then she asked the simplest question she could.

"What was your mother's name?"

The answer that followed was completely unexpected.

"*Gua she sim pu-a,*" A-zou said without emotion.

Instead of translating, Mama paused. She had a shocked look on her face and simply repeated what A-zou had said as a question.

"*Li she sim pu-a?*"

It was the first question asked and Vicki already felt outside the conversation. She knew "*Gua she*" meant "I am" and something told her she should understand "*sim pu-a*", but she was sure her mother had never said the word. Her feeling of isolation quickly deepened as A-ma jumped in. The three older women began to have what was obviously a debate. A-zou raised her voice and snapped at A-ma. This ended the discussion. Mama turned to Vicki and said, "She was a child bride, a little daughter-in-law."

As soon as Vicki heard this the pieces fell into place. *The Effects of Gender in Asia* with Dr. Liang, it had been a fascinating course. One of the books used was by an anthropologist name Margery Wolf, *Women and the Family in Rural Taiwan.* That was where she had learned the term *sim pu-a.*

"It was custom long ago," Mama continued. "I never knew she was one."

"I know about it, Mama," Vicki told her mother. "Studied it with Dr. Liang."

"Why would she be a *sim pu-a?*" Mama said to herself. "Her family wasn't poor. They could afford a wedding."

A-zou snapped at Mama, bringing her back. A-ma did not look happy and muttered something to her mother, who quickly shot back a reply. Vicki was not sure what her question had started, but any reluctance on A-zou's part appeared to have vanished.

"She said it is time everyone knew the truth," Mama translated. Then A-zou started to speak in a calm voice with Mama translating while A-ma pouted in the background.

"Her birth parents were Chiu Lai-wang and Ho Liang."

"Did she know her biological parents?" Vicki asked letting her curiosity dictate her questions.

A-zou laughed and answered, "Of course I knew my parents. They lived close by. I spoke with my mother once about being a '*sim pu-a*'." She seemed to drift back to another time as she told her story.

****

"Why give the child away? She is your blood," Ho Liang pleaded. Her daughter was only a week old. How could this man consider giving her up and taking in someone else's daughter?

"The Chen family has been kind enough to make this offer," Chiu Lai-wang replied. "I do not want to pay for a large wedding just when I will have to support my parents. You will have a daughter on your breast that you can raise and teach."

"But she will not be my child," she cried.

"She will be your son's wife," he reminded her. "You will have trained her to act as she should for your son and she will help you cook and clean. Why do you have a problem with this? You were a *sim pu-a.*"

"That is why I have a problem with it," she snapped back. He ignored what she said, so she pushed on. "Will the Japanese allow it?"

"The Japanese policy is to let us follow our traditions and customs," he replied. "They will not interfere."

"This other child will not be my own," she begged. "I cannot look at her face and see how she resembles me. She will be an outsider."

"No!" he shouted. "She will be your daughter and our son's wife. Let us not speak about it again."

****

A-zou paused for a moment then said something quietly.

"That is the story her mother told her one day while they were washing clothes by a stream," Mama said. A-zou then continued speaking in a controlled cadence. A-ma was now listening intently.

****

"Why can't I study with *gege*? Chiu Bu asked.

"What would you do with your learning?" her mother asked. "A man has use of reading and math. You will be cooking, cleaning, and raising sons. There will be no room in your world for such skills."

The explanation did not sit well with the ten year old girl. She knew she was better with numbers than her older brother. Using an abacus came naturally to her. *Gege* struggled with even the simplest concepts. She had promised her future husband that she would not tell their mother about her help, but it was not fair. The tutor taught him, yet she was brighter.

"Can't I sit with him when the teacher comes?" she asked. "I won't bother them and I'll be able to help him."

Her mother made a clucking sound which meant her patience was wearing thin. "And who would do all your work? Besides if you were to learn all he did, he would not want to marry you. Learn useful things instead. Come, I'll teach you how to make his favorite meal."

****

A sad look passed over A-zou's face as she finished the story. Then she muttered something forlornly.

Mama finished the translation in a whisper, clearly affected by the words, "She never made that meal for him. He died two weeks later. He was such a good hearted boy; always trying to make her laugh. She lost her brother, her best friend, her companion that day."

A-ma sat in silence, tears in her eyes. Mama was quiet for a moment before leaning toward Vicki and whispering, "I think was should stop now."

Vicki shook her head in agreement, still trying to fully process what she had heard. At least she had the names of A-zou's parents. Speaking about this appeared to be too much for her great-grandmother. A-zou reacted strongly to Mama's whisper. A-ma rejoined the conversation, but the results were the same as the earlier debate. A stern look of determination had slowly crept onto A-zou's face. It appeared to Vicki that the old woman had decided she wanted her story heard. She returned to her controlled cadence, staring directly ahead as if viewing her life on a screen.

****

"It will be difficult to find her a husband," the old matchmaker told Chiu Bu's parents. "One so pretty and so smart is intimidating to most families. This type of woman tends to be strong willed and demanding. She will ruin the harmony of the household."

Chiu Bu sat quietly, knowing if she tried to defend herself it would only reinforce the matchmaker's prejudice. The fact that she was allowed to listen to this conversation had already done that. Her mother responded in a cajoling tone.

"We have taught her well from the time she came to us," she countered. "She knows the duties of a wife and realizes she must pay attention to her mother-in-law."

How humiliating this whole affair had become. Chiu Bu felt no need to marry. She would be happy to just care for her parents, but her mother would not hear of it. Caring for their parents was the responsibility of her brothers. Who would care for her when she grew old and had no son? At twenty she was considered well beyond the proper age to marry. It could be put off no longer. The families in their village were not interested in having her join their households. The women feared her temperament and the young men feared her mind. All remembered the tricks she did with numbers as a child. This had forced her mother to reach out to the neighboring districts for a matchmaker willing to represent her adopted daughter.

"Fortunately, I know of a family that may welcome such a woman," the matchmaker continued. "The Ma family in Ping-dong has an exceptional son who is very progressive. He can even speak Japanese. The family runs a confectionary business. I think I may be able to persuade them that your daughter's intelligence and good looks will benefit their enterprise."

With that Chiu Bu knew her fate was sealed. Who was this progressive young man? Would she be expected to learn Japanese? Numbers came easily to her, but language did not. She could not even write her own name, let alone read. Was she to move to Ping-dong? That was the fate of a woman, to be thrown out of her home and live with people she has never met, only allowed to visit her maiden family once a year. She wanted to scream "no", but did not dare for fear her parents would lose face. They had raised her as their own even after their son had died. Now she was duty bound to repay them for their kindness.

He must be very progressive, Chiu Bu thought as she nervously waited in the front room of the Ma house. It was a neat one story structure that rested behind the Ma's large confectionary shop on the main street of Ping-dong. They appeared to be a prosperous family, but she was not sure if being progressive was a good thing. In fact, she was not even sure what progressive really meant. One thing it apparently meant was she was about to meet the man the matchmaker said would be a good husband before she actually married him! What if she found him to be repulsive? Could she then refuse to marry him? Maybe he has mental problems that have prevented him from finding a bride. What if he is only ten years old? These thoughts were swirling around in her mind when a handsome young man walked into the room alone. He appeared as nervous as she felt.

"I am Ma Lu," he said, looking indirectly at her. After a painful pause he continued, "I have heard that you are good with numbers."

This caught her by surprise. Why was he taunting her? The matchmaker had said this family would accept her even with her math ability. How should she respond? Should she deny it? Her parents felt she needed to marry even if she did not think it necessary. But looking at the young man in front of her, Chiu Bu was having second thoughts about her reluctance.

"I cannot read or write," she replied, staring at the floor, not daring to look at him.

"Oh, that is not necessary," he chortled. "I will do that, but a wife who understands numbers and money would be invaluable."

He agreed to marry her because of her talent with numbers? Was he just going to make her a numbers slave? "I have no experience dealing with money," informed him. "And have no training with numbers."

"But you can use an abacus I have been told," he laughed. "It all comes naturally to you, does it?"

"Yes it does," she whispered, blushing. "You can test me if you wish." Speaking with Mr. Ma was proving to be very disconcerting. He refused to be put off.

"I believe you," he laughed, appearing to gain confidence with each sentence they exchanged. "I will warn you, my father wishes to expand our business into Xingang. That means we will live there and not here. My mother and brothers will not be able to help you and we will have to work long hours in the store."

Xingang? Alone with him? No interference from a mother-in-law? No having to care for his younger siblings? This was not progressive, it was revolutionary. She had worked hard all her life. Hard work did not frighten her. The more he spoke the better this marriage sounded.

"You mother agrees with this?" she asked skeptically.

"My father will see to it," he assured her. "Are you interested in such an arrangement?"

"I will do what my parents wish me to do," she informed him.

"I am not interested in living with a woman who does not willingly want to live with me," he stated. "Do you want to share life with me, to raise my children, to care for my parents when they are old? If so we can tell the matchmaker her job is done."

Her mind was spinning. Ma Lu was telling her she had a choice, but she would have to choose now. Was he always this decisive? Could she be happy with a man like him? She found the courage to look at him and then decided. "You can tell her the job is done."

He laughed for a moment, turned on his heels, and marched out of the room. She knew her world had changed in that instant and was happy about it.

****

A-zou paused for a moment. The room seemed to shrink as the sound of her voice receded. Vicki glanced at her mother and A-ma. It was obvious that both had found the simple, common tale to be as magical as she did. A-ma was transfixed; her body rigid as if moving would somehow break the spell of her mother's words. Mama seemed overwhelmed by the information being passed through her. Vicki had coaxed more family history from A-zou in the past twenty minutes than her mother or grandmother had in their lifetimes. A-zou seemed to be content resting in that moment so many years ago when her life was transformed. Before the sounds of the night market crept back into their awareness she continued her story.

"He was truly a *zhunzi*, a superior man," she whispered. The statement gave her strength. She cleared her throat and resumed in her cadence. "We moved to Xingang, established the shop on the principle road of the town, and called it Xin Yu Xiang. Everyone liked him. He was such a salesman. I took care of the accounts while he took care of the customers."

****

"I spoke with Mr. Wu. He wants to know how much he owes this month," Ma Lu informed his wife.

"He owes 2500 yen," Chiu Bu told him. "It has been a bad month for him. People appear to be waiting until after the new year to marry, so his business is slow right now. But that's the way it has been for the past five years."

Her husband chuckled at his wife's detailed memory. "And you know what he purchased each month for the past five years, don't you?"

Chiu Bu looked at him in bewilderment. "Of course I do," she answered. "I have not lost my mind because of our misfortune."

He immediately regretted his teasing and stepped across the store to her. "I was not thinking of that," he reassured her tenderly. "You need not worry. Now that we have Bong Chie, a son will follow."

She gave him a weak smile. After so many miscarriages, to finally have a child in the house was heartening, but they did not need a daughter to consume the family resources and then leave. They needed a son who would build those resources and then inherit them. She quickly pushed these thoughts to the side.

"Have the architect and builder agreed on the plans?" she asked.

"Yes," her husband answered. "I was going to tell you, but Mr. Wu's matter interrupted. Everything was finalized this morning. Work will begin on the factory next month."

The news lifted one of the many weights she was carrying. At last, they would not have to worry about sugar prices and transport. Within a year, they would be manufacturing their own sugar. The only transporting that would be needed would be to his father's shop in Ping-dong. Business had been expanding so quickly that shortages had occurred. There had been a slowdown over the past few months, but that had given them time to plan the next expansion. Things would surely pick up by the time the sugar plant opened and they would be in a position to take full advantage of the increasing need for their products.

"The Japanese are going to confiscate our sugar plant!" Ma Lu hissed angrily. "They intend to convert it into a plant to manufacture an additive for gasoline."

Chiu Bu sat speechless while their daughters listened quietly. They had realized since the beginning of the war with China that restrictions would be imposed and economic policies might change. When America entered the war, they knew change was inevitable and had planned for it. But the confiscation of their sugar plant had not been anticipated. The war had made the business environment so challenging and now this.

"How can we maintain our business without sugar?" she whispered to herself.

Ma Lu was pacing the floor, as he did when he was deep in thought. "We will have to see how much sugar we can obtain," muttering his thoughts. "If there is no sugar to be had, then we will have to make more fruit based products. Perhaps we can develop some sort of food the military can use since they have taken over the economy with their war."

"But what of the girls schooling?" Chiu Bu reminded him. Knowing their income would drop precipitously.

"Bong Chie will have to help in the shop full time," her husband pronounced. "She has no real desire for school and is getting too old for it anyway. It would be a waste of talent if Lei Ga was to leave school. She is so bright and has your talent with numbers."

"Then we will find a way," Chiu Bu asserted. "I have heard that the Japanese are looking for Taiwanese men to enlist. That will mean young men will leave, so we will need help in the shop."

****

"A-ma is Lei Ga?" Vicki asked, guessing from the similarity to the Mandarin pronunciation of A-ma's name.

Mama shook her head yes. "A-ma has A-zou's math talent."

"Who is Bong Chie?" Vicki asked quickly. This brought a chuckle from A-zou and a frown from A-ma.

"Bong Chie is *Yi-nai-nai*," Mama answered. "A-hong's grandmother."

A-zou said something with an understanding smile.

"She said Taiwanese is much harder to understand than Mandarin, isn't it?" Mama translated.

Vicki smiled and muttered "You've got that right." Then she looked at A-zou and answered with another of the few Taiwanese words she knew. "Dee oh, li dee oh." By now the sun had slipped behind the buildings to the west of them. A-Ma shook off her mesmerized daze and jumped up to turn on lights as A-zou thought for a moment.

"It was difficult, but the business adjusted and Lei Ga passed the high school entrance exam. Then the bombing started"

A-ma suddenly breathed in sharply and said something that Mama did not bother to translate. A-zou responded with an exasperated "Ah yo" followed by an impatient sentence. The bearing of the three older women changed as they prepared to relive a trying part of their lives.

"The Japanese had airfields and bases around Taiwan," A-zou sighed. "These were the targets of the Americans. There was an airfield by Xingang. As soon as they finished building it the American planes came and destroyed it. Bombs fell on the high school, so Lei Ga could not attend. A bomb fell on a meeting of business leaders the Japanese had called together. It killed my husband. I was alone, no man in my life to comfort me, two daughters to care for, a business to run, and no son. It seemed to be my fate."

Chapter Four

"Then she said she was tired. I helped her stand and walk to the bedroom," Vicki told Sue. They were sitting in the coffee shop of the Grand Hotel. The excitement from the day was still pulsing through Vicki's veins.

"A-zou let you help her get up and walk?" Sue asked in amazement. "Telling her story must have drained her."

This only made Vicki feel guiltier. How asking for the name of A-zou's mother had evolved into a life story still eluded her. A-zou had taken control of the interview and was apparently using it to preserve her stories. Mama had mentioned that the elderly in Taiwan often made a point to remind their offspring of the sacrifices made for them. But this was much more than that. A-zou was recounting experiences with little reference to how they affected others. The tales she told that evening were personal ones filled with emotions. Could her great-grandmother continue like this? The effort was exhausting her.

Sue was sipping her coffee, decaf because of the late hour, and glancing around the coffee shop while waiting for Vicki to respond. They had been coming to this shop since they were children. It was a way to have time away from the parents without leaving the safety of the hotel. Now it was a room filled with memories which were quickly turning nostalgic. The price they had to pay for growing up. Vicki needed an unbiased opinion. Where was Joe when she needed him? Somewhere over the Pacific Ocean right now, totally unaware of the hornets' nest she might have stirred up with her simple question.

"It's not only telling the story that's draining her," Vicki pointed out, knowing she was trying to assuage her conscience. "It's the debating with my mother and A-ma. There's more here than A-zou's story. I mean my mother didn't know she was a *sim-pu-a*."

"No one knew except maybe A-ma," Sue reminded her. "It's not one of those subjects people talk about. Even if there are a lot of women in A-zou's generation and even younger who were. It's just not talked about. She really said Zou-gong died in an air raid? What happened to pneumonia?"

Vicki shrugged and took a sip of her tea with a dozen questions in her mind vying for attention. The most pressing one was should she continue to speak with A-zou about her life experiences? Right behind that was how can she tolerate me when the Americans killed her husband? Feeling it would be better to get Sue's input than to let these queries fester, she blurted them out.

"Should I subject her to more emotional stress?"

"Emotional stress? You mean ask her more questions?" Sue asked.

Vicki shook her head yes.

"From what you told me, you weren't asking a lot of questions," Sue reminded her. "And the ones you asked had nothing to do with any stress. A-zou seems to have decided her story should be told and you are the one to hear it."

"Me, my mother, and A-ma," Vicki reminded her. "I'm not making it stressful, they are."

Sue placed her cup on the table and looked at Vicki sympathetically. "Are they really causing the stress or is A-zou putting herself through it for a reason? I think she knows she's dying."

Vicki sat quietly for a moment digesting what her cousin had said. If A-zou wanted someone to know her story, why pick me? Sue or A-hong would be better repositories for preserving the memories. Someone had to translate and explain things to her. She could give no comfort or feedback other than a smile or sympathetic look.

"Why would she want me to hear her story?" she asked. "Why not my mother or you or A-hong?"

"Maybe because you are at a safe distance," Sue guessed. "You can't condemn or judge her. You don't speak Taiwanese. You don't really know the nuances of the culture she lived in. You're an American. We Chinese don't like to air our dirty laundry and we expect everyone to conform to our world view. You Americans are more flexible. You accept and even respect different points of view. Doesn't your father always say he's worried about how three people live their lives, him, your mother, and you? Other than that, everyone is on their own."

Vicki laughed at her cousin's imitation of her father. As for the "we Chinese" and "you Americans" part of Sue's monologue, she ignored it having grown used to these broad classifications. There was no longer a need to comment.

"You don't really believe him, do you?"

"No, not literally," Sue answered. "But there is a tolerance implied by it that not many people around here have. Did he ever really worry about what other people thought? I mean when he made his life choices?"

Vicki knew exactly what she meant. "You mean when he married my mother."

Sue chuckled and looked down at the table for a second before responding. "You see, American directness, not easy for the Chinese to do."

Vicki let that assessment slide also, even though she had witnessed numerous cases of "Chinese directness." Perception was always more important than reality and she knew there was little chance of changing her cousin's perception.

"So, I've become A-zou's confessor," she muttered. "Still it seems to take so much out of her. It's no easier for Mama or A-ma. Should I continue?"

"Do what A-zou wants you to do," her cousin advised. "She wants to be heard."

Vicki accepted this and immediately moved on to her other question. "Do you think she might resent me because of how Zou-gong died?

Sue looked at her in astonishment. "A-zou resent you?" she questioned. "She could never. She's too proud of you. Listen, you have to take a step back. If she told you it was her fate, she meant it. Her Buddhist beliefs teach her that. She accepts misfortune because it is payment for transgressions in a previous life. That's what she believes. She's incapable of placing blame on you for something that happened before you were born. It was simply her fate."

Vicki knew she was right. That realization brought a release of her anxiety. A feeling of utter exhaustion began creeping into her body to replace it. Time to set Sue free and get some sleep. Mama was already up in the room probably sleeping soundly.

"Joe's getting in early and I promised to meet him," Vicki hinted. "He seems to think he'll get preferential treatment if I help him check in."

"I know, he told me," Sue chuckled. "He probably will. I intend to stop by on the way to work to make sure he's settled in."

"Settled in?" Vicki laughed. "I'm going to have to warn him."

They both laughed and walked down to the lobby. After seeing Sue to a cab, Vicki dragged herself to the elevator and her room for some much needed rest. Unfortunately, when she opened the door the lights were on and Mama was writing at the desk.

"Sue went home?" her mother asked, taking off her glasses and looking up from a pad filled with Chinese characters.

"Yes," Vicki answered. "She has to work and she wants to stop by beforehand to see Joe. I thought you would be asleep by now."

They were in a "superior" room of the hotel which was an improvement from the interior "deluxe" rooms of her childhood. Two full size beds stood on a wall, ancient Chinese characters decorating the dark wood of their headboards. The floor was covered by a thick Chinese rug. A couple of chairs occupied the space directly across from the beds, with the dresser and desk placed so they would benefit most from the floor to ceiling windows. Heavy drapes covered the windows, but were parted in the center at the moment. The opening revealed a sliding door which opened onto the balcony, the lights of the city stretching out as far as the eye could see.

Mama put down her pen and glasses then turned to face her daughter. "I wanted to write down what I remembered of A-zou's story before it faded," her mother sighed.

"I took notes, Mama," Vicki assured her. "You should get some rest."

"Don't worry, rest is one of those things that comes to me whether I want it or not," she chuckled. "If I use your notes alone, I get your view and then have to translate it. I'll need them anyway. She spoke so fast, I had to translate the words without trying to remember them. She seems to be determined to do this now. When I asked her about being a *sim-pu-a*, she snapped at me and said to just translate or she will find someone else to do it."

They both chuckled at this last point, Even with her liver failing A-zou retained her feistiness.

"I want to thank you for what you did today," she began. "It seems you really do have a special place in A-zou's heart."

Vicki felt uneasy with Mama's comment. She saw no reason for her to have such a special place. That honor belonged to A-hong because of his devotion. What her mother said only added to her confusion. She suddenly realized that one of the consequences of the evening's revelations was her Roger problem had been considerably diminished. She had not anticipated speaking with Mama until the next morning. Having elicited Sue's opinion on interviewing A-zou, she decided to get her mother's view. First she had to understand why A-zou might think of her as special.

"Why do you think that?" she asked. "Wouldn't A-hong be the special one?"

"He is but in a different way," Mama chortled. "A-ma and I discussed it on the phone while you were with Su-hui. Do you realize how extraordinary today was? How would your father say it? She bared her soul to you and told you things she never revealed to A-ma or to me."

That seemed to be a bit of an exaggeration to Vicki. Her grandmother was sitting there and her mother was translating. "But the two of you were there," she protested.

"And if you had not been, her old habits would have ruled. She would have been silent."

"Even if that's true, it still doesn't explain why I would be special."

"A-ma said it best. It is because you allow her to dream," Mama pointed out.

This last assertion took Vicki by surprise. How could she allow A-zou to dream? They could not even communicate effectively. It was just smiles and the affectionate gestures a great-grandmother would give to her granddaughter's child. In that way Vicki's relationship with A-zou was almost like that of a much beloved pet. In twenty-three years, this was their first real meeting of the minds.

Claiming she allowed A-zou to dream was more than a bit of a stretch.

"How can I allow her to dream when she knows so little about my life?" Vicki asked, immediately regretting the cold tone of the question.

"A-hui, she is your great-grandmother," Mama sighed. "Only after you have children of your own will you understand the strength of maternal love, even if it reaches across three generations."

This was a favorite theme of hers, often used when Vicki was growing up. It was "I am grounding you to teach you because I love you more than you can imagine." It did not play well then, but she had to admit as she matured there was some truth to it. Even with acceptance of this point, allowing A-zou to dream was too much.

"I understand the love part, but the dreaming bit is hard to process," Vicki confessed.

"You are different than your uncles, aunts, and cousins," Mama said quietly. "You were the only one who could never hurt her with your words. You could never disappoint her by making promises you didn't keep. You never told her of your dreams, so she could only imagine. Since she only heard of your triumphs, you can imagine how successful you have been to her. Her life seems to have been filled with frustration, but yours will be filled with success. That's how you allow her to dream."

Vicki sat quietly for a moment, letting the words percolate through her consciousness. To have as bright a mind as A-zou obviously did, but be stymied throughout life by the cultural limitations she faced must have been all but unbearable. She was like a flower unable to bloom for want of a little water. The thought of being in the same position was terrifying. This realization led to an understanding of how her great-grandmother might view her as special, even if she did not agree. She may be different from her relatives, but she was not special. The label made her feel uncomfortable. Placing that subject into the "cannot be resolved right now" bin, she moved onto her question.

"A-zou seemed so tired after telling her story," she began. "Should I continue to interview her?"

Her mother looked directly into her eyes. "I don't think you have a choice. You are no longer in control; she is."

"Then we better get some sleep," Vicki sighed, wondering what it was she had gotten herself into. "Tomorrow is going to be a busy day for both of us."

Mama shook her head in agreement, slid her glasses back on, and turned back to her writing. Vicki walked to the bathroom to prepare for bed. Neither knew what the next day held for them.

Chapter Five

Vicki sat in the same coffee shop seat she had abandoned the night before. She was nursing a cup of coffee and sorting through the short and long term issues facing her. The immediate worry was Joe. He should have landed an hour before and so should be arriving shortly. The last time they had spoken she had been winding herself up to split with Roger. Joe, usually the sympathetic surrogate brother, had tried to listen, but had been preoccupied with something himself. When they had parted, neither she nor he had revealed what was eating at them. He would know by now about the demise of her relationship, but she had no idea what was bothering him. Sue had not indicated anything was wrong with their relationship. Since Joe fixated on the woman in his life and his career, the only thing she could think of that might be worrying him was his job. But he worked for her father and Uncle Ed treated him like a son. Her dad had actually created a paid internship in the company so Joe could get a feel for the family business. She was sure it would become a permanent position if Joe wanted it. Was he thinking of going with some other company? That would break her father's heart. She said a prayer, hoping it was not that, finished her coffee, and started down to the lobby.

While she eased herself down the regal staircase leading from the mezzanine level to the lobby, Vicki reviewed her other concerns. Long term was the decision of continuing on to graduate school or just working with mom and dad for a year. The tests for grad school had been passed easily. She had been accepted into a program. All that was needed was a commitment on her part. That had been derailed by the Roger fiasco. Coming to Taiwan was supposed to clear her head so she could make the leap or wimp out and defer for a semester or two. After yesterday's surprising revelations, her mind was focused on A-zou. The troubles with men had faded a bit. That was a good thing. A-zou's story had begun to put things into perspective. The healing process was beginning. Today would belong to her great-grandmother and she was comfortable with that.

Vicki looked at the lobby while her shoes sank into the thick carpet of the stairs. It was after eight and the activity around this central part of the hotel had begun to pick up. People were checking out at the main desk while their luggage was transferred to the front entrance. Others were making their way across the floor from the elevators to the breakfast buffet. The subdued chatter of a large hotel waking up permeated the first floor. Joe should pull up around eight-thirty if he followed the same itinerary she and her mother were on the day before. Mama had said she would meet Vicki in the buffet room around nine. That would give her about thirty minutes to help Joe check in and orient himself. She made her way to the entrance to wait, hoping she could do so without disrupting the routine of the doormen. When Sue would show up was still a mystery.

Joe stepped out of a cab before Vicki reached the door. Why had he taken a taxi instead of the hotel van? What was the rush? The doormen pulled his luggage out, showing signs that they felt her cousin was familiar, but obviously not recognizing him. When Vicki stepped up, they immediately put the puzzle together and gave him a welcome worthy of a Wei. Joe looked up when he noticed the subtle change and saw Vicki. He laughed, stepped over to her, and gave her a peck on the cheek.

"You see," he smiled. "That's why I wanted you to meet me. The Phaff magic makes things so much more pleasant."

"The Phaff magic?" she laughed. "You are a Phaff. It's the Wei magic you're after."

"Please, nothing too complicated right now," he moaned. "My brain is fried."

"I know," Vicki sympathized. "Remember, I'm only on the ground a day, so I'm not much better. Why the taxi? Kind of pricey compared to the hotel van."

"I figured it would give us a little extra time before Sue or your mother joined the party," Joe answered.

Vicki instantly became concerned. Why would the two of them need time alone? Did it have to do with the unspoken business of their last meeting? She was not sure she could handle another emotional hit right now.

"Mama said to meet her at nine for breakfast," she told him knowing there was no need to ask questions right then. He would tell her the reason for his need of privacy soon enough. "I don't know when Sue will be here."

"She told the boss she'll be a little late," he informed her "She intends to roll in about eight forty-five."

Eight forty-five, that would give them half an hour. They turned and followed his luggage into the hotel. As they marched to the front desk, Joe began to explain.

"I've been chasing a problem around in my head for a little while now," he said. "And I need to bounce it off someone I can trust."

"Is this the issue that was bothering you back in Jersey?"

"Yeah, yeah," he confessed. "While you were trying to tell me you were giving Roger the heave hoe."

"Oh, you figured that out, did you?

"Sorry, It's just that I had this thing on my mind. It kind of ate up the storage space in my brain."

They were approaching the front desk. Vicki did not think that this conversation should be had in front of the staff there. "Let's get you checked in then we can sit and talk."

He shook his head in agreement as they stepped up to the counter. Shouts of *"shuai ge"* greeted him. He blushed a little and switched to Mandarin to deny being a ladies' man. Joe had been coming here as often as he could to see Sue. The doormen may have had a little trouble placing him, but the girls at the front desk knew him, his connection with Vicki, and his interest in one of the Wei woman. This led to some goodhearted teasing. Vicki was always amazed at his embarrassment when teased by the opposite sex. When guys did the teasing, Joe came back with guns blazing, holding his own against all comers. Keeping his time at the counter brief as much to minimize the teasing as to talk with Vicki, he picked up his key and moved toward a couple of chairs in the center of the lobby away from everything. The significance of the choice of seating was not lost on Vicki. She prayed it was not bad news.

"I've been thinking," Joe jumped in as soon as they sat down. "I really enjoy working with your dad and he's offered me a permanent position."

"Oh, Joe that's great!" Vicki interrupted, feeling that worry lift.

"Yeah, it is," he continued. "It would involve a lot of travel between the States and Asia. Your dad's convinced trade with China is going to grow vertically and, well, so do I. But, you see, I've been getting some pressure from Montana."

"You mean your folks want you to move back?" Vicki asked. Joe seemed to grow more distraught as his tale unfolded, but she still could not figure out what was bothering him. He must have been obsessed with this conversation his entire flight and seemed to have planned it out down to where they would sit in the lobby. After they had settled in the seat, she had noticed that this position not only allowed for privacy, but also allowed him to see the entrance and the elevators. Neither Sue nor her mother could arrive unnoticed.

"No, no," Joe reassured her. "It has to do with settling down. Jesus, I'm only twenty-five, just earned my MBA, and they think I should settle down."

"What do you mean settle down?" she asked confused. "They don't want you to travel?"

Joe shook his head no, getting a bit more agitated with each moment. This had to be settled before Sue or Mama showed up. He needed a quick discussion and resolution to whatever was chewing him up. She knew from experience with her cousin that he was building up to a major decision. If she gave him a few more minutes, it would come pouring out.

"That's the thing, mom's thrilled that I'll be working for your father," he spurted out. "Thinks it's a growth industry and she's jealous about the travel. Easy for her, but the time on the road and the jetlag are a bitch. But you see, she just loves Su-hui; won't call her Sue; doesn't consider it her proper name. Funny, she has no problem calling me Joe instead of Joseph, but I don't try to understand. When it comes to Sue, mom's particular. But anyway, my folks love Sue, which is convenient because I love her too. But now mom's making all kinds of subtle and not so subtle hints that I should settle down. You know, ask Sue to marry me and start a family eventually. I'm not ready to be a father right now, but in a few years. Only problem is I have to ask her. So what do you think?"

Vicki could not believe that the verbal barrage she had just been subjected to had come from Joe. She was shocked at his question and delighted at the same time. They were two of the most precious people in her world. She had known since the first vacation they had spent together ten years before that they would be happy as a couple. She laughed at what she had just endured for such a simple question and quickly blurted out an answer before Joe could misinterpret her mirth.

"Joe, how could you ask me what I think?" she exclaimed. "I think it's wonderful!"

He seemed to take things down a notch after that, but the pressure was not entirely off just yet.

"Do you, ah, do you think she would say yes if I asked?"

"I'm sure she would. She loves you," Vicki reassured him.

"Yeah, but it won't be easy," he pointed out clinging to his worries. "There are so many questions. Where will we live? What about all that travel? Will her parents agree if she moves to the states? Will my parents agree if we move here? What about kids, where would they grow up?"

"It will all sort itself out," she told him. "It did for my parents."

"Not the same, not the same," he pointed out. "Your folks met in Jersey, so your mom was already out of the country by her own choosing."

She thought that was a funny way to put it, out of Taiwan by her own choice. Vicki had never looked at it that way, not that she ever really thought about it. The way Joe had put it made it almost sound as if Mama had been running from something which was ridiculous. She had been back here countless times over the past twenty-five years and had managed not to be chased out of the country. Joe was just nervous.

"It will all work itself out," she repeated. "That's the fun part of life."

He loosened up more, but was not quite finished. "So, I couldn't bring a ring with me because the duty on it at customs," he explained. "Do you know where I can pick up something respectable without going bankrupt?"

Of all the questions he had asked, this was the easiest. A-hong had an uncle in the jewelry business. They had a showroom in Taipei. If she could talk with him on the side, they could set something up without Sue knowing.

"Harry's uncle owns a jewelry business," she informed him using A-hong's English name.

"Harry's uncle? Not your's?"

"On the Liu side."

"My man Harry," Joe laughed. "I'm gonna have to take him out and get him drunk."

Vicki laughed. The thought of her cousins getting drunk was comical. Before she could point that out, Joe straightened up and smiled broadly. Turning she saw Sue beaming as she jogged across the lobby to him.

"You have to swear you won't say anything to her about this," he demanded. "Not even a hint."

"You have my word," she answered as he stood up. Sue threw her tiny frame at him and squealed with delight. What happened to the reserved Chinese nature? It was heartening to watch two people so obviously in love. The funny thing was she did not miss Roger watching this. She missed A-hong.

Chapter Six

"Are you going to try the *xifan*," Mama asked with a mischievous smile. She had become playful after seeing Joe and Sue together, having always encouraged the two of them. Vicki knew Mama considered herself the matchmaker for the young couple. It took everything she had not to say anything to her mother about Joe's intentions. She knew if a word of it leaked out, it would be on the national news that night. Wei Jia-yi found it impossible to keep happy news to herself.

"Mama, you know I tried it last year," Vicki answered her halfheartedly. "Unless they've changed their rice congee recipe drastically, it will be as unappetizing as it was then."

They were seated in the buffet room enjoying breakfast. Joe and Sue had excused themselves after saying hello to their aunt. Ostensibly, Sue went up to Joe's room to help him settle in before she went to work. Mama had turned a blind eye to them, muttering something about Sue getting to work on time. Vicki found it interesting how the black and white of a decade before had slowly faded to gray. Back then she and Sue had a motel room to themselves because it would not have been proper for Joe to sleep in the same room. But that was a subject she wanted to avoid for fear it would lead to an assessment of their relationship. Instead she opted for her cousin's other obsession.

"Were you aware dad had offered Joe a permanent position?" she asked while constructing a scrambled egg sandwich on her plate.

"Of course I was," Mama answered between bites. "It is a business decision. Your father and I are in business together."

Well, that was one secret she had kept, but that did not give Vicki the confidence to share her news. She washed down a bite of her sandwich with a swig of coffee, not really surprised by the answer. Her parents were a coordinated team that avoided surprises, recognizing long ago that business decisions affected the home front in a big way. She quickly left that subject behind and pushed on to A-zou, hoping to get a feel for what the day would bring.

"Sue said her father took A-zou to the doctor's office," she told her mother.

"That's good," Mama commented. "A-ma said that she wanted to talk with you. That would give us the time we need."

Vicki was surprised by Mama's comment. She had not anticipated A-ma's interest and was completely unprepared. Of course, if things evolved as they had yesterday, she would not have to ask many questions. It remained to be seen how much more A-zou was willing to share, but it was apparent all that she required of Vicki was an attentive look. She had said it was time the truth was known. If A-ma approached it with the same attitude, then there was no need to worry about preparedness. The only question Vicki had about that attitude was whose truth would come out, A-zou's, A-ma's, or Mama's? If there was any filtering it would be Mama's, although A-ma would try hard to influence that. After this quick sorting, she returned to the Sue and Joe conundrum. How to ask Mama about A-hong without it becoming an issue? Memories of the lecture in

Anchorage airport were still fresh, but she had to get hold of him quickly. Joe was only here for a week.

"Is A-hong coming up?" Vicki asked surrendering to her fatigue and opting for the simple question. Mama's facial expression changed instantly.

"A-hong?" she asked, her voice laced with suspicion. "Why do you ask?"

"Joe wants to see him."

Mama relaxed a little. "I'll give him A-hong's phone number. Why does Joe want to see A-hong?"

Her mother's questions were beginning to grate. "Maybe they want to go out drinking," she snapped back.

"Drinking wine?" Mama responded with a puzzled look. "They don't drink like that."

Vicki let that drop. There was no need to burst her mother's little bubble. Neither Joe nor A-hong indulged often, but both were quite capable of earning a killer hangover once or twice a year. While she could let that pass, she could not keep from expressing her annoyance at Mama's attitude.

"So, can I ask you?" she began innocently. "You don't think I should see my cousin at all?"

Mama put her fork down and looked directly at her daughter. "Just remember he is your cousin."

"What's that supposed to mean?"

"Nothing," she answered in a tone that told Vicki her mother had made her point. "So, tell me," she continued picking up her fork. "What was wrong with Roger? You seemed so happy at first."

This caught Vicki off guard. Mama had a way of doing that when she did not want to continue with a subject. The question was put in a reasonable way and tone. It sounded like her mother was genuinely curious, even concerned.

"Roger had a problem with control," Vicki explained choosing her words carefully. "He needed to control me and I didn't react well to that. I just couldn't reason with him or even talk with him. He talked to me not with me."

Mama sat listening intently. "Those are traits people outside a relationship don't always see," she commented.

Vicki felt she was finally communicating with her mother after two days of avoidance. It was a good feeling that was sometimes hard to come by.

"Have you thought more about grad school?" was Mama's next question.

Sometimes her mother amazed her. It was as if she had downloaded the list of concerns Vicki had reviewed and prioritized while waiting for Joe. The mother/daughter relationship between them ran deep, making it difficult for Vicki to keep things secret. Remembering that put her on guard. Do not spill the beans about Joe she thought before continuing.

"A little," she replied. "But at the moment I feel responsible to A-zou and her story."

Her mother smiled, finished the last bite of her breakfast, and reached for her coffee.

"I think you have pushed A-ma into telling you hers as well," she said before finishing the coffee and standing. "We have to leave for A-ma's; it will be an interesting day."

Vicki stood up and walked to the exit while Mama handed the breakfast coupons to the cashier. Breakfast was included with the room. Her mother drove a hard bargain.

A-ma was waiting expectantly when they stepped into her apartment. Mama slipped out of her sandals, quickly slid into house slippers, and stepped into the apartment to begin speaking with her mother. Vicki was a little delayed because she had chosen to wear running shoes. This put her at a distinct disadvantage when it came to shedding footwear. If the conversation between her mother and grandmother began in Taiwanese, it rarely converted to Mandarin. A-ma's Mandarin was not very fluent, but it was good enough to express major points she wanted to make. Vicki spoke directly to her often. Of course, as with diplomacy, the devil would be in the details, but at least she could be part of the conversation. If the exchange between mother and daughter picked up a head of steam, then Mama would end up translating. Vicki dropped her troublesome footwear and quickly hopped into the apartment.

"*A-ma, zao an,*" she interjected into a pause in the conversation.

"*Zao an, A-hui,*" A-ma replied. "*A-zou qu kan yisheng, kuai yao hui lai. Wo yao gen ni tan hua.*"

"Hao, hao," Vicki agreed. Why was she so anxious to speak with her while A-zou was away? It was not a question she could or should ask. Instead she sat on the couch as she had the day before while A-ma reclaimed her television seat. Left to fend for herself, Mama pulled out a chair from the table and sat between them. A-ma began speaking at a rapid pace, obviously concerned with her time limit. She spoke in Taiwanese. Mama was going to have a long day.

"She always hated the name 'Bong Chie," Mama translated. "She never called *Yi naina*i Bong Chie. She called her *jiejie,* but her name was Li-an."

The emphasis on the name of A-ma's sister piqued Vicki's curiosity. When A-ma paused for a moment, Vicki inserted a question. "What does Bong Chie mean?"

The query caused a perceptible shift in A-ma's tone. A hint of confusion laced with bitterness crept in. Her answer became defensive.

"I never understood why," she began. "How can you be so cold to your own daughter? I don't want to make it sound as if A-zou didn't love my sister, but to call her that . . . The name means 'might as well raise her.' As if she was an afterthought and not a child. I guess that was the way they did things back then and she was only a daughter after all."

As Vicki listened to her mother's translation she studied Mama's face for any reaction. It was apparent this was the first time she had heard it. The last sentence hit her hard. Vicki had a feeling she would hear more about it later, but right now A-ma had moved on.

"She was my best friend," A-ma continued. "She was smart, kindhearted, and helped me through some very difficult times."

****

"You are smart," Li-ya said to her sister. "I don't know why she calls you that."

"Oh, that doesn't bother me," Li-an answered. "I know she is not being mean. It is her little joke on the world."

"Your name should not be a joke on the world!" Li-ya insisted.

"It is not my name. Remember I am called Ma Li-an," she chuckled. "It is a family nickname only."

The two sisters were walking home from their school along Fu De Road. The family candy store occupied the corner a hundred yards ahead. Li-ya still could not understand her sister's nonchalant attitude toward the name their mother called her.

"If you were a son she wouldn't call you that," she pointed out in a final attempt to sway her sister to ask Mama not to use that name anymore.

"A son? *Meimei* don't say that," Li-an warned. "You know how much it bothers Mama."

She was not calmed by her sister's acceptance. It was not right to call her *jiejie* "Bong Chie". Li-ya also felt guilty about what their parents had told them the night before.

"Why do you have to work while I go to school?" she asked "You are older and should continue in school. Then you can teach me."

Li-an chuckled. "*Meimei,* I don't have your talent. It would be a waste for you not to continue in school. Besides you are too young to work all day in the shop. I have all the education I need to be a good wife and mother."

The sound of airplanes drew their attention away from their conversation and to the clear autumn sky. Japanese planes were common over the area. An airfield was under construction a short distance away. But there was something different about what they were hearing. The planes were very high, so they could not see details, only the color of them. Some were the standard beige with red circles they saw every day. But flying among these were dark blue planes that they had never seen before. The aircraft were dancing around each other. Suddenly black smoke began pouring out of one of the beige planes. As this plane fell from the sky, another beige plane began to burn, then another. The girls were not sure what it meant. Was the war now being fought in the skies above them? They began running for the candy shop. When they arrived, two Japanese soldiers who guarded their parents' former sugar plant were pointing toward the sky and shouting.

The two girls quickly slipped into the shop, remembering their father's warning about staying away from soldiers.

"Baba," Li-an shouted. Ma Lu rushed from the rear of the shop.

"Baba, there were planes in the sky," Li-ya told him earnestly. "Japanese planes and other planes. The Japanese planes began burning and falling."

"Are you sure the other planes were not Japanese?" he asked.

"They were a different color," Li-an answered. "They looked blue and after one plane started burning, another one did then another."

Their father looked at them anxiously for a moment. "Stay indoors and help your mother," he instructed them. "I have to go out for a few minutes. Tell Mama I'll be right back. Just stay inside, okay?"

"Okay, Baba," the two girls answered in unison.

He returned with a grim look on his face. Closing and locking the door, Ma Lu stepped to the rear of the shop and motioned for his family to sit at the kitchen table.

"The Americans are coming to free us from the Japanese," he told them. "We will be part of China again. Don't repeat this to anyone. It will not happen quickly. The blue planes were American. Do not go near the new airfield they are building. And you must all promise me, when I tell you to do something, do not question me, just do it."

Li-an and Li-ya agreed quietly. Chiu Bu looked at her husband and asked, "What did the soldiers say?"

"They said nothing," he answered. "I did not speak with them. I spoke only with our neighbors. All agreed it was American planes. Taiwan is too valuable to the Japanese war effort to be left alone. There will be more American planes and they will not stop at shooting down Japanese planes. The harbors will be bombed. The airfields will be bombed. The army bases, the factories, the railroads, everything will be destroyed. Everyone agreed, but no one thought they would bomb our homes.

* *

"They never did bomb our homes," A-ma said quietly. "But they destroyed the airfield a few days after it was completed. The high school was hit by a bomb, so I never went to high school."

Vicki sat quietly as her mother finished the translation. The next logical question would be, "How did your father die?", but she did not have the nerve to ask it. The short tale A-ma had just told had been difficult for her. Vicki had no intention of prolonging her suffering.

"The bombing became frequent," A-ma continued. "Then one day the Japanese ordered all the business leaders of the city to attend a meeting in another part of town."

* *

"Why are they demanding you go to their meeting?" Chiu Bu asked anxiously. "You are too old to learn how to fight. What can you do for them?"

Li-an and Li-ya sat as quiet witnesses to their parents' discussion. The Japanese had become increasingly demanding as the war progressed. First it was the requirement that schools teach in Japanese. Then efforts to suppress Chinese culture and replace it with Japanese culture began. After that young men were encouraged to volunteer for the army. Now they were drafting them. "Could they force Baba into the army?" Li-ya wondered.

"All I can do is keep the local economy working," he answered. "They do not trust Taiwanese men to fight for them. The Taiwanese are only coolies. It is a meeting. They don't want to bother with us. Maybe they want to protect us so they have rice to eat."

"Rice to eat!" Chiu Bu snapped back. "We make sweet treats, not rice. I don't feel good about this meeting. You should just ignore it."

"And have them come with the three of you here?" he returned. "It is better if they ignore you. I will go to the meeting, listen to them, make some pleasant sounds, and come home. Then no one will bother us."

"Please don't go," she begged. "What if something happens? I don't trust them."

"It will cost us nothing but a little time," he reassured his wife. "It is for your protection."

****

"I never saw him alive again," A-ma whispered. "Where ever this meeting took place was bombed. So many of the business men in our neighborhood died there. My father had always spoiled me. He treated me like his doll. Then he was gone. All of us were devastated. My mother found she was pregnant the following month. She had to run the shop, deal with the workers and customers, and raise the two of us."

"She was pregnant?" Mama interjected. "What happened to the baby?"

"The child was still born," A-ma told her. "It was for the best, but it only added to her sorrow."

Vicki remained silent. No matter how much she understood Buddhist beliefs, no matter how reassuring her mother was, she still thought there must be a kernel of bitterness towards America. The least she could do was honor the memory of her Zou-gong by being quiet while A-ma relived those days. The doorbell chirped loudly, ending A-ma's story. Mama walked over to the button that opened the street door and pushed it. Vicki could hear Sue's dad helping A-zou up the stairs. As Mama opened the hallway door, her brother's voice came through the screen of the security gate. He was speaking to A-zou in Taiwanese. Then he gave instructions to someone else. A male voice answered in Taiwanese. It was A-hong's voice! Vicki tried not to smile too broadly for fear of upsetting her mother, but she could not help herself. The quote from the Analects popped into her mind. It was wonderful when friends come from afar and A-hong knew exactly what the Master had meant.

Chapter Seven

A-zou came through the door with a slow, careful gait. Wei Shan-ji followed closely behind, ready to help if necessary. Mama's older brother was a thin man who was shorter than his sister. She always claimed she had inherited the tall genes from her grandma Wei. At five foot four inches, she was the height of the average American woman, but was considered tall for a woman from Taiwan. Because of her height, many people mistook her for a *waisheng ren,* someone whose family came from mainland China in 1949. It led to some embarrassing assumptions which Mama corrected with a quick Taiwanese sentence. She was a *Daiwanlam* through and through, just taller than average. This allowed her to claim that Vicki's height came from both sides of the family, insisting that "tall" was a relative term and she was tall in Taiwan. Vicki had learned to acquiesce whenever the subject came up.

Mama appeared conflicted to her daughter, although Vicki realized it could just be a projection of expectations on her part. A-hong had earned a special place in her mother's heart. When he was studying at Rutgers the two of them had talked, Vicki thought they really commiserated, about the difficulties of navigating through American culture. He had asked questions and sought advice from Mama often at the beginning of his stay. Gradually some of those duties had migrated to Vicki because so many of the people A-hong had to deal with were of her generation. However, Mama remained an important interpreter of America for him, even if she did not always get it right. It was during this period that she also became aware of the gradual change in A-hong's relationship with her daughter. Mama began to remind Vicki that A-hong was her cousin with whom she shared too much DNA. No matter how much Vicki reassured her mother that she was well aware of it, the cautionary remarks continued *ad nauseam*. It was clear Mama was happy to hear A-hong's voice, even if a conflict existed. The sounds of the street floated in through the open windows of the balcony, masking any rustlings A-hong would make climbing the stairs. They would both have to wait for him to darken A-ma's doorway.

Before any comment could be made on the absence of A-hong, Shan-ji *Jiu-jiu* enthusiastically greeted his sister in Taiwanese. This left Vicki fending for herself. A-zou shuffled over to A-ma's favorite chair and dropped into it. When she was settled in A-ma offered her fruit which was declined with an explanation. Mama broke from her conversation to tell Vicki what was going on.

"A-hong is here to help with the translation," she informed Vicki in English. "Right now he's buying some food on the street. He'll be up in a moment."

Vicki could not believe her luck. Now she would not have to chase A-hong down over the phone. They just had to find a private minute so she could pass on Joe's request. Although her mother's apparent internal conflict did make her nervous. Would they be able to get a moment alone? No matter what she told her mother, Vicki knew Mama remained skeptical. All her denials had been ignored, only producing muttered comments of body language. How could she defend herself against claims of body language? The sound of A-hong stepping in left this question unanswered.

Liu Huang strolled in wearing jeans, a T-shirt, and a broad smile. It was amazing what one year in Jersey had done for his sartorial style. A bag of street vendor food was daggling from his fist.

"Yi-nainai, A-yi, Biaomei, nimen hao?" he asked cheerfully. Vicki's smile was uncontrollable now. She knew her mother might comment later, but she had a hard time not being genuine around A-hong. If there was a tall gene in the family, he had it even though he did not have any Wei genes. A-hong stood head to head with Joe, although he had a slimmer physique than her American cousin. He was as handsome as ever. She remembered a nickname given him by some of her classmates when they found out the Taiwanese pronunciation of his name. A-hong was immediately dubbed "a hunk". An unwanted retinue of college coeds began to pester him. One of her tasks was to run interference so he could study. He had taught her a quote from Confucius that he claimed helped him resist these flirtatious temptations. "If men would pursue virtue the way they pursued women the world would be a better place." Some of her friends thought the remark condescending, but Vicki understood A-hong's need.

A-ma laughed and reached for the bag of food while motioning for him to sit down. He walked over to Vicki before settling in.

"Hello, Vic," he said in English smiling. "It's good to see you. I just wanted to thank you for what you're doing for A-zou."

Vicki found this unexpected expression of gratitude bewildering.

"I don't understand," she countered. "I should be thanking you for all you do for her. What have I done?"

A-hong looked to the floor and chuckled. "You've given her something to fight for," he told her. "She's determined to tell her story to you. That's why I'm here. She wants me to translate, seems to think your mother will only muddy the water. How did you get her to open up about her life? The subject has been so taboo."

It was Vicki's turn to chuckle, although her mirth had an ironic tone to it. "I asked her what her mother's name was," she told him. "She ran with it after that."

"Vicki," Mama called a little too sharply. "A-zou is ready."

"Okay," she replied then quietly slipped in one last comment to A-hong. "Joe needs a favor." A-hong answered with a nod of his head while Vicki retrieved a writing pad from her purse and sat on the couch. A-ma steered A-hong to the seat Mama had occupied yesterday then retreated back to sit with Mama in one of two chairs just behind A-zou.

A-zou began to speak as soon as everyone settled in. Vicki wished she had been able to warn A-hong. If yesterday was any indication, he was in the midst of three feral felines. Cat fights were inevitable. She knew he did not do well when women began spitting words at each other. All that could be done now was to pray he knew when to translate and when to keep a polite silence.

"After my husband was killed," A-zou said, picking up where she had left off. "I had to decide how I would raise my daughters. So I went to speak with my father-in-law."

****

She could tell he had been crying. How could she comfort a man whose first born son had died when she was the wife of that son? Could they console each other? He did not appear to be consolable. Chiu Bu was still too numb and frightened to mourn. She had grown to love and respect Ma Lu; had made him the center of her universe. To have him torn out of it so suddenly had left her terribly wounded. Responsibilities overshadowed emotions. The business had to continue so she could care for her children. Choices had to be made for them. What of the little one just beginning to grow inside her? If it were a boy, he would be his father's heir and the Ma family name would be passed on. If it were another daughter, she would be too much of a drain on the family resources. Chiu Bu needed to know how her father-in-law felt about giving away the last piece of his son.

"Dou Jiang," she called loudly to him, attempting to shake his attention away from their loss for a moment. "I need your guidance."

This seemed to resonate with the old man. He calmed down and focused on her. "I am sorry. You have lost as much as I have. What do you need?"

"I am pregnant," she whispered. "If it is a son, we will celebrate the return of Ma Lu's spirit. Your line will continue. If it is a girl, what do we do?"

Her father-in-law became very stern. "If it is a girl, you cannot afford to raise it. It will have to be given away. When you are a little further along, I will begin making discrete inquiries."

This brought her a moment of peace. After a breathe she pushed on to other concerns. "I am only a woman," she began. "How am I to run a business? I cannot read or write and have only daughters to help. If the Japanese approach me with demands, how can I respond? If there is a business dispute, am I to resolve it alone?"

He smiled for the first time since being told of his son's fate. "You are the one who takes care of the accounts. That is the hard part. You have a good baker in Mr. Shi. He will represent you if needed, but I don't think you will need his help. You have the respect of the businessmen in this city. That will carry you a long way in running this business. As far as reading and writing are concerned, you have two daughters who can do that for you."

Listening to her father-in-law relaxed Chiu Bu. As her stress diminished, her sorrow grew. "Thank you, Dou Jiang," she whispered before being overwhelmed with grief. He tried to console her, but could not. His own pain was too great.

✱✱✱

"He never recovered from the loss of his son," A-zou said quietly. "He cried so much he went blind. His business was sold and he came to live with us. I gave birth to another daughter, so she was given to a family that wanted to lead in a son."

A-ma inhaled sharply when she heard this revelation and immediately began asking questions. A-hong did not attempt to translate the torrent of words flowing from her mouth. Instead he waited for A-zou's response.

"I am sorry, but what difference would it have made if you knew of another sister?" A-zou asked. "Her family did not want contact between you and her. I have always been in contact. Her name and information are among the instructions of what to do after I die. A-hong will be able to reach her."

A-ma was close to tears. She angrily stood up and left the room. Mama sat quietly, a shocked look covering her face. A-zou gave out a bitter chuckle before saying something. A-hong hesitated for a moment before A-zou waved her hand telling him to translate it. "My daughter led in a son for them, but I never gave birth to one." The look on her face became more determined as she continued her story.

****

"Dou Jiang, I need your advice," she said. "It concerns Mr. Shi."

Her father-in-law sat quietly for a moment, staring straight ahead with eyes that could no longer see. "I have been waiting for you to ask," he stated. "You are young and recover more quickly than an old man like me."

She was not sure what he was referring to and so waited to be sure he had finished his thought. After a few moments she continued. "I have developed feelings for Mr. Shi, but don't think it wise to marry him."

Her father-in-law sat up straighter and smiled. "I see," he chuckled. "How am I to guide you? Mr. Shi is a good man. You should not lead him on in a relationship that cannot blossom."

"I cannot marry him," she stated in anguish. "If I do I will lose control of my business, my children, my life. He will be my husband and so will control everything."

"That is the law and our customs," he stated avoiding any commitment. "Since the Japanese have left, Chinese laws and customs are to be followed. That is what the government says."

"There is no law that says I have to marry a man," she pointed out defiantly. "I don't need one to support me. Mr. Shi works for me and yes; he is a good man. His wife died shortly after Ma Lu died. He helped me through my trying time and I helped him through his. We have need for each other."

"And how do you propose to fill this need?" the old man asked.

"He has agreed to move in with me," she told him revealing the results of her negotiations. "Any children born would bear the Ma name. It is the only way I can give you an heir."

"And give yourself a son?" he asked knowingly.

"Yes, and give myself a son," she admitted.

"What of the neighbors and your business associates?"

"I would hope they could see I am striving to be filial toward you and the memory of my husband," she answered.

"Some will and some won't," he reminded her.

"I do not care," she stated. "I will not give up everything, even to him. And I will not give up living."

"I only want you to be happy," he sighed. "It is what my son wanted more than anything."

****

A-ma marched back into the room. Her eyes were red from tears; her face was red from anger. She hissed something to A-zou who responded sternly. Mama began speaking in a conciliatory tone, but both her mother and grandmother ignored her. A-hong sat quietly with a nervous look on his face. Vicki knew the argument was about the taboo subjects of her mother's youth. After A-zou left, Mama would be busy translating A-ma's response to her mother's revelations. It was going to be a long day.

A-zou spat out an angry sentence that subdued her daughter. A-ma dropped into the seat she had vacated, folded her arms, and glared at her mother. A-zou continued.

****

"She is beautiful," Mr. Shi reassured Chiu Bu as he leaned over to see his daughter for the first time.

"I wanted to give you a son," she cried. "Why can't I bear a son?"

"You will," he smiled. "There will be others. We are not finished."

She laughed at his optimism. This was her fourth daughter. How many more children could she bear?

"I will tell your Dou Jiang," he told her. She drew the baby to her breast, closed her eyes, and cried silently.

"They came here as if they were conquering us not liberating us," Mr. Shi shouted. "The Taiwanese have been excluded from all important government posts. These people don't even speak our language. How can they govern when they are ignorant of the conditions on our island? This is not mainland and we are not a conquered people!"

He stood in front of Chiu Bu, their one year old daughter clinging to her leg. Li-ya and Li-an hovered in the background waiting to see if their mother could reason with him.

"Ah yo, we are all aware of the problems these mainlanders brought with them," she said in an attempt to calm him. "Undisciplined, poorly trained; criminals is what they are. But just because they are corrupt and ineffective doesn't mean they are powerless."

"They are cowards," he hissed. "Beating a woman to death for selling cigarettes. They control everything. We cannot make a living."

"They have guns," she reminded him. "If they can beat a woman to death because she asked them to return the cigarettes they ceased, they can shoot you for protesting!"

This appeared to have no effect on him. She was desperate. What news they had heard from Taipei told her these people were capable of creating a blood bath. How could he not see that? "I beg you, please do not go!" she pleaded.

"Do not interfere in the affairs of men," he warned her. "If we do not respond to these actions, they will treat us worse than the Japanese treated us. We will be dogs to them." With that he stormed out of the house and joined a group of men marching to Chiayi to voice their protest.

****

"He never returned," A-zou said mournfully. "Those mainlanders shot him. Then they arrested the leaders of the protest and shot them in the public square. Bodies were floating in the rivers, so many died. I was alone again with three daughters to care for."

When A-hong finished his translation, the room became silent. Noises from the street drifted in through the open windows to fill the vacuum. Vicki completed her notes mechanically and then waited expectantly, looking at A-zou to see if she could read what her great-grandmother was feeling. A-ma sat defiantly, her anger not allowing other emotions in. Mama sat quietly, a tear tracing down her cheek. A-hong was looking at the floor, unable to look at A-zou and her pain.

"My father-in-law died shortly after that," she whispered. "The loss of his friend was too much for him."

She paused for a moment as if trapped in the past then she rallied. Her voice brightened a little and she said, "Now I am tired of talking about yesterday. We can talk again later. Why don't you young people go out and have lunch? We can eat the *baozi* A-hong brought up and argue. You can catch up on all that has happened in your lives since you last saw each other and talk about your poor A-zou."

Vicki listened to A-hong's translation and noticed Mama stiffened. "I will take them to lunch," Mama insisted. A-hong glanced at his cousin as the three of them stood up. His look told Vicki he knew they were being monitored.

Chapter Eight

Mama, Vicki, and A-hong made their way down to the street in silence. Motor scooters, small trucks, and Japanese cars passed sporadically. Scooters were parked on the sidewalk, so the three strolled along the side of the street walking toward Neihu Road. The sun was bright, the humidity was high, and the temperature was climbing. It was a typical summer day in Taipei for most of the people traveling down the street, but the day was extraordinary for the three of them.

Vicki's head was abuzz with unrelated questions. How did her mother feel about what was said this morning? What of A-hong? He had not heard yesterday's revelations. How to get Joe's request to A-hong without Mama hearing it? The last question was the most pressing of all. They had to act quickly given Joe's time constraints. There was also the nagging question she could not voice. Why could she not control her smile when A-hong walked in? She dreaded Mama's comments.

"*A-yi*," A-hong broke the silence. "I know a great dumpling shop not far from here. The food is good and the prices are better."

The thoughtful look on Mama's face melted with this. "The food is good and the prices are better?" she asked. "You sound like an American advertisement."

A-hong laughed while Vicki just looked up at the sky. They were surrounded by similar ads as they walked the short distance to Neihu Road. Why place the blame on America? She knew better than to ask.

There had been more than one occasion where Vicki had pointed out the difference between Americanization and modernization. In her mother's mind they were the same. If it had not existed in Taiwan when she had lived there, it was Americanization. She had seen it first in America had she not? Vicki and A-hong had dissected the issue often, debating the pros and cons of modernization, its chipping away at traditional cultures, and whether or not it was Americanization. As far as she was concerned science trumped everything and science was universal. A-hong allowed for the universality of science, but saw no need to abandon all of society's traditions, especially when those traditions supported whatever point he was trying to make. She called him a convenient modernist. He thought she should delve a little more deeply into her heritage. They often agreed to disagree.

"I think you want to eat dumplings because your *biaomei* is partial to them," Mama opined.

A-hong laughed while Vicki feigned shock. "Who says I'm so partial to dumplings?" she protested. "For all I care we can go to Pizza Hut." She pointed to the Pizza Hut located in a modern office building across the street as if adding an exclamation point to her statement.

"It's good that Vicki likes dumplings," A-hong countered. "But I seem to remember you also enjoyed them and this shop makes delicious *shui-jiao.*

Mama laughed enjoying her little joke at Vicki's expense. Her daughter decided to reply with a question to A-hong that she knew would annoy her mother.

"So, do they have good pot-stickers?" she asked mischievously using the English translation in place of the Chinese to add a little extra to her poke. It produced the desired response.

"*Guo-tie?*" Mama asked shaking her head. "Yesterday's left over *shui-jiao*. Why do you always order leftovers?"

"I'm sure they're freshly made, Mama."

"You can never know," her mother warned.

"I will make sure they are fresh," A-hong reassured them, always the diplomat.

They arrived at the dumpling shop as he said this. The shop was located on the first floor of a typical four story poured concrete building. Its whitewashed walls were in need of some touch up, but the table and floors were clean. The "kitchen" consisted of a few gas burners with pots of boiling water behind a deli style counter. This ran for half the forty foot length of the store, occupying the left wall as customers walked in. Seating was in the back. As with so many Taiwanese establishments, the street side of the store was open to the outside. Above the rear seating hung an elongated air conditioner which played down on the guests.

Mama waved toward the back, directing her daughter and cousin's son to find seats. She intended to schmooze the store owner and guarantee the pot stickers were fresh. Vicki and A-hong found an unoccupied table for four with small stools encircling it. This was a traditional Mom and Pop store that eked out a living along Neihu Road. The sheer number of eating choices in the area made earning money selling food difficult. A-hong said the dumplings were great and Vicki trusted him. As she sat it struck her that the battle between the traditional and the modern was being fought right in front of them. The Pizza Hut she had pointed out had delivery scooters in front of it. Each scooter had a number stenciled on it. The highest number was ten. To add insult to injury, there was a Domino's Pizza just down the block with its own troop of scooters.

She thought of telling A-hong about Joe, but reconsidered when she noticed Mama walking towards them. Instead she let the last thoughts that crossed her mind start the conversation.

"Every time we come back to Taiwan I'm floored by the changes," she began. "We're sitting here in a traditional dumpling shop and across the street is a modern office building with a Pizza Hut and there's a Domino's just down the block."

A-hong had a quizzical look on his face. "How would Joe answer something like that?" he asked himself. "What wall did that come off of?"

Vicki laughed at her cousin's command of colloquial English. He had always been a quick learner.

"It's complicated, but let's just say that something my mother said reminded me of our little debate about tradition and modernizing."

"Ah," he shook his head knowingly. "The American advertising comment. So, do you think Pizza Hut and Dominos are an improvement over *guo-tie*?"

She laughed at how well his mind was in synch with hers. "No, but I don't count," she asserted. "I'm here for a few weeks a year at most. It's what the folks in the neighborhood think that matters."

"The modern Taiwanese like a little variety," A-hong countered. "They frequent traditional and modern restaurants."

Mama reached them as he finished his point, so Vicki let their sparring match go for now.

"A-hong, I ordered ten *shui-jiao* for you and ten *guo-tie* for A-hui," Mama told them as she pulled up a stool and sat down. "Did you understand what A-zou was talking about and why?"

"I understood what she said," he answered politely. Vicki resisted a sarcastic remark about her mother doubting her cousin's Taiwanese, knowing the question was not about the meaning of the words, but about their meaning in A-zou's context. "It was a different world then," he continued. "I think I understand why she made those choices. As far as why she is talking about it now; that seems obvious."

He did not have it within him to say she was dying and Mama did not push the issue. Instead she changed the subject. "Do you know what a *sim-pu-a* is?" she asked him.

"A *sim-pu-a*?" he asked thoughtfully. "That's a child bride." It took a moment to connect the dots. "You mean A-zou was a *sim-pu-a*? How could that be? Her marriage was arranged when she was twenty."

"She told us yesterday," Vicki interjected. "The boy she was betrothed to died as a child, so her adoptive parents arranged a marriage."

"Really?" he replied.

"Did she ever tell you how Zou-gong died?" Mama asked.

"He died of pneumonia," he answered.

"He died in a U.S. bombing raid during World War II," Vicki informed him as she played with the disposable chopsticks on the table.

"She ran the store, raised her daughters, and cared for her father-in-law alone," Mama muttered almost to herself.

"She had Mr. Shi for a couple of years," Vicki pointed out. "Then she lost him. God, she was made of steel."

The three sat quietly for a moment before A-hong shifted subjects. "Vic, I have a question for you," he began. "Did you understand the phrase 'lead in a son'?"

Vicki thought for a second. She remembered it being somehow related to a *sim-pu-a,* but knew that was not quite it. A-zou had used it when describing adoption. "I can only guess," she admitted.

"It's an old custom," Mama informed her. "A couple who was having trouble conceiving or bearing sons, would adopt a daughter. It was felt this would 'lead in a son'."

"I'm sure it worked half the time," Vicki commented wryly. "She seemed so forlorn when she said the daughter she gave away led a son in, but she never had one."

"In her world, without a son there would be no one to take care of her in her old age," Mama pointed out. "There was no social security, no assisted living homes, no nursing homes. All you had was family and daughters became part of their husband's family."

"I care for her now," A-hong assured them.

"And I thank you," Mama smiled. "Now tell me about what has happened since we saw you last."

A-hong looked down and laughed. Vicki had always thought he was too modest, too hesitant to take credit for the help he gave others. He needed a good woman to give him a swift kick in the ass. He side stepped Mama's compliment and went straight to his studies.

"I am working on my dissertation," he told them. "The working title is 'Macro-economic Changes in Developing Countries and Their Effect on the Traditional Role of Women.'"

"That's a mouthful," Vicki laughed.

"It's inspired by what I have seen in Taiwan," he continued.

"How far along are you?" Vicki asked.

"The research is done," he replied. "I'm beginning to write."

"Is that a useful topic?" Mama asked.

The dumplings arrived with a pot of tea as she finished her question, so the answer was put on hold until the dishes were settled. Vicki removed the chopsticks from the paper sleeve, pulled them apart, and rubbed them together to remove any splinters. The habit had been learned as a child and still attracted some curious glances in New Jersey. In Taiwan it was expected behavior. This task completed, soy sauce, vinegar, chili oil, and sesame oil were mixed in a small dish. She nabbed a fried dumpling with her chopsticks, dipped it in her creation, took a bite, and leaned back to see how her diplomatic cousin would handle the question.

"Many businesses are interested in this research," A-hong began as he reached for a dumpling, having completed the same preparatory ritual as Vicki. "Asia is changing rapidly. The economic power of women is increasing. Since women traditionally handle the finances in many Asian societies, it's really a subject that should have been studied long ago."

He paused to take a bite of his dumpling; the sounds of the restaurant mixed with those drifting in from the street and filled the momentary void. After washing down the first bite of lunch with a swallow of tea, he continued. "The changes happening now are giving women financial independence. Spending decisions are being made for personal consumption instead of solely for the family. Discretionary spending is growing rapidly, especially in the luxury goods sector. Companies will need research on the demographic and economic trends so they can target their products most effectively."

Mama sat shaking her head gently as she listened and enjoyed her meal. Vicki could tell her mother was already thinking about how the family business might be able to benefit from A-hong's research. She wondered if those thoughts could be used to somehow shake free a little time for Joe and A-hong to get together. They could say the two were going to discuss the economic trends in Asia and how the business might be able to take advantage of them. A business meeting to discuss engagement rings, Vicki smiled at the thought.

"Where is your data coming from?" Mama asked now in full business mode.

"Government statistics on demographic change in some countries," A-hong answered. "U.N. stats for others. In Taiwan I also did interviews."

"Were they all as freely given as A-zou's" Vicki asked.

"I didn't even attempt to speak with A-zou," he laughed. "Growing up I was taught everything was a secret. But now you've broken through the barrier. I'd love to add her story to my collection. Would you consider lending your notes to me?"

A-hong awaited her answer with a boyish grin. Vicki considered how to answer to get the most out of this rare opportunity to tease her cousin. The two of them were looking directly at each other, ignoring Mama entirely. The lunch table had suddenly become a bargaining table and Vicki was looking for the best deal she could get.

"I don't know," she answered coyly. "What can you offer a girl for her work?"

"Victoria Phaff! *Sanba!*" her mother scolded, calling her a Bohemian.

It snapped both of them back to reality. The bargaining table quickly receded.

"It was only a joke, Mama," she said nonchalantly. "No need to get excited."

"That was very inappropriate," her mother chided. "It will give people the wrong impression entirely."

A-hong's face had turned red which caused Vicki to react in kind. Had she begun to flirt with her cousin? Rejecting the idea immediately, Vicki answered A-hong's question. "Of course you can copy my notes," she assured him. "I hope they can add another dimension to your work." It was a little stiff, but would hopefully calm her mother.

"*A-yi*, what do you think of A-zou's story?" A-hong asked changing the subject quickly.

Mama accepted the subject change, releasing Vicki and A-hong from their embarrassment.

"I understand better all the hushing," she sighed. "There were so few choices for her. She did what she had to do for her daughters, but did not stop being a woman."

Vicki listened, trying to appear as neutral as possible for fear of interrupting the flow. The last sentence was loaded with questions. What did Mama mean by "did not stop being a woman"? What did she mean by "did what she had to do for her daughters"? Both statements burst with ambiguity and were wide open for interpretation.

"Vicki, you did not understand A-ma's complaints," Mama pointed out. "They were as eye opening as A-zou's story. I think she will want to talk with you again, but let me tell you what A-hong wisely let go."

Vicki pulled her pad out and prepared to take notes, instinctively knowing A-ma's comments were half the story.

"A-ma never knew she had a younger sister," Mama stated. "She told you the child had been still born; that is what she knew all these years. To have her mother keep such a secret was shocking. She was very angry and let her mother know it. She told A-zou she and Yi-nai-nai could have helped care for the child. There had been no need to give away the last part of your Zou-gong. That was when she walked out."

Vicki shook her head in understanding, imaging how she would have felt if her parents had given away a sibling. This effort quickly showed her that is was not possible to compare her situation to A-ma's. The cultural and economic differences seemed to be insurmountable. A-hong picked up on her struggle.

"It might be hard to understand now, but if you think of the practice in the context of her times, it was not that unusual," he interjected. "It was actually mutually beneficial. The family that adopted the girl received a child and hope for a son. The family that gave up the girl had less of a financial burden to carry. It was an agrarian society and infanticide is not unheard of in such cultures. If you keep that in mind, it was a very humane practice in a subsistence farming society. With economic advancement these types of practices tend to die out."

Vicki had an instantaneous negative reaction to the points her cousin was making, but let it go, knowing it was the doctoral candidate speaking. She realized that any conclusion she reached on the subject would be corrupted by cultural differences. Her personal situation would taint a conclusion further, making a comparison impossible. The struggle and failure of her parents to have a second child made giving a child away incomprehensible. Intellectual acceptance of what had happened was all she could hope for. The deep empathy she felt for A-ma was so magnified by personal feelings that it could not be considered legitimate. Just having these thoughts made her feel heartless, so she pushed them to the back of her mind for reconsideration at another time. Mama jumped back in when A-hong completed his explanation.

"A-ma came back in because she did not want A-zou to tell you about Mr. Shi," Mama continued. "She had felt so ashamed of the whole affair and saw no reason for you to know. They exchanged some hard words. When A-ma objected, A-zou said that Americans wanted to hear the truth no matter how much it hurt and reminded A-ma of the Watergate scandal as proof. She appears to be tired of keeping secrets and wants you to know she did what was necessary to care for her family."

"Americans want the truth?" Vicki asked in disbelief. A-hong began to chuckle. "It's not funny. I know a lot of Americans who would rather hide from the truth."

Mama smiled in agreement. "It does not matter to her. That is her excuse to talk to you. Now I have to use the Ladies' room."

She stood up and walked away, leaving Vicki an opening to speak with A-hong about Joe.

"Real quick, Joe wants to buy an engagement ring for Su-hui," she blurted out. "I told him about your uncle's shop. Can you get him there fast? He's only here a few more days and wants to give her the ring before he leaves."

A-hong had a huge grin on his face. "Of course," he answered shaking his head and chuckling. "I'm not surprised, been expecting it really, just not here. I thought he would take her to Hong Kong or Europe, some place romantic."

"Hong Kong is romantic?" Vicki quizzed.

"For them it is," he answered before turning more serious. "What do you think of the match? You have so much experience with that type of couple."

Vicki was confused. Why would she have experience with "that type of couple"? To what type of couple was he referring?

"What do you mean?" she asked. "What experience?"

"You know the whole cross cultural thing," he answered averting his eyes in embarrassment. "Your parents struggled with it, right?"

With that Vicki remembered the conversation he was talking about. "Sometimes I talk too much," she chided herself quietly.

"No, not at all," he reassured her. "It was a rough time and you needed to talk. Your mother had already spoken with me about her frustrations, so what you said wasn't surprising."

"She still goes wacky every now and then," Vicki sighed. "The whole 'living in a foreign language environment' thing gets to be too much. Dad tells her to speak Mandarin, but that's like a foreign language also. She just wants to speak Taiwanese and she never taught it to him or me."

"It's just language?" A-hong asked knowingly.

"No, it's culture too," she admitted, looking at her tea cup while she swirled her finger around its edge. "Most of their fights center on either language misunderstandings or child rearing. Mom's more of a 'spare the rod, spoil the child' parent and dad's a 'speak rationally spelling out what is expected and encouraging appropriate behavior' kind of guy. It's funny; he grew up with 'the strap'. Grandpa would hit his rear end with a belt to discipline him. Nothing extreme, but still it must have hurt. Anyway, you can imagine where those differences would lead."

A-hong chuckled at this, but she knew an answer to his question about Joe and Sue had yet to be given. "What do I think of the match?" she sighed while keeping an eye on the Ladies' room door. "A-zou would say *'qian shi de guanxi'* wouldn't she?"

"Probably," he laughed. "9000 miles couldn't keep them apart. Seems to be pre-ordained. Fortunately they're from different sides of your family."

"Fortunately or it would get complicated. Even so, it will be a challenge," Vicki said. "Not as much as my parents. They've known each other for a decade and the attraction was there from the beginning. Still the differences in their childhood experiences and how those color their view of the world will have to be accepted. My parents are still married, so there's hope."

They both laughed to her assessment. Vicki noticed the Ladies' room door open, so she rushed in one more thought on the subject. "Give Joe a call at the Grand and set something up."

"Okay," A-hong acknowledged then did a complete change of subject. "So, how about you? What's going on in your life?"

"She's thinking of graduate school," Mama interjected as she pulled her stool out and sat down. "Possibly an MBA."

"Slow down Mama," Vicki cautioned. "I've taken the GRE and GMAT, but am still unsure. When I get back home, I'll take the leap."

"And now we should get back to A-zou," A-hong reminded them. "She wants to talk some more."

The three of them stood up to leave with Mama leading the charge to the door. She stopped to pay the bill while A-hong and Vicki walked out into the midday heat and waited on the street.

"We'll talk later," Vicki whispered with her back to the store. A-hong nodded his head in agreement.

Chapter Nine

A-ma was waiting for them. "A-zou is lying down," she said quietly. "Let her rest. I can talk to you for a little while."

Vicki felt a pang of guilt when she heard this. Even though her control of the interview had been swept away the day before, she was ultimately responsible for the emotional stress A-zou was experiencing. A-ma motioned for them to sit down while she went to gently close the bedroom door. She appeared to still be shaken by her mother's revelations that morning.

"I cannot understand why my mother hid so much from me," she muttered to herself in Mandarin, obviously wanting Vicki to understand. "How could she give away my father's child? It was the last of him we had. I remember the night she went into labor." She switched to Taiwanese and A-hong began to translate.

****

"Bong-chie," Chiu Bu called out. "Come and help me get to A-jim's. Li-ya, run to Mrs. Lin and tell her it is time." She stood up with a struggle and staggered to the door, her daughters jumping up to follow the instructions she had shouted out. Li-ya leaped ahead of her mother and sister, running to the mid-wife's home. She did not understand why her mother was going to the home of her father's youngest brother. Uncle had left his wife, moved to another town, and started a new family. A-jim was alone here. Why risk walking the distance to another house? The teenager knew how dangerous child birth could be, having had classmates whose mothers had died in labor. Even if her mother felt particularly close to this aunt, it made no sense to risk the exertion of leaving home and walking when in labor. By the time she arrived at A-jim's with the mid-wife, her mother was lying on the bedroom *tatami*. Mrs. Lin moved in quickly while A-jim shooed her and Li-an away.

"Go home," she told them quietly. "There is nothing you can do here. Your mother is in good hands. A-gong will need you to run the store."

The two sisters walked home quickly. There was no one on the streets. The war had ended weeks before, but everyone was still unsure who was in charge. Some Japanese had been attacked by Taiwanese men after the surrender to America. Could they still maintain order in Xingang? The Chinese army was supposed to take over, but there were still no troops in town. At least the street lights were still on. The two girls moved quickly to home, remembering how nervous their father had been about their being outdoors without him. They stepped into the house quietly, looked in on their grandfather, and then sat to wait for word.

"What if it's a boy?" Li-ya asked her sister.

"Then mama will have something she has always striven for," Li-an replied. "A son will care for her when she grows old."

"And if it is a girl?" Li-ya asked.

"She will be crushed with disappointment," Li-an sighed. "Pray it is a boy."

They did not see their mother for three days. With each passing day, the chances they had a brother diminished. The two worked in the store with A-gong and waited. Mrs. Lin stopped to talk with A-gong on the second day, but he had been very closed mouth. All he had said was mama was alright. Mrs. Lin had left with a piece of paper clutched in her hand and a stern look on her face. When their mother returned the following day she looked crushed. There was no baby with her.

"Mama, the baby?" Li-ya asked nervously.

"Dead," was the answer. "It is my fate."

****

"She never wanted to speak about it again," A-ma said. "We learned quickly not to raise the subject."

A-zou was still sleeping and her daughter gave no indication she wanted to wake her.

"I don't know how she kept it a secret all these years," A-ma sighed. "It's a shame *Yi-nainai* never knew. My sister loved all of her family so. She would have been overjoyed to add a sister to it."

A-hong smiled at this comment. Vicki knew he had been close to his grandmother. When she had died suddenly after suffering a stroke, he had taken it hard. Much of her time in Taiwan that year had been spent giving comfort to A-hong and his father. A few months later, her mother's uncle passed away, many said it was from a broken heart. The strength A-hong showed through this period still amazed her. Vicki doubted she could suffer two such losses and still remain mentally stable.

"Why had she insisted on talking about Shi *Shu-shu*," A-ma whispered, snapping Vicki's attention back. "I was always so ashamed. It was less than a year after the war had ended."

****

"Shi *Shu-shu* is going to live with us," Chiu Bu informed her daughters. "It will be easier for all of us."

As soon as Li-ya heard this she looked at her sister. Li-an had been predicting this would happen. How would this be easier for them? Now the gossip that had been whispered around the neighborhood would be proven true. It would only complicate her life. She had just taken the test for a position at the bank. Would they want the daughter of a widow living with a man? Xingang was a small city. Everyone knew your personal business.

Why not just marry him? Mr. Shi was a good man. A-gong would not forbid the union. The two men were close friends. Li-ya knew it was her mother's insistence on remaining independent. Baba had given her too much freedom. She was too proud of what she had accomplished with that freedom to give it up by becoming a wife. The neighbors' talk did not seem to bother her. She had A-jim to talk with, A-gong to care for, and Mr. Shi with whom to share life. No one else seemed to matter, least of all her daughters. Li-ya knew her sister was not bothered by the situation. *Jie-jie* was content to be married off and start a new life with her husband's family, even though there was so much more that she could do.

With this thought, the inherent contradictions of her mind set became obvious to the teenager. It made no sense to condemn both her mother's ambition and her sister's lack of the same. She turned and fled the room, choking on her contradictions, knowing she had no choice but to bear the shame in silence.

* *

"I did not understand why she did that until today," A-ma confessed. "She had little choice if she wanted to honor my father's memory. My A-gong understood that. *Shu-shu* must have loved her deeply to agree to such an arrangement. It's so obvious now; they were two wounded souls looking for comfort. I was too young to understand then and too full of shame to see it until today. Thank you A-hui. You have helped open you're a-ma's eyes."

Vicki found her grandmother's gratitude unsettling. She had done nothing other than ask A-zou the name of her mother. If A-ma felt grateful, her gratitude should be directed at her mother not her granddaughter whose question was simply a catalyst. Mama and A-hong sat silently waiting for A-ma to indicate she was finished and wanted to wake her mother. A-ma broke the room's stillness with a whisper.

"Two wounded souls clinging to each other," she sighed. "Then there was only one."

* *

The sound of wailing came from the street. Li-ya rushed to the front door to see what had happened. She had a bad feeling in her heart. *Shu-shu* had not returned home last night. They had waited expectantly all day, numbly attending to the few patrons who came into the store. The streets had been deserted as rumors of violence in Chiayi spread fear.

"Chiu Bu," a voice called from outside.

Li-ya froze instantly. The wailing and tumult continued outside. Her mother walked past the family altar in the front room, handed the baby to her daughter, and called back to Li-an.

"Bong Chie, come here and stay with your sisters," she shouted while staring at the door leading out to the street. She turned to face Li-ya and said, "Don't worry. They will not come to bother you. The three of you should stay inside. I will go out to see what has happened. I cannot run from it. I must face it." Li-an took the baby from her sister as their mother walked with a deliberate stride out the door into the chill of the early evening air.

****

"We heard someone tell her that *Shu-shu* was dead," A-ma whispered. "She came back in very stiffly. Told my sister to care for us, stepped into her room, and slid the door closed. We could hear her quiet moans, but that was all she allowed herself. The baby was still breastfeeding. When she cried, we opened the door so she could feed. A-zou was sitting staring off into nothingness and muttering. One of us would place the baby at her breast. When *mei-mei* finished eating, Li-an would carry her out and I would close the door. This went on two days. Then she suddenly opened the door and asked for the baby. After feeding her, she said we had to open the shop, but *Shu-shu* was gone so we had no baker."

Sounds of A-zou waking came from the bedroom. A-ma stopped her narrative and went to open the bedroom door. Vicki jotted down the last notes, glad she did not have to speak. Saying anything at that moment would have released the sorrow that was burrowing into her soul. All seemed to have come to an unspoken agreement not to add to A-zou's distress. Whatever anguish A-ma felt was hers alone, not to be shared with her mother. Vicki wanted to be certain there was no hint on her face of the hidden emotions she felt.

A-zou slowly shuffled in with a smile on her face. "Did the two of you enjoy each other's company?" A-hong translated. "It is wonderful to see you together again. I feel younger just looking at you." She laughed when the last sentence was finished. A-hong and Vicki blushed. Mama stiffened. Then A-hong said something to his great-grandmother who laughed while she moved to her seat.

"I heard what you said," A-zou told her daughter with a smile then signaled A-hong to translate.

A-ma sucked in a quick breathe. "You heard?" she said in disbelief. "But I closed the door so you could sleep."

"My ears are still good," A-zou chuckled. "And I had slept enough. It's good that we understand each other. You wonder how I could send your sister away. Would you not have done the same at that time in my position? I did not know what would happen. I only knew that I had two daughters whom I loved and lived for. They had to be taken care of."

She became quiet for a moment as long suppressed emotions rolled over her. The tale continued after she regained control. "I could not afford to become too attached to the child," she explained. "A-gong arranged for a respectable family to adopt her. She has had a good life. It took three days for me to return home because I cried for two of them. When they lifted her out of my arms I hated the world. When Li-mei was born I swore never to let her go. I almost did when I slid that door closed after those mainlanders killed her father. Thank you for the care you gave her. I don't remember those days. I only remember waking up."

****

The pain from her bloated breasts brought Chiu Bu back to the world. How long had her soul left her body? The last thing she remembered was being told that her love was no more. However dizzy and weak she felt, the most compelling sensation was the discomfort of her breasts. This pushed her to crawl across the *tatami,* slide open the door, and call for her daughter.

"Bong Chie," she called. "Bring A-mei to me."

Li-an and Li-ya came scurrying to her, tears of joy in their eyes.

"Mama, you're awake!" Li-ya cried.

"Of course I'm awake," she snapped back. "That's how I called you. Now bring your sister. She has to drink."

The pain of the baby sucking brought tears to her eyes, but there was no time to sit idly feeding her child. What had happened in the days she was lost to sorrow?

"Have the soldiers come here?" she asked.

"No. mama," Li-an answered. "No soldiers here, but we heard there were bodies in the river. They say the soldiers have been arresting and shooting many. People who came back from Chiayi said it was horrible. Rumors say it was worse in Taipei."

"Have people been on the streets?"

"Not many," Li-an replied.

"We have to open the store," Chiu Bu insisted.

"But who will bake?" Li-ya asked.

"*Shu-shu* trained his helpers; they can bake until we find someone."

****

"It was hard. We opened, but it was so hard," A-zou whispered. "In the end, my sister said we should move to Ping-dong so we could break the bad luck."

"Your sister?" Mama blurted out. "Not your cousin. I thought she was your cousin."

"No, how could you think that?"

"Her name."

"I was a *sim pu-a*. What does a name mean? I called her *jie-jie*," A-zou said sounding annoyed.

"You called everyone *jie-jie*."

"You couldn't see the family resemblance?"

"Of course I could, but cousins resemble each other, don't they? A-hong and Su-hui resemble each other," Mama insisted.

"Vicki doesn't resemble them," A-zou insisted.

A-hong started to laugh as he finished the translation. Vicki was in shock, caught totally off guard by this exchange. She gave A-hong a scathing look that helped calm him down.

"Vicki is different," Mama muttered. "I'm sorry. I didn't mean to interrupt."

"She is my *jie-jie*," A-zou stated. "We share the same parents. Your mother never told you?"

"It was not a permitted subject," Mama answered. A-ma sat quietly accepting that assessment.

"My sister and her husband owned three rice processing plants," A-zou said, moving back to her story. "I managed the one in Ping-dong. We did quite well. Then the matchmakers began to call."

****

Li-an stood in front of her mother. At no time in her eighteen years, had the two of them shared a conversation like this one. "The Liu family is nice," Chiu Bu reassured her daughter. "They feel you are a good match for their son. Your birthdates and times show good fortune. How do you feel?"

"I will do as you say, mama," Li-an answered quietly.

Her mother was torn between conflicting emotions. Happy that a good family had sent a matchmaker to inquire about her eldest daughter, but frightened because there was no man in their lives to ascertain where the young man stood among the men in town. The Lius seemed eager, asking for only a token dowry and willing to forego the usual inquiry into lineage and character. She just wanted to be sure her daughter would be content with the arrangement.

The move to Ping-dong had indeed been fortuitous. Her luck had changed immediately. Li-an happily looked after her youngest sister and seemed fulfilled. Li-ya worked in the local bank, receiving a promotion from teller to loan officer six months after starting. She herself managed the rice plant easily and the baby was thriving. Then the matchmaker came and immediately threw their settled life into turmoil.

The problem was neither affording the dowry nor caring for Li-mei. Along with their insistence on asking for only a token dowry, the Lius had made it clear they were quite willing to welcome Li-mei into their household during the work day. The past months of caring for her sister and the household had shown that it was Li-an's destiny to be a wife and mother. Li-ya was the problem. She would have a hard time dealing with the coming separation from her sister. Chiu Bu knew she would find it difficult to arrange a marriage for her second daughter, but that was a problem for another day.

"I think the Lius are right," she smiled. "You will match their household well. I will tell the matchmaker we accept the arrangement."

****

"It was a good match," A-zou opined. "Your grandparents were a happy couple, A-hong. I wish all my choices were so good."

A-hong smiled at his great-grandmother's comment, but Vicki noticed A-ma stiffened. She was certain there would be background comments later.

"My life back then was full," A-zou sighed. "My older daughters were grown, yet I had Li-mei. Ping-dong had schools she could attend, although she did not have her second sister's talent. She tried to pass the bank exam, but never could. Instead she went into real estate," she chuckled proudly to herself. Vicki knew her grandmother's youngest sister had done very well in the Taipei real estate market.

A-ma shot a question at her mother that removed the self-satisfied smile from A-zou's face. Her mother snapped back, causing A-ma to leave the room. Mama did not appear happy with the exchange, but remained silent.

"Li-ya, Li-ya," A-zou sighed. "So pretty, so smart, she had the same problems I had, but it was a different time and I was not as willing to let her go."

****

"They no longer want a dowry," Chiu Bu told her second daughter. "They have been asking for more than a year. The father is very impressed with you."

Li-ya stood before her mother with a stubborn look on her face. "I do not want to marry," she repeated what she had told her mother all those months. "I only want my work and to care for you. Besides, the bank needs me. Their policy is to have both a man and a woman involved in every loan interview. I am the only woman in our branch. It would not be right for me to just leave."

Chiu Bu had accepted this justification, but knew the real reason she had been wrestling with this marriage proposal was selfish. This daughter was the only one able to support herself. This gave Li-ya an independence that would permit caring for an elderly mother. But if she were to remain single, then Li-ya would have no one to care for her later in life. Deep down Chiu Bu knew it was the comfort of Li-ya's company she desired most. A husband would restrict that comfort. Investments and whatever her daughters could give would be enough financially, but the emotional support of her daughter was irreplaceable. In the end, she could not condemn Li-ya to the uncertain life that would result from not marrying.

"You do not understand what you are saying," she pointed out. "If you do not marry, you will have no one to care for you later on. There will be no better opportunity than this one. He is the first born son of a respectable family. I cannot sit here and condemn you to a life of loneliness and a beggarly old age."

"My husband does not want the boy," Li-ya cried to her mother. "He says it was born prematurely; it is bad luck. How can a man say that about his own son?"

Chiu Bu could not answer. Her daughter had done everything society expected of a daughter-in-law and wife. Her in-laws loved her. She helped care for her husband's younger siblings, managed the grocery store attached to the family business, and now had provided an heir. Her son was the first born of a first born and should have held a special place in his father's heart. All of his grandparents doted over him, but the father would not acknowledge his birth. The situation had grown so bad over the past weeks that her daughter's milk had dried up. Now the baby was feed by his aunt.

The sound of her son-in-law climbing the stairs caused her to stand up and prepare for another irrational diatribe. She hoped he had not been drinking or arguing with his father. Li-ya had been through so much already. How much more could she take?

Wei Wu stepped into the room and sneered at his mother-in-law. "What is she doing her?" he demanded then thought better of it. "It's good that she's here, now you won't have to tell her later. I've decided we're moving to Tai-dong."

Li-ya reacted in disbelief. "Who do you know in Tai-dong?" What will we do there?"

Her husband laughed. "I don't need to know anyone. The city is expanding. People will need businesses to supply them with food and clothes and fuel. The market there is wide open. That old man downstairs can't see that, but I can."

"What about little Shan-ji?" his wife whispered. "My sister can't move there."

"The rat? Give it to her," he scoffed, pointing at Chiu Bu. "She has always wanted a son. We are leaving here. I can no longer stand those people downstairs."

****

A-ma came storming back into the room in tears, shouting at her mother. A-zou snapped back. Vicki waited for an explosion, but then saw her great-grandmother soften. A-hong sat rigidly without translating the exchange.

"It is your story and I am tired," A-zou sighed. "It does not take much to get me tired these days. Perhaps tomorrow we can continue. Now it is time for the young people to go enjoy themselves."

Vicki breathed a sigh of relief before noticing the effect of A-zou's last sentence on her mother. She was not that worried about Mama's reaction since A-hong was meeting Joe while she was keeping Sue busy.

Chapter Ten

Vicki sat in the hotel lobby waiting for Sue. The normal light traffic of late afternoon flowed through, with guests stopping at the front desk asking for directions or exchanging money. She enjoyed the people-watching this large space allowed. Why did Sue want to meet here? Her cousin claimed it was conveniently on the way to where she would meet Joe for dinner, but Vicki knew better. One of the selling points of this hotel was its isolated feeling. You had to ascend a hill to get here. There were no walk-in guests, no casual, curious tourists who just happened to glance in the window. This was a destination of choice, not chance.

She was grateful for the wait. It gave a little down time to digest the plethora of information that had come her way over the past few days. There was also time to think of how to occupy Sue and redirect any questions about what Joe and A-hong were doing. The rich vein of family stories that was coming from A-zou and A-ma could be used for hours if Sue was open to it. Then there was the all but forgotten subject of Roger. They had only begun to plumb the depths of that problem. Feeling confident that she could have a long heart to heart with one cousin without betraying the confidence of another, Vicki leaned forward in her seat to enjoy the ever changing panorama that was the lobby of a large international hotel. Sue arrived shortly after and immediately began challenging her cousin's confidence.

"Where did they go?" Sue asked without so much as a hello.

"Where did who go?" Vicki replied evasively, trying to slow down or redirect the interrogation.

"You know who," Sue insisted. "Don't try to be cute, Joe and A-hong of course."

"Ah, so you know A-hong is in Taipei," Vicki laughed.

"My dad told me."

"Well, I'm not sure where Joe is," Vicki lied. "A-hong said he was meeting someone, but I can't say who that someone is. Maybe he has a secret girlfriend he wants to check in with."

Sue looked up at the ceiling. "You're hiding something, Vic. I know it."

Vicki shifted nervously in her seat, then just gave up and stood. She was not good at lying and felt looking up at her cousin only made things worse. At least when she was standing, Sue was the one looking up.

"If I'm hiding something and I am not admitting that I am," Vicki teased. "Then there would be a good reason for it and it would be happy news."

She regretted the last sentence immediately. Sue was too smart to be put off by such lame reasoning. What if she put two and two together? Vicki was well aware she was incapable of pulling off an outright denial. The two of them knew each other too well for her to be convincing. Sue's face had a calculating smile on it. She appeared to be weighing her options before making a decision.

"What is that English expression about he who waits?" she asked with a playful grin.

"He who waits?" Vicki replied. "You mean 'Everything comes to he who waits'"

"Or she who waits, right?"

They both laughed, allowing Vicki to gracefully change subjects. Sue suspected it would be a special night and Vicki intended to say nothing to dissuade her.

"So, Joe said it would be a late dinner," Vicki reminded her cousin. "Can you hold out or do you want to get a little something now?"

"I know the cutest little beef noodle place not too far from here," Sue said. "How about we share a bowl and you can tell me how it went today."

Vicki shook her head in agreement and began to walk toward the door. Sue joined her with a question, "Taxi or bus?"

"Bus, it's more interesting."

After they placed and paid for their order, the two young women found space at the long communal table and pulled up stools. They sat facing the plate glass exterior of the shop. Advertisements for the shop's wares partially covered the glass, but Vicki could still continue her people-watching while they ate. Purses were slid to the floor between their legs as they each reached for disposable chopsticks and settled in to await their snack, gazing out the plate glass barrier that served as the exterior wall of the building.

"What do you know about the two twenty-eight incident?" Vicki asked.

Sue hesitated for a moment before answering. "A subject not covered in history class," she said with a dry laugh. "That attack on the Taiwanese is just beginning to come out now and marshal law ended in 1987. From what I've read the army killed about twenty thousand people because they protested against the government."

"One of the men killed was A-zou's live in boyfriend," Vicki told her.

"Live in boyfriend?" Sue asked in astonishment. "What do you mean 'live in boyfriend'?"

"After Zou-gong died, A-zou fell in love with the head baker in the family store," she explained. "He eventually moved in with the blessing of Zou-gong's father. *Xiao A-yi*, the real estate aunt, well she's only A-ma's half-sister. She's the daughter of the baker."

Sue sat silently taking all this in. Vicki felt badly. There was a lot of information in those few sentences.

"How did A-ma react to that?"

"Not very well, they had some words, but A-hong didn't translate them. A-ma insisted on telling her side when we came back from lunch. She's been ashamed of the whole affair all these years, but after hearing A-zou's explanation, she understands and has peace." Vicki purposely left out A-ma's expression of gratitude.

"You're writing all this down?" Sue asked.

"Both my mother and I are," Vicki reassured her.

"I have to read it," she insisted before changing subjects. "So how is A-hong doing? We've both been so busy we haven't had time to talk."

A large bowl of steaming noodles arrived as she finished her question, so they broke their chopstick in half, rubbed them, and began eating with the help of disposable soup spoons.

"It's so hard to get a really good bowl of beef noodles in the States," Vicki said between bites. "I look forward to this every summer."

"And I thought you came back to see your family," Sue teased.

"That too," Vicki replied playfully. "But it's hard to compete with a good bowl of beef noodles."

"Ah huh," Sue agreed with a full mouth.

They ate quietly for a few minutes, watching the world stroll by between the window advertisements. After the edge of their hunger was satiated Sue repeated her question. "How is A-hong?"

"A-hong?" Vicki sighed. "He's still focused on his dissertation, wants my notes so he can add A-zou's experiences to his study. He looks great. From what my mother said, he spends a lot of time taking care of A-zou, but we didn't get a chance to talk about it."

"My dad said the same thing," Sue said. "He was always close to her. They lived nearby, so A-zou did a lot of child care when A-hong was small. She did the same thing for my father."

This reminded Vicki of what A-zou had said. A-ma's first born son should be Sue's father, unless something had been omitted. Those women had thrown so many curve balls over the past two days, nothing was certain.

"What has your dad told you about his childhood?" Vicki asked.

Sue thought for a moment before responding. "Something about A-zou looking after him while A-ma and A-gong started the business."

Vicki instantly began weighing her options. Should she reveal the true reason A-zou raised her father the first years of his life? What purpose would be served by telling Sue the shortcomings of their grandfather? Was being superstitious at that time even a shortcoming? Realizing that she had promised her notes to Sue, Vicki decided to tell the story.

"From what A-zou said today it was a little more complicated than that," Vicki told her.

"More complicated? How so?"

"A-zou said your dad was born prematurely," she began. It only took five minutes to tell the story, but the myriad emotions that crossed her cousin's face made it seem much longer.

"How can a man reject his infant son?" Sue asked in disbelief. "It's not that he was some uneducated farmer out in the countryside. My dad told me he grew up in Tai-dong. His childhood pictures are all of him there. How did he get back to his family?"

"Haven't gotten that far yet," Vicki admitted.

"That explains why he feels so close to A-zou," Sue muttered. Then she brightened up. "But I can read your notes. How about Roger? Need to talk about him?"

Vicki marveled at her cousin's resilience. If only it were a family trait.

"Roger," she sighed. The subject could be pushed to the back burner, but not off the stove. Hearing A-zou's story had taken the edge off. Her little bumps in the road of romance paled in comparison. With this new perspective as a foundation, Vicki took a deep breath and plunged in.

"Like I told you," she started. "He just doesn't know how to speak to a lady's heart."

"Who broke it off, you or him?" Sue asked.

"I did," she chuckled wryly. "Which really pissed my mother off. 'Roger was perfect, so smart, so handsome, so respectful.' I'm sure she liked the respectful part the most. Respectful to her, but not to me. And he was so one dimensional."

Sue laughed when she heard this. "That's the way most people are," she reminded Vicki. "They stay with what they know, what they're comfortable with. The only two people I know who are not like that are you and A-hong."

"Me?" Vicki was surprised. "I'm not a math and science whiz. I stick to words and philosophy, things like that."

Sue thought about it then shot back. "Maybe you're not a math genius, but you do okay. You're missing my point. You can have a conversation with a math whiz and be fascinated. I just fall asleep."

Vicki was still not clear about the point her cousin was trying to make. Was it that she was a good conversationalist or that she found many subjects interesting. Deciding it was the latter she countered, "I just have an innate curiosity."

"Innate curiosity?" Sue muttered.

"Yeah, you know, it's just part of me.'

"I know what innate means," Sue assured her. "Others might call it intelligence. But really, whatever it is, it's rare. You have it. A-hong has it and I don't." She laughed at herself.

Another disconcerting moment, Vicki thought. What was it about this visit? She did not feel comfortable with Sue's assessment. If nothing else, it was seriously overdone.

"I think you're getting carried away," she insisted.

Sue threw her hands up in the air. "There you go again," she moaned. "The two of you never take credit for what you've achieved, never give yourself enough credit."

"And you do?"

"If I don't, I'm learning fast," was the response. "In business, if you don't let people know what you are capable of, you won't get anywhere."

Vicki was astonished at what her cousin had said. It was not so much the content of the statement, but who said it. Sue had been raised in Taiwan. Vicki could not remember how many times her mother had told her a Chinese woman does not talk about her achievements. Sue sounded like a modern woman. Had Joe corrupted her or had she? Whatever the source, Vicki could not pass up the chance to tease.

"Doesn't that go against the traditional model of a Chinese woman?"

Sue had a sassy look on her face when she answered. "It's the twenty-first century, got to change with the times. Besides, it's what attracted my man."

"Whoa!" Vicki exclaimed. "That's too hot for me."

They both laughed and then finished the last of the noodles. The restaurant was beginning to fill. There was always the outside chance, however slight, that someone would be able to understand English too well. With an exchange of glances, they silently agreed it was time to take it outside. Bowls and chopsticks were deposited in the trash and they walked back out into the humidity.

There was still a little time to kill before Sue had to hop a bus to meet Joe, so they strolled along the street. Vicki searched her mind for a topic that was not too random. Since Sue had taken away the subject of A-zou, the only natural subject was Sue's relationship with Joe and maybe men in general. As long as they stayed away from specifics, she should have no problems.

"You know, I am jealous of you," Vicki confessed.

Sue looked bewildered. "Jealous of me?" she asked. "Jealous of what?"

"Oh, the whole long term relationship bit," she replied. "I can't seem to find someone I would want to be with long term." Vicki expected her cousin to laugh and make light of her remarks. Instead Sue's continence changed instantly. The cheerful companion vanished. In her place emerged an anxious, confused young woman. A raw nerve had been inadvertently hit. They walked in silence the next few steps. Sounds of traffic mixed with the blare of music from storefronts and the hum of conversations along the sidewalk to fill in the awkward gap. Vicki swore at herself for being insensitive as she watched Sue struggle with her feelings.

"It's not that easy," she said softly. "Sometimes I think you are the lucky one. You just walk away. I can't. I'm exposed, emotionally naked before him. There are so many questions. What if he doesn't feel the same? Does he really know how I feel? "

Vicki remembered Sue's squeal when she greeted Joe in the hotel lobby. There was no doubt Joe knew how she felt. Anyone in that lobby knew how she felt about him and his reaction to her was not exactly tepid. What other questions did she have? This was beginning to sound like a replay of her conversation with Joe. How could she turn the conversation away from the emotions her words had unmasked? They were in dangerous territory. The deeper they delved into this subject, the more likely Vicki would say the wrong thing and ruin Joe's surprise. Thinking the best way to avoid slipping up would be to play on her genuine surprise, Vicki asked "Haven't you and Joe talked about your future?"

Sue laughed as tears welled up in her eyes. "Of course we have," she admitted. "He wants to have a firm job offer before we commit to anything. It was great of your father to give him that internship, but we can't live on an intern's salary."

Vicki felt a quick shot of adrenaline pulse through her system. Thank God she had not mentioned her father's job offer. Holding her breathe for a second to slow down her mouth, she searched for a way to ease out of the situation without sounding cold. "Did Joe say anything about a job?" she asked tentatively.

"Not yet," Sue sighed. "I've been expecting something. That's why I was waiting for you when you arrived. But you didn't say anything and your mother didn't. Then Joe came and he didn't, so I'm kind of hanging here. Then there are all the other questions. Maybe he thinks it's just too complicated and he should find some girl from Montana. Oh! I don't know." With that she threw her hands up and shut down.

Watching her cousin drowning in anxiety was heartbreaking, but she had promised Joe, not a word. "He hasn't been interested in a girl from Montana for a long time," she reminded Sue. "That's what long term relationships are all about. I'm sure it will work out. If you're nervous, tell him. It'll give his ego a boost. A sassy twenty-first century woman finds him attractive. Works every time."

Sue laughed when she heard this. It seemed to calm her down. As they strolled up to an intersection and waited for the light to change, she tossed the ball into Vicki's court. "That might solve my problem, but you still have yours."

"Mine?"

"Can't find someone to be with long term?"

Vicki was amazed Sue could remember that detail after the emotional high-jacking she had just experienced. "I've been bouncing around looking for a fascinating mind and none have shown up," she sighed.

"Other than your cousin?" Sue asked.

"He doesn't count," Vicki scolded. "Probably gets in the way because I see there is someone like my dream guy out there. I just can't have him, so do I hold out for a perfect copy or do I settle for an inferior version?"

The light changed as she finished. They crossed with a cohort of pedestrians that had been waiting with them, listening to but not understanding their conversation. There was a time when Vicki would have been cautious about what she discussed with Sue on the street. Her cousin had assured her that even though English was a required subject in Taiwan's schools, very few people could understand anything but the basics. Considering her own lack of fluency in Spanish after years of study, Vicki had relaxed some. She remained vigilant, constantly scanning people within earshot for signs they might understand her conversation. There were no signs of recognition among those around them, so their words remained unguarded.

"It's funny," Sue commented. "A few generations ago it wouldn't have mattered."

"What wouldn't have mattered," Vicki asked incredulously. "Marrying your cousin?"

"Didn't you tell me King Tut married his sister?"

"That was four thousand years ago."

"Well, three or four generations ago, it was okay for A-hong to marry his *biaomei*."

"Yeah, then they discovered genes and DNA," Vicki reminded her. "You mix two recessive genes together and you give birth to a three headed baby."

They both laughed at the absurdity of the conversation. Vicki took Sue's comments as an attempt to make her feel better. She also realized that her cousin had fallen back on traditional customs, ignoring modern science. A-hong was not the only convenient modernist in the family. The conversation died down as they reached the bus stop. It was much too crowded here and on the bus to continue talking. Each was left to her own thoughts. Vicki was excited for her cousin. Provided she did say yes, this night would change her life.

Chapter Eleven

Where was Joe taking Sue? Vicki wondered while waiting for the elevator. A-hong had mentioned that Hong Kong was romantic for both of them. Maybe a Cantonese restaurant? There were some great ones in Taipei. The lower level of the hotel had one, but she was not sure Joe would want to go there tonight. At heart, he was a reserved, quiet kind of guy. Everyone knew him here so there was bound to be a lot of noise after he popped the question. A-hong probably suggested a nice quiet restaurant where Joe could request Sue's hand in anonymity. The elevator door opened as she came to this conclusion. She stepped in, pushed the button for the eighth floor, and then leaned on the mirrored walls.

What an exhausting day it had been. Apparently she was now the designated recorder of family history, with A-hong bearing the burden of official translator. The emotions that surrounded her throughout the day had been draining. Hopefully, Mama would just want dinner nearby followed by a quiet evening to review their notes. Stepping out of the elevator, Vicki turned left and counted five doors down. Knowing the number of doors her room was from the emergency exit next to the elevator was a habit she had acquired from her father. Basic hotel safety is what he called it. If there was a fire or an earthquake knocked out the lighting, she could easily get to the exit and down to safety. It had been considered a ridiculous habit by her until the roof of this hotel had caught fire. Now the calculation was performed without thought when staying in any hotel.

She unlocked the door and stepped into the room. A feeling of relief passed through her while closing the door to this little refuge. Unfortunately the feeling was short lived. A-ma and Mama were seated in the room's chairs waiting expectantly.

"Oh, you startled me," Vicki said. "Are we going out to dinner or something?"

"No, not now," Mama told her. "Sue went out?"

Vicki paused before answering. How much should she tell her mother? It no longer mattered. Joe had probably already received an answer, but Vicki did not need anything else complicating her day. All will be known in good time, she thought. "She went to dinner with Joe," was the abbreviated answer.

"Good," Mama sighed. "A-ma has come here to do as A-zou suggested, to tell her story. She does not want to talk in front of A-gong's picture because that would be bad luck."

Bad luck? Vicki thought as she dropped her purse and reached inside for the note pad. Why would talking about your husband in front of his picture be bad luck? This was not going to be pretty. After retrieving a pen from her bag, Vicki sat on the edge of the bed, the two chairs in the room already being occupied, and prepared to listen. A-ma hesitated for a moment then took the plunge.

"A-zou did the best she could," Mama translated. "But there was no way for her to determine the true character of the man being proposed by the matchmaker."

****

"I have met the father," Chiu Bu reassured her daughter. "He is a gentle man much like your A-gong. The son will be like his father just as your father was like A-gong."

Li-ya listened to her mother, accepting her fate. Was not Li-an happy? Her future husband's family appeared to be respectable. His picture showed he was handsome. They were a business family like her family. Their doors matched each other, was that not a good sign?

"You get along well with your mother-in-law?" Chiu Bu asked her daughter while preparing food on the gas burner.

"Yes. Yes," Li-ya assured her. "Everyone in the family has been very welcoming. They would like me to leave the bank and work in the family business, but that is hard for me."

Chiu Bu could not hide her disappointment. Li-ya tried to stop by every day to visit on the way home from the bank. Her mother made sure she was back from the rice plant so they could share this time together. It would be more difficult after leaving the bank. Mama stirred the rice and fish congee then scooped the mixture out into two bowls. These were carried back to the table.

"How does your husband treat you?" she asked while placing the bowls down.

"Mama, I can't eat with you," Li-ya protested. "If I do, I won't be able to eat the food my mother-in-law prepares. Then there will be questions about how I feel and whether something is wrong with her food."

"Ah ya, you need only have a taste," her mother insisted.

Li-ya sighed, picked up a spoon, and tasted the congee. "My husband is impatient with me at times."

"You do not learn quickly enough?"

"No, it's not learning that bothers him," she answered thoughtfully. "He wants to teach me things I already know and is disappointed when he cannot."

"Things you already know?" her mother asked while placing a spoon into her food.

Li-ya laid her spoon down next to the bowl and looked at her mother.

"Yes, the other day he wanted to test me on the abacus, so he could teach me a faster way to use it. When I told him I was the bank champion, he became angry."

"You have to be mindful of his ego," Chiu Bu advised. "Men are like that. They want to feel they can teach you the ways of the world. It makes them feel important and needed."

Li-ya considered this as she took another sip of the congee. Her husband was not as easy to live with as she had hoped. He had a mercurial temperament which led to outbursts when he was frustrated. The target of those outbursts was whoever caused them. If the frustration grew from the circumstances of life, then he vented on the most convenient target which was usually her. After the words had released his anger, he would treat her tenderly as if apologizing. But he never apologized. When her in-laws admonished their son for his treatment of her, he would explode at them, criticizing everything about her. She did not want to share all of this with her mother, but needed to vent.

"He is not as easy to be with as I had hoped," she began.

"You are still adjusting to each other," her mother reassured. "As you get used to his moods, it will become easier."

"He sometimes has a temper," Li-ya whispered. "I do not always know what angers him which makes it difficult to predict his moods."

"Ah yo, you hardly know the man," Mama reminded her. "As you learn his ways, you will be able to calm and manipulate him."

"I hope so," Li-ya sighed. "Now I have to get home, they will need me to help prepare dinner." She stood up, gathered her things, and began the last leg of her daily trek from the bank, still unconvinced that her mother was right. The man she married was not ordinary. In what way he was exceptional was still to be seen.

Li-ya collapsed on the stairs holding her enlarged stomach. It was too soon. The child should not arrive for at least another month. Her mother had warned about climbing the stairs so much, but managing the grocery store required many trips up and down each day. The contraction passed. She knew the child would come by tomorrow. The bile of frustration welled up in her. It was imperative that this child be a healthy boy if she was to solidify her place in the family and calm her husband. Since she announced the pregnancy, her husband had become kinder, gentler, and more considerate. His pride knew no bounds. The baby would be a boy he guaranteed, a healthy, handsome child who would grow up to be like his father. How would the father react if his child was a small premature girl? She stood up and continued climbing the stairs unaware that a stream of fluid trailed behind her.

When she stepped into the office, her father-in-law saw her distress and called for his wife. Li-ya dropped into a chair and waited. Memories of the next twenty-four hours were a blur. What would remain etched in her mind was her husband's reaction when he saw the tiny son she had produced.

****

"Everyone was shocked," A-ma whispered bitterly. "How could a man reject his new born son? His parents scolded him which only made him angrier. His anger was directed at me and our son. He said we both should die, so he could start over. The stress of that time caused my milk to dry up. *Jiujiu* had no strength to suck hard enough, so my sister helped. She had just given birth to A-hong's father."

Vicki sat stiffly trying to do nothing that might interrupt the flow. Mama said something to her mother which brought a sharp response. It appeared to be a reenactment of the spats A-ma had with A-zou and bore the same result. The older generation demanded to be heard.

****

"I have decided we are going to move to Tai-dong," her husband informed Li-ya and her mother.

As soon as she understood these words, desperation began to build inside her. If they moved to the southeast coast, he would be beyond the controlling influence of his family. She would become like a mainlander's wife, bereft of the social safeguards provided by family obligations. There would be little to regulate his behavior since his family could not lose face from his misdeeds. Such a simple statement, but it planted seeds of fear in her heart.

"Who do you know in Tai-dong? She asked. "What will we do there?"

He laughed derisively. "I don't need to know anyone there." This was followed by an assessment of business opportunities in the region. She did not listen. All she knew was her obligation to follow this unpredictably violent man who had rejected her child. He seemed to criticize his father in the background, but it was her son who held her thoughts.

"What about little Shan-ji?" Li-ya whispered momentarily unable to gather the strength for a more vocal response. "My sister can't move there."

"The rat?"

These words cut deeply into her very soul. The baby was his son. What kind of man had she married?

"Give it to her," he sneered pointing at her mother. "She always wanted a son."

Li-ya did not hear the rest of her husband's rant. He had suggested a loving way out of the situation, even if he did not know it. Her mother would be the perfect caregiver for the baby. She was sure Mama would happily raise him. Her sister could continue feeding him, so her child would be safe even if she was not.

"Wei, mama," Li-ya spoke into the phone. "How is my little Shan-ji?"

"He is happy," Chiu Bu assured her daughter. "He is eating and sleeping and laughing and growing. I take him to *jiejie's* every three hours, so he sees his cousin and he's out in the air. Is everything going well there?"

Li-ya felt tears well up in her eyes. She should be witnessing her son grow stronger, should hear his cries and laughter, should smell him and touch him. Swallowing her bitterness, she answered her mother's question.

"Business is good," she informed her. "My husband appears happy with his decision. I have to admit, he was right."

"Right about what?"

"About the business opportunities here."

"How does he treat you?"

How does he treat me? Li-ya thought. What she had feared the most had not happened. His family obligations still had an impact on him. At first establishing the business had taken every ounce of energy from both of them. She had proven to be invaluable to him, so his treatment of her had improved commensurately. But they had been isolated. Now they were beginning to make friends in the community and his behavior seemed to be reverting back. How to answer a simple question in a complicated situation?

"He treats me better than when we were in Ping-dong," Li-ya explained. "Most nights he takes clients to dinner and doesn't get home until late. I spend the days in the store or visiting customers' shops taking orders. We've hired help to deliver the orders."

Half-truths and outright lies, she thought. There was no mention of the physical violence that happened when he came home intoxicated. Help was hired because he was not able to get out of bed some days to deliver the orders himself. What purpose would be served by telling her mother these details? Mama had sacrificed so much to help, even leaving her position at the rice plant to care for her grandson, all to placate her son-in-law.

Mama accepted the answers without asking for any details. Instead she moved on to the subject of health and Li-ya had news.

"Your health is good?" Chiu Bu asked.

"My health is very good," her daughter bubbled. "I am pregnant."

She heard the sound of her mother's gasp through the phone. "Pregnant again so soon?" she asked. "Is that good? Is he happy?"

Is that good? What did she mean by that? Interpreting it as a mother's concern for her daughter, Li-ya tried to calm those fears. "I feel strong," she answered. "This pregnancy is much easier so far."

"How does your husband feel about it?"

His cocky laughter still resonated in the back of her mind. "This son will be strong and healthy like me," he had laughed. "That woman can keep the other one."

"My husband is happy," she assured. "He feels his second son will be healthy and strong."

"How does he know it will be a boy?" Chiu Bu asked knowingly.

How does anyone know? Wives' tales about predicting the gender of a child by how the mother carried it during pregnancy abounded, but she had never seen a correlation between those tales and an accurate prediction. If it was a girl, how disappointed would he be and how would he react? Would the violent streak he had begun to exhibit become more pronounced or would he become calmer with the realization that his son was truly precious? There was no way to predict. "He didn't say how he knew and I didn't question him."

After cooing to her son over the phone, Li-ya said goodbye, hung up, and began to cry silently. She did not want to disturb her sleeping husband.

"Who is the boss?" he screamed at her in a drunken rage. Fear caused her to hesitate for a moment which produced a hard slap to the side of her head. The room began to spin. She dropped to the floor and whispered "You are."

"Say it louder!" he shouted.

"You are," she answered as loudly as she could while remaining on the floor protecting the child inside her. The baby should arrive any day. Did he not have any sympathy?

Sales had been up, but not from his drunken parties with "clients". She had been solely responsible for the increase. Her mistake had been asking if there were any orders from the night's dinner.

He reached down, grabbed a fist full of hair, and pulled her head up. "Don't you forget it," he hissed before throwing her head back down to the floor. She remained on the floor clutching her stomach and sobbing. The sound of his panting filled her ears. Not daring to look at him for fear of provoking another violent outburst, she closed her eyes and turned away.

"Why do you try to anger me so much?" he asked. "Can't you watch your tongue? Just because you are pregnant, doesn't mean you can be disrespectful. You must try harder to improve yourself."

His words told Li-ya that the worst had past. These episodes followed the same pattern, explosion, placing responsibility for his violence on her, and then advice on how to improve. Her husband had made it clear that he was never responsible for his anger. He did not become angry. She made him angry. Since the responsibility for his rages rested with her, she was the only one who could control them. The thought of self-control never entered his mind. After she heard him move away, Li-ya attempted to stand up, but slipped on fluid. She looked down and saw a puddle on the floor and wet stains on her dress. It was time. Would her drunken husband be able to call the mid-wife?

"Mama," Li-ya shouted into the phone. "I have a daughter."
This was greeted with silence.
"Mama?"
"How does your husband feel?"
The question was not surprising, but the answer was. "He loves her, Mama," she laughed. "She is beautiful and happy. My breasts feel full and she is feeding well."

The tone of her mother's voice changed. "Does she look like you?" she asked.

"No Mama, she looks like you."

"Can you talk now?"

"Yes, he took her to show off to his friends."

"Your husband is truly happy?" Chiu Bu queried in a doubtful voice.

Li-ya remembered how he took the news. A look of doubt had passed over his face. She was afraid he would reject his daughter also, but when he saw the tiny bundle in the mid-wife's arms an expression of joy replaced any doubts. So tiny, so pretty, she did not scream like her brother had. Only a quiet whimper had escaped from her before she opened her eyes. When she was placed by her mother's breast, the newborn began sucking strongly. She was everything her brother had not been.

"Yes, he is truly happy," she replied. "I don't know why; at first he appeared doubtful. Then he saw her and lit up." Li-ya stopped her description there, leaving out the return of his doubtful appearance as the day wore on. The edge of cockiness that had informed his every word before the birth had been dulled. Maybe the reality of how precious their son was had begun to dawn on him.

"The boy must come home to join his sister," he pronounced. "He cannot learn to be a man living with an old woman."

Li-ya had watched her husband change gradually over the past few months. He was no longer so flippant about having a son. Life and its hard reality had caught up with his over confident vision. He seemed to realize for the first time that he could not dictate to it. Instead of two sons, he had a son and daughter. Even though he was enthralled by his second child, he knew she would one day leave their family to become a wife. It was his son who would provide for them in their old age, so that son had to come home. She turned away from her husband so he could not see her tears. Were they tears of joy because she would finally be reunited with her little boy or were they shed out of fear for him? How was this spoiled, overgrown child going to teach their son to be a man?

"Mama, I hear him coming," Shan-ji shouted.

"Quiet, A-ji," Li-ya warned her son. The sound of her drunken husband singing came down the lane. She steeled herself for another sleepless night of placating his false sense of pride.

"Go wake your sister and take her to the Lin's," she instructed him softly. "I will come to get you when Baba is asleep."

"I don't want to leave you alone with him," he protested. "What if he begins to hit you again?"

The question broke her heart. Her little man wanted to protect her, but his father was much too unpredictable after a night out with friends. Any hesitation to strike her was lost to the alcohol. It was not safe for a five year old boy to be around such a man.

"I will tell him his children are sleeping so he should be quiet and go to bed," she assured him. "He won't want to wake your sister or you." She had to quickly add the "or you" to her explanation even though it was not true. Her husband treated his daughter like a princess and his son like a soldier. She needed sleep to be pretty for her father. He needed to be toughened up to face the world. "Hurry, he will be here soon," she warned. "Go out the back door."

As her son scooped up his sister and fled out the back, Li-ya turned to face the bitterness of her life. The bastard she called husband spent most of his nights entertaining his friends. He was quite popular among the men in town. Their wives hated him. She stood in the living room on the second floor of their recently completed building. The first floor was occupied by their wholesale business. The second and third floors were their home. The fourth floor was to be a tutoring school where he planned to teach Japanese. Classes would have to be given in the afternoon since it was the only part of the day he was coherent. If only he could take a fraction of the time he spent entertaining and instead use it to increase sales, her life would be immeasurably easier. As it stood now, he partied while she ran the business and raised the children. How much longer this could go on was questionable. Touching her extended stomach, she eased into a chair for a moment's rest before he came in and demand her attention. This pregnancy was not as easy as her last. She had put on more weight and was much larger. How would such a large baby get out of her small body? What if there were complications beyond a mid-wife's abilities? Then they would have to rush to the missionaries' hospital and her husband would be furious.

The sound of him climbing the stairs pushed her up from the chair. He stepped into the room with an unsteady gait, saw her, and immediately began talking.

"My cousin told me of a business opportunity in Hua-lian," he pronounced. "I want to go there to see for myself."

"Hua-lian?" she asked in surprise. "There are only farmers and tourists up there."

"Yes, and they will want our bean paste for their cakes," he laughed. "If it is as my cousin said, a bean paste business will thrive there also."

Li-ya took a second to analyze what he had said. She had spoken with A-Bong after they had started the bean paste business in Tai-dong. He had told her that Hua-lian would be a great place for expanding, but she had ignored it because they were just establishing that part of their business. The large pool-like vats for soaking the beans had only been installed a few months before. Their production of bean paste had begun last month. Should they try to expand so soon? However, she did agree Hua-lian would be an ideal location for expansion. She had no time to do the research, but if he were willing then it might work.

"Will you go before or after the baby comes?" she asked acquiescing to his plan.

"Why do you need me?" he laughed. "That is women's work, just provided me with another son."

He continued to chuckle to himself as he made his way to the bedroom. Li-ya had not asked the question to solicit his help, only to get the information. She had already spoken with the Lins about watching her children until Li-an arrived. A-ji knew where the mid-wife lived and was excited about helping his mother give him another sibling. The thought crossed her mind that Hua-lian had an additional advantage. The man could visit his sister. She was a nun at the Buddhist temple there. Maybe his *mei-mei* could shame him into being more responsible and less violent.

****

Mama stopped translating. She appeared thunderstruck and whispered something to A-ma who responded in bitter anguish. After this she turned to Vicki with tears in her eyes.

"I was a twin," she told her daughter. "That was why she was so large, a boy and a girl. He was born a few minutes after me. I never knew."

Vicki sat transfixed. The pain of this revelation was etched in the faces of her mother and grandmother. She did not dare ask what had happened to her uncle. Instead she sat quietly waiting for A-ma or Mama to take the lead. A-ma spoke first, switching to Mandarin so her granddaughter could understand.

"That is enough for today," she said quietly. "I have no strength to continue."

Vicki escorted A-ma down to a taxi, knowing Mama would have more to say when she returned. Her head was spinning with the revelations of the evening. Now she understood why Mama refused to speak about A-gong. His story was not one that a daughter would be proud to pass on. The feeling that important points had been left out of the translation taunted her. Certain all would be made clear by the end of the night, Vicki returned to the room wondering if she had the strength to act as confessor for an additional generation of her family. It was apparent her mother had been crying when she stepped back in. Mama looked up from her seat on the bed as her daughter gently closed the door.

"I know it is *buxiao* to say this," she began, her hands shaking as tears flowed down her cheeks. "And your father would say it is not the Christian thing to say, but no matter how un-filial, how un-Christian, I cannot help it. I hate that man!"

Vicki stood frozen. She had never seen her mother so distraught. Even when threatening to divorce her husband, Mama had not reached the level of despair she was displaying now. Deciding it would be best to simply listen to her mother; she walked over to the bed and sat next to her.

"I didn't translate A-ma's last sentences because I was so shocked," Mama explained quietly while looking at the floor. "She said 'My little son, he killed my little son.' I had a twin brother and my father killed him."

Vicki felt the blood drain from her head. Killed him? Her grandfather had murdered his own son? It made no sense if everything A-zou and A-ma had said over the past days were true. Questions poured into her mind like water cascading over a falls. Was it possible to commit murder without prosecution back then? She doubted it, especially if the victim was your son.

"Killed him?" she asked. "How did he kill him?"

Mama looked up, pain gripping her face. "I don't know. A-ma stopped after saying that. She muttered 'tomorrow, sometime, not now' then changed to Mandarin."

The phone rang as she completed the explanation. There was a silent agreement to ignore it. "He killed my brother, her little son. How could a man do such a thing?"

With so many questions exploding in her head, Vicki needed basic information. How could her mother not know she had a twin brother? Did the child die as an infant? Why would A-ma call him her little son if he had died so young? Would she not then say he killed my baby? The logical answer implied the boy was older.

"You don't remember him?"

"Who? My brother?" Mama asked in a daze. "No. I was sent to *Amitoufu Gugu* at the Hua-lian temple to be raised as a nun. Then they brought me back to Tai-dong when I was three. It was never explained to me, never spoken about, never even hinted."

How could that happen? Vicki thought. Her siblings said nothing? "Your brother and sister said nothing?"

"No. not directly. Sometimes they mentioned something that made no sense to me. They were immediately hushed. A-gong controlled everyone. We saw what he did to my mother. No one dared to speak. Then I became a stewardess, so I was no longer around to hear after that. They would just follow A-ma's lead. What good would it do to tell me anyway? So many things were never discussed."

There was a knock at the door before Vicki could ask any more questions. She walked over and opened it a crack. Sue stood outside dressed in a stunning outfit and beaming as she held out her left hand. A diamond ring sparkled in the hallway lights. Vicki stood motionless, unable to respond because of all the conflicting emotions inside her. She felt like a computer that had frozen and needed a reboot.

"Who is it?" Mama asked sounding genuinely puzzled. Her speechless daughter threw the door wide open thinking a picture was worth a thousand words. Mama gasped, stood up, and walked briskly to the door. A broad smile had instantaneously replaced her anguish.

"He asked you!" she exclaimed. "Where is he?"

"He's upstairs," Sue told her happily. "We thought you were asleep since no one answered the phone, but I had to let you know before anyone else, *Gugu*. You are responsible for it more than any one."

"Your father doesn't know yet?"

"You're the first."

Mama demonstrated how Americanized she had become by giving her niece a hug. Tears of joy had replaced those of sorrow.

"You should all go out to celebrate," she insisted.

"Won't you come?" Sue asked.

"No, I'm too old for late night celebrations," she replied. Then she turned to Vicki and said, "Go celebrate the future. The past can wait until tomorrow."

Chapter Twelve

Vicki glanced at Sue as they made their way across the plush red and gold of the hallway rugs to the elevators. Which of her cousin's personas was beside her? Certainly not the serious, stoic student she had grown up with. The bouncy, bubbling young woman walking with her had more in common with the squealing, diminutive beauty who had thrown herself at Joe a few days earlier. Vicki realized that no matter how in love with a man she might be, it was not possible for her to pull off a stunt like that. There were just too many German genes in her genetic makeup. The men she had dated used words like fascinating, intelligent, exotic, even beautiful to flatter her. None had used the word diminutive or any of its synonyms in their descriptions. One or two of these men had looked up to see her eyes, while too few had to bend down to kiss her.

"You knew didn't you?" Sue asked snapping Vicki back to reality.

"Not the details," she laughed in response. "But yes, I knew he was going to ask."

"Did he tell you in the States?" Sue continued as Vicki pushed the elevator button.

"No," she answered thoughtfully, remembering her conversation with Joe that left so much unsaid. "We had this conversation where I never got around to telling him about Roger and he never got around to telling me about his plans."

Sue shook her head in acknowledgement as they stepped into the elevator. Vicki went to push the floor button, but paused before doing so. "We are going up to his room right?"

"Oh," Sue giggled. "Yes to his room. He's waiting there for us."

Vicki pushed the button for the floor Joe was on and waited for Sue's next question. The elevator doors slid closed and the hum of machinery working provided background for their conversation.

"When did he tell you?"

"When he arrived, but before you leaped into his arms squealing like a Beatles fan in 1964."

"A Beatles fan?" Sue asked in shock. "Was I that crazy?"

"I wish I had a camera," Vicki chuckled. "I admit to being jealous. I was just thinking what would happen if I tried that. It wouldn't be a pretty sight."

Sue laughed at the thought. "Don't try it with a Taiwanese guy," she warned. "You might find some mainlanders who are big enough, but you'd have to search."

"They'd have to be from up north," Vicki agreed before changing the subject. "So how and where did he ask you?"

Sue had a faraway look in her eyes as she smiled then sighed. "He took me to dinner at the American Club."

"The American Club?" Vicki asked in amazement. "He's not eligible to be a member. How'd he pull that off?"

"A business associate set it up for him," Sue explained.

Vicki felt a tinge of envy. She had been coming to Taiwan her entire life, but had never set foot in the American Club in China.

Membership was restricted to expatriates. Granted it was only a curiosity thing; she had no need or desire to belong. It gave those Americans living in Taiwan a taste of home which she did not need, especially this year when she was running from troubles at home. The envy passed quickly as Sue continued her tale.

"We had a nice American style steak dinner," she informed her cousin. "Then he made an excuse about wanting to look at the wine list and walked to the maître d'. He came back with two roses bound together at the bottom and presented them to me stem first, which I thought was a little strange even for a *yang guizi.* "

Vicki chuckled at the comment, remembering the first time Sue had called Joe a foreign devil. That time she had spit out the term in anger. Since then it had evolved into a term of endearment. He was her foreign devil.

"I figured since it was strange, he had a reason for giving them to me that way, so I looked at the bottom of the stems," Sue continued. "And saw what bound them together." With that she held up her left hand and pointed at the ring.

"He held the roses together with the ring?" Vicki asked in wonderment. "How clever, I never knew Joe had such a romantic side."

"And how would you know?" Sue laughed. "Anyway, that's not the most romantic part of the evening. After I saw the ring, I made a little noise . . ."

"You didn't squeal again did you?" Vicki interjected.

"I don't think it was a squeal," Sue defended. "But I made some noise. I was trying to control myself since we were where we were. He waited for me to calm down and then said the roses symbolized the two of us and this ring bound us together."

With that Sue's voice cracked and tears escaped from her eyes. A subdued smile crept across her face as the elevator door opened.

"Wow," Vicki commented. "That's a side of him I've never seen."

"And why would he show his romantic side to his cousin?" Sue laughed. "That's reserved for women outside the family isn't it?

"No," Vicki chortled. "In Joe's case, that has been reserved for one woman outside his family."

They stepped out of the elevator and turned left toward Joe's room.

"Are my eyes red?" Sue asked before either of them knocked on Joe's door.

"Don't worry, you look great," Vicki reassured then knocked.

Joe opened the door with a sheepish grin on his face, still in his suit jacket, but absent the tie. Sue jumped up and gave him a bear hug while Vicki stepped in marveling at the transformation of her cousin from Su-hui to Sue. It was like a modern version of *The Americanization of Emily*. With that thought she began to wonder, was it a personal transformation or was it societal, the influence of Joe or a change from traditional values to modern? That was a discussion to be had with A-hong. Right now her cousin's behavior made her feel like a third wheel.

She took in the contents of the room after stepping past the happy couple and could not help but think "a guy is staying here." The closet was wide opened revealing a few shirts, a jacket, and a pair of pants draped over hangers. The hotel bathrobe remained in its wrapper on the shelf. Joe's luggage rested on the luggage rack, opened for all to see. His socks, casual shirts, underwear, and short pants still folded inside. At least his shave kit had apparently made it to the bathroom. He would not have to check the drawers when he felt. Nothing had been placed in them. The bed was made, but she knew credit for that went to the housekeeping staff. Chances Joe would go through the trouble of throwing the bedspread over the pillow were meager at best.

While Vicki was absorbing all of this, her cousins were laughing quietly. Then Joe noticed her and whispered something to Sue, who quickly released him from her grasp as she turned red. This made Vicki feel even more like an intruder.

"How did it go?" Vicki asked desperate to start a conversation that would dispel the embarrassment Sue was experiencing.

"How did what go?" Sue asked recovering quickly.

"Buying the ring," Joe informed her.

"You bought the ring here?" Sue sounded amazed.

"Didn't want to pay duty on it," Vicki chuckled.

Joe gave her a look that said she was only half right. "It was more than avoiding the duty. I needed a job offer first don't you think? Your dad didn't talk to me about that until just before I left. By then I was too busy prepping to look for a ring."

Vicki considered this a lame excuse. How could he doubt her father would offer him a job? The question had never been would a job be offered; it was would he be willing to stay in the family business.

"Where did you get the ring," Sue asked pulling Vicki back.

"A-hong's uncle," Joe chuckled.

Sue looked at the ceiling in disbelief trying to act overwhelmed by the conspiracy of her cousins. "A-hong also knew?" she sighed.

"Just found out today," Joe told her. "He set up the trip to his uncle's shop." There was a pause then he changed the subject completely. "You know, I think A-hong is holding out on us."

"What do you mean," Vicki asked.

"Well, when we got there his uncle was all excited. They spoke in Taiwanese, so I can only give an impression of what was said, but it was obvious his uncle thought Harry was buying the ring."

"A-hong?" Vicki spurted out. "But who would he give it to?"

They both looked at Sue who immediately pleaded ignorance. "Don't ask me. As far as I know, he's still the focused doctoral candidate. I've never seen him with a woman who would be considered a girlfriend."

"Maybe his uncle thought he was going for an arranged marriage," Joe wondered.

"Arranged marriage? You've been reading too many history books," Vicki laughed. "There are no more arranged marriages. Modern young people won't go for it."

Joe did not look convinced. "Maybe not, but there was something going on between the two of them."

"The uncle who owns the jewelry business is really his grandfather's brother," Sue pointed out. "That generation might still think an arranged marriage is a possibility."

This seemed to bolster Joe's conviction. Vicki wondered, what did A-hong do that put such an idea in Joe's mind? She chose not to ask the question. They were celebrating an engagement, not analyzing A-hong's love life, although the whole conversation left her with a strange feeling of ambivalence.

"There was one other thing I noticed," Joe remembered. "His uncle kept repeating something that sounded like it might be a name. Something like 'bwei mwei'"

"*Beu mwei?*" Sue asked.

"Yeah, that's it!" Joe said triumphantly.

Sue started to laugh. "That's me," she told him. "I'm his *beu mwei,* his *biao mei* or his cousin. I guess his uncle knew more about what was going on than you thought."

"Well, I don't know," Joe replied unenthusiastically. "A-hong seemed put off by the whole thing. He seemed to be explaining a lot."

Sue looked at Vicki. They both came to a silent agreement to move on.

"If he's holding out on us, then you should simply ask him," Vicki suggested. "So where is your partner in crime?"

"Ask him?" Joe chuckled. "No thanks. When the man wants to, he'll tell us all about it. As for where he is now, he's at Prince Albert's on Zhongshan Road."

"Prince Albert's?" Vicki puzzled.

"Yeah it's a new English style pub. A-hong says it's great."

Great for the English or the Taiwanese, Vicki wondered. She guessed it was a fusion type of place probably offering fish and chips or fired rice. Her trust in A-hong's opinion of an English pub was limited, but she was hungry. The lovebirds in front of her had just finished a steak dinner. They might want to continue this little discussion, but she needed sustenance quickly. "You two have eaten," she reminded them. "But your poor little cousin has not, so how about we suspend our discussion of A-hong's love life or lack thereof and reconvene at Prince Albert's. We can share a pint and ask the man himself."

Joe put his arms around Sue and looked down into her eyes. "Sounds good to me," he said. "How about you?"

Sue looked up with the most adorable smile and shook her head in agreement. That was when it struck Vicki that they would expect to share a cab. The third wheel feeling gripping her stomach hardened. When they arrived at the pub A-hong would be there to quell the sensation of intrusion. Before then she wanted to let her cousins share a little private time, but they would insist.

"Okay," Joe exclaimed. "Let's go. Just have to shed my jacket and grab my keys."

Vicki's mind began to race. She needed a polite, believable excuse fast.

"Why don't the two of you go ahead," she suggested. "I want to stop and check on my mother. It's been a tough day for her."

Sue looked surprised. "You're coming aren't you?" she pleaded.

"Yes, of course," Vicki promised. "Just want to see if she's settled down. Maybe I can talk her into coming. You go ahead. I won't be long. Remember, I'm the one who hasn't eaten. Besides I wouldn't miss this celebration for anything. It's been ten years in the making."

With that the three of them headed for the elevators. Joe and Sue went to the lobby while Vicki got off on her floor. She paced up and down the hallway for a few minutes, killing time to be sure her cousins left before she hit the lobby.

When Vicki arrived at the Prince Albert Pub, Joe and Sue had already gone in. The pub was on the ground floor of a typical poured concrete structure. The exterior was covered with a façade of heavy wooden timbers giving the front of the building the look of an eighteenth century London public house. As she made her way to the entrance, Vicki wondered if this place would resemble the family oriented pubs of England or the young adult pubs of New Jersey. She needed the former. No food had entered her system since lunch. The beer and burgers of Jersey would not do.

Stepping in revealed a restaurant setting which put a smile on her face. After the day's labor, it would be nice to enjoy good company and an order of fish and chips. Scanning the tables, she spied her cousins at the far end of the restaurant. Joe and A-Hong were laughing while Sue appeared to be scolding her newly minted fiancé. The girl needed an ally so Vicki hustled back to join the fray.

"Here she is," Joe exclaimed. "Now we can get an expert's opinion."

Being called an expert by Joe did not bode well. Vicki could think of nothing she knew that deserved that title. At twenty-three, the only thing she could claim expertise in was picking the wrong men.

"I have many opinions," she warned. "None of which rise up to the expert level."

"Oh, but you are at the expert level when it comes to balancing two cultures," Joe insisted. "You've done it with such finesse your entire life."

"Oh shit, not that again," Vicki muttered as she dropped into the empty seat beside Sue. A-hong sat across from her with a grin on his face that told her there would be no help from that quarter.

"Careful Joe," A-hong warned. "That sounded like you have awakened the Jersey girl in her."

"Now that was an impressive use of English," Joe chortled. "It showed an excellent command of the language and an in depth knowledge of American culture."

"Joe!" Sue scolded. "What are you on? You haven't even had a glass of beer."

"I'm drunk with love, my dear," he countered.

This produced a groan from everyone. Vicki had never seen her cousin act like this, but forgave him his exuberance. It was not every day the woman you love agrees to marry you. A Taiwanese waitress came to the table before anyone could respond.

"A-hong, how are you love?" she asked with a British accent. It was then that Vicki noticed she was not Taiwanese at all, but a Eurasian girl.

"Hello Nikki," A-hong smiled. "Let me introduce you to my two *biaomeis,* Sue and Vicki, and my good friend Joe. Everyone this is Nikki Salisbury. Nikki, we're here to celebrate. Sue and Joe just got engaged."

"Congratulations!" Nikki beamed. "I've heard a lot about all of you."

The three of them sat in quiet surprise. Was this the interest that A-hong's uncle was thinking about?

"Nikki is my English tutor," A-hong informed them.

"No, I wouldn't say that," she responded. "He just practices with me."

"She tries to correct my Americanisms," A-hong laughed.

"And he helps me with my Mandarin," Nikki told them. "Corrects my Cantonese-isms"

They both laughed at their descriptions. "Now I'm sure your cousins are hungry, so what will it be?"

Orders were quickly placed with Sue and Joe asking for drinks while Vicki and A-hong ordered meals. As Nikki left, Vicki noticed Joe motion to A-hong, who waved him off. It was obvious to Vicki that they were hiding something. She decided to let them enjoy their little inside joke. Sue could tell her all about it later. Looking up, she noticed Nikki stop and speak with the bartender who looked directly at her and waved. Vicki meekly returned the gesture, assuming it was meant for her. He could not be waving at A-hong because her cousin's back was turned toward the bar. It must be the whole Amerasian/Eurasian acknowledgment thing. They were always aware of people with similar backgrounds.

"Do you think she'll do?" Joe asked in mock seriousness.

"She's just a friend," A-hong told him. "Besides she has a boyfriend in London and that big burly guy behind the bar is her father. He's a retired Royal Navy man and is very protective of his daughter."

"Is that why she has a boyfriend in London?" Sue asked. Vicki purposely let her cousins lead this conversation. Nikki seemed like a wonderful girl, but for some reason Vicki felt uneasy. If Joe and Sue could pull out more information from A-hong maybe Vicki could figure out why.

"I doubt it," A-hong answered. "It probably has more to do with opportunity and proximity. She attends the University College of London and this guy is a grad student there."

"She goes to school in London?" Joe asked. "How does she tutor you here?"

"Her parents own the pub and she comes back every summer to help out," A-hong told him. "I met her last year and we've been listening to each other's worries and complaints since then whenever we're both in Taipei."

"That's a shame," Joe sighed. "She would be perfect."

"Joe!" Sue admonished.

"Oops, you're right," he apologized. "We're off subject anyway. If I remember right, we were soliciting the advice from our resident expert on mixed cultural relationships."

This pulled Vicki out of her neutral corner. The mystery of the conversation from the time Nikki left was forgotten. They were beginning to push the wrong buttons. How could she get it across to them that her experiences growing up would have little to do with their relationship?

"You're asking me for advice about relationships?" she chortled. "Remember Roger? I chew men up and spit them out, but don't recommend anyone follow my method. It doesn't lead to Nirvana."

"Roger never had it," Joe insisted.

"No one seems to have it. You shouldn't ask me about relationships."

"We don't want advice on relationships," Sue calmed her. "Just suggestions on mixing both cultures on a day to day basis."

Vicki thought about what Sue requested. It brought back some hard memories. As far as she was concerned her parents did not mix cultures so much as smash cultures together. It had led to some horrific arguments that still resonated in her mind. She could not give them the advice they were looking for without giving out the dark side of her family life. How much of a bearing would her experiences have on their relationship was debatable.

"I really don't see a connection between my parents' relationship and yours," she said in a final bid to beg off the subject.

"We know every relationship is unique," Joe assured her. "But there are similarities in all relationships. Neither of us grew up in a culturally mixed household, but you did. I realize it's unfair to just dump this on you and we're not looking for a definitive guide to cross cultural marriage. Any pointers come to mind that might help us avoid stupid misunderstandings while we plan our wedding?"

Joe's plea showed Vicki this was not going away. If she was going to be thrust into the role of counselor, she was not going to sugar coat anything. "You have advantages that they didn't have," she began. "They were married a year after they met. The two of you have had a decade to get to know each other.

"Not really," Sue pointed out. "Most of that time we were in separate countries."

Vicki held her hand up, signaling they had to let her finish. "You met when you were teenagers, so you were more open to accepting differences," she reminded them. "They were in their mid-twenties and more set in their ways."

"So, you're saying it should be easier for us?" Joe asked.

"Easier?" she pondered. "No, but you have an advantage. Remember my father started studying Chinese because he thought there was a business opportunity."

"Smart man," Joe interjected.

"Shush, let me talk," Vicki scolded "He became fascinated with Chinese culture after. You did it in reverse order, Joe. That gives you an edge. And Sue grew up with a mixed up cousin which gives her an edge."

"You never struck me as mixed up," Sue chuckled.

"Well, I was, possibly still am," was Vicki's response. "But all that was just a preamble. How did they mix the cultures day to day? Sometimes I think they never did. They've had and still have some tremendous blowouts. My mother throws the word divorce around liberally. Luckily for her, dad just ignores it. But you're all aware of that to some extent."

She included that last little comment for Sue. Joe had seen the tip of the iceberg over the years, especially after he began his internship. A-hong had provided a sympathetic shoulder to cry on during the year he spent at Rutgers. Sue had been more distant. Memories of childhood long suppressed deep within Vicki's consciousness began to flash across her mind. Her mother's obsession with grades, her need to control everything about their family life and her sometimes extreme negative reaction to surprises were a few of the subjects Vicki had kept to herself. They should have enjoyed celebrating holidays from both cultures, but Mama could not handle a proper Lunar New Year celebration and had learned to despise the commercialization of Christmas so there were no holidays in the Phaff household.

These points had little to do with Joe's and Sue's questions. What was everyday life like when she was growing up? At times her childhood was a clash of modern American middle-class culture and traditional Taiwanese culture. Did they want to hear that? She did not think so.

"I can only give you a child's view of their attempts to intermingle East and West," Vicki continued. "As you might expect since we lived in America, my dad spent a lot of time explaining to my mother. He used to tell me that she was a permanent ten year old child. A lot of her questions were pretty basic, things that American kids learn in grammar school. She knew that and would get very frustrated. So, the first thing I would suggest is being prepared to be a teacher. She taught dad in Taiwan and he taught her in America. Just be ready to deal with each other's frustration."

Joe and Sue were now listening intently. A-hong sat quietly watching the proceedings. His face had the look of a proud brother watching his sister perform. Vicki scanned through her memory trying to ferret out other relevant subjects. What had precipitated most of her parents' clashes? They often hovered around either child rearing issues or the English language. Dad had wanted to restrict the speaking of English to outside their home. He had only partially succeeded. Mama had refused to teach him Mandarin. Taiwanese was not even a consideration. Arguments were almost exclusively in English which caused frustration for both partners. Mama felt frustrated because she could not always express complex ideas in that language. Dad's frustration came from her attempts to express those ideas which often created incomprehensible sentences. Before she could point this out, Nikki returned with their order.

"My father says the drinks are on the house," Nikki smiled. "And he wishes you all the luck in the world."

Joe and A-hong turned around and raised their glasses in thanks. Nikki's dad smiled and nodded his head in acknowledgement.

"You're right A-hong," Joe admitted. "This is a capital place."

"A free beer swayed your opinion?" Sue teased.

"Don't underestimate the power of beer," Joe advised.

The meal gave Vicki a bit of a respite to think. What bothered her most about the evening so far was the way she had felt when Nikki had arrived. Was it a desire to protect her cousin that drew it out of her or was it something else? Why would she feel threatened by or even jealous of Nikki speaking with A-hong? Knowing her blood sugar levels would not support any analytical thoughts she put it off to protectionism and concentrated on her meal.

"We've been dealing with the teaching aspect all along," Joe reminded everyone between sips of beer. "But it is something we should keep in mind."

Sue nodded in agreement, so Vicki considered that topic covered.

"Have you discussed which language will be the primary one in your home?" Vicki asked between bites.

All three of her cousins stopped what they were doing and looked at her. Apparently it was not a subject that they had touched on. The four of them had fallen into the habit of speaking the language not spoken in whichever country they were in. Since trips to America for A-hong or Sue were a relative rarity, they usually conversed in English. She knew from her mother's experience that not speaking the language of your youth could become an issue. It would also give one of them an advantage in any argument. No one responded, so she decided to let that question hang for the moment.

"Something to think about," she said then moved on. "Have you talked about child rearing? Will it be the *jia fa* and *gui xialai* method or the reasonable discussion and grounding method?"

"The what?" Joe asked. Sue and A-hong had knowing smiles on their faces.

"They didn't teach you those terms in college?" Vicki asked factiously. She knew A-hong and Sue would understand the concept of "groundings" because she had taught them. It had never occurred to her to teach Joe the Chinese terms. Sue stepped in, allowing Vicki a chance to sip her beer.

"*Jia fa* literally means family law," she informed her fiancé. "And *gui xialai* simply means to kneel down."

"The *jia fa* around the Phaff house was a thick wooden ruler," Vicki sighed "Caused many major blowouts between my parents. Dad hated it as much as I did. He would tell my mother that she hit me to release her anger not to teach me. As you can imagine that didn't go over big."

"Your mother hit you with a wooden ruler?" Joe asked incredulously.

"Yeah, one of those thick ones we used to get from the volunteer fire department during fire prevention week. You know the type. You can use them to pull the rack out of a hot oven. They have a twelve inch ruler marked on the edge. 'Spare the rod, spoil the child' was

Wei Jia-yi's motto. Dad had more of a child psychology approach. Never discipline when you're angry. He'd send me to my room and calm down then give me a punishment that was commensurate with the offense. It had to either teach me or make me do something constructive. So, when I pissed him off, I cleaned the bathroom or read a book of his choosing and discussed it with him. I hated *The Hobbit* for the longest time," she chuckled then reached for her beer.

The emotions these revelations were releasing made it hard to continue. A-hong noticed and stepped up to fill in the gap. She was sure he understood her feelings more than Sue or Joe, having been there to listen during the darkest time.

"Sometimes when Chinese children are disobedient they are told to *gui xialai,*" he picked up the explanation. "That means kneeling with a straight back and placing your hands behind your head. Usually it's for a set period of time. Occasionally, you might have to explain your actions and apologize while you kneel there."

"It's not as bad as the *jia fa,* but it is humiliating, especially as you grow older," Sue pointed out. "I would never use either method. One of the things that most impressed me about my American uncle is his ability to control his temper and teach proper behavior without violence."

Joe had a shocked look on his face. The Phaff brothers raised their children the same way and Joe's mother came from a quiet loving family. Vicki had overheard a conversation between her aunt and her mother about raising children. Her aunt had stated emphatically that she believed in raising children with love. There were no misused rulers in Joe's home.

"That was the traditional way of raising children," A-hong pointed out. "Not just in China. Remember 'Spare the rod, spoil the child.' Now people are starting to use psychology more than the rod. Grounding your child works better for everyone, don't you think?"

Vicki smiled at that, happy to see A-hong starting to participate more in the conversation. She finished her beer and decided it was time for a visit to the ladies' room. The gift from Nikki's dad was having the usual effect. Her face felt like it was glowing red and her bladder was full. "If you'll excuse me," she said with a smile. "I have to visit the ladies' room."

"I think I'll join you," Sue said as Vicki rose. As soon as they were out of ear shot, Vicki began grilling Sue. "What's with A-hong? He's so quiet."

Sue hesitated for a second, made a decision, and dove in. "When you came in the lighting around you was very flattering," she explained "You probably didn't notice because you were looking for us, but just about every guy in the place turned to look at you."

Vicki began to feel very self-conscious. Not many patrons had left since she arrived. As soon as she heard Sue's explanation, she had the feeling every eye in the place was on her.

"There were some whispered comments I overheard," Sue continued. "The standard 'Ah, yo she's an *ainoko,* so pretty."

With that Vicki felt her face glowing; thank God she could blame it on her reaction to the beer. How would she have explained it otherwise? "What do you mean 'the standard'?"

"I know you never believed your father when he told you about the comments he overheard on the street, but that's what people in Taipei say when you walk by," Sue repeated what she had told her so many times before. "But what I want to tell you most is that Joe commented rather proudly about how good you looked and then A-hong said 'If I could find a woman like that who wasn't my cousin, I'd marry her.' And don't you tell him I told you!"

Vicki stopped short in the little hallway leading to the restrooms. She was trying to process what Sue had just said, but was having a time of it. Was A-hong doing the same thing she was? Using her as a litmus test by which to judge all potential mates? "I promise not to say a word," she reassured Sue. She could not think of anything else of intelligence to add, so they went into ladies' room and then returned to their table. All the while Vicki was trying to sort through her feelings. Had A-hong's comment really changed anything? What did he mean by 'a woman like that'?" Did it indicate he wanted an *ainoko* for a wife or a tall woman or someone of similar personality to her? All were questions that were impossible to ask. She felt exceptionally flattered that he had said it, but it also bothered her that she enjoyed the comment that much. Thinking back on her feelings over the course of the evening, Vicki discovered that A-hong's opinion did not really surprise her. She was as special to him as he was to her. That was the reason she had reacted to Nikki. Deep inside was a need to protect this special cousin.

By the time they reached the table, the guys had paid the tab and were ready to go. Joe had a meeting in the morning, Sue had work, while she and A-hong had a date with A-zou. It had not been much of a celebration. As far as Vicki was concerned, it had been more of an interrogation. They had not even mentioned the revelations of the day. A-hong had no idea what A-ma had told her while he was shopping for rings with Joe. That had to wait until tomorrow. She felt drained by the day's activities and prayed Mama would be asleep when she arrived back at the hotel.

Chapter Thirteen

Vicki pulled herself out of bed. Mama was straightening the room without any effort to be quiet. Easy for her, she was sound asleep when Vicki quietly crept into the room. It had been past one o'clock when she had finally slipped between the sheets. The extra rest her mother had was going to be an issue for the entire day. Shorting oneself of sleep when not yet over jetlag was incredibly poor form. Standing up, Vicki tried to remember when A-hong said he was bringing A-zou to the Neihu apartment. She glanced at the clock and noted it was eight. Less than seven hours of fitful shuteye translated into a groggy mind. If today were anything like yesterday that was not acceptable. Remembering that A-hong would be in the same condition gave her some solace. Misery does love company after all.

"You are awake," Mama stated the obvious. "Good, we have to go down to breakfast before they close."

Vicki could not help but feel a little annoyed by her mother's exuberance. She grunted a "good morning', placed her feet into the throw away slippers provided by the hotel, and staggered numbly into the bathroom to begin her day. A quick shower would improve her outlook immensely.

The lively sounds of the lobby only added to Vicki's angst. Her mother danced her way across the space to the breakfast buffet, greeting everyone she met with a smile and a compliment. Times like these were fraught with the tensions of their unique mother/daughter relationship. When her mother exuded energy at the same time Vicki was dragging, the crevasses that broke the landscape of their relationship widened dramatically. Knowing that any explosion would be the result of her lack of patience, Vicki vowed to be extra vigilant. "Sickness comes in from the mouth; disasters go out from the mouth." It was one of her mother's favorite expressions and one that should rule this day. A glance at the glass wall that was the hotel entrance revealed a dank, rainy day. She would get no comfort from the sun today. The day promised to be as dark as her mood.

She rolled up to the buffet entrance behind her mother in time to overhear a conversation in Taiwanese with the maître d'. After this short exchange, Wei Jia-yi did the unthinkable and stood to the side so others could be seated ahead of them. This was so out of character for her ultra-competitive mother that Vicki snapped out of her doldrums.

"Is something wrong, Mama?" she asked.

"No, no," was the reply. "Just want to sit along a wall, maybe in a corner, so we can talk before going to A-ma's."

Vicki's heart sank. Her duties as family historian were beginning earlier than anticipated. Scanning the edges of the room for candidates likely to exit quickly, she spied a businessman folding his newspaper. After a final swig of coffee, the gentleman rose and walked briskly to the check out. Mama would like the corner location, but Vicki would find the soaring plate glass windows intimidating. There was something about a wall of glass twenty feet high rubbing up against her elbow that she found unnerving. Her mother would call that silly, so Vicki played the dutiful daughter and followed the receptionist to the table.

By the time Mama was ready to talk, Vicki was on her second cup of java. Not normally a coffee fanatic, the brew's jolt of caffeine was having the desired effect. Hopefully there would be no yawning as her mother laid herself bare.

"I thought about the questions you asked before Su-hui came last night," Mama began quietly. "It must have sounded crazy, but you have to know the environment I grew up in."

Vicki listened attentively, not having taken her note pad she would have to rely on caffeine kicking her memory into gear.

"My father controlled everything in our house with his temper," Mama told her staring off into the distance. "We lived in fear. No one dared to disobey him. When my brother tried to protect A-ma, A-gong became like a possessed demon. The physical abuse *Jiu-jiu* endured no child should even witness."

"That's why you never talked about him," Vicki stated.

"That's why," was the answer. "It is why I went to America to study. It is why A-ma did not oppose me marrying your father. It is the why of so much of my life. All the hushing, all the secrets are because of one sick man whom I called father."

The last sentence was cut short. Leaving Vicki with a brood of questions she dared not ask. Mama reached for her coffee and sipped a little as she struggled to control herself. Her daughter could not discern whether it was anger or sadness that was overwhelming her. After a brief pause, she rallied and promptly changed subjects.

"So, how did the celebration go last night?"

This caught Vicki off guard. Many of the subjects discussed at Prince Albert's could not be mentioned here. Going with a subject that would obviously meet with approval, Vicki began by describing the pub.

"We went to an English style pub on Zhongshan Road," she said feeling the caffeine kick into high gear. "The owners are a retired British navy man and his Cantonese wife."

The comment had the desired effect, piquing Mama's interest and drawing the focus away from any dinner conversations.

"And they have a lovely Eurasian daughter who is quite friendly with A-hong." She purposely left out mention of Nikki's London based boyfriend. Maybe that would keep Mama calm when the subject of A-hong came up.

Her mother was now all smiles. It seemed nothing made her happier than seeing young people find a soul mate. The thought made Vicki feel a bit guilty about her little subterfuge, but it was for the common good.

"We should go there sometime," Mama suggested. "It might be interesting."

Suddenly her little lie of omission threatened to become complicated. Now Vicki had to dance around one more issue. "Well, it was cute," she replied. "But the food was pretty basic. We only went there because A-hong was friendly with them. He goes there to practice his English with her."

"He has another *ainoko* tutor?" Mama laughed shaking her head.

Vicki did not like the trajectory of this conversation. Unable to think up a way to change it for her benefit, she decided to end it.

"It's getting late," she pointed out. "We had better get going in case A-ma wants to talk before A-zou arrives." With that she picked up her purse and stood up. Mama seemed a little bewildered at first, but slowly followed suit. A quick stop was made to hand in breakfast coupons at the cashier and then a taxi to Neihu.

They arrived at A-ma's in short order and climbed the stairs to her apartment quietly. The clanking of the metal security gate let them know A-ma had no intention of waiting to greet them. The door was ajar when Mama reached the landing. Her mother had already retreated to the living room. Vicki shed her shoes quickly and hopped into the apartment first. Her grandmother was in her television chair wearing a stern look. It was apparent A-ma had lost her inhibitions about talking in front of her husband's picture. Vicki dropped into the seat she had been occupying for the past two days, muttered a good morning to A-ma, took out her note pad, and waited for Mama. Since A-hong was escorting A-zou, her mother would do the translation duties.

Mama began a conversation with her mother that quickly bogged down in bickering. She apparently surrendered and took a seat between grandmother and granddaughter.

"I told her about Sue and Joe," Mama informed Vicki. "She said my brother had already told her, but right now was not the time to talk about it."

A-ma said something, paused for a moment, and began reciting with a blank look on her face.

"I realize when I stopped last night it might have given the wrong impression," she stated. "You're A-gong was not a murderer. He was abusive, out of control, irresponsible, but also haunted by something in his past. Some of the things he said hinted at bad experiences when he was in the Japanese army."

****

A shout woke Li-ya. Her husband was having another bad night. These nights were becoming more frequent. He would shout things out in Japanese. If he woke up, she would feign sleep, not daring to let him know she was aware of his nightmares.

"It happened again last night," Li-ya told her mother-in-law over the phone. "He shouted to someone 'get down', laughed, cursed, and said the sergeant is dead."

Her mother-in-law listened patiently. "He has had these dreams since he came back from the army," she sighed. "His father spoke with him, trying to help, but it did little good. There was a sergeant in his unit who had served in China before being stationed here. He hated us Chinese."

"That's where the sergeant's ghost comes from," Li-ya interjected.

"Sergeant's ghost?"

"Yes, when he is drunk," she explained. "He sometimes whimpers about the sergeant's ghost looking for him."

"That's why I said he was haunted by something," A-ma said, pausing her story. "He was haunted by his sergeant's ghost, but I don't know why."

"So, he was a soldier suffering from some sort of post-traumatic stress?" Vicki interrupted.

Mama did not appear to appreciate her daughter's conjecture, but passed the question on. The response was harsh.

"If you want to give him an excuse that is a possible explanation, but it does not release him from responsibility for his behavior, for decades of abuse, for causing the death of my little boy."

The last statement hung in the air like a storm cloud, dark, brooding, full of destructive potential. Vicki did not dare hazard another question. They were only minutes into the day and she already feared A-ma would shut down like the night before. The pain from the loss of her little boy was still palpable. After gathering her wits for a brief instant, A-ma plunged into the darkest waters of her life.

"I have made another son," he crowed. "He is strong like me. We have no need of the other one."

Li-ya lay on the *tatami*, exhausted. Shan-ji sat beside her cradling his brother, Shan-bao. He showed no reaction to his father's biting words. Jia-luan cuddled her little sister, Jia-yi, cooing and ignoring the conversation. The mid-wife had left after cleaning up and settling the newborns. Her mother-in-law would arrive tomorrow to help with *man-yue*. For a month Li-ya would have the help and comfort of her husband's mother, after that there would be little to control him. The twins were less than a day old and their mother was already worried. Her husband had not even acknowledged there were two babies in the room. He had briefly looked at his new daughter, grunted, and began doting on her twin brother. Ironically, the girl resembled a Wei more than a Chiu. Her father was not impressed.

A deep disappointment welled up through the haze of exhaustion that clouded her mind. He had been to Hua-lian and had spoken with his sister. There had been hope in her heart. The visit had changed him subtly. It was as if he had suddenly become aware that he had a soul and his actions might impact on it. Her hope died when he ignored his new daughter and disparaged his eldest son. If he could not change for his children, he would not change for her.

"I have spoken with my sister," her husband announced. "I told her how hard it is for you with twins and asked if her temple would be open to the daughter being raised there."

She listened in disbelief. "You want to send my daughter away to live in a temple? How will they feed her?"

"There is a woman who works in the kitchen," he told her. "She has a child who is still breastfeeding"

Li-ya took in what he was saying, trying to comprehend. Then the calculating began. He had not touched this daughter since his mother had returned to Ping-dong and had only reluctantly done so while she was here. Breastfeeding both babies was draining. Nannies helped with the childcare, but between what they could not do and managing the business she had little energy or time. If they were to expand into Hua-lian, then her time would be at a premium. She did not expect him to take responsibility for the new branch. He could not even take responsibility for himself. But more than any other consideration, her husband's nightly drinking pushed a decision on her. Before she could agree, he made a comment that revealed an additional reason he wanted to send their daughter to the temple.

"She can pray for us when she gets older," he pointed out.

Pray for us? Now he was worried about his next life! The irony was not lost on her. If he could only worry about this life, there would be no need for prayers. Then the full meaning of his statement struck her.

"As she gets older?" she asked. "How long do you intend for her to be in Hua-lian?"

"I have no need for a second daughter," he snarled. "My sister can raise her to be a nun."

"A nun?" she snapped back. "She is two months old. How can she make the choice to be a nun? They will not accept her. This is not the Tang Dynasty."

He laughed at her protest. "She will become accustomed to the temple. After her schooling it will be the sensible choice for her to make."

"Your sister knows this plan?" She asked knowing the answer. His sister was a sweet, pious young woman who had made her choice three years before at the age of fifteen. The temple would not accept girls before that age.

"It will happen naturally," he assured her before turning and walking away.

"Where is Shan-bao?" he asked.

It was clear he had been drinking, even after swearing he would not. Li-ya glanced out the second floor window to see if the van was parked outside. Seeing it at the curb confirmed her worst fear. Her husband was a wild driver when he was sober. It was a miracle he had arrived home in one piece. She should have sent one of the workers on an errand so the van would not be available.

"*Didi* is where all two year olds should be at eleven o'clock," she snapped then regretted her tone. The potential for this to turn into an explosive situation was high. Tread softly she reminded herself.

"Get him up," he commanded. "I have to take him back to the restaurant."

"You have to do what?" she asked incredulously.

"They don't believe me," he explained with a laugh.

"Believe what?"

"They don't believe he can use numbers," was the proud response. "I told them he can add and subtract numbers, that he has math talent. They said I am lying, so I will bring him back with me and show them."

What he said was incredible. The child could repeat what she taught him, but she never dreamed her husband would take that to mean the boy understood numbers. It was just a little game she played with her son, just as she had played with her other children. Now the father was bragging to his drinking buddies.

"Didi only repeats what I say," she reasoned. "He does not understand. You should go to bed. There is no need to go back to the restaurant."

The slap struck her left ear and drove her back.

"I gave my word that I would bring back my son and he would show them I was not lying," he hissed. "Now get the boy."

"You can't drive like this," she insisted. "These men will not remember what you said come morning. Please come to bed and let your son sleep."

With that he grabbed her by the shoulders and threw her to the ground. She landed hard, driving the air from her lungs. As she tried to catch her breath, he leaned over and began to punch her about the head. Her only defense was to curl up in a ball and use her arms as a shield.

"Please don't!" she sobbed. "Please just go to bed! It is not safe for you to drive. I beg you! Leave the boy alone. He is so small. Let him sleep."

He reached down and pulled her head up by the hair. "My honor is at stake," he growled. "The boy will come with me now. We will settle your account later."

A sleepy toddler was carried out to the van by his father. After placing the boy in the front passenger seat, her husband climbed into the van, started the engine, and sped off into the night. It was the last time she saw her little boy alive.

✱✱

"I should never have taught him about numbers," A-ma whispered. "His father would not have taken him to show off that night if I had not."

Vicki sat transfixed as A-ma sobbed. Mama had struggled to finish the translation then descended into her thoughts. The apartment became silent as pent up pain overflowed. All three women rested in the moment allowing A-ma to cleanse the debris of this tragedy from her soul. The sounds of rain striking the windows filled the void.

Chapter Fourteen

A-ma was the first to pull herself together. She suddenly stood up and announced that they all needed a cup of tea. Neither Vicki nor her mother protested, although Vicki suspected there were entirely different motives for their silence. Mama probably wanted the tea for the calming effects of drinking something hot, even if the air was warm and muggy. Her daughter felt the need for caffeine before the jolt from the morning coffee wore off. While A-ma was in the kitchen the doorbell chirp broke the quiet.

"That must be A-hong with A-zou," Vicki said as she rose to push the release button for the street door. Her enthusiasm for the day's labor had been dampened by A-ma's grief. She walked to the apartment door and opened the security gate. When they reached the landing, A-zou said something to A-hong who turned around and went back down umbrella in hand. Vicki assisted her great-grandmother in without A-zou protesting, not a good sign.

By the time A-zou was settled, A-hong had returned with two bags of food. Vicki smiled at him and said a good morning. He reacted with a contrite look and a muttered reply. This sent her mind into overdrive. It was so unlike him. Why would he be acting so strangely? A quick review of the previous night produced only one possible answer. He suspected Sue had told her about his remark when she had stepped into the restaurant! The thought made her stomach lurch. How would she be able to handle such an embarrassing topic with a brain dulled by exhaustion and running solely on caffeine?

A-hong carried the bags to the table then began moving chairs around so they could sit with A-zou. Vicki moved back to her place, deciding to focus on the task at hand. Any questions or explanations her cousin might have would have to wait until later. She picked up her note pad and waited for the show to begin. Before A-ma could be seated, Mama threw a question at her mother. A-ma responded and then looked at A-hong. The room went silent for a moment, all eyes on the unofficial translator who did not seem to notice. A-zou said something to him that snapped his attention back.

"A-zou asked if your grandmother had told her story," A-hong said to Vicki, still avoiding looking directly at her. "Your grandmother said yes. Then A-zou said good; she was going to explain hers."

A-zou looked at Vicki and began speaking in the same cadence as the previous day.

****

Give the boy to me? What does he mean by that? Chiu Bu stood frozen in shock at the possibilities of what her son-in-law had said. Could it be possible to raise her grandson as a son, even adopt him? She quickly rejected the thought. If the boy were a second son, the custom of the child being given his mother's surname existed. But this boy was not only a first born son, he was also a first born grandson. No matter what this man said, his parents would not allow it.

"I will care for the boy," she assured her daughter. "I am not afraid of any bad luck that might accrue from his early birth. He is my grandson. My blood is in his veins."

She could see this comforted her daughter. As for the father, he did not appear to have heard what she said. "When do you intend to leave?" she asked Wei Wu.

"As soon as we can," he laughed.

"It will take a few days to make arrangements," Chiu Bu told him. "If that is not fast enough, then you can leave the baby with Li-an."

"But Mama, what about the rice plant?" Li-ya asked with concern.

"Ah yo, I do that to stay busy," she claimed lightheartedly. "There is nothing more important than my children and now my grandson."

"Thank you, Mama," Li-ya whispered.

"Have you spoken with *mei-mei*?" Li-an asked, passing her nephew to his grandmother.

Chiu Bu positioned the boy on her shoulder and rubbed his back, marveling at how well her grandson was growing. Li-an seemed to be handling her son and nephew with little trouble. Of course, she was only responsible for feeding little Shan-ji, but between his aunt and his grandmother the child was thriving. They all enjoyed his laughter. The pity was his mother rarely heard it.

"Yes and I have news," Chiu Bu told her daughter. "She is pregnant."

A look of concern passed over Li-an's face. "Pregnant so soon? Shan-ji is only a year old. She has no one to help her down there."

"Yes, yes I know, but she said her health is good, that this pregnancy is easier than the first."

"How does Wei Wu feel about it?"

"He is confident it will be a healthy boy," she snickered.

"What does he know about predicting the gender of an unborn child?" Li-an asked derisively. She never put any effort into hiding her contempt of Li-ya's husband. "If it is a daughter what will he do? That man cannot handle disappointment."

The question only reinforced Chiu Bu's doubts. "I wish all my choices had turned out as well as the one I made for you," she sighed.

"You did the best you could," her daughter consoled.

If only I had borne a son, she thought, he would have known the Wei boy had problems.

"Mama, I have a daughter!" Chiu Bu heard Li-ya shout through the phone. The news stole any words she had from her throat. Her daughter's tone was reassuring, but it did not mean the husband was accepting. If he rejected this child, what would they do? The girl could join her brother, but how would they feed her? Li-an was no longer breast feeding.

"Mama?"

Her daughter's shout pulled her back. "How does your husband feel?" she asked with trepidation.

"He loves her, Mama. She is beautiful and happy. My breasts are full and she is feeding well."

Chiu Bu could feel a weight lift off her. This was quickly replaced by a recurring worry. Would her son-in-law demand his son return home? She knew from the day she accepted responsibility for Shan-ji that her hold on him would be tenuous. So much of her day to day happiness now came from this little boy. Li-mei was at school or in tutoring classes. Shan-ji provided company and filled the day with his laughter. If he went back to that man's home, his soul would be crushed and she could do nothing to prevent it. With this thought came the question, was she really worried about the boy or was she saddened that his returning home would leave her lonely? Determined not to dampen her daughter's happiness, Chiu Bu pushed aside her concerns and asked, "Does she look like you?"

"No Mama, she looks like you."

She felt a sudden rush of pride fill her heart then doubts flooded back in. Unable to control these worries she asked, "Can you talk now?"

"Yes, he took her to show off to his friends."

His friends, she thought. Were these the drunks he spent his nights with? Concerns were beginning to overwhelm her, so Chiu Bu reached for a question of reassurance.

"Your husband is truly happy?" She knew her voice was full of doubt, but could do nothing about it.

"Yes, he is truly happy," was the reply. "I don't know why. At first he appeared doubtful. Then he saw her and lit up."

When she hung up the phone, Chiu Bu knew why her son-in-law had appeared doubtful. There was nothing unique about a cocky young man. She had witnessed the doubts of so many of them when the reality of life came crashing down onto their shores. A feeling of resignation filled her as she accepted the fact that her little Shan-ji would soon be returning to his father's house.

"*Gege* come, you have to get ready," Chiu Bu told Shan-ji.

"A-ma, why do you call me *gege* now?" his little voice asked.

She was busy gathering the boy's clothes into a bag while trying to hide how upset she was. A phone call that morning had confirmed her fears.

"Mama," Li-ya had whispered into the phone. "Wei Wu now insists *gege* has to come home. He will pick him up this evening."

"I understand," was all Chiu Bu had said. Both women knew from Li-ya's whisper that the situation could become volatile. This was the environment her precious grandson would enter. Neither mother nor grandmother could change that simple truth.

"I call you *gege* now because that is what you are," she told Shan-ji trying to sound cheerful. "You have a *mei-mei* and you are going to meet her tonight."

"Will Mama be there?"

"Of course she will. Your father is coming for you now."

"Who is my father?"

"You don't remember him?" the question was absurd. The child could not remember his father. He was an infant the last time that man was anywhere near him. "Well, you will meet him in a little while. When he comes in you must bow to him and say 'Hello, baba.' He is a very busy man, so listen to him and do what he says."

"When will I come home?"

Chiu Bu found it all but impossible to answer this question. It took everything she had to turn to her grandson and say, "Shan-ji, this is not your home. Your home is with your mother and sister. You are going home tonight."

He grew quiet and had a look of confusion on his face after this. When her son-in-law arrived, the boy was frightened by all the noise his father produced. Wei Wu noticed and immediately began questioning her.

"Why is he so quiet?" he snapped after silence followed his son's bow and hello.

"He is not accustomed to loud noise," Chiu Bu defended.

"Well, he will become accustomed to it very soon," he shouted. "I will make him into a man."

"Into a man?" she asked. "Let him be a boy before you try to turn him into a man."

"What do you know about men, old woman?" he laughed. "It is good I came to get him now. You would have him cooking and cleaning before long. Come here boy, it is time to leave this woman's world."

"He is only two years old," she begged. "He belongs in his mother's care."

"That's where I am taking him," he told her. "To his mother." With that Wei Wu picked the boy up and walked out the door, ignoring the terrified screams this produced.

Chiu Bu walked to Li-an's home from the rice plant just as she had before little Shan-ji had arrived. All hope of her grandson becoming a permanent fixture in her life had vanished when Wei Wu carried him away. It had taken months to fill the void. Work and visits to see Bong Chie and her children only partially covered the emptiness. Li-an's life was still the center of tranquility for her mother. These daily visits gave her some solace and the children looked forward to the treats she picked up at the local bakery along the way.

As she began climbing the stairs to her eldest daughter's apartment, a small voice shouted out, "A-ma!" Chiu Bu heard the pounding of five year old Liu Xing-ren's feet running to greet her. This brought an instantaneous smile to her face. One grandson to help fill the emptiness left by another.

"Don't run, A-ren," Li-an warned her son. "Let A-ma come in before you get excited."

Chiu Bu reached the door, gently pushed it open, and stepped into the apartment. A-ren saw the paper bag in his grandmother's hand and began making a fuss.

"What did you bring?" he shouted.

"Have you been *guai-guai?*" she asked him.

"Yes, I help Mama with *didi* and *mei-mei,*" he claimed proudly.

Li-an looked at him dubiously. "Sometimes you teach your brother and sister the wrong things," she grinned. "But, yes you have been good today."

"Then you can have some *shin koa me,*" his grandmother said before placing the treats on the table. A-ren quickly reached up for a piece then waited for his mother to give him others for his siblings. He scooted out of the room to deliver his catch while his mother and grandmother settled at the table with cups of tea.

"I spoke with *mei-mei* yesterday," Li-an sighed. "She said this pregnancy is the hardest. Her stomach has grown so much larger than the first two. I think she is worried the baby is too big."

Chiu Bu sipped her tea and sighed. "I have the same worry. How can she continue like this? This baby is drawing all her strength away and yet she must manage a business, care for her children, and deal with that man."

Li-an became agitated at the mention of her sister's husband. "I do not want to talk about him," she spat out. "I offered to go to Tai-dong and help, but he refused to allow it. Why does he insist on isolating her? We must find a way to help. When this child is born, she will have no strength to care for the other two. Who will help with the *man-yue*? He does not want me to do it."

Her mother perked up a little when Li-an asked about her sister's after birth care. "I have been speaking with Mrs. Wei," she told her. "We agreed that Wei Wu will listen to his mother when it comes to this matter, so she intends to go down for Li-ya's *man-yue*. That will give her some rest."

"Good, good," Li-an said before changing the subject. "How is Li-mei?"

"She does well in school, but she does not have Li-ya's math ability," Chiu Bu chuckled forlornly. "She wants so much to be like her sister, but I don't think she will be able to pass the bank test."

Li-an shook her head in agreement. "Li-mei is much better with words and relationships. But that is a concern for another time. Right now Li-ya is the worry, one worry at a time. Did she tell you about his idea for Hua-lian?"

Chiu Bu placed her cup back on the table and recounted the conversation with her second child. "Yes, bean paste for farmers in the mountains," she chortled. "There might be a market there. I think they should first solidify their paste business in Tai-dong, but his cousin could be right. If they start before anyone else, they will become the primary supplier in the area. She said he is going to do the research, so at least she won't have more to do in the beginning."

"I feel better about it now that you put it that way," Li-an breathed while reaching for her tea. "And his sister is a nun there. Maybe she can help him with his troubles."

"That would be a miracle," her mother laughed.

The two grew quiet. Sipping tea and thinking of the woman in Tai-dong they desperately wanted to help.

Twins, how could Li-ya cope with twins? Chiu Bu sat in her kitchen, heating water and waiting for her daughter's mother-in-law. Mrs. Wei should arrive at any moment. She could not stay long, but had insisted on speaking before boarding the bus for Tai-dong. It would take five hours over mountainous roads that gradually descended to the ocean before she arrived at her destination. The two grandmothers had never been close, but Chiu Bu now felt a deep gratitude towards this woman. The sound of her ascending the stairs announced her arrival.

"Wei Tai-tai, welcome," Chiu Bu said as she held the door open. "Please have a seat. I am boiling water for tea. It will be ready in a minute."

"Oh, I shouldn't drink too much tea," she laughed. "The bus won't stop for an old woman's bladder."

They both laughed in agreement then sat at the table; each bundled in layers of clothing against the damp chill of a Taiwanese winter. Warm tea leads to warm conversations, Chiu Bu thought as she sat.

"I want to thank you for agreeing to go down and help my daughter," she began stiffly before noticing the water was boiling.

"There is no need to thank me," Mrs. Wei insisted as Chiu Bu stood to prepare the tea. "She is my daughter-in-law. Someone has to help her and my son can be so particular." The last part of the sentence was laced with sadness. There was a pause in the nascent conversation as they enjoyed the comfort of hot tea. When Mrs. Wei resumed, it took a dark turn.

"My son was still a boy when he went into the Japanese army," she recounted sadly. "He came back to me a stranger. My husband spoke with him, trying to help, but the memories wouldn't fade. The boy saw friends blown apart by bombs. His sergeant was a sadistic man who hated anything Chinese. Wei Wu was a favorite target of his abuse. When this man was killed, they celebrated. Afterwards A-wu began to feel guilty. He felt guilty that so many of his friends had died and he had lived. He felt guilty about celebrating the death of that sergeant. Then after he came home, he felt guilty about the dreams and the shouting out at night. And now I feel guilty about what he puts my daughter-in-law through."

Chiu Bu sat quietly, unsure what to say or do to ease the pain. She sipped her tea and waited for a sign from her guest.

"I fear for our grand-daughter," Mrs. Wei blurted out. "A-wu said he does not want a second girl. He intends to give her away."

These words struck like a physical blow. Memories of the sorrow felt when she gave away her daughter flooded Chiu Bu's mind. Before she could regain her balance, Mrs. Wei made a proposal.

"My daughter is at the Shan Li temple in Hua-lian," she began hesitantly. "She is a sweet eighteen year old novice nun. We have supported this temple for years. My husband has spoken with the superior nun and they are open to allowing my daughter help in raising her niece. The temple has a large staff of young women. One or the other is always breastfeeding. It would be a safe haven for the baby."

She listened quietly, weighing the pros and cons of the proposal. How would Li-ya react? If the man was determined to give his daughter away could anyone stop him? The pain she felt revisiting her decision to give up a child showed the wound never heals. Was this a viable alternative?

"How would you convince your son to go along with this plan?" she asked.

"I am not worried about him," Mrs. Wei answered. "I can sway A-wu easily. Can you persuade Li-ya that it would be for the best?"

The advantage of this arrangement was that it was not irreversible. If the man was already making noises about sending the baby away, then giving her to an aunt was the best proposition available.

"I will speak with Li-ya," she assured Mrs. Wei. "I think she will see the wisdom of it, but what about your daughter? She has no experience dealing with one so young."

Mrs. Wei smiled. "Thank you for your concern. She helped with her younger siblings as she grew up. It is not so foreign to her."

"Then we will send the girl to Hua-lian," Chiu Bu agreed. "She will be safe there and still be part of our family."

The two women quietly finished their tea, each lost in her thoughts.

"The two of you had it all arranged before you even saw my daughter," A-ma hissed bitterly. "Give away my daughter for his salvation."

A-hong seemed reluctant to do the translation, but had begun it before realizing how toxic A-ma's words were. A-zou accepted his translating, responding to her daughter without hesitation.

"It was for her safety," she snapped back. "He was your husband."

"And you arranged my marriage."

A-zou became quiet for a moment then sighed. "That is enough for the morning. The young people should go out for some fresh air away from us."

Mama stood up to accompany Vicki and A-hong, but A-zou said something that stopped her.

"A-zou wants to speak with me alone," Mama told her daughter with a concerned look.

"So, A-hong and I go to lunch alone?" Vicki asked unsure if it was a good thing. He had been so distant, so preoccupied. It might turn into a very quiet meal.

Mama shook her head affirmatively, but with obvious reservations.

"Don't worry, Mama," she reassured. "He's my cousin and I'm not fifteen anymore."

"I know you are not fifteen anymore," her mother replied. "And I am worried because he is your cousin. Don't forget that."

Chapter Fifteen

What did her mother mean with that warning? Of course he was her cousin. It was humiliating to have A-hong subjected to that. Vicki let the issue slip away as she and A-hong stepped out of the stairway and its reverberating concrete walls that amplified a whisper into a shout. As soon as he stepped out onto the sidewalk, she turned and hit him with a broadside of American directness. There was no way they were sitting through lunch with him staring off into space and muttering. Thank God the rain had stopped. This was not going to be a conversation to be had huddled under an umbrella.

"What is with you?" she asked a little too harshly as they stepped into the street.

A-hong looked at her directly for the first time that morning.

"She told you didn't she?" He asked bluntly.

Apparently, it took only a year in Jersey to become direct, but the question did not shock her. How to dance around the topic without embarrassment? Start slowly Vicki told herself. Let the conversation evolve so they could become more comfortable with the subject.

"Who told me what?" she parried.

"Sue told you about my, how would those nineteenth century novels put it? About my indiscretion," he chuckled to himself.

Vicki congratulated herself on her choice of strategy. Ease into the subject then divert the conversation whenever possible. His choice of words gave a perfect opportunity to divert.

"Your indiscretion with whom?

"With my words."

"Careful in nineteenth century literature, a gentleman's indiscretion could result in a bastard child," she pointed out. This could turn into a fun game.

"Okay, okay," he conceded quickly. "Not the right choice of words. How about my indiscrete comments?"

That one was going to be harder to dodge. At that moment she regretted all those summers of tutoring. So much for becoming a game, it was going to be hard work if she was to keep her word to Sue. Thinking of Sue brought back the memory of her word play when Sue had accused her of knowing what Joe was up to the night before.

"So, hypothetically, if Sue had told me something," she countered coyly. "Would you find my knowledge of that something to be good or bad?"

A-hong stood quietly working through her question. It was purposely wordy, meant to give them more time to become accustomed to this topic. Knowing her cousin, it would not take long to work through it, so she needed to quickly come up with responses that would put him off.

"Hypothetically? You mean like *jia ru shuo*?" he confirmed.

"*Jia ru shuo*? Supposing?" Vicki considered, playing this for all it was worth. "Yeah, that would work. Suppose she told me something? Good or bad?"

"Then you might find it flattering, but embarrassing," he answered.

"And you?"

"Me?" A-hong looked at the ground and chuckled. "I would just find it embarrassing."

"Then I absolve you of your embarrassment. Now where are we going to eat?"

"Absolve me?" he quizzed. "What do you mean by that?"

"Absolve?" she chuckled, happy that her strategy was taking the sting out of his discomfort. "To free from or release."

"So you have released me from my embarrassment," he laughed. "I wish it was that easy."

"It is if you want it to be," she reminded him. "Now food, your poor little cousin is about to drop from lack of nourishment."

"You are not poor and are certainly not little," he countered jovially. "How about Pizza Hut today?"

Another bullet dodged, Vicki thought. How she pulled it off in her current mental haze was beyond her. The only explanation was sharp reflexes.

"Pizza Hut?" she teased. "In Taipei? Why Pizza Hut?"

"Nostalgia I guess," he answered. "It's not La Familia, but we're not in New Brunswick. Jersey pie is hard to come by around here."

"You're not going to get good pie anywhere west of the Mississippi," Vicki laughed knowingly, having traveled to Montana by car a few times with her parents. "But I'm curious, so let's do it."

"Okay," A-hong chortled.

They began strolling along the side of the street toward Neihu Road, stepping around puddles and avoiding the splash of cars rolling past. They finally climbed onto the sidewalk at a break in the parked scooters. The final few yards to the corner were obstacle free. At the intersection, they waited for the light to change. Four lanes of roadway and a steady stream of motor scooters along with the occasional taxi stood between the cousins and Pizza Hut. A-hong appeared to have last night's comment behind him. His face bore a tired smirk which told Vicki he was about to spout out something he thought was humorous.

"I'll warn you," he chuckled. "Some of the toppings might seem a little strange to you."

"Don't fret," she countered. "I've been to California. They put just about anything on top of a pie there. But I'm not getting a topping anyway. Always have a simple cheese pie when I'm trying somewhere new. Toppings would mask any deficiencies."

"You're a real Jersey girl, aren't you?" he teased.

"What's that have to do with anything?"

"A pizza connoisseur or maybe a pizza snob," he poked.

She put a shocked look on her face before defending herself. "Just because I know what good pizza tastes like does not make me a snob!" she insisted. "You've had Jersey pizza and loved it if I remember right."

He laughed and shook his head, conceding the point. "Yes I am a convert to New Jersey's thin crust pie."

The light changed so she stepped off the curb and barked, "Let's go. Talking about food is just getting me hungry. With that she began marching in front of a wall of idling motor scooters impatiently waiting for the light to release them.

A pizza snob, she thought. He knew she had grown up with Ms. Anna Guliano. Vicki Phaff may not be Italian by birth, but her best friend's family had given her palate an Italian education. A-hong had been a guest at a few of their Sunday dinners. That was where he had learned what good authentic Italian food was. How dare he call her a snob!

"You know that comment - - - " she started.

"About being a pizza snob," he interjected. "Is unfair or maybe annoying or did it just piss you off?"

"All of the above," she laughed as they stepped up onto the sidewalk in front of Pizza Hut. It was spooky sometimes the way he could finish her sentences. They walked past the delivery scooters on the sidewalk. Only two were there out of the ten that were parked there when they went to the noodle shop. The lunch business must be good. "So are you going to apologize now or wait until we sit down?"

A-hong burst out laughing while reaching for the door. "Okay, maybe that could have been put a little more diplomatically," he apologized. Vicki nodded her head to accept his contrition and stepped into Pizza Hut.

I can't believe they don't have a plain pizza." Vicki complained as she finished her seafood slice.

"You could have ordered a special," A-hong reminded her. "Hold the toppings except the cheese."

That was not a true option and he knew it, Vicki thought. He was baiting her to see if she would react. Even after this thought she could not help herself, there had to be a response to such a preposterous statement.

"Then we would have had to order an entire pizza," she countered. "And they won't know how much to charge us."

"We could have just paid for the toppings," he said with a smirk.

"Oh, no," she snapped back. He was playing with her. Why was she reacting? Still she continued, enjoying the banter. "I'm too much my mother's daughter for that."

A-hong chuckled and looked down as he fooled with the paper cup that held his guava juice. "You are a fascinating mix of East and West," he said without looking at her.

"What do you mean by that?"

"Nothing, just an observation."

She was taken aback by this comment and found herself floundering, searching for words.

"Roger didn't think so," she blurted out.

"Roger?" A-hong queried. "So, who broke it off, you or him?"

God, how could he always know the right question to ask to push her off balance? She really was not comfortable with this swerve in the conversation. How to get it back to center?

"You know the answer to that," she whispered. Then regained her voice and jumped the subject back to more stable ground. "Do you realize that was the first pizza we have shared since you left Rutgers?"

A look of surprise crossed his face before he responded. "I think you're right. We didn't go to any unusual restaurants last summer. You were in a beef noodle, dumpling frenzy at the time."

"Beef noodle and dumpling frenzy?" she quipped. "Why because they were the only restaurants we went to? What, were you in Taipei for two days? I wouldn't call that a frenzy."

A-hong was laughing at her by the time she finished. He was suddenly in a playful mood and she was going to play right along with him. "What do you miss about Rutgers?"

"Miss about Rutgers?" he repeated. "Haven't really thought about it. Let's see, there are the grease trucks with their overstuffed sandwiches. I already mentioned La Familia before. All those buses with all those campuses and all those students, but I can't say I miss the crowds."

"Crowds?" she huffed. "New Brunswick can't compare to Taipei."

He conceded the point by raising his hand, but added "Those crowds in New Brunswick are a lot younger."

"Yes they are," Vicki agreed. "And all those young coeds who wanted me to introduce you to them," she just could not resist the opportunity for payback.

He burst out laughing. "I owe you for running interference for me."

Vicki smiled, appreciating his use of the phrase she had taught him.

"You know what I miss the most about Rutgers?" he asked turning serious. "I miss your help and company. I owe you a lot, Vic. Won't have made it through without your help."

This caused a pause in the exchange. How was she to reply to that? Deciding to ignore the company part of the comment, she instead focused on the help.

"Which help are you referring to?" she asked. "The coeds, the English, or the food?"

"Ha," he snorted. "Well the English was a lifelong commitment on your part. Already mentioned the food."

"Only the junk food."

"Isn't it sacrilegious to call pizza junk food?"

"The grease trucks are not exactly health spas."

"No, but their sandwiches taste so good."

They shook their heads in agreement. By now she had regained her equilibrium and decided to squeeze in a response to his statement in between the nostalgia.

"You don't owe me anything," she assured him. "I owe you. That was the most trying time of my life. I needed a sympathetic ear and you were there for me. I don't know what I would have done without your support. My mother was going crazy and you helped me understand her."

They rested in her acknowledgement momentarily then Vicki jumped back in trying to guide the conversation to calmer waters.

"But really, no plain pizza?"

A-hong accepted the change without comment. "I'm sure they did a lot of research before making that decision."

Vicki was surprised to feel her nerves unwind and was shocked at how quickly she had become tense. They had wandered into dangerous territory and had touched on subjects that were reserved for Sue and Joe. Honestly discussing her breakup from Roger with the man against whom he was measured would be unbearably embarrassing. Determined to flee from the topic, Vicki forced the conversation toward the philosophical.

"So this is a good example of the contrast between modernization and Americanization," she opined.

"How so?" he asked before continuing into conjecture. "You're saying that Pizza Hut is a sign of modernization not Americanization? Isn't pizza Italian?"

Perfect she thought. They were back on safe turf. "You're supporting my thesis," she chirped. "Pizza is Italian. Pizza Hut is American. But this pizza would die in the States."

"Maybe, but Pizza Hut is a franchise and that's an American concept, no?"

"That is not American," she countered pointing at the menu and enjoying their game of verbal ping pong.

A-hong smiled at her, but did not back down. "American business is like a chameleon. It may change color to blend in with the indigenous culture, but it remains American."

"You just can't admit when you're wrong," she shot back. They both laughed at this then became silent for a moment. A-hong broke the silence and allowed reality back in.

"Will Joe and Sue have to be chameleons?" he asked.

Vicki went still. He had done it again, always asking the hard questions that demanded an answer. "Sometimes I think, in a way, that's how I live my life," she whispered before a surge of emotions forced her to shut down.

"Sorry," A-hong apologized quietly. "Hit a raw nerve, didn't I?"

"Yeah, I guess you did," she replied then after a deep breathe she rallied and skipped to another subject. "You didn't hear my grandmother's story. My A-gong was a hard drinking, wife beating, child abusing son of a bitch."

The statement hit A-hong like a truck. He paused to gain some traction and then slid into the new subject as if they were reading lines from a script.

"That explains why my A-ma won't talk about him," he told her. "My father advised me not to bring it up."

There was another break in the conversation. Vicki realized A-hong was probably gun shy, so she picked up the lead.

"How do you think Sue will handle the split between America and Taiwan?" she posited showing it was the phrasing of his question and not that subject that had put her off.

He chuckled to himself and appeared ready to make a comment before thinking better of it. "That's hard to say today," he began moving away from his first thought. "A few years ago I would have thought she was raised Chinese, so 'You marry a chicken, you follow a chicken.' But she's grown up on me and become a career woman."

Vicki listened intently. These same thoughts had been percolating in the back of her mind since the night before. Sue's world had changed so rapidly. The choices and opportunities afforded her by Taiwanese society and its economy seemed endless. For her generation, it was no longer a given that life would be better or richer in America. She would lose opportunities by emigrating.

"What about Joe?" A-hong countered.

"Joe?" she asked. "Well, between studying in New York and working with my dad, he's already been away from home for two years. I think he would find it to be an adventure, but I don't know how long that would last."

"How would you handle it if put into that situation?"

"Me?" She asked sounding a little surprised. "That's not a fair comparison. Joe's parents are thrilled with Sue and he's a son. "A son's a son until he takes a wife."

A-hong straightened up when he heard that. "Did I hear you right?" he asked shocked.

"What? I never taught you that expression?" Immediately knowing the answer. Why would she teach that?

"No, you didn't," A-hong told her.

"It's an old English expression. 'A son is a son until he takes a wife. A daughter is a daughter all her life'."

"Really?" He asked in disbelief. "That makes it easier for them."

"How?"

"You know what's expected from Sue," he reminder her. "She's expendable."

"Expendable?" was Vicki's incredulous response.

"Well, maybe not the right word, but she isn't expected to stay close to her parents. That's her brother's responsibility. But how *would* you handle it?"

Vicki began to feel a little uncomfortable, but quickly put it off. It was a legitimate question. "I don't know," she admitted while playing with her paper plate. "Split the time between if possible, but that would be hard. You'd have to be able to support yourself in both countries or be independently wealthy." Then she laughed at the absurdity of the last part of her statement.

"Do you think they can do it?" A-hong continued.

"If anyone can they can," she stated. "She's becoming a business woman and he travels extensively between Asia and the States."

"Yes, but when children come they'll have to put roots down."

"*Jia ji sui ji,* I guess."

"Really, would you be content to follow a chicken?" he laughed.

"I think we better be getting back," Vicki suggested putting an end to the conversation.

They stepped out of the pizzeria quietly and walked past a gaggle of five delivery scooters. The lunch rush was slowing down.

"You ignored my question about becoming a chicken," he teased. "Although I think I know the answer."

The light was against them, so they waited for it to change and he waited for her answer. Was he leading her on or was there some other reason to push the question? She felt they were drifting to that grey uncomfortable zone again and so decided to respond without answering.

"Since you think you know the answer, I'll just say a lady is entitled to her secrets."

"Entitled? So you're not going to answer?"

"Nope," she chirped as the light changed. Then she stepped off the curb and headed for A-ma's leaving A-hong to trail behind.

Chapter Sixteen

When Vicki pressed the button for A-ma's flat, she and A-hong had still not exchanged a word. She had been reliving her less than stellar performance during lunch. Why was she criticizing herself? She had lunch with A-hong, not a unique experience. How come it felt like a first date? Not just her average first date, but one where she screwed up and left the entirely wrong impression. Something was happening deep inside her psyche that was incomprehensible at the moment and it made her nervous. A-hong rolled up behind her as the buzzer sounded and the latch releasing the door clanked.

Her uncle's voice greeted them as they ascended the stairs. This was joined by laughter then Sue's voice. What was Sue doing here? She had said last night she had to get up for work. Then Vicki heard Joe's voice. It was going to be crowded in A-ma's living room. Stepping into the apartment revealed a celebratory scene centered around A-zou. Sue was bending down showing off her ring. Joe stood behind her with a look of bewilderment on his face. This was his initiation into a Taiwanese family. He was in the midst of a language whirlwind with the conversation switching, sometimes in mid-sentence, between Mandarin and Taiwanese. The shifts were so sudden it was impossible for anyone not fluent in both languages to keep up. Vicki smiled with empathy. This was her life when in Taiwan.

Joe saw them at the door, an instant smile of relief creasing his features. A-zou looked up from Sue's ring with a large unguarded grin. She said something to A-hong, who was parked behind Vicki, but he did not bother to translate.

"What did A-zou say?" Vicki asked.

"She wanted to know why you didn't tell her this morning."

"Why I didn't tell her?" Vicki asked in astonishment. "Of all the people here, I was the only one who couldn't tell her. Why didn't you tell her is the question."

"I was preoccupied with something," he reminded her. "That was before I was absolved of my embarrassment."

Before Vicki could respond to this lame excuse, A-zou threw another question at him. A-hong smiled tightly, looked down for a moment then gave a quick answer. A-zou shot another statement at him that was followed by a knowing smile on her part and silence on his. Joe, Vicki, and Mama were the only ones who did not laugh. Vicki understood hers and Joe's lack of mirth. Her mother's abstinence made her nervous. A-ma said something to A-zou which drew the attention toward them.

"Why aren't Sue and Joe at work?" Vicki asked A-hong while A-ma had everyone's attention.

"Work?" he laughed. "It's Saturday, only half a day remember?"

Is it Saturday? She had no idea what day of the week it was. Between jetlag and not having any required activities, the day of the week had become irrelevant. Another burst of laughter brought her focus back to what was happening around her. Much to her consternation, Vicki saw she had become the center of attention. A-zou and A-ma appeared to be having a discussion about her, pointing proudly and commenting.

"What's going on?" she asked A-hong quietly without bothering to turn toward him.

"You don't want to know," he told her.

"Yes, I do," she insisted. "Tell me or I'll un-absolve you and you'll melt from embarrassment."

She heard him laugh behind her while her grandmother and great-grandmother seemed to be bragging about something.

"Okay, but I'm not the one who will be melting from embarrassment," A-hong relented. "They're telling Sue that she has a challenge ahead of her. Will be she able to produce a child who is as tall, smart, fair, and attractive as you are?"

"No, they are not," Vicki protested, using denial to relieve her discomfort.

"Sorry, but they are," A-hong chuckled. "I warned you."

Now Vicki wanted to crawl into a corner and hide. She knew they meant well and were in fact bragging, but she felt objectified, the *ainoko* on display. Sue looked as embarrassed as she felt. Mama and Sue's dad were all smiles. Then the sound of Sue's mother came from the kitchen. She walked into the room with a tray of tea cups, spouting her opinion. Vicki prayed the three women would not take their game any further. She had no intention of modelling for them. Not in front of her cousins, especially not in front of A-hong. Joe noticed how uncomfortable she had become and walked over. Sue handed out the tea to the older generation then slipped away to join her cousins and fiancé, bring tea with her.

"Your A-zou is a live wire," Joe smiled. "Now I really understand what Vicki goes through not speaking Taiwanese."

"You don't know the half of it," Vicki sighed. "I knew they were talking about me, so I had A-hong translate. He said I didn't want to know and he was right."

The chatter continued in the background as Sue handed out the tea. "She wasn't the only object of their attention," she told Joe then turned to A-hong. "What did A-zou mean by that last remark?"

Vicki and Joe looked at her with a quizzical expression. "A-zou asked him if he was also ready to move onto the next stage of life."

All four laughed before A-hong attempted to give a clearer translation. "She actually asked if I was ready to grow up," he said, "I told her I was married to my dissertation and when we divorced I would be open to whomever heaven sent me."

"After that she said maybe heaven had already sent him someone," Sue added.

His cousins moaned while Joe shook his head quietly. Vicki wondered if her mother had mentioned Nikki from The Prince Albert Pub to A-ma and A-zou. She prayed the little lie of omission she had used to make things easier was not going to come back to bite her.

"I don't know what she meant by that," A-hong confessed. "Sometimes she's a little impatient with me, wants me to find a wife before she goes."

This revelation put a temporary damper on the conversation. Sue picked it up after a loud burst of laugher came from behind her. "Did A-hong tell you what they were saying, Vic?"

"Yes, he did, at least most of it."

"A-hong, why don't you tell Joe?"

A-hong looked up at the ceiling and waved his hand at her. "Don't Sue, there's no need."

"No need, why not?" Vicki insisted. "It was very obvious they were talking about my height and appearance."

"Yes," he admitted. "But it goes deeper and involves more than you."

Vicki took a sip of tea and debated whether or not to push the issue. "If Sue is willing to talk about it, then I am."

The noise emanating from the rear of the room began to throttle back, so Vicki glanced up. A-zou seemed to have suddenly lost her sparkle. Whatever reserve she had before lunch had been washed out by Sue and Joe's announcement. Her great-grandmother appeared to be losing her vitality quickly. There would be no interview that afternoon.

A-hong saw where she was gazing, looked at A-zou, and then simply said "I agree." There was no need to explain her thoughts.

"So, is Sue willing to reveal the secrets of her ancestors?" Joe quizzed.

"Is Joe prepared to feel embarrassed?" Sue retorted.

"Embarrassed?" he asked. "This sounds bad, but I'm sure I can take it."

"She would have eventually told you anyway, Joe," Vicki insisted.

"Yes, but I don't know if my translation would have been right," Sue confessed.

"Okay," A-hong stepped in. "If you're all in agreement. The conversation revolved around Sue and Joe, as it should have. A-zou said they have a challenge ahead of them. Not the challenge of marriage. I don't think they look at that as a challenge, that's more like something women put up with."

This brought more moans from all around. Vicki was not sure where he was going with this. It was more involved than his translation to her. Knowing better than to interrupt when he was playing a story for maximum dramatic impact, she quietly waited for him to continue.

"The challenge they face is having children as tall, as fair, as capable, and yes, as beautiful as their A-hui," he finish by raising his cup to Vicki.

"As beautiful?" Vicki laughed. "What happened to simply attractive?"

"Didn't want you to get too big a head," A-hong smiled.

"Oh, you dirty bastard," she snapped back.

"That is a challenge," Joe interjected obviously trying to bail out A-hong. "But I think we're up to it eventually, just not too soon."

"Yeah, let's get married first," Sue sighed. "They were off to the races as soon as they heard. We have careers to start and decisions about our life together to make. They seem to think this is 1950."

Vicki appreciated Sue's effort to move the conversation away from her. As A-hong had said, this should be about an engagement. The apartment was beginning to heat up despite the cooler weather. She looked up to see how A-zou was faring. Her great-grandmother appeared to be fading fast. Even with all the chatter around her A-zou was quietly dozing. Vicki looked at A-hong who shook his head in agreement, then leaned toward Sue.

"I think we should let A-zou rest," she whispered.

Since the reunion surrounding the sleeping A-zou showed no sign of breaking up any time soon, Sue walked over to her mother and whispered in her ear. Shortly afterwards Sue's dad went to bring his car around, A-ma gently woke her mother, and A-hong helped her down the stairs. Sue went ahead of them to open doors. Her mother gathered her things and approached Vicki with a broad smile. She was a petite woman in her mid-fifties who could still live up to her nickname of "little beauty." Sue looked like her younger twin.

"A-hui, it's good to see you," her aunt bubbled. "I want to thank you for giving A-ma a chance to tell her story. So much bitterness held inside for so long is bad. It eats away at one's heart."

Vicki was surprised at how her aunt put it. Giving A-ma a chance to tell her story? What happened to A-zou's story? Before she could ask any questions, her aunt hurried on. Obviously trying to get as much conversation in as possible in the short period before her husband arrived with the car.

"It's such a blessing for Joe and Sue," she sighed. "When will the two of you do something?"

The two of us? Vicki thought then realized she must be speaking about A-hong and herself. "A-yi they've known each other for ten years. I haven't spent a lot of time with anyone. It will take a while."

Her aunt had a quizzical look on her face. "You've know each other forever."

This caught Vicki completely off guard. "Who have I known forever?"

"Why A-hong of course."

"A-hong?" Vicki with a stamper. "A-yi, he's my cousin."

This made no impression on her aunt, who quickly made the transition to matchmaker.

"Ah-yo, you're his *biao-mei*. You don't share the same surname," she pointed out. "It is easy to see there is a connection, an attraction there. I can see it just like A-zou. It's understandable you want to keep it quiet right now. He has to finish his dissertation, but don't put it off too long. He's a good man. A lot of the men in my family are like him. They are good men. Your A-gong was not the usual Taiwanese man. If only your A-ma had such a relationship, how happy her life would have been."

The sound of a car horn ended their conversation. Her aunt hurried out the door and down the stairs, leaving Vicki in utter shock. How many of her relatives shared this view? She can see it just like A-zou? What does A-zou see? Is her mother aware of it? So many questions without answers were darting around her brain. She had to speak with Sue. That was the only way she could get a real handle on what her aunt had said. The pizza she had for lunch had suddenly become a stone in her stomach. Then the thought crossed her mind. Is A-hong aware of this? The stone in her stomach now felt like it was going to come back up.

Chapter Seventeen

The festive atmosphere that had permeated the apartment vanished with the departure of Sue and Joe. Vicki was struggling to avoid showing how shaken she was. The conversation with Sue's mother had been surreal. The difficulties of processing what was said seemed insurmountable. It would take a major shift in her life view to understand. Now was not the time to begin that adjustment.

She turned away from the apartment entrance to see A-ma enthroned in her seat. A-zou was too exhausted to continue her story, but A-ma was intent on being heard. Mama quietly slipped into the chair next to her mother. No one gave any indication they were waiting for A-hong, so Vicki took up her position on the couch. She had the presence of mind to reach for her pad despite the rollercoaster ride the day had become.

"After the accident, our relationship changed," A-ma started. "He stopped drinking and was not violent. It was as if he needed someone to console him, but I could not, so he fled to Hua-lian. A-zou and his mother came to visit me after he left."

* *

Each day seemed darker than the last to Li-ya. Her little Shan-bao was gone. She should have resisted that man. It would have been better if he had beaten her senseless. Then he would not have had the strength to return to his drinking buddies. Instead she curled up on the floor and protected herself.

"Li-ya," Chiu Bu whispered. "You cannot continue like this. I know you have the strength to overcome it. Your children need you."

"My son is dead," she sobbed. "That man killed my son."

"You have three other children, A-ya," her mother-in-law reminded her. "Little Shan-bao would want them to be happy."

"He was only a baby," was her bitter response. "Too young to want anything. I gave in and allowed Shan-bao to get in that van with a drunken wild man. What kind of a mother am I?"

"You were a good mother, but unless you remember your other children you will no longer be one," her mother scolded.

Li-ya knew the truth of these words. The world remained dark. She would never forgive her husband and doubted she could ever be happy again. But her children needed her, if she focused on them, maybe she could get through one day without tears.

"Mama," Shan-ji called. "Baba is here." After this announcement, the boy scooted away, knowing better than to stay around his father.

She had not seen her husband since he had fled. After two months absence, what did he want? She steeled herself and hoped Wei Wu was sober. He walked in quietly. Li-ya was sitting at her desk working on accounts. She did not bother to turn around and face him.

"The machinery has been installed," Wei Wu informed his wife. "We should be able to begin production in Hua-lian in a few weeks."

She continued to look at the account books, still unable to meet eyes with him for fear her rage would explode. Instead her head remained down perusing the accounts; the sound of the abacus beads moving filled the silence. "Good," was the only syllable she could muster.

"I stop at the temple to see little Jia-yi," was his next attempt to reach her. "She is happy and healthy."

Li-ya struggled to contain her emotions. This was the man responsible for her daughter being sent away. How dare he try to placate her with talk of *mei-mei.* "Does she pray for your soul?" she asked without thought.

This was followed by silence. The abacus beads clicked while she worked and he waited. Although she could not see his expression, she knew he was struggling to understand this new dynamic in their relationship. Guilt had shifted control to her.

"I would like to see the children," he stated.

The clicking of the abacus stopped as she drew in her breath to maintain control. "The children are afraid of you," she informed him coldly. This produced an angry outburst.

"What have you been telling them?" he snapped.

She sat up straight and became rigid, no longer intimidated by her husband's voice. The pain in her heart consumed any fear that might have developed. The truth was all that was needed to silence him.

"I do not speak of you," she assured him. "And they are not permitted to mention you."

Another period of stillness followed. Li-ya felt no empathy for him. In this matter they were not equals. She had lost her baby boy. He had killed her son. There could be no commiseration between them. As the quiet dragged on, she began to work with the abacus again.

"I have stopped drinking."

"I am glad to hear that. You are such a good businessman when you are sober."

"The Hua-lian shop needs cash," he told her. "I want to stay here tonight and go to the bank in the morning."

It took all that she had to control her emotions. With clenched fists and shaking arms, she hissed, "I don't think that is a good idea."

"There is a price to be paid for treating me like this!" Wei Wu shouted.

"A price!" She screamed losing control. "You owe me the life of my son! What debt could I possibly owe you?"

The sound of something being placed on a table was followed by that of his shuffling feet receding. When the door closed behind him, Li-ya laid her head down on the desk and sobbed.

****

"The next day he came back with your mother," A-ma told Vicki. "He told me, 'Here is the life I owe you.' Then he returned to Hua-lian. He travelled back and forth. We both lost ourselves in work. In the end it was not that much different than it would have been. One of us had to be in Hua-lian to expand that part of the business. He did not spend a night in Tai-dong, so there was no drinking. It went on like that for months. Your mother was home, but still did not know her father. Then I received a phone call from his sister."

✱✱

"Li-ya, I have disheartening news," Wei Wu's sister said quietly. "There is a young woman named Lee Mei who works in the temple kitchen. She is an orphan and not unattractive. My brother spends too much time with her. That is all I will say. These are not matters I should deal with."

"I understand, *mei-mei,*" she whispered. "Thank you, I will take care of it."

As soon as she hung up the phone, Li-ya began weighing her options. Her husband was having an affair with a young woman who was an orphan. This woman probably had nothing and was employed as an act of mercy. Such a woman would latch onto any man she could attract since she had no family to arrange a marriage for her. But she was still a woman and so would calculate the pros and cons of a man before becoming involved. Part of Li-ya wanted to demand a divorce and walk away from him, but there were the children. A divorce would place them with him. She loved her children too much to condemn them to such a fate. In order to protect them she would have to meet this challenge head on. Imagining the convoluted lies Wei Wu must have told, his wife began formulating a plan that would solve the problem without a confrontation.

"Shan-ji, get your sisters together," she called. "We are going to Hua-lian to visit Amitofu *Gugu* and baba."

"Miss Lee," Li-ya called. The young woman stopped at the temple kitchen entrance and turn around, her hands clutching an empty basket.

"Me?" she asked.

"You are Lee Mei?"

"Yes, I am."

"Do you know Wei Wu?"

"I do, why do you ask?"

"I am his wife," Li-ya informed her.

A look of shock replaced the friendly smile on her face. "I don't believe you," was all she could say.

This confirmed one of Li-ya's suspicions. Her husband did not deny he had a wife, but gave an unflattering description of her.

"I am Ma Li-ya. Wei Wu did not tell you about me?" she asked with sarcasm. The woman placed the basket down and approached her.

"You cannot be his wife," she insisted. "He told me his wife is ugly, fat, and barren. He said he was going to leave her."

Li-ya laughed contemptuously. "He said I was barren? You do not know about his daughter who stayed here?"

Confusion informed her every movement as Miss Lee struggled to make sense of what Li-ya said. "He said she was adopted."

Li-ya turned around and called, "Shan-ji come, bring *jie-jie* and *mei-mei.*" When the three children approached, their mother could see that Miss Lee recognized Jia-yi. Li-ya's heart broke as she watched the hopes of this young woman crumple.

"If he leaves me," Li-ya whispered almost to herself. "I will miss them so."

The statement had the desired effect. Miss Lee took a step back involuntarily at just the thought of becoming the step-mother of Wei Wu's children.

"Children, introduce yourselves to *A-yi*."

"Hello, *A-yi*," Shan-ji said with a smile. "I am Wei Shan-ji and they are my sisters."

"Mama said to introduce yourself, not me," *Jie-jie* interjected. "*A-yi* I am Wei Jia-luan." She turned to her sister and encouraged her to speak."

"I am Wei Jia-yi," *Mei-mei* whispered shyly, not daring to look at the young woman in front of her.

Miss Lee was visibly shaken. She began to back away muttering apologies.

"Please, there is no need to leave," Li-ya assured her. "I just wanted to come to an understanding with you." She then reached into her bag and produced a red envelope filled with cash. "I understand you have cooking talent."

"So I am told," she answered reluctantly, wanting only to leave.

"I have a proposal for you," Li-ya informed her as she presented the envelope to her husband's mistress. "We can call this a down payment to make up for all the trouble my husband's lies have caused you. I hope it will allow you to begin a new life."

The woman understood immediately what was being asked of her. "Where will I go?"

"Have you been to Xin-gang?"

Miss Lee shook her head no.

"I have a cousin there. I think he will be happy to help. I'll talk with him if you wish. There is surely room in Xin-gang for a small eatery run by a woman with your talent. I am willing to invest in such an establishment if you are willing to work hard at building it."

"You are much too kind," she cried. "I do not deserve this. No one has ever given me such an opportunity. I have worked hard all my life. You won't be disappointed."

"I'm sure I won't be," Li-ya smiled. "It is the least I can do after my husband's deception. We women have to help each other or the world will fall apart."

After exchanging information, the two women parted. One to pack what little she had to go to Xin-gang and begin a new life of hope, the other to drop in on her husband and implement the second stage of her plan to save their family.

Wei Wu was standing next to the newly installed vats speaking with a worker. His back was turned to the door used by Li-ya and the children. She leaned over and motioned for her children to be quiet then strolled over to surprise her husband. A part of her pride would die this day, she thought, but she would not give her children to be raised by this man alone.

The worker glanced up and saw her approaching. She could see the outfit was having the desired effect. His eye were eating her alive.

Wei Wu noticed his colleague's foolish stare and turned around. The expression on his face told her he was defenseless.

"A-wu," she purred. "*Mei-mei* wanted so much to see her aunt and I wanted to see the progress you spoke of, so we came up for a short visit."

"A short visit?" he asked sounding disappointed, as the worker excused himself and slid away.

Perfect, she thought. His mind had already begun to calculate the possibilities implied by the effort she had made in front of the mirror. An attractive outfit and a little makeup can go a long way, especially when he had given her the outfit as a peace offering.

"I can't be away from the Tai-dong store too long," she hummed. "Just the night. The children can stay with their aunt in the temple so we can talk about the future of our business. Do you think we can cover that in one night?"

A broad smile now lit his face. "I'm sure we can do that in an hour."

"Then whatever time we have left is ours to enjoy together." Then she motioned for the children to come over to greet their father.

****

Vicki sat in shock. "You seduced him?" Mama muttered.

A-ma laughed at this interpretation.

"He was my husband," she reminded. "That was my power over him. He had no feelings for that woman. It was purely a physical need."

Vicki felt a deepening respect for A-ma. People are all prisoners of the times in which they live. A-ma had used the knowledge and tools available at that time to protect her children.

"Do you know what happened to the woman?" Vicki asked.

A-ma chuckled. "Of course I do," she replied. "We were in business together for a time, although your A-gong didn't know that. She settled in Xin-gang and opened a small eatery. It was successful, so we expanded it into a restaurant. She married a veteran and had a family. We keep in touch. She had nothing before and so was very appreciative of my help. That was a peaceful time. He was not drinking. Our business was growing. The children were happy. But the shadow of my little boy never left our relationship. The peace only lasted until he came back to Tai-dong and started drinking again."

A-ma paused, looking dispirited. Vicki finished her notes and waited, doubting her grandmother would continue. This was a good place to stop for the day, she thought. A-ma had re-lived a seemingly rare triumph. There was no need to delve into the turmoil of her last sentence. It would be better to rest in the peace of that short period.

Mama appeared to be of the same opinion. She stood up, walked over to A-ma, and spoke quietly in Taiwanese. A-ma shook her head in agreement then turned to her granddaughter and spoke in Mandarin.

"We can continue tomorrow," she suggested. "A-hui, your A-gong was a nice man when he did not drink. I think he was proud to have me as his wife and actually loved me in his own way. When he drank that part of him was lost."

Vicki was surprised by the comment. Was this the woman who had scolded her for making excuses for his misbehavior? How long did this period of sobriety last? Mama retrieved her purse and gave every indication they were leaving. Vicki put A-ma's last comment off as nostalgia, stood up, and stepped over to her grandmother to give her an American hug before they left. She had no clue where they were going. All she knew was the problem of her aunt's comments remained and Sue was not around to help sort it all out.

Chapter Eighteen

The two women made their way to Neihu Road quietly. Vicki was certain her mother was thinking about what A-ma had said. However impressive her grandmother's story was, she could only think about what Sue's mother had blurted out while leaving. Those short sentences combined with A-hong's comment the night before added up to mental turmoil. It felt as if her world had hit an ice patch and was spinning out of control. That was an odd analogy considering the heat and mugginess they were pushing through. There were fewer puddles to avoid as they trod down the street, but the humidity was rising off the road surface like an invisible fog.

They reached the intersection as the light stopped traffic on Neihu Road. This allowed Mama to calmly scan the stopped traffic for a cab. She spied a yellow Toyota sedan in the middle lane and waved. The driver motioned for them to move to the other side of the light, allowing him time to maneuver through traffic to the curb. Vicki had no idea where Mama might be going until after they slid into the cab. Her mother told the driver Zhongshan Road north in Mandarin. He started the meter and eased into traffic.

"The Prince Albert," Mama asked. "It's on Zhongsahn Road north, right?"

The question only added to Vicki's stress. She should have known better than to mention Nikki to her mother. It was inevitable that she would be drawn like a magnet to the pub. Knowing her mother would not want to pay for two cab rides when one would suffice, Vicki resigned herself to an early dinner.

"Yes," she sighed. "A few blocks from the hotel."

"You don't sound enthusiastic," her mother commented. "Was the food that bad or was your lunch too big."

Vicki felt physically and emotionally exhausted. She did not want to get into a discussion that would require thought. The omission of Nikki's London based boyfriend could be glossed over easily. It had been a few hours since her pizza. Now that her stomach had worked through the nervous reaction to her aunt's words, she thought dinner was an option. Quick assessment complete, she turned to answer her mother's question.

"I'm just tired, Mama," she sighed. "Dinner would be nice. The meal I had last night was tasty. You might enjoy it."

Mama patted her daughter's leg in sympathy. "It's been a long day for you, I know," she said with understanding then began speaking to the driver in Mandarin. "Do you know where the English Pub is on Zhongshan Road?" she asked.

"Yes, yes," the driver assured them. "By the Grand Hotel. The place with the wood timbers on the outside wall."

"That's the place," Mama said while glancing at the cabbie's license. When she read his name her language immediately switched to Taiwanese leaving Vicki in the dark. The conversation droned on for a minute before Mama attempted to bring her daughter in.

"Mr. Chen says he's been to this pub and seen their daughter," she told Vicki. "He said you are taller and prettier."

Unsure what answer her mother expected, she simply said *xiexie* hoping a modest thanks would suffice. Mama switched back to Taiwanese and continued to chat while Mr. Chen dodged Taipei traffic. When the conversation slowed, the cab driver switched to Mandarin and spoke directly to Vicki.

"You mother is a very talented woman," he laughed. "She goes so easily between three different languages without so much as a pause."

She could see the compliment took Mama by surprise. Considering the source was a metropolitan cabbie who must hear people struggle with foreign languages daily, it was no idle statement. She had always been proud of her mother's language talent, having grown up boosting about it. This was a rare time when she could make Mama squirm a little by bragging about her. Never let rare opportunities slip away without taking full advantage.

"Those are not the only languages she speaks," Vicki boosted. "She also speaks fluent French." Mama slapped her knee playfully while the driver shouted "Ah-yo" in amazement. The conversation then reverted back to Taiwanese while Vicki returned to her quandary of how to handle her aunt's comments.

Mr. Chen got them to Prince Albert's in one piece. They climbed out and Mama paid the fare including a generous tip. She then led the way into the restaurant. The day was so dank their eyes did not have to adjust to any change in light. Of course that was helped by one of the concession made to the locals, a brightly lit dining area. Vicki scanned the room quickly. There were plenty of free tables as expected at this time of day, too late for lunch, too early for dinner. Tourists sat at the few occupied tables. She caught herself paying attention to the patrons, looking for a reaction to their arrival. Thank God no one seemed to notice they had stepped in. No one except a short middle aged woman who marched up with a smile, eyes on Mama.

"Welcome," she said in accented Mandarin. "Just the two of you?"

"Yes," Mama replied.

As the woman turned she glanced at Vicki and stopped. Her smile broadened from a polite business like crease to a genuine friendly grin. "Please follow me."

From the woman's reaction, Vicki suspected this was Nikki's mother. Her energy level had jumped noticeably as soon as she realized Mama's daughter was an Amerasian, Although Mrs. Salisbury would think of her as Eurasian.

"My daughter will be here shortly to take your order," Nikki's mum told them, confirming Vicki's suspicion. She hurried away calling her daughter in Cantonese.

"I think that would be Nikki's mother," Vicki laughed.

"Yes, I noticed her change as soon as she saw you," Mama agreed.

"You don't speak Cantonese, do you?" she asked knowing the answer. The question was more to remind her mother of Nikki's background than anything else.

"You know I don't," her mother replied. "She speaks Mandarin with a heavy Cantonese accent. I hope her English is better."

Vicki chuckled at the thought of two Chinese women forced to converse in English. They could always write their questions on napkins or speak through their daughters. This could prove to be an interesting meal. Something to quell the beginnings of panic she felt rising deep inside.

"Hello love," Nikki gushed as she stepped up to their table.

"Hey, Nikki," Vicki replied in kind. "This is my mom, Jia-yi Phaff." She used Mama's married name knowing that was the rule in situations like this.

"Hello Mrs. Phaff," Nikki said politely. "I'm Nikki as you've already heard. You just met my mum, Aggie Salisbury and my dad is behind the bar." With that she pointed her pen in the direction of the bar behind her. Vicki glanced over and saw Aggie speaking with her husband. He smiled and wave to them.

"What can I get for you?" Nikki asked.

"What would you recommend?" Mama replied as she always did in a restaurant new to her.

"Oh, I think you would want to ask my mum that, not me," Nikki laughed. Then she turned around and invited her mother back to the table. Aggie laughed and propelled herself across the room, energy radiating from her.

"Mum, this is Mrs. Jia-yi Phaff," she paused for a moment to confirm the pronunciation was correct. "And her daughter Vicki."

"Oh, so nice to meet you," Aggie exclaimed. "You know A-hong? He is such a nice boy."

Mama's mood improved a notch. "Yes, he is my *biao-ge*'s son. He does so much for his great-grandmother, very *xioashun.*"

Nikki had to help a little with the Mandarin words, but it appeared the two mothers were off to the races. Before they delved too deeply into a conversation, Nikki reminded everyone why she had asked her mother over.

"Mrs. Phaff was asking what we would recommend."

"I don't know," Aggie anguished. "Do you not eat some things?"

Mama shook her head no.

"Then the braised lamb is good," Aggie suggested. "Or you could try the chicken and mushroom pie. My husband makes delicious pies."

"Why don't we try both," Vicki offered wanting to make up for her lack of adventure the night before. "That way we can share them and taste both."

Mama agreed which sent Nikki off to place the order.

"Nikki seems so *xiaoshun*," Mama said before realizing Nikki had to translate for her mother. She naturally began using her finger to trace the characters in the air. Aggie watched closely with a stern look of concentration then broke put into a grin.

"She is a good girl," she replied. "She comes from London for the summer to help us."

"All the way from London?" Mama marveled. "She doesn't live here with you?"

Vicki heard the astonishment in her mother's voice. She doubted Mama would go for such an arrangement. If her daughter settled in London, Mama would move to London. It would be a battle royal for Vicki just to settle so far away. Ma Jia-yi would use every manipulative ploy she knew before surrendering her daughter to the world. That was an anticipated battle to be fought another day. There was too much on her plate right now to raise the subject.

"No she doesn't live here all year," Aggie told Mama. "She goes to university in London, to UCL."

"Ah-yo!" Mama exclaimed. "Such a good school, but you must miss her."

"Yes, I miss her when she is away, but it is better for her father," she laughed. "She draws too much attention here."

Vicki did not like the drift the chat had suddenly taken. It sounded like conversations she had had with her father who swore she would never travel to Taiwan alone. He said she drew the wrong kind of attention from the boys here. It was supposed to be a tongue in cheek comment, but she had yet to come to Taiwan by herself.

"Too much attention from boys?" Mama asked with a knowing smile.

Aggie shook her head yes and laughed. A young couple stepped in through the entrance, ending their conversation for now. As Aggie hustled to greet them, Mama announced a visit to the ladies' room. With a few minutes to herself, Vicki settled back in her seat to think. The conversation had been a pleasant distraction. Now with her mother away she could spend a minute trying to put together the puzzle her life had become over the past twenty-four hours.

The first thing she needed to know was who shared her aunt's opinion. Does Mama and if she did how to solicit that opinion? What did A-hong's mother think? There was no way she would ask that question of Mei-zhi *A-yi* and she certainly was not asking her son, so those were dead ends. How about Sue's dad? She might be able to get an idea from Sue as long as her cousin swore eternal silence. From what Sue's mom said, A-zou certainly shared the same opinion. How did this happen? Did she inadvertently do something to encourage this view? Remembering her spontaneous smile when she heard A-hong's voice the other day gave her pause. Was she in denial of her true feelings? The thought made her dizzy. Was A-hong aware of or even share her aunt's opinion? Now her head was swimming. Nikki returned with tea to pull her out of the hypothetical and back to reality.

"It's so nice to see you again," she enthused. "A-hong spoke so much about you. Oh, and your cousin Sue is a doll. She does resemble A-hong so."

Vicki smiled at the ball of energy Nikki had become. Unknowingly, her new found friend had touched on some hot button issues, but Vicki thought one of them could help. Before she could insert herself into the flow of words, Nikki realized one of her faux pas.

"And I shouldn't have made that last comment," she apologized. "Your mouth did it again Nikki Salisbury."

Vicki chuckled. "Don't be so hard on yourself."

"I should know better. I experience the same thing."

"You mean the 'She's not quite one not quite the other' routine?"

"Yes," Nikki answered. "Sometimes you just don't seem to fit in at family gatherings."

"Oh, don't I know that," she agreed.

"It's not that they don't adore me, don't get me wrong," Nikki clarified.

"No, no don't worry about that," Vicki reassured her. "If your family is anything like mine, they smother you with love and attention and expectations and God knows what else."

The two women laughed then Nikki brought up another subject about family without knowing it. "Sue's fiancé is gorgeous isn't he," she cooed.

Vicki laughed, realizing that Joe had been introduced last night only as A-hong's friend. "Joe is, well he's Joe," she stuttered trying to come up with a way not to embarrass Nikki. "You see, Joe's is also my cousin."

"No! You are joking aren't you?"

"God's honest truth," Vicki swore. "Joseph Phaff is my *tang-ge*."

"Oh, you poor girl," Nikki sympathized. "You're related to all the good looking guys."

"Yeah," she sighed then changed the subject, trying to divert their attention. "So, how is your Cantonese?"

"My mum made certain I could talk to her family," was the response. "How about your Mandarin?"

"Mandarin is just part of me," she stated. "But it's a little more complicated here. My mother has a tendency to converse in Taiwanese which she never bothered to teach me. So, I'm left out of most of the conversations. Then my grandmother's Mandarin is limited and my great-grandmother's is non-existent."

"Your A-zou?" Nikki asked. "A-hong told me a little about her. She sounds remarkable."

"She is and he probably didn't know a fraction of her story when he spoke with you."

"I'd love to hear it someday," she smiled. "A-hong is your cousin, right? I mean your blood relative."

Vicki laughed at how the question was framed. It always amazed her how the precise meanings of Chinese familial terms could be instantly corrupted by the habit of using them for close friends. "Yes, I'm his *biao-mei*," she sighed. This was really not a good subject right now. She glanced up to see where her mother was. Mama was at the bar talking with Vicki's parents, so it was safe to continue. "His grandmother and my grandmother are sisters."

"Your grandmothers are sisters?" Nikki confirmed. "Then you're not first cousins."

As far as Vicki was concerned, their little chat had suddenly taken on a more serious tone. She was not sure where it was going, so decided to go in what seemed the natural direction. "You said A-hong told you about me," she began. "What exaggerations do I have to deny?"

Nikki chuckled nervously. "Oh, he just bragged about his cousin, probably because you and I are both a mix of East and West. He's a gentleman after all and quite handsome too."

"Yes I know," Vicki replied then decided to take a plunge into unknown waters to see if she could shake loose a hint of A-hong's view. "Too bad he's my cousin."

Nikki laughed. "That shouldn't bother you. The royals have been marrying their cousins for centuries. Prince Albert was Queen Victoria's cousin."

"That's right, he was," Vicki acknowledged. "Wasn't there some sort of issue with genetics? Hemophilia, that's it. Some of their descendants had hemophilia. Have to be careful of those recessive genes."

"Oh, I don't think you have to worry about something like that," Nikki reassured her. "And he's so taken by you. The way he looks at you when you're not looking, anyone can see it would be a good match."

This threw Vicki for a loop. Was it that obvious to everyone but her? She pushed herself to get through the shock, not wanting to lose the opportunity to get a point view outside the family. "My dad, ah, my mom said my dad would never go for it," she stuttered.

"You talked it over with A-hong?" Nikki asked in a breezy way.

"No, never even thought to discuss it," Vicki admitted.

"Then your mum must have noticed too," she pointed out. "Mums pick up on these things before we're even aware. At least Chinese mums do. Did your dad talk with you about it?"

This chat was turning into hard work. Did her father ever speak with her about A-hong? She could not recall one instance and knew it would have been very awkward if he had. Mama was the sole source of all the opinions about her cousin. "No, he never did," she confessed.

"Well, if my mum tells me my dad's opinion, I always ask him separately," Nikki laughed. "Mum has a way of projecting her thoughts onto him." She looked up and saw the newly arrived couple was ready to order, so she excused herself and went back to work. Her departure seemed to pull some of the atmosphere with her. That was one big personality in a small package. What an extraordinary chat they had. Unfortunately, it raised more questions than it answered.

She tried to pull her mind back to the problem of Sue's mother. Should she just ignore her aunt's comments? Maybe she should speak with A-hong so they can both deny there was anything beyond familial affection between them. But people seemed to see something she did not. What if he refused to deny it? The questions were becoming increasingly complex. Vicki could not come up with answers now. The situation had gone way beyond people misunderstanding and thinking she might be trying to attract her cousin. The thought of staying in her hotel room until they left crossed her mind. That was no longer an option. A-zou and A-ma now controlled her day. Vicki looked up with this thought and saw her mother approaching. Her personal predicament had to be pushed into the back recesses of her consciousness. A-zou and A-ma were not the only ones controlling her time.

Chapter Nineteen

"Such a fascinating couple," Mama bubbled as she sat. Hearing this allowed Vicki to relax a little. If her mother was focused on Nikki's parents, there would be fewer probing questions to deal with. Being well aware of Wei Jia-yi's propensity to dominate a conversation, Vicki eased back into her chair and accepted the role of audience.

"Michael is from London. He was in the Royal Navy. That's where he learned to cook. They met when he was on leave in Hong Kong. They dated, then he left the navy, came back to Hong Kong, married her, and they moved to London. He worked as a cook in a pub there until they saved enough money to move back to Hong Kong and open a pub."

"They owned a pub in Hong Kong?" Vicki asked to show she was listening.

"Yes, they still do," Mama continued. "Nikki has an older brother. He runs the Hong Kong pub."

"She has a brother?"

"Yes, but he's married to a nice Vietnamese girl," Mama's answer was laced with disappointment.

Vicki did not comment on the tone, knowing it was her mother's natural tendency to play matchmaker that gave birth to the inflection of her answer. The pub had begun to fill with patrons. They were not the only ones looking for an early dinner. It was Saturday, Vicki reminded herself. That allowed for a relaxing meal and maybe an evening of entertainment. Since the end of martial law, the Taiwanese had gradually moved away from the Spartan existence imposed by curfews. If she were lucky a good number of the diners who frequented the Prince Albert would be British ex-pats and Mama would be reluctant to talk about family history. Vicki really needed a short intermission from the monsoon of information pouring on her.

"They came to Taipei for a short vacation," Mama rolled on not noticing her daughter's muteness. "Michael saw it was becoming an international city and thought they could open a pub here for the European businessmen. Oh, and Nikki has a boyfriend in London, but she comes back to help every summer. She's such a good girl."

Vicki sipped her tea and listened, her mother's words and opinions flowing around her like a gentle mountain stream. Nikki delivered their meals as Mama finished her report.

"You didn't say who ordered the lamb and who ordered the pie," Nikki reminded them.

"We are going to split them," Vicki told her. "So it doesn't matter."

Nikki placed the lamb in front of Mama and the pie with Vicki. "Tell me what you think of my dad's pie," she requested before dashing off to another table.

"Looks like we got in just before the rush," Vicki commented.

"A-ma warned me," Mama replied. "She told me weekends are not the same as when I left Taiwan and suggested we get here early."

After some shuffling of dishes, they settled down to their dinners. Vicki found her appetite was sharper than expected. After tasting the pie, she realized appetite did not matter. This was one of those treats enjoyable no matter how satisfied your palate felt. The lamb was good, but the chicken and mushroom pie was to die for.

"What do you think of the pie?" she asked wondering if taste buds first educated in the East would appreciate such a humble Western meal.

"It is delicious," Mama exclaimed. "Although I am not sure the average Taiwanese person can fully appreciate it. It is not gourmet food, more like *bianfan*, unsophisticated but delicious."

"You've been reading too many culinary magazines," Vicki laughed marveling at her mother's description. "It is everyday fare, I'll admit and it's great."

"Your father would love it, but not the lamb."

"Yes, you're right, dad doesn't like lamb," Vicki agreed. With their requisite culinary review completed, they concentrated on dinner. Vicki's mind still preoccupied with her newly discovered troubles. The problem with Roger seemed light years away.

Mama patted her lips in a ladylike manner reserved for Western restaurants. She reached for her tea and blurted out a question Vicki had hoped would not come up.

"What did *A-yi* say to you before she left?"

Vicki knew she had a dumbfounded look on her face. The complete truth was not an option, so she quickly dissected the short conversation and picked out appropriate pieces to share.

"She thanked me for allowing A-ma to tell her story," she began. "Which I found puzzling because she didn't mention A-zou."

Taking a sip of tea to play for time, she continued to review her aunt's words. After spending so much energy focusing on just one sentence, she was finding it hard to pull up the rest of the conversation. Then *A-yi's* comment about the men in her maiden family came to mind. Could that be used to indirectly ferret out Mama's view of A-hong's feelings? Quickly deciding it was a possibility, she dove in head first. "Then she said something odd. She said A-gong was not the usual Taiwanese man, that the men in her family are more like A-hong. What do you think she meant by that?"

The way it came out was more than a little indirect, but it placed the subject on the table.

"The Lin family," Mama smiled ignoring the comparison to A-hong. "It is surprising she didn't mention A-zou. A-zou is close to them. She was the one who arranged for Shan-ji *Jiu-jiu* to meet *A-yi*. Then she did everything to encourage them. *Jiu-jiu* was always special to A-zou. It's funny, when someone suggested A-hong's father might be a better match, she was adamantly opposed to the idea. She had made her choice. Any other match would be bad luck."

Vicki felt a little frustrated at her mother's omission of any comment about A-hong, but saw no way around it without setting off alarms.

"The usual Taiwanese man?" Mama chuckled. "What did she mean by that? There are many different types of men in Taiwan. There was a Hakka family that lived next door when I was a girl. The father was not like A-gong. I spent a lot of nights there when my father came home drunk. They taught me Hakka."

"Hakka? You can speak Hakka?"

"All forgotten now," Mama laughed then sighed. "I always had a niche for languages. If my childhood had been more normal I would have applied myself. Instead of escaping, a Ph.d would have been my dream. I owe so much to A-zou."

A simple question about her neighbor's language had suddenly opened up a part of her mother Vicki did not know. She did not want to let the opportunity slip away. It had taken twenty-three years for Mama to mention her dreams. Was it possible to understand someone without knowing their dreams? It had been her lifelong desire to understand her mother. What to say that would not shut this newly cracked door.

"A-zou?" was all she dared say.

"She paid for my schooling."

"A-zou did?" Vicki asked then immediately pushed on. "You never told me much about your childhood."

"Tell you about my childhood?" Mama chuckled bitterly. "There is not much to tell. A-zou and A-ma will tell you their stories then I will correct them."

"Correct them? Why correct them?"

"They will tell you my story the way they saw it. I was the youngest daughter, the forgotten one, the opposite of you. You were always the most precious thing in my life. I was only noticed when I grew up and left the country."

This truncated explanation left so much unsaid. Vicki wanted desperately for her mother to continue, needing to understand Mama's experiences. Only then could she comprehend her thoughts and feelings. Since both A-zou and A-ma had already mentioned her return from Hua-lian, that was a legitimate topic.

"Do you remember the temple or coming home?" she asked hopefully.

"I was only three," Mama laughed. "I have vague memories of fear. It was a loud household I returned to and the temple was so peaceful. I don't remember the quiet period A-ma mentioned. It ended too quickly. All I remember is fear and anger, running and hiding."

"You don't remember the temple?"

"The temple before I was sent home?" Mama asked then continued talking without waiting for an answer. "I spent my childhood moving back and forth between there and Tai-dong. I also stayed with A-zou and Wei A-gong and A-ma in Ping-dong. My parents found me troublesome, always under foot. A-ma had to travel during the day to take care of customers. At night she did the accounting. There was no time to care for such a young child."

Vicki wondered if that was why her mother suffocated her with attention. What was just revealed helped explain the violent reaction Mama had to anyone raising their voice. Should she hazard another question or would pushing cause a shutdown? Deciding A-zou had unleashed the forbidden topics of conversation, Vicki attempted to get her mother to focus on what she experienced coming home.

"What are your earliest memories?" she gambled.

"Oh, I have vague impressions of being with my *Gugu* in the temple. They were teaching me how to massage," Mama smiled. "My earliest memory is of running and hiding from my father."

"Run, *mei-mei*, hide!" Shan-ji warned Jia-yi. "He's coming."

Shan-ji vanished before she could ask where to hide. Frozen in terror with her heart pounding, she just wanted to cry but knew better. Tears only brought derision down on her from Baba. Feeling desperate she looked around feverishly, panic rising within her. Was he going to hit Mama again? Would *gege* be the target of his rage? When would he begin hitting *jie-jie* and me? The sound of her drunken father singing floated in through the open windows. Then her eyes latched onto the space under the *tatami* platform. Who but her could fit in there?

Jia-yi scurried over to the gap and squeezed into it. He would never look for me here, she thought. As soon as she crawled under, she regretted her choice. The space was filled with cob webs and dust. Tears began to well up in her eyes, but she controlled them and waited for her father to settle down and fall asleep. Jia-yi could not believe this was the same man who had come to see her in the temple. He had been so nice to *gugu* and her. Now she was petrified of him.

The sound of her father climbing the stairs told her the wait would soon be over.

"Ma Li-ya!" Wei Wu shouted. "Is there no one here to serve me?"

"Ah-yo, you needn't talk so loudly," Li-ya chided gently as she stepped out of the kitchen. "The children are sleeping."

"They should be here greeting their father as he comes home," Wei Wu insisted.

"But they are asleep so they can do well in school and make you proud."

"Ha, that rat do well in school?" he spat out. "With his curse, he will be lucky to be a street cleaner."

Jia-yi hoped Mama would not try to defend *gege* tonight. Whenever she did Baba became angry and dragged *gege* out of bed to test him. If her mother interfered, her father would become violent. At those times Jia-yi ran out of the house, but she could not run out tonight, not from this hiding place. They had so little warning. Baba had not started singing until he was almost home.

"Come, I will give you a cup of tea and then you can go to bed," Li-ya cajoled. "You worked so hard tonight. You deserve a rest."

"That's right," he agreed. "I have worked hard."

Jia-yi froze when she heard her father enter the room. He walked over to the *tatami* and dropped down heavily. A tiny shower of dust floated down around her. She struggled to stifle a sneeze then felt a spider drop onto her leg. A small muffled sound escaped from her before she could gain control. Jia-yi prayed to Buddha her father was too drunk to notice. Sounds of him preparing to sleep followed. These movements unleashed another sprinkling of fine dust. Fear could not suppress a tiny sneeze.

"Eh," Wei Wu muttered. His face appeared at the opening of the space Jia-yi occupied.

"Get out!" he shouted. "Can't a man get some rest after working all night? Get out!"

Jia-yi crawled out quickly and dashed out of the room.

"Run you little mouse before I bite your head off and hang your bones out to dry!" he laughed derisively, the sound cutting through her as it chased her out of the room.

Mama came running from the kitchen, quickly scooping up her youngest. She carried Jia-yi to the children's room quietly admonishing her, "*Mei-mei* you mustn't hide in Baba's room. It upsets him when you do."

"That laughter still haunts me," Mama confessed. "To me he always seemed proud that his children feared him. Your father could never understand that, to desire your child fear you. He said it was a violation of a sacred trust, that it broke a pact with God and nature. Fathers are supposed to protect, not frighten."

Vicki heard the revulsion in her mother's voice. She knew her dad took his role as father very seriously and would find her mother's tale disgusting.

"I think that is enough for today," Mama declared. "I'll pay the bill and we can get to bed early tonight. You look like you could use a good night's sleep."

While Mama paid for dinner and chatted with Aggie, Vicki thought of the day with its emotional ups and downs. A good night's sleep sounded great. The trick would be convincing her mind to shut down long enough to pull that trick off. She was not sure it was possible.

Chapter Twenty

The sound of her mother leaving shook Vicki out of a light sleep. Mama had said she was going to meet an old friend this morning. That gave time for her daughter to catch up on her sleep and try to work through the puzzle of her life. In spite of the air conditioning, she felt uncomfortably warm. The oversized cotton tee shirt that served as her sleep wear was not doing it. Remembering the nighty she had slipped into her luggage at the last minute, Vicki dragged herself out of bed and retrieved the light sheer sleep wear Roger had given her with the hope of spending the night.

It was a strange gift considering their six month affair had been one of afternoon tete-a-tetes in her dorm room while her roommate was in class. She had never suggested he spend the night and he had never done so. Even as she slipped out of her tee shirt, Vicki knew the room temperature had little to do with her choice of sleep wear. The truth was her body was in mid-cycle and she missed Roger. Actually she missed the attention of a man. Her aunt's comment had set in motion an internal reassessment of the past few years. She was not sure where that would lead, but was certain she owed Roger and all the other guys she had played with an apology.

As she put the nighty on a feeling of pure femininity flowed over her. The sensation came as a reassurance after three days filled with the woes of womankind. The feeling did not assuage another more ominous one stirring inside. Vicki felt she was building to some sort of epiphany and was terrified. She slid back into bed caught between melancholy and terror. Lying on her side with her back toward the door, a tear escaped from her eye. It was then that she realized Roger and the others had been used to fill a gap, one that could only be filled by her cousin. Nikki had pointed out he was not her first cousin, but that seemed to matter little to her parents. Was she prepared to alienate her mother and father by claiming a love that might not be reciprocated? Both Sue's mom and Nikki had said A-hong's attraction was obvious, but that was no guarantee. You are a fool Victoria Phaff she chided herself before trying to sleep.

The click of the door opening pulled her awake. She swore to herself, having wanted to be up and dressed before Mama returned. Now she would have to explain the nighty. Her mother's opinion of the effect Vicki had on young men would be reinforced. That was not a good thing. At least Dad was not here. The sound of the door being closed gently was followed by silence which pulled her up to look. A-hong was standing there smiling with a look in his eyes that said he saw her as a woman. Instead of embarrassment, Vicki felt the situation titillating. Surrendering to emotions she had denied for too long, she slowly moved the sheets away and stood facing him. His smile widened as her hands signaled he was welcome.

A-hong moved toward her and gently kissed her lips. She reached for his belt and began to help him shed his clothing. Taking his hand, Vicki led him toward the bed.

"Is this what you really want?" he asked quietly.

"Yes," she answered. "More than life itself."

The sound of the toilet flushing woke Vicki from a sound sleep. She was breathing hard and sweating. What had she been dreaming? Her mother stepped out of the bathroom already dressed.

"I'll meet you at A-ma's around noon," Mama reminded her. "A-hong will bring A-zou. If we get there early enough, maybe A-ma will tell us a little more."

Vicki sat up in bed, still shocked and trying to get her bearings. "At noon," she muttered. "A-hong will bring A-zou, got it."

"Are you okay?"

"Yeah, just was in a deep sleep."

"Sorry, I tried to let you sleep as long as possible," Mama apologized.

"No problem," Vicki reassured. "Who are you meeting?"

"Oh, a childhood friend from Ping-dong."

"Okay, enjoy yourself."

With that her mother stepped out, leaving Vicki struggling. Where did that dream come from? One sentence from her aunt had sent her cascading into forbidden territory. Yet the dream left her with a feeling of a woman claiming what was hers. Was she that woman? A week ago the answer would have been an unequivocal no. Now she was unsure. It had felt so right to seduce him in the dream, even if he entered the room for the expressed purpose of being seduced. What would she do if the opportunity arose now?

Sun-zi had written, "If you know yourself and know the other, in a hundred battles you will have no concerns." Vicki was beginning to doubt how well she knew herself. She wished she could talk with A-hong, but that was becoming harder to do with each passing day. She certainly could not speak with him about the dream. Who else could she talk to? She was not mentioning it to Joe. Did she dare tell Sue? Speaking with Mama was laughable. Vicki felt so alone. Her whole support network seemed to be excluded from discussing her quandary. One sentence had unleashed tectonic forces in her inner world. Was her mindset shifting? Nikki reminding her about their not being first cousins came back. That memory created a natural division to her problem. She decided to split it between two cousins. Sue would get the half created by *A-yi's* question. Joe would get the half presented by Nikki's observation.

Where was Sue? Joe's room? Vicki jumped out of bed and reached for the phone.

"*Wei*," Sue answered in a sleepy voice.

"Sue, good," Vicki exclaimed. "Is Joe there with you?"

"No, he had a business meeting," Sue replied with a little more energy.

"A business meeting on Sunday? How long will he be gone?"

"Your father's a slave driver," Sue teased. "You're not going to get hold of him until the afternoon."

Perfect, thought Vicki. "I don't want him. I want you."

"Uh-oh, this sounds serious," Sue replied. "Does it have to do with my mother's unfiltered mouth?"

"She told you?"

"We'll talk," Sue assured. "You have to give me time to get ready."

"Don't rush, I just got out of bed," Vicki confessed. "Have to be at A-ma's by twelve. How about we meet at the breakfast buffet in twenty minutes?"

"Give me twenty-five."

"See you there."

Vicki hung up the phone and hopped into the bath. It was good Sue asked for an additional five minutes. She was not the only one who would need it. As she shed her tee shirt, Vicki smiled. No one ever had the nerve to give such a presumptuous gift and she had never felt a need for such a nighty. After finishing her morning routine, she stepped to the dresser. Her mind raced through the clothing options available there. Thinking of the day ahead, she decided on a blouse made from thicker fabric. Today would not be one for flouting her femininity. She would feel more comfortable emotionally in something a bit more modest than the outfits of the past few days. Decision made, she threw on a plain pink cotton blouse and a pair of white capris then dashed for the elevator, confirming she had two breakfast coupons in her purse before stepping out.

With the hum of the elevator providing background music, Vicki's mind worked through assorted strategic approaches to this most sensitive of topics. A bull in the china cabinet style would not do. It was not that Sue could not handle it. The topic was too fraught with subplots and implications for Vicki. She was bound to leave too much out to get an informed opinion from her cousin. No, she would have to use a gradual approach starting with a discussion about the comments of Sue's mom. Having noticed she had a tendency to dress a little more provocatively in mid-cycle, she took one last look in the elevator mirror to be certain modesty ruled the day. The doors opened at the lobby level and she stepped out to begin the trek across the lobby to the breakfast buffet. The sunlight shone in brightly through the glass wall at the entrance. It looked to be a typical hot, sunny day.

Letting her mind take a rest and just wander allowed her to marvel at this familiar space. The red columns ascended three stories before encountering a white ceiling covered with large three dimensional square tiles. Their design reminded her of a stylish flower. As a child she would run across this part of the lobby with her arms out like the wings of a bird. The thick cushion of the rugs had reminded her of a grass field. She would circle with her eyes fixated onto the ceiling until she became too dizzy, finally tumbling safely onto the cushion of the rug. Dad would laugh. Mom would scorn. From the beginning her cultural balancing act had been challenging. Although, now that she thought about it, it may not have been a cultural divide. The staff had enjoyed her antics and obvious pleasure.

Vicki stepped under the more mundane ceiling of the hallway leading to the buffet. A bank of elevators lined the walls while a thick plate glass wall much like the hotel entrance wall but on a smaller scale created a barrier at the end of the corridor. The sun shone brightly through the exterior glass wall. The rain had spent itself, the clouds had dissipated, and the heat had been turned up. It promised to be another cozy, comfortable day for lizards. Those creatures that produced their own heat would be miserable.

Sue was nowhere in sight, so Vicki approached the maître d' and made the same request her mother had made the morning before. Even if she wound up seated next to a twenty foot high sheet of glass, Vicki would tolerate it. The upcoming conversation required all the privacy she could arrange. Fortunately, a table in the far corner away from the outside wall was available, so she quickly claimed it and went there to wait for Sue. Her cousin stepped in before Vicki could place her purse on the floor between the wall and the chair.

"You look stressed," Sue commented as she settled in her seat.

"It shows does it?" Vicki sighed. "Why don't we gather up breakfast before we chat?"

They stood in unison and made their way to the buffet tables, purses dangling from their shoulders.

"How detailed an account did you get from your mother?" Vicki asked while reaching for two plates. She handed one to Sue, absently noting it was quite warm, probably fresh from the dishwasher. The two sorted through the breakfast offerings while Sue pondered a response.

"It was pretty detailed," she began obviously choosing her words very carefully. "My first reaction was 'You didn't say that did you?'"

Vicki laughed, "Yes she did."

"Oh boy," Sue breathed. "You requested that table?"

Vicki shook her head yes.

"Good choice, too many people speak English around here."

That had an ominous ring to it, Vicki thought. What have I gotten myself into? She began strolling back to the table with a light breakfast on her plate, sensing it would be a demanding chat and unsure if her stomach could handle it. After picking up a cup of coffee, she completed her retreat to the corner and sat expectantly.

"Mom said she stated the obvious," Sue said between a sip of coffee and a spoonful of congee. "Seems it never crossed her mind that there would be any complication with what she said. Her only concern was you not presenting yourself to him assertively enough."

"Assertively?" Vicki was astonished.

"Okay, okay," Sue surrendered. "She really said aggressively not assertively."

"That's supposed to make me feel better?"

"Do you love him?" her cousin asked bluntly.

"We are talking about A-hong, right?"

"Yes."

Her breakfast was now forgotten. How did she appear to her cousins? Asking the question implied Sue already knew the answer, but Vicki could not bring herself to verbalize a direct reply.

"He's my cousin," she blurted out. "Of course I love him."

"You're dodging the question," Sue told her. "But you don't have to answer me. You have to answer yourself."

"I need to know how I appear to the family," Vicki insisted.

"The family?" Sue asked putting her spoon down. "Well if you mean your mother, she seems to be convinced you're trying to attract him. At least she does everything she can to prevent the two of you from being alone together. Joe's convinced the *biaomei* A-hong's uncle mentioned at the jewelry store is you. I'm not quite there yet.

You know my mother's take. A-zou, A-ma, my father, they're all harder to read. From what my mother told me, A-hong's mother agrees with yours."

"Mei-zhi *A-yi* agrees with my mother? Oh, shit!" Vicki muttered. "How did this happen?" Part of her felt the world was imploding, pulling everything she had thought to be true into a bottomless abyss. Yet another part of her felt almost a joyful explosion. This was quickly reigned in. "Even if he was interested, how could it ever work out? My parents would be opposed. His mother doesn't sound thrilled. We would have to give up our families. What am I saying? This is ridiculous."

"Ridiculous?" Sue laughed. "Ridiculous is me sitting nine thousand miles away from my teenage crush waiting for him to come and scoop me up. That's ridiculous."

This stopped Vicki. Stranger things have happened. What of A-hong? The degree of humiliation she would feel by approaching him only to be rejected would be immeasurable. She picked up her cup of coffee for a sip and noticed her hands were shaking. Needing an indirect way to query her cousin, she decided to revert to the hypothetical method that had worked so well over the past few days.

"Hypothetically, if a cousin in Taiwan approached another cousin in this type of situation what would happen in the average Taiwanese family?"

At first Sue chuckled at the word "hypothetical" then sat quietly working through the question. This is payoff for all those summers of tutoring, Vicki thought.

"Hypothetically?" Sue asked. "Well, this hypothetical couple are not first cousins. It's illegal to marry your first cousin. So, ideally they would have to receive the blessing of their families, if not both, at least the man's family. Even today, the woman is marrying out of her family and into his. Of course you shouldn't share the same last name, but that's about it."

Vicki analyzed Sue's explanation quickly and muttered, "So it's up to the families and that doesn't look good. Have you noticed a change in how A-hong looks at me?" She asked pushing onto a subject inspired by Nikki's comment.

"Looks at you?" Sue wondered.

"Nikki said the way he looked at me said something," she informed Sue.

"Nikki?"

"The waitress from Prince Albert's. She said it would be a good match."

"Really, she noticed?" Sue chortled. "As far as a good match is concerned, the two of you as a team would be a frightening match."

"What do you mean 'she noticed'? That sounds like you agree," Vicki asked ignoring the comment about a team and getting increasingly flustered.

"Agree? Agree with what?" Sue chortled. "The way A-hong talks about you, the way he looks at you all changed after that year at Rutgers. I think he noticed you were on longer a cute little girl, more like a beautiful woman."

Vicki was stunned. Everything was changing. Her mother had sensed it. It had become obvious to everyone. How could it work? Her father thought they were too closely related. At least that was what Mama had said. A-hong's mother seemed not to approve. More importantly the two of them had never openly acknowledged anything. What was she thinking? She had not acknowledged anything to herself! Then she remembered last night's dream.

"I, ah, I had this dream last night," She began. By the time she was finished, Sue was fanning herself and Vicki was laughing.

"Wow, that was hot," Sue exclaimed. "I'm no psychologist, but the meaning seems to be pretty obvious."

"Obvious?" Vicki protested. "What's obvious?"

"You can sit there in denial if you want to Victoria," Sue stated. "But your feelings toward A-hong appear to run deeper than you want to admit."

"It was only a dream," Vicki insisted. "And don't you dare share it with anyone."

"As always, you secret is safe," Sue assured her. "So what do you plan to do?"

Vicki found she could not answer. It was the ultimate conundrum. Allow herself to fall in love and alienate her family or remain in the cycle of searching for the perfect substitute.

"I don't know," she admitted. "I have to talk with Joe or my dad or both."

"Looking for a guy's perspective or an American's perspective?"

"I've got the American part down all by myself."

"Are you American or Chinese?

"Don't even go there."

"Well, you can try Joe later on or maybe just give Roger a call," Sue teased.

Vicki swore quietly in Taiwanese then stood up to pay the bill.

Chapter Twenty-one

Vicki climbed down the stairs leading from the hotel to the street. Trees covered the walkway protecting her from the summer sun. She had not used sun screen and so was grateful for any cover. Being fair skinned in Taiwan may be fashionable, but it could also be painful. So much of the time had been spent indoors or in taxis that she had not bothered applying protection. Taking the bus to A-ma's was the first test of her skin tolerance this trip. The hassle of rubbing on sun screen was always weighed against the probability of sun exposure. Gambling that she could catch the bus without a prolonged wait under an unimpeded sun, her skin remained unprotected. Probably not the brightest move, but a tube of protection rested in her purse just in case.

She stepped onto the sidewalk from the hotel stairs and walked briskly to a crosswalk, taking advantage of any shade along the way. The crosswalk light changed just before she reached it, so she trotted the short distance and crossed the street. Even this tiny exertion brought up beads of sweat. It was going to be challenging at A-ma's. Vicki parked herself under a tree close to the bus stop and waited. The light traffic of a Sunday morning flowed past. Whether caused by the passing traffic or by nature, there was a subtle breeze that combined with the moisture on her skin to provide cooling. She would take anything she could get. Her attire did not allow for the usual relief of a thin silk blouse and shorts.

The number 237 bus for Neihu pulled up after a short wait. Vicki climbed up into the air conditioning, looked at the sign and saw she was expected to pay her fare getting on, so dropped her fare into the coin collector and sat down behind the driver. As she leaned back into the seat a temporary shock of coolness swept across her back. She enjoyed the momentary relief from the heat, but knew her back would soon be sticky with sweat caused by the plastic seat cover. There was a comforting familiarity to it all. At least this part of her existence remained stable. Reminding herself that the day belonged to A-zou and A-ma, she did her best to push away any thoughts of her troubles. Thinking of A-zou created a rush of these thoughts to the forefront of her mind. Her aunt had said A-zou saw an attraction between her and A-hong. How could Sue's mother say that? Had A-zou said something to her? Mama said *A-yi*'s family was close to A-zou. Close enough that her great-grandmother would confide in *A-yi* but not Mama or A-ma? Did they all know of A-zou's view? Was that why Mama was so nervous when A-hong was around? "Stop!"she commanded."You will drive yourself crazy." Vicki realized she had a Pandora's Box in her mind that she was afraid to open. Once the feelings were out, they could never be put back and she was not sure there was any hope to lighten the disappointment that would follow. Today is for A-zou. Everything else can be sorted out later. She leaned her head back and distracted her mind by trying to read the bus advertisements. Chinese school had been so long ago, but she could still pick out a few characters.

When she arrived at A-ma's, Vicki found Mama waiting impatiently, even though she was early.

"How was your friend?" she asked, hoping it would calm her mother.

"My friend?" Mama replied curtly. "She has her problems like we all do. Come quickly A-ma wants to talk before A-zou comes."

She stepped to her assigned seat while her mother went to the bedroom to tell A-ma they were ready. Before A-ma could come out the door bell chirped. Vicki moved to the door button and pushed it. A-ma would not get a chance to share before her mother. Hopefully Mama would not be too annoyed. Her body language said the chat she had with her childhood friend had not gone well. Once in a funk, the entire day was usually ruined. She breathed in deeply trying to calm her nerves. It felt like a vice was squeezing her. One jaw of it was last night's revelations; the other was Mama's attitude. Hopping to the door, Vicki was still uncertain how she would react to A-hong. The sound of her cousin and A-zou climbing the stairs came through the security gate. Her great-grandmother did not sound well at all.

It took an inordinate amount of time for the pair to reach the second floor landing. When they stepped into the apartment A-zou looked exhausted. The shock of her appearance distracted Vicki until A-hong had her seated. When he turned around to greet her, Vicki involuntarily looked away.

"Hello, Vic," he said cheerfully.

"Hey, A-hong," was all she could produce in reply.

Out of the corner of her eye, she could see he was confused. Before he could greet anyone else, Mama began snapping orders.

"Let's go, Vicki you take your place. A-hong you know what to do. A-zou wants to get this over with, I'm sure."

Both complied without comment while A-ma took up her position. Mama was the last to sit.

"Good morning," A-zou greeted her family. "Last night was difficult for me, but I have enough energy for the two of you."

The two of us, Vicki thought. What of A-ma and Mama? She noticed Mama became a bit more agitated with this. It was promising to be a hot day in more ways than one.

"We ended with Jia-yi going to the temple, didn't we?" A-zou asked.

"Yes," A-hong agreed.

"I never felt the pain of losing a child," she began. "Even when I gave my daughter away, I knew she was alive and would be treated well. How do you console a grieving mother?

****

"I gave in and allowed Shan-bao to get in the van with a drunken wild man," Li-ya cried bitterly. "What kind of a mother am I?"

Chiu Bu struggled to retain her composure. The memory of her little grandson's laughter was all she had left of him. Her daughter was being consumed by grief and anger. Now was her time to be strong, as strong as her daughters had been when the mainlanders had robbed her love.

"You were a good mother, but unless you remember your other children, you will no longer be one," she scolded, sounding harsher than she intended. It appeared to have the desired effect. Chiu Bu knew the only way out of this dark cavern was to concentrate on children and business. That was how she had survived her loses. It was how she would guide her daughter to daylight.

"I think he is drinking again," Li-an said over the phone. "He was still in bed when I called *mei-mei* at noon."

Chiu Bu was not surprised by her eldest daughter's conjecture. Wei Wu was spending too much time in Tai-dong. She was certain he was meeting with his old friends. There had been hope for a short period. Before she had had a chance to speak with Mrs. Wei to have her suggest Jia-yi go home, he had brought her back. Li-ya had handled his affair masterfully, opening up the door for reconciliation. Their family appeared to be mending itself until Wei Wu began to spend more time in Tai-dong. If he was drinking, then the violence would surely follow. There was no escaping the bitter taste of agreeing to this marriage. She chastised herself frequently, but could do nothing for her daughter. This frustration ate away at her soul. It might not be possible to improve Li-ya's situation, but she could work to minimize the children's exposure.

"Did she mention anything about his behavior?" she asked Li-an.

"Mama, you know she will not say such things to me. *Mei-mei* is too proud."

"The children should not be exposed to his behavior," Chiu Bu asserted. "I will speak with Mrs. Wei. We have to come up with a way to limit their time with him."

"They will have to attend school in Tai-dong," Li-an reminded her mother.

"Yes, that is required now, but when school is not in session, they can come here to Ping-dong to be with their grandparents."

"And their aunt and cousins," Li-an agreed.

"How are the children?" Li-ya asked.

"Oh, they are being helpful," her mother answered before she switched the phone from one ear to the other. She reached for a cup of tea before continuing. "Some days they help me, others they are at the Wei's. All the family children play together and they play with the Lin children also." She did not want to tell her daughter about the nightmares and acting out of Shan-ji. At times the boy was skittish while at others he was overly aggressive. "Jia-luan takes care of Jia-yi and helps Li-mei around the house." She wanted to say Jia-luan was the most cheerful and well-adjusted of the children, but knew that would produce too many questions. None of this would be a revelation to their mother. A summer away from madness could not erase the damage of ten months in hell.

"How is *mei-mei?*" Li-ya asked.

"Mei-mei is as smart and as stubborn as ever," Chiu Bu laughed. "If the older children don't pay attention to her she yells at them. A *Hakka* family moved in close to the Wei store. She plays with their

little girl. It is a wonder to hear her switch between languages so easily."

Her daughter laughed along. "Yes, language comes so easily to her. But not numbers. She has to work harder with numbers."

"We all have our talents," Chiu Bu said after sipping her tea. "Is business doing well?"

"Business has been falling off since that veterans' store opened," she sighed. "Business in Hua-lian is better. My husband was chosen as district leader here, so he spends more time in Tai-dong. I have to go to Hua-lian more often to cover for him. The children will have to come home in two weeks for school."

"Yes, I know," her mother replied. As she hung up the phone she repeated "I know" to herself. Shan-ji would start high school this year. Jia-luan would be in junior high, and little Jia-yi would start third grade. Comments from their neighbors made it clear they were exceptional children. They performed well enough in school even though there was no opportunity to study. Instead they spent any nights their father was home running.

"A-ma, it would be such a waste if she doesn't continue her language study," Jia-luan begged.

Chiu Bu sat in her living room listening. There was no arguing with what her granddaughter said. How could she influence Wei Wu to allow Jia-yi to develop her talent and blossom? The child had been all but ignored by her father, a second daughter who had never won his heart like her elder sister. Was she destined to be a hairdresser as Wei Wu insisted?

"I agree," she answered. "How will we convince him to allow this for your *mei-mei?*"

Jia-luan smiled, happy to have an ally. "I have spoken with the missionary doctors in Tai-dong. Jia-yi has always practiced her English with them. They are willing to speak with my father. But I know he will refuse to pay for any more schooling. He was not happy paying for mine and he likes me so much more."

It saddened Chiu Bu that a fourteen year old girl on the verge of womanhood should have her life decided for her so arbitrarily. "Do you think they can convince him?" she asked.

"I think between my begging and their persuasion he will allow it," Jia-luan stated confidently. "But I don't think he will pay for it. Mama will try to convince him. It is a dangerous game."

Chiu Bu became angry with herself once again. She had condemned her daughter to this life with her choice. It took only a moment to decide on a solution to this problem. She owed a debt to Li-ya that could not be repaid directly. The debt would be paid through her daughter.

"You can tell him when he objects that I will pay for it," she promised.

****

"It was a good investment, don't you think?" A-zou queried. "Look at the returns." With that she motioned toward Vicki and laughed. A-hong shook his head in agreement and smiled. Vicki did not appreciate the attention.

It was shocking how much the telling of this part of her story took out of A-zou. Vicki wanted to end it there, but knew she could not. Mama said something which gave her grandmother renewed energy. She snapped back at her. A-hong declined to translate the exchange. A-ma joined in with a gentle suggestion. Her mother seemed to relent, which only added to Vicki's worry.

"They discussed whether A-zou should continue right now," A-hong told her. "At first she refused to even consider it then A-ma suggested she rest for a little before going on. She agreed to that, so she's going to lie down and you're A-ma is going to talk to you."

Vicki found it a little easier to look at her cousin after listening to A-zou. "Thanks for the explanation," she said a little too formally. He was bound to pick up on her sudden reticence if she could not push to be more like her usual self. It was only a dream and he had no idea what was going on. Before she could say anything further, A-zou spoke with him then struggled to stand up. A-hong jumped up to help and aided her to A-ma's bedroom. Mama had a puzzled look on her face.

She turned to Vicki and told her, "A-zou wants him to go pick up something for her from a lawyer's office."

"From a lawyer's?" Vicki asked in shock. "Did she say what it was?"

"Only that it was an envelope," Mama answered.

"I'm sure it has to do with preparations for leaving us," A-ma interjected sadly.

A-hong came out and gently closed the bedroom door. "She's lying down," he assured them. "Something is going on, but she won't quit right now. I asked her and she only said she is almost finished and she has a doctor's appointment tomorrow. What should we do?"

A-ma looked at him with sympathy and sighed. "This is what she wants, what she is living for right now. As long as she does not collapse we should let her finish. After all this time, she has earned to be a little reckless with her health." This was followed by a resigned chuckle.

Chapter Twenty-two

After A-hong went on his errand, the three women sat down. Sunlight was streaming in through the living room windows, raising the room's temperature and making Vicki regret her choice of clothing. The reason for modesty had been sent away. She was sitting in a sauna needlessly. Picking her pad up from the glass top of the table in front of her, Vicki waited for A-ma to begin.

"A-zou was right," she sighed. "The violence returned when he drank and he drank when he was in Tai-dong. As the time went by it became almost a daily ritual when he came back from Hua-lian. It gradually worsened until one night."

****

Li-ya heard her husband shouting greetings and singing. By the sound of it, he was just down the block.

She stood up and called to Shan-ji, "*Gege*, gather up your sisters and go to bed."

Hopefully, Wei Wu would be sober enough to listen to reason and do the same. When she first allowed him back into their lives, her husband had been on his best behavior. He had gradually reverted back to his former habits, although not to the extreme he had exhibited in the time before Shan-bao's death. Time away from Tai-dong was the key. The noise he was making tonight made her uneasy. His singing and shouting were too boisterous. It told her the alcohol had control of him. This would be the first time since the accident he had consumed so much. The cold, clammy air clung to her. A thick sweater provided some protection, yet she had still felt chilly up until his dissonant singing had floated through the window glass. Now her heart began to race and her hands were sweaty. The cacophony that was her drunken husband entered the house and assaulted her ears as he climbed the stairs.

"Ma Li-ya," he shouted after stepping into the living room without removing his shoes. "I have decided to hire my cousin to manage the Hua-lian store. They want to choose me as district leader, so I will stay in Tai-dong."

"Stay in Tai-dong!" she thought. The idea was fraught with danger. Not only would it expose her and their children to his bouts of drunkenness, it would also increase their expenses. Wei Wu would almost certainly feel the need to provide food and drink to his buddies. That would increase spending dramatically.

"We cannot afford it," she stated. "Competitors are drawing customers from us. The Hua-lian store needs to grow and you are the only one talented enough to do it."

"My cousin will be able to do it," he insisted, slurring his words more as he became adamant. "Tai-dong needs my talent to deal with these outside born politicians and their laws."

"It's too risky," she pleaded desperately. "We need the income from the Hua-lian store." She could see he was getting agitated, but needed to dissuade him from this idea.

"I have been chosen as the district leader," he bragged. "I have to be here!"

"If we have no money you will not be district leader for long," she told him.

This was too much for Wei Wu's pride. He grabbed his wife by the shoulders and pulled her to him. She could smell the alcohol on his breath as he hissed, "They have chosen me to be district leader because of my leadership abilities, not my money!"

"Leave her alone!" Shan-ji yelled.

Li-ya was shocked. He should be in the children's room with his sisters reassuring them. The man was too drunk for a boy to challenge. There was no telling how her husband might react.

"Shan-ji, go to your sisters!" she ordered, praying her son would comply and his father would ignore him. Wei Wu threw her down and reached for his son.

"Come here you disrespectful little rat!" he grabbed the boy's arm and slapped him across the face. Shan-ji reacted with silence, glaring unflinchingly at his tormentor. "You look like you need a lesson," Wei Wu laughed as he dragged him to the stairs.

"No!" Li-ya shouted. "Leave the boy alone. He was only trying to protect his mother."

He ignored her and pulled Shan-ji to the first floor bean factory. Li-ya chased after them, but could not pull her son from Wei Wu's grasp. They made their way to the back of the factory, Shan-ji struggling the entire time. The two came to a stop at the rear of the building. Wei Wu appeared undecided, scanning the factory floor. She found herself fearing for her son's life and lunged at her husband. He kicked her violently in the abdomen, knocking her to the floor. A sinister chuckle escaped from his mouth as he pulled their son toward the large vats used to soak beans.

"You should stay out of a man's business," he advised angrily. "Trying to protect your mother? She is my wife. I own her and will do with her as I please." When the two reached the vats, Wei Wu wrestled Shan-ji under a hoist used to lift barrels of beans into the vats. As he attempted to tie his son's hands together, the boy swung at him with a closed fist, landing a blow on Wei Wu's cheek. This only enraged the man further. He began beating the boy with his fist, Li-ya lay in the background pleading for him to stop. Ignoring his wife entirely, Wei Wu completed binding Shan-ji's hands behind his back and then attached a hook from the hoist to his belt. The father then lifted his twelve year old son up and out over the water filled vat. The boy was suspended above the cold water for a moment before his father released the locking mechanism, sending the child plunging into the water below. A hideous laugh escaped from him as he hoisted Shan-ji out of the water and then sent him plunging down beneath the surface again and again. Li-ya screamed and begged for it to stop. Shan-ji was gasping for air, but made no other sound. His sisters watched from the doorway.

Tiring of his game, Wei Wu dropped his son on the floor beside the vat and turned his attention to his wife. "See how you make me treat your son!" he shouted. With that he reached down and grabbed her by the hair. "Get up woman and stop making so much noise."

Li-ya realized she had to keep his attention away from Shan-ji. Following her son's example, she slapped her husband. This had the desired effect. He became blinded with rage, seeing only her, forgetting about the child lying on the floor shivering and gasping for air. Too livid to say a word, Wei Wu began dragging his wife by her hair toward the front door. Li-ya fought to remain on her feet and keep up with him, her mind frantically searching for a way to end the hell of this night. As they passed through the door, she saw her daughters rush to help their brother. At least they could give him some comfort.

Her husband reached the street and paused for a moment. His hold on her hair prevented Li-ya from raising her head; she had no idea what he was doing. Her husband had the strength of a mad man at that moment. She was certain he was quite capable of killing her. Suddenly he pulled her forcefully forward and released his hold on her hair. The ground began to rush up, but before she completed the fall her head hit something solid.

Dazed, Li-ya struggled to stand. She heard Jia-yi scream. Blood dripped down her face from a wound on her head opened by the light pole she was lying beside. Wei Wu looked down at her, eyes glaring with rage. He reached for her, but stopped when a man's voice called his name.

"Wei Wu, did that stupid wife of yours get you angry again? Having so much *qi* in your body is not good. Come, I have a new bottle of *sake*. We can open it and talk about how stupid our wives are. The Master was right. Relations with women are the most difficult."

Wei Wu straightened up and chuckled. "Yes you are right; too much *qi* is not good. *Sake* should dissipate some of it. You are a learned man, quoting from the Four Books." The men laughed and walked to the neighboring house. Before disappearing inside, the neighbor surreptitiously signaled for Jia-yi to help her mother.

****

"The next morning when he saw the damage he had inflicted he seemed apologetic and never reached that extreme again. His insistence on living in Tai-dong continued. When he finally moved back, the abuse became common. We all lived in fear. The children could not help but be effected. They fled as soon as they could."

Mama sat quietly, shaken by having to relive such a traumatic night from her childhood. A-ma looked at her daughter and said something that did not get translated. Whatever it was appeared to cause tension between the two women. Then A-ma gestured toward Vicki and insisted Mama translate.

"A-ma said she is going to tell you something I am not yet aware of."

"That man had tried to control everything around him for so long. When the children began to grow up, he did not want to accept that he could not do it any longer," A-ma began. "First it was Shan-ji going into the army. His father said he could not, but the law said he had to. Then he wanted Jia-luan *A-yi* to marry his banker's son. She did not want to marry. Since he had always treated her like a doll, his anger had little effect. She knew he would not harm her. Instead she made him bargain with her."

****

"I do not want to marry," Jia-luan told her parents.

"You must," her father insisted. "Who will take care of you when you are old?"

"Times have changed, Baba," she reminded him. "I can work and support myself. A-ma does it."

"A-ma," he said derisively. "What does that old woman know? She has family that allows her to work for them. We are not rich. Mr. Ye's son is a respectable, capable young man. It will be a good union for both families."

"Will it be a good marriage for me?" she asked.

"A good marriage for you?" was the exasperated response. Before he could go further, she put her hand up to quiet him.

"I will consider this marriage if you allow *mei-mei* to continue her language studies."

"What does that have to do with you? You already brought those foreigners here. No matter what they say, no matter what you do, I will not throw money away on educating a daughter. She needs a skill, not an education," he insisted.

Jia-luan smiled when he said this. "So if someone else pays for her expenses, you will allow her to continue?"

Mama held her breath. This daughter was the only one who could speak with Wei Wu like this. Anyone else would have precipitated an explosion by now. *Jie-jie* had backed him into a corner and he did not know it. Li-ya waited quietly for her eldest daughter to close the trap and open a future for her sister.

"Who would waste so much money on a second born daughter?" he laughed. "Yes, if you can find a fool who will sponsor her, then she can continue."

"A-ma said she would pay *mei-mei's* expenses," Jia-luan informed him. This was greeted by shocked silence. Her father quickly regained his composure.

"You will marry the Ye boy if your sister attends school?"

"Only after she is enrolled and you tell your friends and family."

"If that fool of a woman wants to throw her money away, I have no problem with it."

****

Mama struggled to complete the translation then stood up and walked quickly to the bathroom. Before closing the door, she burst into tears.

Chapter Twenty-three

Vicki dropped her pad on the couch next to her, dumbfounded. She knew her aunt's marriage had been rocky which made this newly revealed debt Mama owed that much greater. A-ma turned to her and spoke in halting Mandarin. "Jia-luan *A-yi* was like a second mother to your mama," she said. "She did everything she could to make sure her *mei-mei* had a better life and never regretted what she did. Even in the hard times, she would look at pictures of you with your cousins and know she had made the right decision."

Me with my cousins? Vicki thought. Her Ye cousins were so much older than she was. They had never been close. She had not seen them in years. Why would pictures of her as a child with her cousins bring solace to her aunt? Before she could consider this question, Mama stepped out of the bathroom. Her eyes were red and her mannerisms were controlled.

"I am sorry," she apologized. "Do you want to continue?"

"Yes, if you can," A-ma replied. "I think we should let A-zou rest more."

Mama moved back to her seat while Vicki picked up her notepad. After her daughter was settled, A-ma continued her story.

"With your mother out of the house, I was determined not to tolerate my husband's drinking and abuse. I prepared myself and then confronted him."

****

"I want a divorce," Li-ya told Wei Wu calmly. "There is no need to continue this farce you call a marriage."

Wei Wu had just woken up after a night with his buddies. He responded with a smile at first. The smile slipped away after the sense of her words meaning set in. She knew he had done a quick calculation of their circumstances and had realized with the children out of the house there was nothing to hold over his wife.

"No you don't," he laughed. "You would starve without me."

"Li-mei has that real estate company in Taipei," she reminded him. "She is doing quite well and has invited me to join her."

A look of rage passed over his face, but quickly dissipated. He had been enabled by the environment, but that was changing and Wei Wu knew it. They both had silently acknowledged long ago that Li-ya had run the business. She would be the first to admit her husband was an excellent entrepreneur. He just did not have the discipline to run what he created. She could support herself and no one would condemn her for wanting out of such a poisonous relationship.

"You can't. I won't let you," was his desperate reply.

"Won't let me," she spat. "After all you have done to me? After your drinking killed my son? You think I need your permission? I am leaving this hell that you created."

With that she walked to the door and picked up the suitcase placed there after he staggered in that morning. Wei Wu moved to stop her, but she easily shook free of his grasp and stepped out. His body had been so weakened by the alcohol consumed the previous night he did not have the strength to prevent her. Instead he dropped to the ground and vomited.

"Li-ya, *gege* told me you left him and want a divorce," Wei Wu's sister said over the phone. She was speaking softly because the temple's phone did not allow for much privacy.

"Yes, *mei-mei,*" Li-ya sighed. "I no longer see a need to live with his drinking and shouting and abuse. Even if he wanted to, he cannot change."

"I knew this day would come," the nun sighed. "Until he stops drinking, you will have no chance for peace."

Li-ya had expected an attempt to pressure her not to go through with her plan. Now that it had not happened, she knew her sister-in-law had a plan of her own. No matter what it was, there would be no return to her previous life. She waited patiently to hear what might be proposed.

"He cannot change himself without changing his environment," the nun stated. "I think I can help there. I have been speaking with Ma Li-mei. She thinks purchasing an apartment in the Neihu section of Taipei would be an excellent investment. I will make the payment. I want you to move there with him."

Li-ya considered ignoring the nun, but knew the social ostracism would affect more than just her. She had no desire to become a pariah or make her children outcasts. Before she could respond to her sister-in-law, the nun continued.

"The two of you can pay me back when you are able," she instructed. "You have to give him one more chance in a changed environment. I have spoken to him about his sergeant's ghost. He says he now understands it was the man's destiny. If the ghost returns it will come to apologize for the pain it inflicted not to haunt. Maybe that will help *gege* leave his past behind."

****

How could he not see the Taidong store was draining them? Li-ya thought as she worked the last numbers Jia-luan had sent. The store had not turned a profit in years. Pride had blinded her husband. Wei Wu could not admit that his brain child was dead. The sound of him closing the street door two floors below came up the staircase and through the apartment door. They could put it off no longer. The store had to be closed so their energies could be focused on the Hua-lian store and the Taipei real estate market. After five years of sobriety she had learned his strengths and weaknesses and how to manipulate them. All of this knowledge would be needed to turn his mind around.

"The Chens have decided against the apartment on Neihu Road," Wei Wu told her when he stepped in. "They said they are looking for something on a quieter street."

"On a quieter street?" she asked. "It will be difficult to find a place in their price range."

"I'm going to speak with A-mei," he sighed. "Your sister has a way with dreamers. I'm too up front." He walked over to her and glanced at the papers on the table. "What are you up to?"

Perfect, she thought. He had unknowingly solved her puzzle of how to begin this difficult conversation. Wei Wu sat across the table from her and groaned in relief.

"A-luan sent up the accounts for Tai-dong," she informed him. "We have to decide on some sort of plan. That store is bleeding us dry."

He became impatient as soon as he heard this news. "What plan? *Jie-jie* and Xiao Ye have to work harder," he insisted. "They have let the business slide. When we were there it was very profitable."

Li-ya did not want to be reminded of their time in Tai-dong. The peace they had achieved in Taipei seemed miraculous. She could not thank his sister enough for the gift of this new husband. The only vestige remaining from those dark days was that store.

"They can work no harder," she reminded him. "The competition in the area from those large stores is too much. We can't buy low enough to match their prices."

He became more agitated when she reminded him of this fact. "If I could go down there and meet with my friends, we could increase sales and turn it around," he bragged.

Just the thought of her husband going to Tai-dong to meet with his friends infuriated her. She controlled her tongue and used the anger to focus on the problem of a proud dreamer not willing to admit defeat. "That store hasn't been viable since I stopped doing my sales routes," she pointed out. "Your meetings never increased sales."

Wei Wu jumped up in anger. "What do you mean never increased sales," he shouted. "They are what kept that business going."

In their previous life she would have felt threatened by his actions, but the time away from Tai-dong had mellowed him. Although he had not reached this level of agitation so quickly since they had relocated, she was not put off.

"I did the books," she reminded him. "Sales came from my meeting with customers in their stores, not from you drinking with your buddies." As soon as these words were out she regretted them. Her rule had been to never mention his drinking and subsequent behavior. Even though it was springtime and the temperature was moderate, Li-ya began to feel warm.

"You're lying!" he shouted. "Trying to take credit for my hard work!"

Memories of her past existence flashed through her mind. Now her wish was to end the discussion, but they were too far into it and could not afford to put it off. Then she remembered something Jia-luan had mentioned a few weeks before.

"*Jie-jie* also mentioned that the language instructors at our tutoring school were thinking of buying the business and building," she shot out trying to divert his attention away from her last statement. "This would be the perfect time to take them up on it. Jia-yi graduated and has some free time before she starts at the airline. Jia-luan can move to Hua-lian and run that store. *Mei-mei* can run the tutoring school until we close the deal."

"Jia-yi? We never see her. She's always with your mother. You really think she'll go to Tai-dong for you?" he doubted. "Running the tutoring school? She can't speak Japanese. What good is French and English?" Scoffing loudly after this.

"They got her a job as a stewardess," she reminded him. He had shown real pride for the first time in Jia-yi's life when she had told them.

"You are wasting my time," Wei Wu snarled. "I won't sell my store."

Damn men and their foolish pride, Li-ya cursed to herself. "Then what will you do with it? Right now you are throwing money away."

The truth of what she was saying became too much for him. With frustration strangling his mind, he exploded. "Who said you are the boss?" he yelled. "We will not sell the store!"

Six years before the shouted question would have terrified her. Now it produced blind rage. "Who said I am the boss?" she shrieked. "Shan-bao said I am the boss! We will sell the store!"

This mention of crimes from their previous life drove him back. He made no attempt to counter what she had said. The discussion was over. "If you think we must sell it then sell it," he said quietly before walking away.

Ma Li-ya sat nervously in her living room waiting for her youngest daughter. Jia-yi must have called form the airport right after landing. She was usually exhausted after working the New York flight and so did not call for a day or two. Today she had called within an hour of landing, found out her father was not at home, and then said she was on her way over. The abrupt click left her mother to ponder what subject would require a private mother daughter chat. Jia-yi had mentioned nothing about a love interest, but that was normal. Her parents knew nothing of their daughter's love life. Would she hide involvement with a man until deciding to marry him? There was no way to know until she arrived, so Li-ya walked to the kitchen to make tea while she waited.

"Over the past two years I have become friendly with an American business couple," Jia-yi began. She was a bundle of nervous energy. The cup of tea sat on the glass top of the coffee table ignored. Whatever the news, it appeared to be exciting. Li-ya refrained from asking questions, knowing the quickest way to an explanation was silence. "They have been coming here every month or two and have always complimented me on my English."

Her mother nodded and smiled. That someone would think *mei-mei* had language talent came as a surprise to no one who knew her. Li-ya sipped her tea and continued to listen. "Today they told me of their plan to open an office in Taipei," she squealed. "And they want me to manage it!"

"Really?!" Li-ya exclaimed. No more in and out of the country. She could settle into a more peaceful life and begin to think of moving beyond this new stage of life her generation seemed to have developed. There would be time now to find a good man and start a family. By the time she was Jia-yi's age she had two children. If she could somehow arrange a marriage for this youngest daughter, Li-ya would. . . . She stopped herself and would have laughed if her daughter was not there. Remembering the discussion with her mother about arranging a marriage, she knew that the world had changed for the better. It would be Jia-yi's choice no matter how much Wei Wu disagreed. That disagreement is what precipitated the question concerning his whereabouts. The arguments between the two had grown increasingly acrimonious. Her daughter did not want to see him if she could avoid it.

"It will take a few months to set up," Jia-yi continued. "But I should be able to leave the airline soon. The salary they offered is better and they hinted about helping me study in America."

"How could you study there and run the office here?"

"That wouldn't be until the office was established," she answered. "And they didn't say the company would pay for it, just that they might be able to help me choose a school and get accepted. So it will take me a few years to save the money for tuition and expenses."

"You're still young, a few years isn't bad," her mother reassured. "And think of the experience you'll gain."

Jia-yi was beaming, making it obvious this was what she wanted. "I'll support you in any way I can," Li-ya promised. "The first hurdle will be your father." How would she convince her husband that this was a better choice than pushing for marriage? A door slamming two stories below told her the discussion might take place sooner than she wanted. *Mei-mei* jumped at the sound then muttered "shit." She silently stood and marched to the bathroom, leaving her mother to deal with her father.

Li-ya quickly scooped up the tea cup on the coffee table and carried it into the kitchen. When she came back into the living room, Wei Wu stepped into the apartment. He wore a scowl on his face and bandages on his hands.

"What happened?" his wife asked in shock.

"Some crazy brat knocked me down with his scooter," he growled. "I was lucky to break the fall with my hands. These young people, they don't know how to be responsible. Where is our country going? No one has respect for tradition anymore."

Li-ya listened sympathetically, letting him vent but cursing her misfortune. He was not supposed to be back for hours. It appeared his only injuries were scrapes and a little pride, but *mei-mei* was still holed up in the bathroom. He was in pain which gave him a dark mood. Jia-yi did not want to interact with her father on a good day. To have him and this daughter in the same room right now would be a nightmare.

"Why don't you go lie down," she suggested. "I'll pour you a cup of tea and you can rest."

"Okay," he sighed. "I just have to go to the bathroom first."

Jia-yi came out as soon as she heard this. "Oh, hello Baba," she greeted. "You hurt your hands. What happened?"

"Some brat hit me with his scooter," he complained. "Why are you here today? Aren't you tired from your flight?"

His tone suggested he was suspicious. Their daughter's reaction showed the question was poorly put. Father and daughter had unconsciously begun to square off. She had inherited his temper. Li-ya struggled to come up with a way to defuse the brewing clash, but could not think of any.

"Yes, I am," Jia-yi replied. "I just wanted to speak with mama about something."

Wei Wu's mood seemed to lighten when he heard this. His wife immediately realized her husband must have drawn the wrong conclusion from their daughter's explanation.

"Can you tell me the news now that your mama knows?" he asked expectantly.

"I'm not announcing my engagement, if that's what you mean," she laughed. "I have a job offer that could allow me to study in America."

The statement hit him hard. His disappointment quickly became annoyance.

"Job offer?" he chortled. "You have a job. Now you should start thinking of a family. There is no need to study. Who will want to marry you?"

Jia-yi was becoming agitated. Li-ya tried to get her attention, motioning with her head to dissuade her daughter from responding. There was no stopping the downward spiral.

"From what I saw of marriage growing up," Jia-yi laughed derisively "I am not interested."

"What do you mean?" her father scolded. "There are three ways to be un-filial. The worst is to not have children."

"You mean the worst is to not have a son, don't you," she snickered. "That doesn't apply to me. I'm a daughter. Your son is responsible for the family name, not me."

Li-ya was grateful Wei Wu did not pick up on their daughter's thinly veiled criticism of their marriage. Instead he turned away from her and shouted, "Do not expect anything from us when you need support."

"I can support myself!" she screamed back. "Why do you suddenly care? A-ma had to pay for my school because I wasn't worth your investment, remember? I don't need some man controlling me, abusing me, living off my labor. I don't want a child! I don't need the pain!"

With that she stormed out, leaving her father fuming and her mother befuddled.

Li-ya hustled out of the kitchen to answer the phone before it dragged Wei Wu out of a deep sleep. He had gone to bed early after an exhausting day. Who would be calling at this time of night? Only Jia-yi, it was eleven A.M. in New Jersey. She scoped up the phone before it rang a third time, grateful that her husband had closed the bedroom door.

"Wei," she said softly.

"Wei, Mama," Jia-yi's voice jumped through the receiver.

Li-ya suspected this was not a social call. The cost of a phone call in the middle of the week was too high for a simple hello. What could have happened? She waited in nervous anticipation.

"I have met someone new and unusual," her daughter continued.

"What do you mean new and unusual?" Li-ya asked. "You are in America. Isn't that what you expect?"

Jia-yi laughed. "Yes, but he is different."

"Different?"

"Exceptional."

Li-ya was struggling to understand exactly what her daughter was trying to say. Since pronouns in Chinese languages do not differentiate between a man and a woman, she was not even sure of the gender of this exceptional person. Hoping beyond hope she asked, "Who is this exceptional person?"

"His name is Ed Phaff."

"Ed Phaff," she muttered wrestling with the pronunciation. "It sounds like a man's name."

Her daughter laughed uninhibitedly. "He is a man and seems to be the type of man I find interesting."

The words were understated, but the excitement in her voice was unmistakable. Her mother felt that energy pulsing through the phone and could not resist being caught up by it. After all the acrimonious debates with her father, had her daughter found a man worth committing to?

"Is he from a good family?" she inquired anticipating her husband's questions.

"Yes, it seems so. His father is a researcher at Bell Laboratories. His mother is from a business family," she reported. "He has an older brother who is studying engineering."

Li-ya understood the description of the mother and brother, but the father's occupation was still unclear. "What is this Bell Laboratories?"

Jia-yi laughed then responded as if everyone in the world would know. "It is one of the premier research labs in the world. The transistor was invented there. They are the research part of the American telephone company.'

"How am I supposed to know about such things?" Li-ya scolded playfully. "I am not a scientist."

"But in America you could have been," her daughter claimed.

She scoffed at the idea. :"How did you meet this man?"

"He is my economics tutor, but his major is Asian Studies."

"Asian Studies? What part of Asia does he study?"

"China and Mandarin, he can read and write Chinese and speak Mandarin," she bragged. "But he is also studying business."

"Are you serious about him?" Li-ya asked hopefully. All she was hearing sounded too good. The only down side so far was Mr. Ed Phaff was an American and America was a long way from home. With that thought she realized that Jia-yi might consider that the most important point of all. If this daughter were to marry, she would do so on her own terms and put as much distance between herself and her past as possible. A sudden sadness overcame Li-ya for an instant, but was quickly suppressed by Jia-yi's squeal.

"I think I love him, Mama," she announced. "We have been gradually getting to know each other and the more we do the better we feel."

They spoke for a few more minutes about the pros and cons of this deepening relationship. By the time she hung up the phone, Li-ya knew she had to tell Wei Wu. How should she broach the subject? What would his reaction be? He had always insisted his daughter marry, but to an American? That was a problem for the morning. Right now she wanted to enjoy the afterglow of her youngest daughter's happiness.

"She wants to marry a foreigner? How will that help the family?" Wei Wu asked.

"She is dating him. We don't know if they will marry," Li-ya reminded him.

"Dating?" he muttered. "Is he from a respectable family?"

"Yes, but they are not rich."

"He is an American college student. In America they are not rich. Here they would be well off. At least there will be no need for a dowry."

Their conversation was taking place over the rice congee and tea of breakfast. Li-ya had begun the talk casually. Even on his best days, Wei Wu was not good in the morning, but they had a busy day ahead of them. This would be the only chance for a private conversation until evening. The morning sun was chasing away the night's chill. She thought the bright light and warmth might lighten her husband's mood and so mentioned the subject. Apparently her judgment had been right. He appeared to be receptive to the idea of a foreigner joining the family.

"So you feel it is a good match?" she asked.

He laughed at her question. "It is not a match. It is her choice," he reminded her. "And it is a gamble. Americans seem to divorce so easily, but she has always liked foreign things."

Li-ya ignored the divorce comment entirely. It was not a good subject for them considering their past. Instead she focused on the glow in her daughter's voice the night before.

"She sounded so happy, so in love."

"In love? What does she know about love?" he asked. "As for happy, that is to be seen. She has become a stubborn woman who does not always accept her responsibilities."

"Stubborn or just strong minded?"

"Both are not good traits for a wife." With that he stood up and walked to the bedroom to prepare for his day. Li-ya now knew he would accept this choice of their daughter. If this liaison became a marriage, her husband would be worried but happy. She stood up, picked up the dishes, and carried them to the kitchen. Of all her children, Jia-yi had been the most neglected and yet she seemed poised to be the happiest.

Vicki jotted the last of her notes before looking up. A-ma had paused as if enjoying another rare triumphant moment from her past. Mama sat quietly, a content smile on her face.

"Your parents sent us money so we could attend their wedding," A-ma told Vicki in Mandarin. "Seeing America affected you're a-gong deeply. He became more humble and considerate, but his biggest change was in how he viewed your mama. She became his pride."

This assertion did not appear to sit well with her mother. Before there was any chance to discuss it, a sound came from the bedroom. A-zou was calling, but did not sound good.

Chapter Twenty-four

"Whose idea was this place?" Vicki queried Sue as they crossed Zhong Xiao Road, The rush hour traffic was just beginning to thin while any evening crowds had not yet started to build. The temperature was easing, but the humidity was relentless. Sue and Vicki were strolling to a restaurant in the district of the city hosting the national government offices, both happy to be leaving the crowded bus behind,

"A-hong called me to suggest it," Sue replied. "But I don't think he's that familiar with high end restaurants in Taipei, so it was probably Joe's idea."

Vicki agreed with her cousin's reasoning, so moved on to the subject that had been stalking her all day. "Didn't get a chance to talk with A-hong one on one. He showed up with A-zou and we jumped right into it. Then when she quit, he was sent on an errand by her. Kind of felt sorry for him. I mean after my little nocturnal fantasy, I felt awkward but he didn't have a clue why I acted so reserved."

"And you would have told him if you had the chance?" Sue asked with a smirk.

"God no!" Vicki reacted. "I'd rather die first, which leaves me in a quandary."

"It was a dream. Just let it go," Sue advised.

"Easy for you to say."

"You need a drink."

"I just turn into a contemplative lush," Vicki sighed. "Alcohol makes me an observer not a participant."

"Are you trying to tell me you're secretly a shy person?" Sue laughed.

Vicki laughed with her. "No, just that alcohol slows my mouth down so I notice things that people like Joe and A-hong see all the time."

"And not me?" Sue protested.

"Wei women like to talk."

They stepped up to the sidewalk and continued at a leisurely pace toward the Dragon and the Phoenix. From what Sue had said, this restaurant was about as far removed from a neighborhood dumpling shop as you could get. Top notch food with quiet live music providing the ambience. A-hong said he would cover the cost, an engagement gift from someone who believed giving extraordinary memories was more appropriate than giving things. He had told her once that things collected dust, while memories soothed the heart. But where was he getting the money to host dinner at such a lavish restaurant? It struck her as an obvious attempt to make up for the tepid, lackluster celebration at the Prince Albert. The natural light of the day had retreated enough to release the glow of the street lamps. Not even seven o'clock and it was getting dark. That was what happened when you traveled south in the summer. Jersey still had a couple of hours of light, Montana even more. No matter where they settled, either Joe or Sue would have to adjust to more than culture.

The two cousins stepped up to an ornate door; a dragon was carved into the dark wood of the top half, a phoenix occupied the space beneath. This entryway was pulled open by a young man wearing a uniform and white gloves. She expected Joe to be waiting for them since he had gone ahead while the ladies had changed into something appropriate for the venue. Vicki had spent an inordinate amount of time deciding on the dress she had chosen. She had plenty of experience dressing to attract the opposite sex, but none in choosing clothes that would discourage men. The fabric she wore wrapped her body loosely without highlighting any feminine attributes too much. The situation was becoming increasingly challenging for her. She was very familiar with the emotions with which she was dealing. If they were directed at any other man, they would be the beginnings of infatuation. Normally she would focus her charms on the object of her interest, but not this time. Her mental survival required that she ignore her heart. Acknowledging it would cause an uncontrolled fall. It was not in her character to do anything in half measures.

They stepped into a space that was a fusion of the East and the West. The interior of the restaurant had an old world European elegance to it, but was brightly lit. Waiters moved about dressed in tuxedos with the same white gloves as the doorman. Classical music floated out of small quality speakers hanging from the ceiling while the aromas of Chinese cuisine invited diners in. Sue stepped over to the receptionist and spoke with him quietly then returned to Vicki.

"Joe and A-hong aren't here yet," she sighed. "So we'll have to wait in the bar."

Vicki nodded her agreement and quietly followed. She had not told Sue about any of the day's revelations. They could discuss some of those while they waited. Before she could settle in and order a glass of wine, Sue started filling her in on the happenings around her home.

"Jia-luan *Gugu* came up from Dajia this morning and A-hong's mother is up from Ping-dong, but you probably know that already."

The last supposition surprised Vicki. "Why would I know that?" she asked.

Sue looked a little confused, but the bartender came over so any answer had to wait. After placing their orders, Sue picked up the conversation where they had left off.

"I thought your mother would have told you," she supposed. "She spent a couple of hours talking with her this morning."

"My mother with A-hong's mother?" Vicki spurted out. "She told me she spent the morning with a childhood friend."

Sue laughed at Vicki's question. "They are apparently one and the same. Your mother never told you?"

"Told me what?"

"She grew up with A-hong's mom," Sue revealed. "They were best friends."

Vicki sat quietly, shocked by this minor omission of her mother's. It was not an important point, but sometimes not sharing such a small detail was alienating. Why had her mother said she spoke with a childhood friend and not A-hong's mother? A-hong had never mentioned this relationship of their mothers. Was he aware of it?

Sue picked up on Vicki's confusion immediately. "She never talked about it?"

"No," Vicki answered. The way Sue put her question reminded her of the silence that had always surrounded the subject of her mother's childhood. "Now that I think about it, it shouldn't surprise me. She never talked about that part of her life."

"They were the best of friends. My father told me they were inseparable."

"Really," Vicki commented. "Do you think A-hong knows?"

"Good question," Sue laughed. "I didn't until this morning. You'd have to ask him."

The bartender returned with two glasses of white wine and a smile. They paid him, but made it clear with mannerisms and the ring on Sue's finger that they were not interested in anything other than a drink. After a taste of their wine, Vicki turned the conversation away from the charged subject of her mother's secrets.

"What has your father told you about his childhood?"

Sue looked at her blankly. "He's never said a word about his childhood experiences besides the basic facts."

She appeared to experience the same reaction to her father's silence that Vicki had just been through with her mother's. Vicki thought for a moment. What had been recounted that morning had been so horrific she was hesitant to share it, but in the end realized Sue had a right to know. "Your father is amazing," she began. "To have gone through his childhood and still become what he is today is miraculous."

By the time she finished her uncle's story, both women were holding back tears. Sue took in a deep breathe to gain composure, attempted to voice something, but had to stop.

"I know," Vicki consoled, patting her cousin's hand.

"So, how is A-zou?" Sue asked, changing the subject out of necessity.

"Well if you could pull yourself away from my cousin long enough to stop home, you won't have to ask," she teased already regretting sharing what A-ma had said. "She's tired, so went back to your place to rest." Even the subject of A-zou seemed touchy. It was a night to celebrate. Vicki hoped she had not ruined it with her revelations. Thankfully Sue laughed.

"Your cousin was supposed to be here before us," Sue reminded Vicki. "I wonder what's keeping him?"

"What about A-hong?" Vicki asked. "He set the whole thing up. When did he say to get here?"

Sue looked at her watch. "He said to be here fifteen minutes ago."

"We have the right place, don't we?"

"No doubt, the name is memorable."

"The Dragon and the Phoenix?" Vicki asked. "That would be the emperor and empress, right?"

"You've been studying with Joe," Sue laughed. "It's memorable for how common it is."

"Really?" Vicki asked with surprise. "I thought it's meant to sound regal."

"No, no," Sue smiled. "It sounds like a roadside food stand. I asked them about the name when I called for reservations. It's an interesting story. The owner is the grandson of someone who had such a stand with that name. He keeps it to honor his ancestor."

"I'm impressed," Vicki commented. "Now where are Joe and A-hong because I'm also hungry?" She was about half way through her glass of wine and was beginning to feel its effect. Without food to slow down the alcohol's absorption, her face was already glowing brightly. Sue was doing no better. They could not sit here drinking wine much longer. If they did Vicki would not say a word all night.

"Here you are," Joe's voice announced from behind them. "Sorry, we were talking and lost track of time. How about we go to the table before they cancel our reservations?"

Vicki doubted they would have trouble being seated. The evening was still a little too young for that. Joe's explanation piqued her curiosity. It was so untypical of either of her cousins to be late that she did not seriously entertain the idea that they had lost track of time. What were they talking about? Whatever it was, she was sure the guys were not going to share it with her. Letting the question go, she scooped up her glass and followed Joe into the dining area.

When they walked in, she noted tables were beginning to fill, but it was not that crowded yet. As they swerved between tables, she saw A-hong standing at a table across from a baby grand piano. He was wearing the suit she had helped him pick out the summer before he went to Rutgers. It still looked good on him, especially with the smile he now wore. Poor guys, she thought, they have to wear jackets and ties in this weather.

"The ladies already have red faces," A-hong noted.

"A girl has to do something to occupy herself when you're so late," Vicki shot back. At least she felt comfortable matching wits with him. They sat at a round table, so there was some personal space for each of them. Joe and Sue might find the arrangement less than ideal, but Vicki needed the breathing room it provided. As they settled in a young couple walked to the piano. The man was dressed in a tuxedo and sat on the bench. The woman, dressed in a white blouse and flowing black skirt, carried a flute and stood in front of baby grand. They were not splitting disposable chopsticks in this place, Vicki thought. She placed her purse beneath the table while A-hong dropped into his seat with a heavy sigh.

"That doesn't sound good," Sue commented.

"It's been a rough day," A-hong confessed. "My mother is up from Ping-dong. We had a bit of a disagreement."

Vicki suppressed an urge to ask what they had fought about, fearing the answer. Did her mother's visit precipitate the argument? Not a subject for tonight she decided.

"You sound like you need a drink," Joe suggested. "I owe you a scotch anyway."

"Owe me a scotch?" A-hong asked with surprise. "Why?"

"Your help with the ring," Joe reminded him.

"Funny you should bring that up," A-hong laughed. "You can't buy me a drink tonight because that same uncle is financing the night's festivities."

"Why does he want to do that?" Sue asked. Vicki had the same question. That uncle was not a blood relative of anyone at the table but A-hong. She sat quietly and waited for the answer, wondering if her reticence was the product of the situation or the alcohol.

"He wants me to enjoy the company of my friends," A-hong smiled. "It got crowded at Sue's house when my mother and Jia-luan *A-yi* arrived. It worked out because he's going to Singapore for a few days, and wanted me to move to his place to keep an eye on things while he's away. When he heard about Prince Albert's, he insisted on something special."

The pianist began to play; after a few bars the young woman joined him. A beautiful flute melody floated through the air around them. To Vicki it created a magical atmosphere that quieted her worries if only for a moment. One of the tuxedo clad young men approached them. Orders for food and drink were placed, with the drinks coming back quickly. Another glass of wine would keep her from saying anything embarrassing. Her only concern was the effects of alcohol on her cousins. She was the only one with her peculiar reaction to wine. Everyone else seated at the table was affected in the usual manner.

"So, have the two of you discussed the points Vicki brought up at our last celebration?" A-hong asked a bit too jovially.

"No, we haven't had a chance," Joe replied. "Been working all day. Maybe we can discuss our options tonight. I heard the two of you were busy with A-zou all day. What stories of old Taiwan can you share?"

This brought Vicki back to life. If they discussed Joe's and Sue's options, she would be in the hot seat again. Stories of old Taiwan were much preferred, but there was a lot of dirty laundry they might want to skip. She wanted to steer the conversation away from any rough seas, so she could not be lethargic. Struggling to shake off the effects of the wine, she dove into the conversation head first.

"You'd find A-zou's story fascinating, Joe," she began. "It covers the colonial period right up to today. The customs it highlights are an anthropologists dream." A little awkward, she thought, but definitely a move away from sensitive topics.

"That sounds like the beginning of a lecture on traditional Taiwanese society," A-hong laughed.

Vicki smiled and quietly conceded the point. She sipped her wine gingerly and waited to see where things ended up.

"What did A-zou have you pick up?" Sue asked.

This put a damper on A-hong's jovial mood. "I don't know for sure," he admitted. "She sent me to a lawyer's office. Turns out, this guy is a distant cousin. Nepotism still reigns supreme in Taiwan. Anyway, I picked up a sealed envelope. Can't say for sure what's in it, but I would guess it has legal papers pertaining to A-zou's last wishes."

"Is she in that bad shape?" Joe asked. "She seemed so animated when I saw her."

Vicki thought the conversation had turned a little too morbid and business like. They were talking about a loved one after all. A loved one who was ninety-five years old she reminded herself. She knew A-zou would scold her for being too sentimental. "I have a feeling she is playing her end game and intends to have things go her way. There was no need to send for her will. That's unsealed after she leaves," Vicki said quietly. "The old girl is up to something and whatever is in that envelope is going to help her."

A-hong and Sue shook their heads in quiet agreement. The melodious sound of a flute filled the void.

"It's funny," A-hong finally broke their silence. "A few days ago I would have laughed at that thought, but hearing her story has changed my perspective."

The waiter came with their appetizers, allowing them to mull over A-hong's thought. It crossed Vicki's mind that Joe might feel a little left out, having only met A-zou a few times. How much had his newly minted fiancé shared with him. She realized it was not A-zou's story that would be hard to share; it was A-ma's. The decision to reveal that tale was Sue's. With that Vicki concentrated on her appetizer, a small serving of fried dumplings. Mama would shake her head in disapproval.

"So, what was the disagreement with your mother about," Sue asked, before sipping an after dinner cordial.

Vicki was still unsure she wanted to hear the answer. Note to self, she thought, do not allow Sue more than two drinks if you want her to avoid embarrassing topics. With that she remembered her dream and had to suppress an urge to flee.

"Oh, we got into a discussion about my future," he answered flippantly. "The usual what will I do when I graduate. She's afraid I'll move away."

"I think that's a given," Joe laughed. "Not a lot of call for economic Phds in Ping-dong."

"She's not worried about me leaving Ping-dong. That would be A-zou's worry," A-hong answered with a wry chuckle. "No, she's worried I'll move to America."

Vicki felt her heart pick up its pace. Why would Mei-zhi *A-yi* be worried about him going to the States? Did that concern involve her? Was that one of the reasons Mama was so sensitive about the subject of A-hong? The music stopped before anyone could react to A-hong's statement. The sudden silence assaulted Vicki's sensibilities. She was not sure she wanted the void filled with words.

"It's not that easy to just move there," Sue scoffed. "Unless you marry an American." She smiled at Joe after finishing.

"That's what she's afraid I'll do," A-hong blurted out. He quaffed down a mouthful of cordial after saying this. Vicki would have sworn he was avoiding looking at her. Did he really have a secret love they did not know about? Why did her stomach flipped at this thought? She could tell he was winding himself up for something, but was unsure what that might be.

"So, Joe is right," Sue laughed, oblivious to how dangerous the conversation had suddenly become for her cousins. "You are hiding someone from us."

"No, he's not," Joe jumped in. "His mother is like all mothers, afraid of what might happen."

A-hong listened to the exchange. A look of resolved determination replaced the contemplative expression on his face. "No, actually I told her I love Vicki," he stated strongly. Then he looked directly at Vicki and said, "She's afraid of Vicki."

His profession was followed by silence. Vicki felt herself falling into an emotional abyss. She noted Sue had a shocked look on her face, but Joe did not.

"Slow down tiger," Joe advised.

"No, she needs to hear the truth," A-hong insisted. "I've loved her since Rutgers."

"A-hong you're drunk," Sue informed him. "Maybe we should call it a night."

"No!" he responded adamantly. "A-zou is right. We are meant to be together just like you and Joe."

Vicki found herself standing up, a bundle of conflicting emotions. There were too many questions, too many possibilities. Before she realized what she was doing, she found herself running out of the restaurant. The space she was in too restrictive for her sensations. When she reached the sidewalk her hands were shaking. Taking a deep breath of the moist air, she suddenly felt it was warmer than when they arrived. The sound of the door opening behind her impelled her to spin around. A-hong was standing there.

"I meant what I said."

"You're drunk."

"I am not drunk."

"Your face is red."

"So is yours, are you drunk?"

Scooters began to whip past them after the light at the corner below the restaurant changed. Cars and buses joined the flow of traffic on Zhong Xiao Road while Vicki thought of a reply. Could she just laugh it off, say she was drunk, and they should forget about what had transpired in the past five minutes? It was not in her heart to lie like that. A-hong was too dear and knew her too well. How to sort this out quickly? Everything about tonight was wrong, she thought.

"It won't work," she replied lamely.

"Why? Are you worried about three headed children?" he asked.

"Children? Where did children come from?"

"I want to marry you Victoria," he told her with conviction. "I want to spend the rest of my life with you."

"No, no, no!" she insisted, the sound of her voice rising with each denial. "Our families would disown us. I'm not willing to give up my family and I don't think you are willing to give up yours."

It was obvious this had no effect on his determination. She knew of his tenacity, had always admired it. Now it only appeared he was being stubborn and unreasonable.

"If we have to live our lives separately from our families then we will," he snapped back. "Doesn't your father say that the trick to life is happiness? That nothing else really matters in the overall scheme of things?"

She was defenseless against his reasoning. He knew her too well, knew all her weaknesses. There was no possibility of winning a debate with him. Her resolve was weakening.

"You're making this so hard," she complained.

"Tell me you don't love me and I'll leave," he challenged.

It would be so simple. Just say it and the discussion would end with the outcome she sought. Just like all the other men she had dated. Except it was not that easy. She understood his underlying threat. He would leave, drop out of her life, and the void would never be filled. Suddenly she was on the defensive, feeling raw and exposed. She could not remember another conversation where she had to work this hard.

"If I told you I don't love you, it would be a lie. We're cousins. Of course I love you" she admitted, stating the obvious as she played for time to think.

"That's not what I mean and you know it," he countered.

The ebb and flow of traffic provided the background for their little debate. Neither Joe nor Sue poked their head out to check on them, Even the sidewalk was void of distractions that would provide some relief. Feeling flustered and unsure of how to resolve the conflict, Vicki began to choke up. Determined not to cry in front of him, she whispered, "If you left your family, you would eventually hate me."

"I can do nothing but love you," he assured her. It is '*qian shi de guan xi.*' A-zou knows it; our mothers know it; and so do you."

"It can't work. No more words. I have to leave." With that she turned and ran down Zhong Xiao Road, tears falling freely down for cheeks.

Chapter Twenty-five

Why had she run? How could she have cried? Vicki passed through the hotel lobby mindlessly, questions battering her very core. Had the night really changed anything? Had it changed everything? Her mind was exhausted. She had wandered the streets around the government district aimlessly. Not paying attention to where she was, fearing her cousins would find her. Time alone to sort through her feelings was needed.

She was shocked, but somehow not surprised by what she felt. Was she willing to gamble everything she had known? Then she remembered what Nikki had said about her mother's habit of speaking for her father without asking him his opinion. Would Mama do such a thing? Vicki knew she could no longer answer that question with certainty. All that had been revealed over the past days showed that so much more could be hidden. How could she speak with her father without Mama knowing? Would she want to put the onus of revealing another deception on Dad? Her parents' relationship seemed so fragile.

It was late and the lobby was quiet. Dragging herself to the elevators, skittish as a cat from the fear A-hong would be upstairs waiting for her, Vicki pressed the up button and waited. An elevator door opened immediately. She stepped in quietly. Her isolation was suffocating. The support system she had grown up with vanished when A-hong said those words in front of Joe and Sue. She certainly could not speak with her mother about it.

When the elevator doors opened, Vicki poked her head out and looked down the hall. She knew it was a silly thing to do. Where would she go if A-hong was standing outside her room? There were few people in Taipei who she knew well enough to impose on unannounced. Taiwan was about family to her and family was her problem. The hallway was clear, so she stepped out of the elevator and made her way to the room. If one of her cousins had spoken with Mama about this night, any chance for peace would have vanished. As long as the evening's events remained at her generation's level, there was hope, although she did not know what to hope for. Quietly opening the door, she found the lights on and her mother writing.

"Such a late night," Mama commented. "Did the four of you enjoy dinner?"

Was she emphasizing it was four of them as a cautionary note? Vicki decided that was a good sign. If Mama was aware of all that had happened, hysteria would reign supreme.

"It was classy," Vicki told her. "A pianist accompanying a flutist played some melodious classical music as we sipped wine and enjoyed our meal."

"That's good," her mother answered mechanically. "I'd like to talk a little about some of the points from today's work."

At first Vicki felt overwhelmed, but then realized this might be the perfect tonic for the kaleidoscopic complexity of emotions with which she was dealing. Mama's review would give her something to focus on besides A-hong's revelations.

"Okay, if you're up for it I am," Vicki answered. "Just give me a second to go to the ladies' room." No matter what had happened, the effects of wine had to be addressed. Her bladder was too full for her to sit down. When she returned, her mother was ready to dive in.

"My first vivid memory is of the night my brother was dunked in that pool."

****

"We have to go to them," Jia-luan told her little sister. "He is crazy tonight."

Jia-yi shook her head, fearing to make a sound. She thought *gege* had been brave to rescue Mama, but *jiejie* was the only one who might stop the madness. The two girls cautiously followed the insanity down to the bean paste factory. Mama begged Baba not to hurt their brother. The pleading had no effect on the man. Jia-yi knew it would not, begging only made him wilder. Both she and *gege* knew not to make a sound when they drew their father's attention.

The two sisters stopped in the entrance archway to the factory's back room and silently witnessed their brother's trial by water. Mama was lying on the floor pleading as she struggled to catch her breathe. Jia-yi cried. With each dunking she held her breathe instinctively as if it would help her brother. She was dizzy by the time Baba tired of his tormenting game.

Her father lowered Shan-ji to the floor then walked over to Mama and grabbed her hair. "Get up woman and stop making so much noise." Suddenly, she reached up and slapped his face. The response was a volcanic eruption. Her father's rage was now focused on her mother. He dragged her by the hair to the street through the front door. Shan-ji was gasping for air and coughing. His sisters rushed to him. Jia-luan quickly untied his hands and helped him stand up. Jia-yi waited to see this then raced to see where her mother was. She reached the front door just as her father propelled Mama into a streetlight pole. Her mother appeared dazed as she struggled to stand up. When Jia-yi saw blood dripping down Mama's face she screamed involuntarily. Did her father intend to kill her mother tonight? Would he kill all of them? It was a mistake to scream. Survival depended on silence. She stood frozen, fearing that his focus would shift to her.

"Wei Wu, did that stupid wife of yours get you angry again? Having so much *qi* in your body is not good. Come, I have a new bottle of *sake*. We can open it and talk about how stupid our wives are. The Master was right. Relations with women are the most difficult."

The sound of their neighbor's voice had broken the curse of this night and released Jia-yi from her trance. She waited quietly for her father to respond.

Baba straightened up and chuckled. "Yes you are right; too much *qi* is not good. *Sake* should dissipate some of it. You are a learned man, quoting from the Four Books."

Even as they walked to the neighbor's house, she stood in frozen terror. This was only thawed by a wave of the neighbor's hand encouraging her to help Mama. Jia-yi ran to her mother and hugged her quietly, always quietly. "Only for you children would I do this,"

Mama whispered. *Jie-jie* and *gege* came up, helped her stand, and then guided their mother into the house.

****

"Your aunt and uncle cleaned her wound and helped her lie down in our room," Mama recalled. "I was so young all I could do was bring wet towels to them. A-gong staggered in a few hours later and collapsed on the living room floor. In the morning he crawled into bed and A-ma opened the store. Her face was swollen and her eyes were blackened. Anyone who inquired was told that she had fallen, but they all knew my father had beaten her again."

"How could he do that?" Vicki whispered. Her worries replaced by empathy.

"You're a-gong was not a normal man," Mama stated flatly. "Drinking was not his only problem. He could not tolerate people touching his things and would constantly wipe everything he touched. Now that I think about it, he was a sad sight. Sometimes he would wipe a bottle, put it down, then pick it up and wipe it again. All with the same dirty clothe. He needed to control everything around him and would become angry when he could not. But the nightly shows from his drinking are what shaped me."

****

"He took Mama upstairs and left the store wide open," Shan-ji told his sisters. The sound of their parents arguing came through the heated, humid air of the night. Mama had always told them not to get involved when Baba was this way. Shan-ji now listened to his mother.

Opposing Wei Wu only led to more extreme abuse. Mama insisted they flee, but the store was unattended.

"How can we watch the store without him seeing us?" Jia-luan asked. They were hiding under the tree across from their building. The tree was too thin to provide cover during the day, but at night the shadows created by the street light concealed them adequately. Their problem was they could not see the front of the store. Jia-yi looked up at the tree and had an idea.

"*Gege* help me climb the tree," she requested. "I can see the store from there. If someone comes, I'll call down to you and you and *jie-jie* can go to help them."

"No, *mei-mei,* I'll climb the tree," Shan-ji insisted. "It is too dangerous for you."

Jia-yi shook her head no. "You're too big. The branch will break and so will you."

She wrapped her arms and legs around the trunk and shimmied up with a boost from her brother just the way he had taught her in Ping-dong the past summer. At the first large branch, Jia-yi cautiously slid herself out and sat down, wedging her body in the natural seat formed where the branch shot out from the trunk. Her heart was pounding from the exertion and fear. Shan-ji had always told her not to look down. Instead she focused on the store front. From her perch the inside of their home was also visible. What she saw there captured her attention. Baba was screaming at her mother. Mama was not backing down. The sound of their words could be heard through the open window. Jia-yi was mesmerized, legs and arms locked around the branch, eyes fixated on her parents. The words ceased when her father slapped Mama hard, driving her to the floor. She could see his arms flaying as he struck her several more times.

Jia-yi cried silently, instinctively fearing any sound would attract her father's attention. Mama's screams for mercy passed through the night air. Jia-yi prayed to Buddha for it to stop, but praying and pleading never worked. How she hated her life. Secretly, she wished her father was dead so this hell would go away.

Her father stopped, stood up, said something, and walked out of view. In a moment he emerged from the store and stormed off. She scurried down from the tree and ran with her siblings to help Mama.

"They all think you are so clever speaking these foreign languages," her father sneered. "You get the talent from me. I got it from my mother. A man has use for these abilities. What you could use them for I don't know, but that old woman said she would pay for it. You can always wash hair and speak to foreigners after you graduate." He laughed to himself derisively as Jia-yi took in the meaning of his words. She would be able to attend Wen Zao!

Gege had attended college and was now in the army. *Jie-jie* had attended junior college and had just told her she was going to marry. When Jia-yi had heard that she had become nervous. Without *jie-jie* to calm that man down, how would they live? To have him focus on her exclusively was terrifying. Mama would not be able to protect her second daughter, being too busy surviving to help. Now this monster had said she could attend Wen Zao Junior College of Modern

Languages for Girls. It was located in Gaoxiong, hours from Tai-dong. That meant she would be in Gaoxiong during the school year and then in Ping-dong during the summer. Free of him except possibly for holidays, but poor Mama. Her mother had always said she endured the abuse for her children. Did that mean she would leave? Jia-yi prayed Mama would walk out on the drunken bastard. He did not deserve such a capable wife.

****

"When they moved to Taipei, there was a noticeable change. My sister took over managing the Tai-dong store. Your uncle left the army and started a career. He let A-zou arrange his marriage or at least suggest who his wife should be. And I attended Wenzao. The nuns liked me and invited me to join their order, but I declined," Mama chuckled at her last revelation,

No matter how hard Vicki tried, she just could not picture her mother as a Roman Catholic nun. Somewhere along the line Mama had converted to Christianity, but had chosen the Baptist denomination. These days she was not particularly devote.

Vicki did not want her mother to stop, fearing more questions about dinner. She did feel a growing admiration for Mama's strength and tenacity. The world being described now was light years from the pictures painted when she was a child. Back then her mother bragged about her entrepreneurial father and her mother's management and sales skills. The dark tale being woven tonight was never mentioned.

"A-ma said you helped when they closed the store in Tai-dong," she reminded. "What did that entail?" It was a minor detail, but one that could keep the conversation alive.

Mama sighed and waved her hand. "Ah-yo, so many words about such a small matter," she chided. "I had just graduated and had applied for a position at the airline. Being a stewardess would take me away from my life in Taiwan. Even though things had improved for my mother, they were still stressful for me. My father could not fathom a young woman who did not want to marry."

****

Jia-yi could tell Wei Wu was going to lecture her again. The topic of the lecture had been the same since she had turned eighteen. Always insisting he contact a matchmaker and begin the process of selling her. A matchmaker? Did such a person exist any longer? She knew of no one in her generation who had any intention of allowing her parents to choose a husband for them. The economy was booming. There were plenty of jobs that would allow a young woman to support herself. The young men no longer depended on their fathers to provide a piece of land for them to farm. With increased industrialization came increased financial freedom. That old man just did not understand the world had changed. How could he have even dared to bring the subject up two years before she graduated? Now she had a job offer that would allow her to flee the insanity of her past. Nothing he could say would stop her.

"Your mother and I would like your help," Baba began.

This threw her off balance. Her help? With what?

"My help Baba?" she replied cautiously. "How can I help you?"

"We are selling the store in Tai-dong," he lamented. "It will take a month or more and Jia-luan is moving to Hua-lian to manage things there. She said you have time before training for your job. Could you close down the Tai-dong store?"

To him it was a simple request. To her it was an emotionally charged issue. She had not spent any length of time in her hometown for five years. Dreams of that horror still haunted her nights. But this was the first time he had ever requested she help him in any way. The derisive laugh that had punctuated her existence so often was absent. In its place seemed to be a reluctant respect. She felt no obligation to the man in front of her, but owed something to his wife who had endured so much for her, even if she was always an afterthought.

"What do you need me to do, Baba?"

****

"All I did was keep track of the school activities," Mama chuckled. "So there weren't two classes scheduled for the same room. After the building and school were sold, I held what you would call a garage sale. Then I went to Taipei for my airline training. That job changed my life more than I could have ever imagined it would."

****

"Mr. and Mrs. Cunningham, how are you?" Jia-yi asked her favorite passengers as they settled into their seats. They were such a nice couple, always talkative, always encouraging. The two flew so often that she had joked they should draw a salary from the airline. It seemed obvious they were trying to establish some sort of business venture, but she had never been bold enough to ask. "Jia-yi," Mrs. Cunningham smiled. "You look your usual radiant self. I wish I had a son to introduce you to."

Jia-yi laughed, finding the comment ironic considering her arguments with Baba, "Now Mrs. Cunningham, you know I'm not on the market just yet. I have to think of my career first. Then maybe I will study in America."

The Cunninghams gave each other a knowing look. "When you get a chance, we'd like to speak with you about your career," Mr. Cunningham requested.

Jia-yi was breathless as she phoned her mother. She was still at the airport, but could not contain herself. The normal post-flight exhaustion had been kept at bay by what the Cunninghams had said. The offer they made would give her the means to study abroad along with priceless experience to use after her studies.

"Wei, Mama," she said into the phone. "Is Baba home?"

"No, he is out with a client."

"Good, I'm coming right over. See you in a bit." She hung up the phone and quickly sought out a taxi. He was out with a client. How long would that give her? There was no need to interact with Baba, not today. Her mother could pass on the news, let him digest it, and then they could talk about her future without the subject of marriage intruding. Surely, with such an opportunity he would see there was no need to commit to an outmoded way of life. What she did need was a quick way to her parents' home so she could talk with Mama while avoiding Baba's questions. Luckily there was a cab waiting at the curb outside the terminal. Jia-ya hopped in, blurted out her parents' address, and sat back to think how to present this offer to Mama without sounding like a school child who had won a speech contest.

"Over the past two years I have become friendly with an American business couple," Jia-yi began. She noticed a cup of tea on the table, but the thought of consuming anything at the moment made her stomach uncomfortable. There had never been a time in her life when she had felt more exhilarated, more alive than she felt at this instant. Life beckoned to her. All she had to do was answer its call. How to put that feeling into words for her mother?

"They have been coming here every month or two and have always complimented me on my English." Mama shook her head and listened, refraining from any interruption.

"Today they told me of their plan to open an office in Taipei," Jia-yi squealed. "And they want me to manage it!"

"Really?!" Mama exclaimed. She appeared to be giving this news careful, quiet consideration. Jia-yi was sure her mother was happy. The thought of her father's reaction raced across her mind again. She needed to enlist Mama's help to avoid a confrontation.

"It will take a few months to set up," Jia-yi continued. "But I should be able to leave the airline soon. The salary they offered is better and they hinted about helping me study in America."

"How could you study there and run the office here?"

"That wouldn't be until the office was established," she answered. "And they didn't say the company would pay for it, just that they might be able to help me choose a school and get accepted. So it will take me a few years to save the money for tuition and expenses."

"You're still young, a few years isn't bad," her mother reassured. "And think of the experience you'll gain. I'll support you in any way I can. The first hurdle will be your father."

A door slamming two stories below told them the discussion might take place sooner than they anticipated. Jia-yi jumped at the sound. That could not be anyone other than her father.

Not now, not when she was sharing the most exciting news of her life with her mother. That man was so unpredictable. She was too tired to deal with his moods and judgments. Knowing that even a hint of disapproval would cause her to snap, Jia-yi tried to come up with a way to avoid talking with him. Other than the stairs her father was climbing, there was no way out of this apartment.

"Shit," she muttered. Even a delay of a few minutes before she started a conversation with him would help, as long as she could hear any discussion her parents might have beforehand. That would give her an idea of his mood, so she could gauge how to present the subject to get the best reaction. Looking around, the only option she saw was the bathroom. She silently stood and marched to it, leaving her mother to deal with her father.

As she eased the door closed, Jia-yi saw her mother scoop up the tea cup on the coffee table and carry it toward the kitchen. Then she heard her father step into the apartment.

"What happened?" Mama asked.

"Some crazy brat knocked me down with his scooter," he growled. "I was lucky to break the fall with my hands. These young people, they don't know how to be responsible. Where is our country going? No one has respect for tradition anymore."

God, why today? Jia-yi could not believe her luck. She was trapped. Unless Mama came up with some sort of imaginative ploy to clear out her husband, she would have to speak with him. From what she heard, he was not in a good mood. Just the thought of interacting with her father made Jia-yi angry. It never went well. He was intent on living her life for her and she was intent on keeping as much distance between them as possible.

"Why don't you go lie down," she suggested. "I'll pour you a cup of tea and you can rest."

Brilliant! Jia-yi thought Mama had come up with a way out. He would go into the bedroom to lie down and she would slip out the front door quietly allowing her mother time to introduce the subject to him.

"Okay," he sighed. "I just have to go to the bathroom first."

With that Jia-yi knew there was no way to avoid contact so she stepped out.

"Oh, hello Baba," she greeted. "You hurt your hands. What happened?"

"Some brat hit me with his scooter," he complained. "Why are you here today? Aren't you tired from your flight?"

"How dare he interrogate me!" she thought. If he wanted an answer to his questions, he was going to have to come up with a better way of phrasing them. He was suspicious, that was obvious. She could see his growing impatience which only made her angrier. There was no need to give him more information than was necessary.

"Yes, I am," Jia-yi replied curtly. "I just wanted to speak with mama about something."

Upon hearing this, Baba's mood lightened. She immediately realized he had fallen back to his obsession with finding her a husband. Bad timing, bad subject, and the day had begun so well. She waited for him to brooch the subject then she would put an end to his fantasy one more time.

"Can you tell me the news now that your mama knows?" he asked expectantly.

"I'm not announcing my engagement, if that's what you mean," she laughed. "I have a job offer that could allow me to study in America." She felt enormous satisfaction voicing this.

The statement hit him hard. His disappointment quickly became annoyance.

"Job offer?" he chortled. "You have a job. Now you should start thinking of a family. There is no need to study. Who will want to marry you?"

"Who would want to marry me?" Jia-yi thought, becoming more agitated with each exchange. That was all there was to life for him. She had no intention of being boxed in to such a narrow existence.

"From what I saw of marriage growing up," Jia-yi laughed derisively "I am not interested."

"What do you mean?" her father scolded. "There are three ways to be un-filial. The worst is to not have children."

The man's views were primordial and had nothing to do with her. "You mean the worst is to not have a son, don't you," she snickered. "That doesn't apply to me. I'm a daughter. Your son is responsible for the family name, not me."

He turned away from her and shouted, "Do not expect anything from us when you need support."

That was it! The man had done everything he could to force her into a subservient position in life, ignoring her and her needs. Now he was threatening to hold back support that he had never given. She could almost hear the effort to control her temper snap.

"I can support myself!" she screamed back. "Why do you suddenly care? A-ma had to pay for my school because I wasn't worth your investment, remember? I don't need some man controlling me, abusing me, living off my labor. I don't want a child! I don't need the pain!"

There was no way to reason with this man or any other. They all wanted to smother you and make you into something you were not. She could no longer abide his presence, so she grabbed her things and stormed out, leaving her father fuming and her mother befuddled.

Chapter Twenty-six

Jia-yi sat staring at the dorm room phone. She could feel her willpower crumpling. It was the middle of the week. The expense of mid-week phone calls was not in her budget. If she called Mama the reason for the call would have to be stated quickly to avoid undue anxiety. What was the reason for the call? The college coed was uncertain. She had never felt this way before. The past week had been magical. Mr. Edward Phaff had finally succumbed to her flirting. After months of interaction and then attraction, she had tired of his gentlemanly ways and had seduced him. Even though she had no experience in such matters, the seduction had been easy. Mr. Phaff shared her sentiments and her hunger.

The following morning he had attempted to cool things down, refusing to say he loved her. After listening calmly and assuring him the previous night had been a gift for each of them, she had laughed to herself. He might not have known it, but Edward Phaff was hers. She had no intention of letting him go. A giddy feeling welled up from deep inside her and propelled her hand to the phone.

"Wei," Mama's voice greeted her quietly.

"Wei, Mama," Jia-yi gushed. "I have met someone new and unusual."

"What do you mean new and unusual?" Li-ya asked. "You are in America. Isn't that what you expect?"

Jia-yi laughed. "Yes, but he is different."

"Different?"

"Exceptional."

Mama sounded uncertain. "Who is this exceptional person?"

"His name is Ed Phaff."

"Ed Phaff," Mama muttered butchering his name. "It sounds like a man's name."

Her daughter laughed uninhibitedly. "He is a man and seems to be the type of man I find interesting."

She was trying not to sound excited, but knew her voice betrayed her. Mama picked up on her energy and seemed to be caught up in it. All the blow outs with her father had become moot, vanquished by a quiet American with a fascination for China. Her mother sounded accepting.

"Is he from a good family?" Mama inquired.

"Yes, it seems so. His father is a researcher at Bell Laboratories. His mother is from a business family," she reported. "He has an older brother who is studying engineering."

"What is this Bell Laboratories?"

Jia-yi laughed at herself. She had not known what Bell Labs was until Ed had explained it. How could she have thought her mother would know? "It is one of the premier research labs in the world," she informed her mother. "The transistor was invented there. They are the research part of the American telephone company."

"How am I supposed to know about such things?" Mama scolded playfully. "I am not a scientist."

"But in America you could have been," her daughter claimed.

Mama scoffed at the idea. :"How did you meet this man?"

"He is my economics tutor, but his major is Asian Studies." She still could not believe that coincidence. How is it that she met a man studying Chinese in her economics class? For the professor to assign him as her tutor seemed beyond credible. Both had sworn they were not interested in anything other than getting through the class. Where the emotions they now felt came from was a mystery. There was no doubt that A-zou would say it was *qian shi de guan xi*.

"Asian Studies?" her mother asked, snapping her back to the conversation. "What part of Asia does he study?"

"China and Mandarin, he can read and write Chinese and speak Mandarin," she bragged. "But he is also studying business."

"Are you serious about him?" Mama asked her voice laced with hope.

"I think I love him, Mama," she squealed. "We have been gradually getting to know each other and the more we do the better we feel."

"These things can be complicated," she cautioned. "Have you thought about where this could lead? He is an American. Do you think he will move to Taiwan or are you willing to live in America?"

Why would her mother ask such question? All of humanity was aware of where these feelings might lead. They both knew that there was little holding her to Taiwan, certainly not any family obligations. Ironically, the debt she felt to the Cunninghams was the only string pulling her back home. But Ed had his own plans that definitely included Asia.

"Where this might lead?" she asked with a laugh. "It could lead to something that will make your husband happy. Will he be willing to go to Taiwan? He has studied Chinese because he plans to go to Asia for business, but it is still too early to talk like this. I just wanted to prepare you if our feelings continue to evolve."

"Thank you, I will let your father know how happy you are with your American," Mama chuckled. "Maybe he will find something else to talk about now that you have found someone interesting."

"Just remember to tell him it is too early to start planning anything," Jia-yi cautioned.

****

"You seduced Dad?" Vicki asked in shock.

Mama smiled. "Of course I did," she bragged. "There was no time for him to be a gentleman. I was a foreign student on a visa. He was too quiet and shy. He needed to be aggressive and see what he had in front of him. I just helped him, that's all."

Vicki listened to the excuse, shaking her head in disbelief. Her mother had been a manipulative temptress when she was young. Dad did not have a chance.

"When we were planning our wedding, your father insisted we send money to A-gong and A-ma so they could attend," Mama sighed. "To have that man attend, I wanted to scream no, but your father would not have understood and I didn't want to explain."

This simple admission piqued Vicki's interest. "How much about your childhood did you tell Dad?"

"My childhood?" Mama asked. "I saw no need to tell him about that. We did not plan to live near my family, so there was no need to burden him with my past."

Burden him with her past? Vicki thought in astonishment. Did her father marry a lie? She knew what he would call it if his daughter withheld information like that. It would be deemed a lie of omission. His talk about how it was just as dishonest as an outright lie still resonated with her. Suddenly she realized why Mama not mentioning her relationship with A-hong's mother had bothered her so. She knew not to mention it. Not if she wanted this conversation to continue.

"How much does dad know?"

"He knows all that I knew before A-zou began talking to you," Mama assured her. "But he never saw A-gong angry. Even if he had, I don't think your father would have been intimidated by him. A-ma was right when she said that A-gong was changed by seeing America. It is such a large, complex country, so diverse. He had never been to any place like it. America humbled him and humility taught him control. Then there was you."

The last sentence caught Vicki off guard. "There was me?"

"Yes, you stole his heart like no one since *Da A-yi*."

"But I don't even remember him," Vicki protested. "He died when I was so young."

Mama chuckled. "One so young could not disappoint him. He did not have to worry about you. That was my job, but he could show you off and he did whenever we visited."

✱✱✱

"Where's Baba and Vicki," Jia-yi asked her husband.

"Oh, they're lying down," Ed answered. "Had a busy afternoon. They went for a walk together up and down the block. Seems they checked in at every store or open door along the way."

"What were they doing?"

"She was laughing and repeating whatever Taiwanese he taught her," he laughed. "And he was simply showing off his American *ainoko* granddaughter. Oh, and you'll have to find a place to put these." He held out two small, solid gold bracelets.

Jia-yi stood in shocked disbelief. This was not the man she had known as a child. Gold bracelets for his daughter were out of the question for that man. She found herself involuntarily shaking her head. "Where is the wandering pair?"

"In your parents' bedroom."

She tip toed over to the closed door, cracked it quietly, and glanced in. The tiny figure of her three year old daughter was lying peacefully in the middle of her parents' queen size bed. Her father was resting beside her, appearing to have fallen asleep looking at his granddaughter. She closed the door quietly and turned to her husband.

"Never in his life has he done anything like this," she told him before slipping off to her mother in the kitchen.

"Mama, come quick," she whispered fearing to disturb the scene in the bedroom. "You won't believe this."

The two women moved to the bedroom door and peeked in. After closing the door they both began laughing quietly.

****

"Your father had a hard time understanding why we found it so amazing," Mama smiled. "He had never seen A-gong in his bad days. With that scene, A-gong's transformation seemed complete. A-ma said that I became his pride, but I don't think that is right. I cannot say for sure that he ever loved anyone unconditionally, but if he did you were that person. He loved you simply because you existed. You needed to do nothing else."

Vicki sat quietly. Of all the assertions of being special she had heard over the past days, this one rested most comfortably. Happy that she was able to bring out the love her grandfather had felt. Looking at her mother, she saw that this memory had given Mama a peace with her father.

"When did he die?"

"Before we came back the following summer. He was killed by a drunk driver," Mama stated. "When he died A-zou told me a debt had been paid. I didn't understand that until now. She must have meant he paid the debt owed for my twin brother's death."

The two rested for a moment. Vicki thinking of the different kinds of love people could experience and wishing she could remember the feeling she must have had basking in the glow of the unconditional variety A-gong had given her. Was A-zou's love unconditional? A-ma's? Mama's? What of the love A-hong had just professed? She quickly came to the conclusion that unconditional love was a very rare commodity and she was too tired to wrestle with the question.

"How about we call it a day?" she suggested to her mother.

Mama shook her head in agreement and stood up to prepare for bed.

Chapter Twenty-seven

Vicki woke to her mother moving around the room. They were only five days into this visit and she was already tired of the routine. Mama would never be able to sleep in, not with the breakfast buffet time limit. After a night of tossing, her daughter only craved more sleep. Acknowledging how elusive that was for her, Vicki reluctantly pulled herself out of bed. Confusion clouded her mind. She was fighting a war on two fronts. Still unable to make sense of her feelings toward A-hong, she tried to focus her efforts on processing what Mama had revealed the previous night.

"Good, you're awake," Mama stated the obvious. "We don't want to miss breakfast." She walked over to the drapes and pulled them aside, revealing a sunny day. Vicki's hand shot up to shield her eyes. Her feet slid into the hotel slippers and she made her way to the bathroom debating when to ask Mama about the one subject that straddle both fronts of her cerebral battle, A-hong's mother. Not wanting to raise the subject directly, Vicki decided to ask about Jia-luan *A-yi,* hoping to ease into A-hong's mom from there.

"How is Jia-luan *A-yi* ?" she asked as she stepped out of the bathroom and walked to the dresser.

"*A-yi?* She is doing alright," Mama answered.

"Did you tell her A-zou's story?" Vicki continued while choosing a blouse. Giving up on the previous day's attempt at modesty, she picked something comfortable. Intuitively she knew the day would be both physically and emotionally hot, so dressed accordingly.

"We talked about A-zou and A-ma, but mostly we talked about where life has taken us. I thanked her for everything she did for me," was the reflective response. "Sisters can sometimes take each other for granted."

Vicki listened quietly, remembering what A-ma had told her as she pulled on her shorts and sat on the bed to put socks on. "A-ma said she was like a second mother to you."

"A second mother?" Mama asked wryly. "At times she was like my only mother. When my nanny wasn't around, *A-yi* took care of me. She protected me, advised me, and secretly released me from hell. That is why I had to thank her."

Vicki's most vivid memories of the relationship between these two sisters were of spats and arguments. Why was it that the strongest memories were negative?

"I don't remember us being very close to her," she pointed out, finishing her sock project. "What happened?"

Mama had been floating around the room as she waited. Now she stopped at the balcony door and looked out over the city. After a moment of thought, she replied in a sad voice. "What happened? Life happened. She got married. I went to school. We haven't slept under the same roof for decades. After school there was work and America. She built her life and I built mine. The years slipped away. I really don't know my sister any more. Life changes you. We will always have those shared childhood experiences, but in many ways, until yesterday, she was almost a complete stranger to me."

The pathos of that statement was palpable. When her mother fled her life in Taiwan, she distanced herself from more than A-gong.

"Our talk was necessary for both of us. We reconnected. I told her about A-zou and asked about my twin brother. She apologized for not telling me, but explained that she saw no reason to upset me. After all these years you're *A-yi* was still trying to protect her *mei-mei*. So, we laughed; we cried; and we have a little peace. Thank you."

"Thank me?" Vicki asked in surprise. "Why?"

"If you had not asked A-zou those questions, we would not have created this opportunity. Now, let's go eat." With that Mama stepped toward the door. Vicki stood up to follow, still unsure how to broach the subject of A-hong's mother.

The two enjoyed a quiet breakfast, each lost in her thoughts. Vicki struggled with the riddle of her mother's omission. Was it really that important? Something told her it was. Maybe if she could understand the relationship between Mama and A-hong's mother, she would have a better handle on where A-hong was coming from. She immediately realized that was a futile hope. He had argued with his mother. Vicki understood perfectly well where she stood on this issue. What she needed was knowledge of why his mother so feared A-hong living in America. It made sense that she would be a little put off by the distance, but the travel time was less than a day's flight. When weighed against her son's happiness, that seemed a small price. Of course that was only half the problem. Part of the other half sat across from her sipping coffee.

How strong was her father's opposition? Vicki had never seriously thought about it having lived in denial of her attraction to A-hong for so long. Who was more opposed, Mama or Dad? Was Dad even against it? These questions had to wait for research on the whole genetic argument. As Nikki had pointed out, the royals of Europe had been marrying their cousins for hundreds of years. Queen Victoria's offspring had problems, but hemophilia came strictly from the mother if she remembered right. Prince Albert's DNA had nothing to do with it. She sighed and reached for her coffee. All of this ruminating had brought her no closer to solving the conundrum of how to start a conversation about Wu Mei-zhi. Giving up on finesse, Vicki jumped right in.

"So, can I ask you something?" she queried breaking the silence. "You told me you spent the morning with a childhood friend."

Mama shook her head yes as she placed the coffee cup on the table.

"From what I heard last night, your childhood friend is A-hong's mother. Why did you put it that way?"

Mama's initial reaction was a blank stare. She recovered and posed a question as her response, "Why say it that way? I said a childhood friend. She is a childhood friend."

"You left out that she is A-hong's mom," Vicki insisted.

Mama was untouched by the veiled accusation. "What difference would that have made?" she laughed. "We just caught up."

"A-hong said they argued yesterday," Vicki informed her.

"Did he say what the argument was about?"

"Nothing specific, just about his future."

Her mother appeared reflective. With a faraway look in her eyes, she explained, "He is all she has, all A-zou has. She's afraid of being alone, afraid of being destitute. She sees A-zou and realizes A-hong is the only thing between her and a future like that. He is her anchor, like you are my anchor."

I am her anchor? Vicki thought. Why would Mama say that? She realized her mother had suddenly developed a habit of dropping loaded comments directed at her at the end of unrelated statements. The woman did have a history of suddenly changing subjects when a conversation did not go her way; this was different. If they had been arguing it might be considered a tactic used to throw an opponent off balance. It certainly did that to her, but appeared to be more of a way to express feelings that were not discussed openly in her family. Vicki knew she was many things to her parents, but had never considered herself an anchor. They seemed too strong and independent for her to deserve that label.

"I'm your anchor?" she asked in disbelief. "What about dad?"

Mama smiled at the question. "Your father? He may be the source of my strength. He is my security, but he is only a companion. You are a part of me. Since I was pregnant, you have been my focus. Everything I did in my life for the past twenty-three years has been for you."

Vicki sat quietly, examining this pronouncement in detail. Having felt her parents' focus for a lifetime, she accepted that part. To claim Dad was only a companion for his wife seemed overly analytical. How can a man be her source of strength and her security, but only a companion? How could the contentious mother/daughter relationship they shared allow for her to be an anchor? There was no doubt in her mind that A-hong had become the anchor of his mother's life. No rational train of thought awarded the same title to her. She looked up from her coffee attempting to gather her thoughts and formulate an intelligent question as a replacement for the emotional blurbs scrolling through her mind. While mulling over options, A-hong entered her field of vision. Vicki felt the blood drain from her head. He marched up to their table without Mama knowing until he announced himself.

"Good morning ladies," he greeted them jovially. The determined expression that had been imbedded on his face melted into a pleasant smile as soon as he came into Mama's view. "How are we this morning?"

"Good morning A-hong," Mama smiled. Whatever questions Vicki might have raised, the man still held a special place in her mother's heart. "What brings you here?" she asked. "I thought you would need a little time away from us ladies before beginning your translation duties."

Vicki sat quietly during the exchange, a bundle of nerves and conflicting emotions, not daring to make eye contact for fear it would reveal her weakened state. Knowing her mother would pick up on any abnormalities, she forced herself to greet him. "Hey A-hong," she blurted out coolly. "Did Joe make it back okay?"

A-hong laughed. "We didn't stay much longer after you left," he replied. "Sue got him back here at a reasonable hour."

"That's good to hear," Mama interjected. "We're almost done. A-zou will be in Neihu around noon."

"Noon? That gives us a little time," he pointed out. "Vic, I was wondering if we could talk a little before A-zou needs us. We can just walk around the hotel grounds, enjoy the scenery, and chat about Joe and Sue."

Vicki sat frozen, unable to respond. She noticed her mother had the same response for a moment. He had trapped her. If she refused to stroll in public to discuss their cousins, Mama would know there was a problem. But the public space he suggested provided privacy for them to discuss a subject for which she was unprepared.

"I don't see any problem with that," Mama pronounced. "You'll be right outside, so it shouldn't delay us."

With that Vicki felt the trap slam shut. He must have thought this out very carefully, taking advantage of his knowledge of her, her mother, and their complex relationship. How could she answer the questions he would ask? How would she respond to his words when her emotions boiled over? Mama stood up, picked up her purse, and turned to pay the bill. "We'll have to leave here around eleven thirty," she reminded them before strolling to the cashier.

"That was masterful," Vicki hissed quietly.

"I know your weaknesses, remember?" he smiled.

"Careful, I am my mother's daughter and am quite capable of making a scene," she warned.

"Easy tiger, I just want to talk," he laughed.

"Tiger? Isn't that what Joe called you last night?" she reminded him.

"That didn't have much of an effect did it?"

"Not the warning to slow down," she teased.

"No it didn't, but it did bring out some heartfelt words," he insisted.

"Slow down tiger," she laughed wryly. "Let's get outside."

Vicki stood up and marched toward the hotel entrance. She did not slow down until they were outside on the marble stairs.

"First, I owe you an apology," A-hong admitted. "I kind of jumped you last night without warning."

Vicki chortled at this. "That's an understatement. Did you realize the implications of what you were saying?"

"Yes, I did," he admitted. "It may have sounded sudden, but it's been building since Rutgers."

Vicki chuckled nervously. "You made that clear to all and sundry last night."

They were moving down the stairs slowly toward the arch, a casual pace for a not so casual exchange. She looked up at the sky and sighed in an attempt to dissipate her anxiety. The words traded so far were controlled and unsurprising. An admission on his part that he realized it would not work would have helped, but that thought brought up strong feelings of disappointment.

"I meant everything I said last night," he told her. "It was well thought out and had been practiced in my head for the past year or two."

Vicki felt her internal battle intensify. Here was the man she measured all other men by expressing his love and she could not respond as she wished. If this were a Greek myth, the gods would be laughing. She needed time to sort through her options, time to see if she could build a case for her father, time to see if she could calm his mother's fears. How could he not see that?

"I will leave everything behind and build a life with you Victoria," he stated. "Our parents will eventually come around when they see how happy we are."

Would the two of them be happy after hurting their families? Vicki wondered. She could easily envision a scenario where something tragic happened before a reconciliation, embittering one or the other family, forever severing ties. That bitterness would permeate everything they touched and drive them apart. "You're describing a fantasy," she warned "Are you willing to alienate your mother? I'm not willing to give up my family."

"What about your personal happiness?"

"I don't know if I can be happy without my family," she admitted. "Can you be happy without yours?" The words of her mother rang clearly in her head. He was his mother's anchor. She was Mama's anchor. "It would kill our mothers. I'm just not that selfish."

These words did not appear to dampen his ardor. The determined look that had marked his face earlier returned. She was not making any headway.

"They would come around," he insisted. "We have a right to be happy."

"You didn't listen to a word I said." Vicki felt her emotions accelerate. Unsure how much longer she could control them, a desire to flee overwhelmed her. "No more words. I need time. It just won't work. Too much pain all around."

The feelings building inside were causing her to speak in a staccato manner, not a good sign.

"That's what you said last night," was his heated reply. "You don't have the courage to face the truth, so you just declare you don't want to talk about it."

"Truth?" she asked with shock. "Whose truth?"

"Tell me you don't love me and I'll leave," he pronounced again.

She stopped moving, frozen at the bottom of the stairs, faced with the same challenge put to her last night. The strength to shout out a denial of her love was still not there. It would be a life altering lie and she could not voice it.

"Just leave me alone!" she begged. "I have to think. And don't you follow me." She turned from him and ran, this time having the strength to hold her tears.

Chapter Twenty-eight

Where could she go? Vicki puzzled. Back to her hotel room? What if he followed her there? Imagining the scene that could play out in front of her mother drove that idea from her. How could the two of them serve A-zou this afternoon? Would he have the nerve to even show up? She felt her resolve weakening each time she debated him. Could she hold him at bay much longer? There were so many questions without clear answers and no one to go to for advice. As she passed through the lobby, Vicki decided the only possibility open to her was Joe. The guys had been late last night because they were talking. Remembering that reminded her about Joe's reaction to A-hong. Sue had been shocked, but her fiancé had not missed a beat.

Arriving at the elevator, a car was quickly summoned. She hopped in and began formulating questions. Joe worked with her father. Guys must talk about what was going on in their lives. Had Dad mentioned anything to Joe concerning A-hong? This thought pattern gave Vicki hope. Stepping out of the elevator with renewed purpose, she marched down the corridor to Joe's room and knocked on the door sharply, ignoring the do not disturb sign. The sound reverberated down the hall despite the thick carpet. A second series of knocks produced a groggy response.

"I'm coming," Joe mumbled. He cracked the door to see who it was.

"Are you alone?" Vicki asked.

"Yeah, Sue went home."

"Good, we need to talk."

"God, sometimes you women are frightening."

"What?" she responded totally confused.

"I've been expecting you, Sue warned me."

"Sue warned you," Vicki sighed. "What did she say?"

Her cousin opened the door and motioned for her to step in. He was a pathetic sight, cute but pathetic. Sue had her work cut out for her if she wanted to smooth out the rough edges. Joe stood sleepy eyed, bare chested, in bare feet, but at least wearing shorts. That was probably a concession to Sue's warning.

"She thought you would want to discuss last night's crazy performance."

"Smart girl," Vicki commented.

"Could you give me a minute to transition from sleep to reality?" Joe pleaded.

"Of course, I just have to meet my mother at eleven thirty," she informed him.

"And what time is it?" he asked while walking toward the bathroom.

"It's around ten."

"Be right with you." He closed the door while Vicki sat in a cushioned chair along the wall. The sound of a flushing toilet was followed by that of running water. She sat impatiently, struggling to collect her thoughts and pin point why she came to speak with Joe. The original plan had been to get a guy's point of view, but now she needed more. She needed her American family's point of view and

Joe was her only option. He stepped out and pulled on a shirt before throwing the bed cover over his sheets and dropping onto the edge of the bed.

"The main actor in last night's little drama showed up this morning while I was having breakfast with my mother," she began.

"And how did his leading lady react?"

"She was terrified at first," Vicki sighed. "But, always the gentleman, he schmoozed my mom and took me for a stroll down the stairs in front of the hotel."

"And what did Romeo have to say?"

"Joe! This is not a time for male levity," she scolded. "I'm in a bind and you know more about this than you're letting on."

"What do you mean by that?"

"When A-hong made his pronouncement last night, Sue was shocked," she pointed out. "You were not. What did the two of you talk about that made you late?"

A guilty smirk creased his face as she finished. It was all Vicki needed to confirm Joe knew what was on A-hong's mind the previous night. "Fess up cousin, I need information."

"First I'll point out that A-hong's words may have shocked you, but you really didn't look surprised," he told her. "In fact, for a moment, just a brief instant, you actually looked delighted."

"Delighted!?" She shot back. "How can you say that?"

"I call it the way I see it," Joe replied lazily. "Sue's mother is not the only one who sees an attraction. Why do you think your mother is so negative? According to my future mother-in-law, it wasn't always like this. Seems before A-hong's father passed, both your mothers tried to steer the two of you together, although apparently your mother began to cool to the idea before that."

"What?"

"That's what Sue said last night," Joe confessed. "A-zou is not the only one talking about the past."

Vicki's head was spinning. What was he talking about? "Steered us together?" she whispered. "How did they steer us together?"

"English," Joe stated bluntly. "You tutored him in English, right? When did that begin? That's when they decided you would make a great couple."

"But I taught him English my entire life," she insisted.

"Really? That's not what he said last night," Joe informed her. "Maybe we're discussing semantics. When did you stop teaching him and start tutoring him?"

With that Vicki began to review her past. She had always spoken some English with her cousins, but seriously teaching them had not begun until Sue entered an English speech contest when she was thirteen. A-hong had sat in on some of the practice sessions. After that Mama had suggested she teach him seriously. There were phone calls and intense lessons for both her cousins from that summer forward until he attended Rutgers. "A conspiracy so immense," she muttered. "What else did you talk about?"

"Who? A-hong and me?" he asked evasively. "Just guy stuff, he ignored my advice so it doesn't matter."

Guy stuff! That was a non-answer. Knowing she would get no further down that road, Vicki made a quick turn and headed in a different direction. "Guys talk, right?" she began tentatively, doubting she would get anything useful from her next question. "So did you and my dad ever discuss this subject?"

"Which subject?" was Joe's perplexed response.

"A-hong and me."

"No," Joe answered after a moment's consideration. "We've discussed A-hong; we've talked about you; but I don't think we ever spoke about the two of you together. It's not a subject that came up."

"Shit," she muttered. Men were all brain dead when it came to relationships.

"What are you looking for?" Joe probed.

"I'm trying to get an American male perspective on this."

"On you and A-hong?"

"Yes, my mother says my dad would flip if I became involved with my cousin," Vicki sighed in frustration.

"Why would he flip?"

"DNA is too close."

"She thinks he would oppose a consanguinous marriage?"

"Consaguin - - - marriage? Who said anything about marriage?" she snapped.

"Consangineous marriage, marrying your cousin. Yes they have a name for it, but that's what it all comes down to, isn't it?"

She paused knowing her response had been a reflex reaction. "Look, this trip has been really hard on me," she found herself admitting while struggling with an emotional swell. "There's been so much coming at me, all these long kept secrets, all these emotions, things I must have felt and denied for God only knows how long. I need someone not in the direct line of fire to bounce things off of."

Joe smiled at her the way he did when they were kids and she asked for his advice. "I'm here for you Vic," he reached out and touched her knee. "How can I help?"

She smiled, got hold of her feelings, and asked, "Do you think my father is really adamantly opposed to me becoming involved with A-hong?"

Her cousin thought for a moment and then answered slowly, "I don't see why he would be. You're not first cousins and even if you were, it's still legal in Jersey to marry your first cousin."

"What?" Vicki could not help but react to the last statement.

Joe laughed at her. "You didn't know that?"

"How would I know that?" she snapped back. "How do you know that anyway?"

"I had to write a paper on the subject."

"Where did you come up with that topic?" she quizzed.

"Well, I really didn't. A professor assigned it to me after I blew a midterm and requested something for extra credit," he explained.

"You blew a midterm?"

"Yes I did. A young woman from Taiwan came to visit just before the test. Midterms were supposed to be over, but this one was rescheduled and she couldn't reschedule her flight."

Vicki started laughing. Her super competitive, studious cousin had been distracted by Sue. "I'm disappointed in you, Joseph," she teased. "You let a woman draw your attention off of your goal."

"Not just any woman," he parried.

Vicki nodded her head to concede the point.

"Anyway, getting back to my story, the professor was from London, part of the Pashua community there. Seems there are a lot of marriages between cousins because they like to marry within their community. Apparently, he was looking for a little understanding of their customs. Never thought the research would be very useful in my life, but now you can benefit from it. People marry their cousins all over the world."

Vicki sat and digested this information. Were her parents aware of it? Was her father really against her being involved with A-hong? Joe broke into her thoughts with a provocative question.

"Do you think your mother might oppose it because of the distance it could put between the two of you?"

"Where did that come from?" Vicki asked in shock. It was not something she had ever thought about, but now that he had brought it up it was a legitimate question.

"Remember that comment Sue said her mother made last night?" Joe reminded her. "She said your mother began to lose enthusiasm even before A-hong's father died."

"So, you think my father is okay with it, but my mother is opposed?"

"No, no. I didn't say that," Joe chuckled. "Your dad and I never talk about your love life. I don't know how he feels about it. But there is evidence that your mother might be against it."

Vicki took this in and processed it carefully. If the problem was her mother's opposition, how would that change things? The two of them had fought incessantly over a myriad of subjects. Would this just be one more point of contention? If this man was the key to her happiness could Mama drop her resistance? Why was her mother against it? This discussion with Joe had given her information for a rational talk with her father. Was it possible to have such a discussion with her mother? Joe interrupted asking another challenging question.

"How do you feel about it?"

"What do you mean?"

"You may not have noticed," he pointed out. "But you can't seem to say you would be dating A-hong or seeing him or going out with him. You only use ambiguous terms like being involved with him. So what do you feel towards him?"

Joe always knew to ask the hard questions, Vicki thought. How could she answer honestly? It was a question she had been wrestling with since that dream.

"It's not that easy," she insisted. "I need time. Everything is coming together so quickly."

"Do you love him?"

"Of course I love him," she shot back with a feeling of déjà vu. "He's my cousin."

"So am I, feel the same way about the two of us?" he smiled knowingly.

Damn him, Vicki thought. He knew her too well. After the initial reaction, Vicki had to admit to herself the feelings were not the same. When she attempted to voice this answer, emotions welled up inside her. A quick sideways shake of the head was all she could produce. Joe sat quietly waiting for his cousin to regain composure.

"Thank you," she finally whispered. "You have given me a clearer way to look at this."

"What are your plans now?" he asked quietly.

"Go back to my room and confront my mother," she sighed. "I need her to answer questions. Then I have to speak with my dad." She stood up and walked to the door filled with dread. How to begin a conversation with Mama about why she opposed her involvement with A-hong and not have it turn into a confrontation? No answer came to her before reaching the hotel room door two floors below.

When Vicki stepped into the room, her mother appeared agitated.

"A-zou is in the hospital," Mama blurted out. "*Jiujiu* said she is weak but coherent and wants us to visit her so she can finish her story."

Chapter Twenty-nine

The two women passed through the lobby without Mama greeting a soul. Vicki had not said a word since being informed of A-zou's condition. When they stepped out into the sauna that was a Taipei summer, the doorman waved to the first taxi of the usual queue of cabs that served the hotel patrons. They slid into the back seat of the car silently.

"MacKay Hospital," Mama told the driver before retreating into her thoughts.

Vicki had so many questions darting through her mind. The most paramount concerned A-zou, but she saw no need to ask them, doubting her mother could give an informed answer. While the cab negotiated traffic, she reviewed the past five days. Thoughts of the all but forgotten Roger flashed through her mind. One reason for accompanying Mama was to forget him. She had certainly done that. Along the way a hidden part of herself had been found. That was a gift from A-zou. Her great-grandmother might be resigned to her fate, but Vicki was not ready to let her go.

The cab pulled up to the main entrance of MacKay Memorial Hospital. They stepped out of it, still having not exchanged a word. Mama paid the driver and marched into the building, her daughter following closely. A large bronze mural depicting Dr. MacKay treating patients in a farming village greeted them as they passed through the lobby. Apparently her mother had the information she needed to find A-zou. They did not stop to check-in with anyone.

Vicki dutifully followed Mama through white air conditioned halls to the elevators, the pungent smell of disinfectant permeating the air. After stepping out of the elevator, they slowed down to get their bearings then her mother launched herself down the corridor and turned into a room.

Vicki walked into a crowded room. Two hospital beds were pushed against one of the whitewashed cinderblock walls. The first bed was occupied by a middle aged woman who appeared to be resting comfortably. Her family surrounded the bed while a white curtain provided separation from the rest of the space.

As Vick stepped past the curtain, she saw A-zou lying in bed with an I V tube going into her arm. A-hong was leaning over her holding a cup as she drank through a straw. When he placed the cup on a small table next to the bed, Vicki noticed an envelope. Was this the envelope A-hong had retrieved yesterday? A-ma and Mei-zhi *A-yi* sat quietly along the wall on the far side of the bed. A-hong's mother caught her eye and quickly turned away. There was no peace between him and his mother. Seeing A-hong gave Vicki a surprising feeling of wholeness. She had crossed a bridge and entered a new land. Finally at peace with herself, the next challenge was to convert the mothers. She was certain the key to that was lying in bed.

"Good, you are here," A-zou said weakly. "Now we can finish."

"A-ma, you should rest," *A-yi* instructed, unaware of A-zou's determination to be heard.

"No," A-zou responded feistily. "It is important that I finish my story."

"Wait until tomorrow when you feel better, Mama," A-ma suggested.

"You can say I will be here tomorrow?" she snapped back gaining strength with each word. "I will explain; I will reveal; I will have peace."

They saw the futility of any further discussion and settled down to listen. A-zou turned to Vicki and asked a question. A-hong translated, "Did you bring your pen and paper?"

Vicki smiled and shook her head yes, thrilled at the energy her great-grandmother had shown. She pulled out her pad and stood at the foot of the bed since there were no open seats. A-zou began to speak as soon as her great-granddaughter was ready.

"If what I am about to tell you upsets anyone I apologize," she began ominously. "I hope you will stay and listen until I finish explaining. I had several miscarriages during the early years of my marriage."

****

"She will not be a *sim-pua,*" Chiu Bu insisted weakly. The baby had been a son! She quickly pushed these thoughts out of her mind. There was no need to torture herself. It was not meant to be. Instead she focused on her husband's proposal.

"We have no son for such an arrangement," Ma Lu reminded her.

"But if she leads in a son?"

"She will be our daughter."

Chiu Bu lay quietly, thinking about this proposed adoption. Her husband's business associate thought they might be interested in a *sim-pua* for their expected son. Everyone said the child would be a boy just from the way she was carrying it. She had opposed the arrangement vehemently, remembering her own experience. The thought of raising an adopted child was also abhorrent. Even though her adopted parents had treated her as their own, she had always felt outside her family. But this miscarriage had happen so quickly there had been no time to call the midwife. The only ones who knew were Ma Lu and herself. If they were to adopt a daughter without the child ever knowing the truth, they would have to do it now.

"I will only agree as long as no one tells her she is adopted," Chiu Bu negotiated.

Her husband paused, thinking if this would be possible. "The Lins are in Ping-dong," he reasoned out loud. "The child was born last week. I can go to bring it back. We will have to register it as adopted. No one can see those records, so you need only stay indoors until I return. Then we can tell your mother that we have a daughter and she can come to help for *man yue*. That is what everyone will know in Xingang."

His wife shook her head in agreement. Ma Lu gently lifted the body of his dead son and carried him out to bury him. Chiu Bu remained behind sobbing.

****

Silence reigned around her bed as A-zou quietly mourned the loss of her son seventy years before. A-ma was visibly shaken, tears streamed down her cheeks. Mama stood stiffly. At first A-hong looked like someone had slapped his face. This expression gradually

---
351

faded as the implication of what A-zou had revealed sank in. Men were so dull sometimes, Vicki thought. The meaning of A-zou's confession was instantaneous to her. She and A-hong were not blood relatives! Glancing at her mother, it was obvious she had had the same realization.

"At first I called her Bong Chie to remind myself that there was a need for a son," A-zou explained. "Then it just became a nickname the child was accustomed to."

"I don't believe you," Mama blurted out.

"The household registry is there," A-zou said pointing to the envelope.

"How could you?" A-ma hissed.

"What would telling anyone have accomplished?" she sighed. "I loved her as my own."

A-hong stopped translating after this. Everyone in the room became quiet and looked at Vicki and A-hong. All understood what was said except Vicki. A-zou finally snapped a sentence that reminded A-hong of his job.

"She said if not for the two of us, my grandmother would have remained her biological daughter," he finished.

"Who will care for you if A-hong leaves?" Mama blurted out.

A-hong appeared ready to reassure her, but A-zou reacted too quickly.

"*Ah-yo*, do you think I will live forever?" she laughed. "He has to finish his dissertation; he has to graduate; he has to find a job. I will not live to see that. When I die I want to know I did not stop what heaven has ordained. Only they can stop it."

With that pronouncement she grew silent. At first A-ma appeared livid, but as the minutes passed and she worked through her mother's revelations, calmness crept into her mannerisms. A-hong's mother appeared shell shocked while her son seemed torn. Vicki knew he was dealing with the same contradictory emotions she felt. A-zou had removed a major objection to the two of them becoming a couple, but it came with a price. Their great-grandmother would need to pass away before that could happen. Looking at Mama told Vicki there were still battles to be fought.

The morning's revelation had drained A-zou. She drifted off to sleep as her family worked through the meaning of what she had said. Vicki and A-hong exchanged glances, not wanting to hazard more. Mama leaned toward her daughter and whispered, "We have to talk."

We have to talk? Vicki thought. That was the understatement of a lifetime. A-ma showed no inclination to leave. She spoke with A-hong's mother quietly, who then walked over to the envelope, picked it up gingerly, and carried it back to her seat. Mama stepped over to join them as they perused its contents. With their mothers preoccupied, Vicki and A-hong looked at each other. He glanced over at his mother then mouthed "I love you." After confirming Mama remained focus on the envelope's contents Vicki mouthed "later." A-hong shook his head yes and reverted his focused to A-zou, where it remained until his mother gave out a mournful groan before standing up and walking out of the room. Mama quickly followed. A-ma motioned for A-hong and Vicki to come to her.

When they reached her, she handed the paper to A-hong and said something in Taiwanese.

"She wants me to read this to you," he told Vicki.

"What is it?"

"A household registry for Xingang," he answered while looking at the sheet of paper.

She looked down and saw a paper covered with boxes containing Chinese characters. A-hong began to point at the different boxes and explain. "This is A-zou's name. These characters say she is illiterate, literally doesn't recognize characters. These are the names of A-zou's biological parents and these are her children."

Vicki had to trust in him completely. The characters could have said anything. She recognized so few and understood nothing of their meaning in this context.

"No, couldn't be," A-hong said to himself.

"What?"

"This is my grandmother," he pointed. "These are her birth parents. I'm almost positive they are Sue's great-grandparents."

"You can't be serious," Vicki laughed. "That means Sue is still your cousin?"

"Yeah, but from the Lin side of my family," he chuckled.

"That woman," A-ma muttered, pulling their attention away from the family registry. She raised her hand and pointed at her mother. "That woman and her secrets, I spent my life with her secrets. So much that could not be said, so much hidden away. I always thought Li-an was different. Why did she look like the Lins in Ping-dong? Why was my mother so opposed to A-hong's father dating Sue's mother? The secrets must have eaten away at her soul."

The last sentence ended with a quiet sob. Vicki stood mesmerized as A-hong finished his translation. Her grandmother seemed so conflicted. Angry at A-zou's lies. Sympathetic with what those lies cost. How did A-ma feel about her and A-hong. Vicki did not dare ask.

"It is good that Li-an never knew," A-ma whispered in Mandarin. "In that way A-zou was correct. Whether or not revealing this now is good will depend on the two of you. But you must remember your mothers are frightened. It is not easy to have your child live thousands of miles away, to only see them for a short period each year."

Mama came back into the room as A-ma finished. "A-hong, your mother would like to speak with you," she informed him softly. The she turned to Vicki. "Come A-hui, we should let A-zou rest."

Vicki shook her head in agreement, sensing a tired sadness in her mother's voice. As they left the room, she turned for one last look of A-zou, wondering how much longer her great-grandmother could hold on, silently thanking her for revealing her secrets, thanking her for reliving her pain.

Vicki sat with her mother in the rear seat of a taxi heading back to the hotel. How should she start what might be one of the most important conversations of her life? Seeking neutral ground as a beginning point, she fell back on the curious transformation of her cousins' relationship.

"So, from what A-hong read to me he and Sue are still biological cousins, right?" she posited.

"I don't think this is the place to discuss it," Mama opined, effectively shutting down the conversation before it could begin. This left Vicki's mind wandering among possible reactions the mothers might have to the evolving situation. Nothing is her mother's expression or demeanor suggested acceptance or at least resignation. Every indication pointed to Wei Jia-yi handling this fabricated crisis in her usual manner, angry manipulation.

They made their way through the lobby in the same manner as they had left. Vicki was sure the hotel staff would be talking about the uncharacteristic silence of Wei Jia-yi. She marched behind her mother who was doing a quick step toward the elevators. Seeing Mama so quiet was eerie. As they rode the elevator up and made their way down the hallway, Vicki could feel the pressure of an expected explosion build. Exhausted from the emotional upheavals of the past days, she did not think she had the strength to control herself if the situation became a confrontation.

After unlocking the door, Mama strode into their room and collapsed in a chair. Vicki gently closed the door and tried to read her mother who had suddenly become an enigma. There were no signs of the anticipated fury so characteristic of Wei Jia-yi. Instead a look of contemplation rested on her facial features.

"Come, we have to talk," Mama invited, patting the cushion of the chair next to her.

Vicki sat, astonished by the calm demeanor of her mother and curious about what was next.

"Wu Mei-zhi lived next door to me in Tai-dong. It was her father who distracted A-gong the night he drove A-ma into that pole. We often ran to their house when my father drank," she sighed to her daughter. "Jia-luan *A-yi* may have been like a second mother to me, but Mei-zhi *A-yi* was like a sister. She was my confidant, my best friend. We were inseparable as children. Often she came to Ping-dong during the summer. There we laughed, played, ran around, and just enjoyed being away from Tai-dong. A-zou introduced her to A-hong's father. It wasn't until today that I understood why she encouraged him and discouraged my brother."

Vicki listened intently, trying to sort through the bloodlines involved. She knew Sue's mother was a Lin. From what A-hong had pointed out on the household registry, his grandmother was from the same family. If A-hong's dad had married Sue's mom it would have been a marriage between first cousins. Would that have been legal in Taiwan back then? No wonder A-zou imposed herself into their love lives. Her little subterfuge would have blown up if she had not.

"Mei-zhi was taken by A-hong's father from the time they met. They seemed to be meant for each other. When he died, I thought she would follow. Instead she put all her energy into A-hong, but her spirit was diminished. Then he returned from America and *A-yi* saw the change in him. She knew he was in love. When she called me about it, we both agreed that you were his interest."

"But the two of you did everything to encourage us when we were younger," Vicki reminded her mother. "How could you think you could stop the attraction once it started? I've spent years denying my feelings because of you!"

Mama looked at Vicki with pleading eyes. "Then his father died. She is a lost soul without him. Can't you leave him be?"

Vicki was stunned by what she heard. "Leave him be?" she whispered. She could no longer just sit and listen. Standing up abruptly, she began to pace the floor in front of Mama. Struggling to come to grips with what was said. Her voice gained strength as she comprehended the implications of her mother's monologue. "It was all a lie, wasn't it? Dad's opposition to me being with A-hong is bullshit."

"A white lie to protect you," Mama confessed. "In the long run, it would end badly. Both of you would be unhappy."

"How can you say that? You don't know," she snapped. "Didn't you see the truth would eventually come out?"

"If A-hong found someone else before that then he would be happy and his mother would be happy," her mother insisted. "If you could see how desperate she is, how helpless she looks, you wouldn't be this selfish."

Vicki knew her mother too well. The supreme manipulator was waging an all-out campaign. Her only concern was what she wanted. What happened to a mother's concern for her child?

"What about my happiness?" Vicki hissed, struggling to control the anger building inside her.

"What about mine?"

"Yours?" was the shocked reply.

"Where will you live?" Mama shot back. "Will you run from me the way I ran from my father? You don't have to run from me."

With that question, Vicki instantaneously understood her mother. It was not just about the fears of Mei-zhi *A-yi*. It was about Mama's fears as well. Before she could respond her mother continued. "I have seen your power over men," she claimed.

"What? My what over men?" Vicki laughed incredulously. "Are you crazy? What, do you think I'm some sort of beauty queen? You and dad have it all wrong. I'm just your average girl."

"I know you can find another man. There are so many who find you attractive at home. Why move here, so far away?"

"What is with you? It's not the nineteenth century. We can go between here and the States."

"But will you?" Mama wondered forlornly.

"Yes, I want to see my father," Vicki responded. With that she knew her limit had been reached. If she stayed any longer it would turn ugly quickly. "I'm going out," she snapped then turned, stomped to the door, and walked out.

Chapter Thirty

In her anger, Vicki had not thought about where to go. She just knew to leave. Even though faced with the same puzzle as the night before, her mind was not as clouded. Today she had an alliance behind her, but how to get hold of them? Joe was probably meeting with a client. A-hong was with his mother, so that was out. Sue would be at work. Where was her office? Then Vicki remembered the card her cousin had given her. Thank God for the Asian penchant of exchanging business cards. She dug into her purse to retrieve what she needed. With a little luck, they could do lunch and talk.

A quick cab ride dropped her in front of the Good Fortune Trading Company. Vicki shook her head and chuckled. Talk about a cliché name. She stepped into the building and rode a tiny elevator up to the sixth floor. The door opened into a small office space filled with cardboard boxes of merchandise that surrounded several desks. There were no mahogany paneled offices with middle aged executive secretaries here. The walls were the standard concrete whitewashed variety with ceiling fans whirling above head. Glancing around the room, she spied Sue at a desk in the room's center.

A young man saw Vicki before Sue looked up. He approached her and asked in halting English, "Can help you?" Vicki smiled, resigned to the fact that she did not always look like someone who spoke Mandarin, and quietly replied in that language, "I'm Wei Su-hui's cousin. Would I be able to speak with her for a moment?"

"Ah-yo, you speak Chinese so fluently," the man gasped then turned toward Sue who was now on the phone. "Wei Xiao-jie, someone to see you."

When Sue looked up. Vicki saw a look of sadness pass over her face. Realizing that Sue might think A-zou had died, Vicki smiled and mouthed "lunch",

The anxiety washed off Sue's face. She smiled and held up her finger. Quickly completing her business on the phone, Sue picked up her purse, announced she was going to lunch, and jogged over to her cousin.

"What's going on?" she asked.

"You won't believe it," Vicki laughed. "Where's a place around here where we can have a quick lunch and talk privately?"

"Privately? That doesn't sound good," Sue commented.

"Oh no," Vicki laughed. "It's wonderful, but it's complicated. How much time do we have?"

"Technically, half an hour, but I can stretch it," Sue informed her. "They're understanding around here. Besides, I'll just work later to make up the time."

"Let's get it done quickly," Vicki insisted. "I might need you tonight."

They hopped onto the elevator. Vicki began explaining the morning before the door was closed.

"You are A-hong's cousin, but I am not."

"So my mother's observation was right," Sue pointed out "Your mother lost her enthusiasm first."

They were sitting in a small eatery down an alley a few blocks from Sue's office. The food was everyday fare, but there were four walls enclosing the dining area and the cliental were working stiffs who had little chance of speaking any English.

"That's the impression I got," Vicki replied sipping her tea. Lunch had been so rushed the brew was still hot. "But when she lost any enthusiasm she might have had is irrelevant. She seems dead set against A-hong now."

"She's not your only problem," Sue reminded her as she reached for her tea. "A-hong's mother is nervous and he's not going anywhere while A-zou needs him, but all of that isn't really important, is it?" She took a sip of tea and waited for Vicki to react.

"What do you mean? Of course it's important."

"Is it? How do you feel?" she asked with a smile, placing the tea cup on the table.

This pulled Vicki up short. The morning had been so filled with revelations and conflicts she had not had time to consider her own feelings. Sue sat quietly waiting with a knowing grin on her face.

"How do I feel?" she sighed. "Haven't thought about it. It's only been a few hours and I've been dealing with my mother."

Her cousin waited patiently for Vicki to continue. When she stopped volunteering information, Sue gave a gentle nudge. "Take the time now," she prodded. "What are your initial feelings?"

"I love him, but it's not that simple," Vicki anguished. "I haven't made the emotional shift from familial to romantic love."

Sue laughed when she heard this. "That dream you had says different," she reminded. "Your problem may be an intellectual shift, but it's definitely not an emotional one."

Vicki felt herself blush. "I should keep my mouth shut," she chided.

"Why, so you can keep lying to yourself and be miserable?" Sue asked. "How long do you think you need? He's looking for an answer. From the way he talks, it's either you or he becomes a monk."

"I don't believe that," Vicki laughed nervously.

"That doesn't matter. What I'm saying is it's up to you," she reassured her. "He's ready whenever you are."

Vicki felt overwhelmed with confusion. Too much was happening too quickly. "He's ready for what?" she spurt out in an attempt to slow down.

"Ready for a commitment."

"A commitment?" she whispered. "Any idea where he is?"

"Probably at his uncle's."

"Where's that?"

After jotting down the address, Vicki quickly paid the bill and walked Sue back to her building. From there she took a taxi to the address her cousin had provided.

She found herself outside the building A-hong's uncle called home, her emotions no more settled than before. She was in the enviable situation of having known the man she loved her entire life. Why was she so afraid to walk in and talk with him? Where could that lead? Maybe they should not stay here to talk. The decision to invite him to Prince Albert's for a drink propelled her forward. It would be best to meet on neutral ground. Experience had taught her intimate conversations in private quarters usually resulted in intimate contact. She needed a controlled burn today. With that thought, her resolve hardened. She stepped purposefully into the building and climbed to the third floor.

Waiting for a moment in front of the door to catch her, breathe, Vicki marveled at the security door in front of her. So this was how the successful people of Taiwan lived. Stainless steel doors with traditional Chinese landscapes etched in. The floor was covered with white marble as were the walls. The hall was actually air conditioned. She could have used the elevator if her preoccupation had not hidden it. Drawing in one last breathe, Vicki reached for the doorbell, pressed it, and waited. Was he even here? Was his mother here with him? She came close to bolting at that thought. The sound of the door being unlocked held her feet to the floor. An exhausted A-hong appeared when the door swung open.

"Vicki," he sighed with relief. "Come on in."

"How about we go to Prince Albert's for a drink instead?" she suggested.

"Prince Albert's?" he smiled. "Let me get the keys to this place."

Vicki stepped through the door held by A-hong and into the cool air of the Prince Albert. They had been very reticent on the drive over, exchanging smiles, but reserving their thoughts for the pub. A-hong followed behind, allowing the door to ease shut. After her eyes adjusted to the pub lighting, Vicki glanced around. Nikki's mother was striding over with a wide grin.

"You two look like such a nice couple," she gushed. "Is your mother also coming?" she asked Vicki.

"No, it's just the two of us today," Vicki smiled back. She suddenly found herself at a loss for words, unsure if A-hong had eaten lunch. Should they ask for a table or just hang at the bar? She looked at him to see if he would provide any guidance. Picking up on her indecision, A-hong chimed in.

"Hello Mrs. Salisbury, could we have a table for two?"

"Of course A-hong, this way. Nikki will be thrilled to see the two of you. Today she's only served business men. No one to talk to," with that she ambled off in the direction of the dining area. Vicki and A-hong exchanged glances and chuckled before following.

Nikki strolled out of the back as they settled in. The forlorn look on her face vanished instantly, replaced by a warm smile. She hopped over to their table.

"Look at the two of you," she squealed. "All by yourselves, is that how your day played out or is something more sinister afoot?"

Vicki laughed at the way their friend put it. "Sinister?" she countered. "What could be sinister about us stopping in to see you?"

"No mum accompanying you dear," the waitress pointed out. "No cousins, just the two of you. I don't think that's happened before. Is that significant?"

The restaurant was empty, allowing them time for banter. Vicki saw this could be a double edged sword. Lively chatter always lifted her heart, but the purpose of the rendezvous was a private exchange between herself and A-hong.

"It could be significant," A-hong laughed. "We got some new info from our A-zou that kind of changes things."

"Changes things?" Nikki asked, her curiosity piqued.

"Yes," Vicki smiled. "We're not really blood relatives. Our A-zou adopted his grandmother."

"No!" Nikki laughed. "That opens up some interesting possibilities, now doesn't it?"

"Yes it does," A-hong agreed while looking at Vicki. She watched his stare and smiled.

"Looks like the two of you have a lot to discuss," Nikki observed. "How about I take your order and scoot out of the way?"

As she went to place the order, the waitress seemed more excited about those possibilities than either A-hong or Vicki.

"She's a diehard romantic, isn't she?" Vicki commented. A-hong smiled as he played with the fork in front of him.

"Yes, she is. That must be the English in her. Americans appear to be more practical."

This comment took Vicki off guard. "What do you mean by that?" she quizzed with feinted offense.

"Oh, nothing really," he quipped. "Just that you Americans seem to do more calculating in matters of the heart. Where the Brits have no problem marrying their cousins, at least Victoria and Albert didn't."

She was tempted to call him a wise ass, but knew she had to concede the point. He had been ready to sacrifice all for love. Was that not what romance was all about? Nikki had encouraged her to do the same, but she did not have the nerve. Was that being too practical or was it simply realistic? She thought the latter and drove her point home with a reminder.

"That is not the only problem we face."

"No, it's not," he sighed. "I've been dealing with the other aspects since we left A-zou."

"So have I," Vicki commiserated. "What was your mom's reaction?"

A-hong became quiet, struggling with his own internal conflict. His answer began in a slow, thoughtful cadence and gradually gained strength.

"My mother? At first she was angry. Angry at A-zou for what she did, angry at me for helping reveal this secret by translating, angry at you for making me fall in love. That one was a bit of a stretch, but she's scared. After the anger passed she began to cry and accused me of wanting to abandon her. From there she began reminding me of all she has done for me, how I wouldn't be where I am today if it wasn't for her sacrifices. Like I didn't work to get into college. I didn't study. It sounded like she did it all. Then she lamented her effort to steer me toward you before my dad died. Oh, if only he hadn't died, life would be perfect. It got pretty bad toward the end. I had to leave to avoid exploding. How does that English expression go about being careful what you ask for?"

Vicki had sat quietly, trying to maintain a neutral posture, biting her tongue when he said his mother was angry with her for making A-hong fall in love. She knew better than to encourage his anger. It would pass, but any harsh words towards his mother would not. His question pulled her out of neutral. She was determined to move cautiously.

"You mean 'Be careful what you wish for, you might just get it?'" she replied.

"That's it," he laughed with irony. "It's obvious now that she spent years wishing for this. Did everything she could to manipulate us into falling in love. Now she can't stop the train she started."

"She actually said she was pissed off at me because I made you fall in love?" she asked unable to contain the question.

"Yeah, she did," A-hong laughed. "She wasn't in on the whole make a fool out of myself pursuing you while you beat back my every attempt."

Vicki laughed. Being caught between two women might have driven him to become a monk. Remembering her conversation with Joe, she decided to give a little encouragement.

"You never know," she chuckled. "It's possible you would have won the lady's heart even if we were cousins."

Nikki came back with their drinks as he laughed at this. The waitress scampered away without a word, giving A-hong the space for a reply. "You think after considering all your options you would have chosen me?" he asked. "That was a very spirited defense to give before a complete capitulation."

"Let's just say it was a lot of bluster, but my defenses were fading rapidly," she confessed.

This was followed by quiet as they enjoyed their peaceful interlude. The restaurant remained deserted. Vicki noticed Nikki and her mother chatting by the bar, their gazes fixated on the drama playing out between the two cousins.

"So now what?" she asked ending their respite from reality. He had painted her as a practical American, so she decided to act the part. "We've caved in to emotions. Now we have to make practical decisions."

"Where to from here? That's the lady's decision. I already made my desires clear," A-hong reminded her.

"Are you dodging the question or making a point?"

"You haven't given me a response to what I said last night."

"I said it was possible you could have won my heart even if we were cousins, right?" she countered partly to play with him and partly to build up the nerve to vocalize her feelings.

"It sounds like you are the one dodging a question," he laughed.

"We are not cousins, so your victory is a given."

A-hong chuckled and relented, not wanting to dally on the point when they had so much more to discuss. "So your question is back with me. Where to go from here? You heard what A-zou said," he moved on. "I have to finish my dissertation, graduate, and find a job. But it's more than that. There's A-zou and our mothers. What about your dad? Any idea where he stands?"

Vicki sipped her drink and gave his question renewed consideration. Where did her father stand? With all Mama had confessed, she felt confident to reply, ""My father is only interested in his daughter's happiness," she stated. "All the DNA questions were simply my mother's manipulative bullshit."

"That sounds rather harsh," he pointed out.

"Like I said, it's been a rough morning," she sighed.

Nikki approached them cautiously with A-hong's meal, clearing her throat to give warning. A-hong held his reply while the meal was placed in front of him.

"You two seem to be making progress," she chirped. "Call me if you need anything." With that she bounced away, giving A-hong time for a question before beginning his meal.

"How rough was it?" he asked while reaching for his fork.

For an instant Vicki hesitated, not wanting to relive those emotions, then plunged in. He needed a true assessment of the situation.

"My mother is a manipulative bitch," she hissed unintentionally. "Who is only interested in herself and what she wants. Tried to convince me that I should leave you to your mother, let you connect with a nice Taiwanese girl so you wouldn't fly away. Then she tells me she doesn't want me to fly away, that she lives for me!"

A middle aged couple came into the restaurant as she finished her statement. Mrs. Salisbury quickly stepped up and led the two to a table on the other side of the room. Nikki stepped up to take their order, glancing over her shoulder to judge the distance. Apparently happy that Vicki and A-hong still had privacy, the waitress turned on her cheerful, bubbly self, quickly bringing smiles to her patrons' faces.

"Our mothers seem to be cut from the same cloth," A-hong observed between bites. "How easy do you think it will be to convince them they will not be happy unless we are happy?"

Vicki laughed at the question. "You are an optimist to the end," she accused. "What makes you think we will be able to achieve such a monumental task?"

"You, my lady, are a jaded pessimist," he counted after sipping his drink. "I am sure they will come around. Their initial reaction is based on irrational fear. When they have time to consider it, they'll see A-zou is right."

"You really think they can be swayed by A-zou's view that it is predestined?" she scoffed.

"Don't underestimate the influence of traditional views on those two. They remain a product of the environment they grew up in. Deep down there are still bad omens and hungry ghosts lurking in their sub-consciences."

Vicki doubted her mother would be influenced by superstition on this issue. Tradition was not going to do it. This would be a modern argument filled with emotions and unspoken fears. "I don't think you have a handle on my mother's mind set yet," she told him. "I have never seen that woman admit she was wrong in my life. If the facts proved otherwise she simply changed the subject or refused to take responsibility for her error. It was always someone else's fault she got it wrong. You can't reason with her. The last thing we talked about this morning was flying and how it wouldn't take that long to travel between here and the States. You know how she reacted to that? She asked if I would go home to see her."

A-hong was taken off guard by this. "And did you reassure her you would?"

"Yeah, I told her I would because I want to see my father."

"Ouch. How to win friends and influence people."

"I was angry," she confessed. "She won't take that seriously. That's just how females fight."

He finished the last of his lunch, unwilling to comment on her assessment of women fighting. Vicki sipped her drink and wondered if it were possible to change her mother's mind. Thinking back on the argument, she could see A-hong was right. The resistance of Mama was based on fear. If anyone could calm her, it would be the man sitting across the table. This realization made him that much more attractive.

"So, the challenges ahead of us are to reassure our mothers and come up with a plan to care for A-zou," A-hong said thoughtfully. "That is if the lady decides to give a direct answer to my proposition."

Vicki giggled at his persistence. She had felt her perspective gradually shift as they talked. He was no longer her cousin. Now, he was fair game. The concern for his mother and A-zou he had shown only made him more attractive. What a good father he would make. She quickly put aside those thoughts. You're getting too far ahead of yourself, she cautioned. Slow down and take one step at a time. He wanted an answer to his proposition.

"If I remember correctly, you made clear a desire to spend the rest of your life with me," she reminded him. "That might be an awfully long period of time. You sure of this?"

"Yes, Miss Phaff, absolutely certain."

"Then we have our work cut out for us," she smiled. "Because I would like nothing more than to do that. We just have to convince some recalcitrant women that it would be for the best. Why don't we go back to your uncle's place and plan our campaign?" She suggested as she finished the last of her drink.

It amazed her how quickly her cousin had changed into a delicious entre waiting for her to enjoy. When they got back to his uncle's, Vicki intended to take a page out of her mother's play book. It would be an easy seduction and a binding one, not that there was any doubt in her mind. A-zou saw it all along, *qian shi de guan xi,* just payment for a debt from their previous lives.

Chapter Thirty-one

His uncle was definitely an artist and a neat one on top of that, Vicki thought. There were no boxes containing items waiting for a decision on disposal here. They were lying in bed as if time had stood still. This is what poems and songs were written about. Her head rested easily on his chest. She could hear his heart beating; the steady rhythm produced a sense of security and wholeness. They had finally arrived at their destination, resting after the release of pent up emotions that had been denied too long.

Scanning the tasteful décor of her surroundings, Vicki wondered if A-hong had inherited any of the talent revealed by it. So far he had not shown any hint of an artistic bend, but when had he had an opportunity? His life had been spent under the watchful eye of an overbearing mother. His room at Rutgers had been neat and without any obvious décor flaws. Remembering Joe's dorm room at Pace University, Vicki saw this as a good sign.

"So, you're sure your uncle decorated this place by himself?" she asked.

"Yes, by the time he moved here my aunt had passed away," A-hong assured her. "He's a bit of a perfectionist, so won't tolerate anyone else's interference."

"I assume he designs his own jewelry," she speculated.

"Of course, and it has the same influences you see around here."

This would be easy to live with, she thought. It was a fusion of East and West that avoided the gaudiness that sometimes surfaces in both traditions. Tasteful, understated, yet elegant in a masculine way was how she would describe it. The work of art breathing next to her made everything perfect. It was like a dream, but the realization that they would soon wake up to a less than ideal reality kept her alert.

"When does uncle come back?" she wondered.

"In a week," he sighed. "Do you think we can just hide here until he comes back? There's food in the fridge and no need for you to worry about changing clothes."

"And why wouldn't I have to worry about clothes?"

"No need to wear any," he laughed.

She slapped him playfully on the chest. "Don't you wish, but we have A-zou to worry about."

"Among other things," he sighed. "How long do you think we can hold the world at bay?"

"Does anyone but Sue know you're here?"

"Yes, they all know."

"Then we'll have to be ready to jump out of bed, throw some clothes on, slide down a brass pole, and respond to some sort of fire shortly," she warned.

With that they both sighed and relaxed, enjoying their short respite from the small drama swirling just outside the apartment door. The phone rang a few minutes later. A-hong picked it up.

"Wei, yes Sue she's right here," he chuckled then had to hold the phone away from his ear. Vicki heard her cousin's squeal loud and clear. The reserved Asian woman was dead, she thought. Sue's temperament had moved from quiet, respectful Chinese daughter right past practical American girl to hot Latin woman. The speed of the metamorphosis was astonishing.

After the squeal, Sue began rattling off instructions to A-hong who could only get in an occasional "okay". Nothing in his mannerisms implied A-zou's condition had worsened, so Vicki let one worry slide off her plate. When he hung up the phone, A-hong had a serious look on his face.

"Sue said we've been summoned back to the hospital," he began. "A-zou is doing great. The doctor said it was dehydration coupled with exhaustion. She'll be released tomorrow. But she insists everyone go back for a family meeting."

Vicki thought about this and instantly saw the advantage of a family conference in A-zou's hospital room. If anything would keep a lid on the melodrama it would be the fear of losing face from a severe meltdown. She might be ninety-five, but A-zou was still sharp as a tack.

"Who will be there and when are we supposed to arrive?" she queried.

"Not sure who, the way Sue was talking it sounded like she would be there and I got the feeling her father was coming," he informed her. "Our mothers and A-ma. I doubt Sue would encourage Joe to come. That would be too risky."

Vicki took this in quietly. If her uncle showed up, would that be a plus or a minus for their cause? After a quick assessment, she concluded he would be the voice of reason in the room. After all, he was not objecting to the possibility of his daughter living in the States.

"Jiu-jiu would be good, I think," she opined. "He'll keep a lid on the drama. So, when are we expected?"

"Now," was the curt reply.

They hopped out of bed in unison, with Vicki robbing a few seconds to straighten up. Her pride would not allow for his uncle returning unexpectedly and finding a disheveled bed. They threw their clothes on, enjoying A-hong's help with her bra equally, and ran out the door. Both were quiet until seated in the back of a cab. A-hong leaned forward and told the driver Mackay Hospital, then sank back into the seat.

The cab eased into rush hour traffic and accelerated smoothly. Vicki gazed out the window mindlessly, so lost in her thoughts she did not notice the scooters and taxis streaming past.

"How do you intend to handle your mom?" she asked without turning away from the window. Her aunt was going to be the major worry tonight. If his mother somehow pressured or swayed A-hong to recant his profession of love Vicki would be crushed. Could she ever recover from such a blow? The evening was shaping up to be an intense competition between the dreams of two women. She loved her aunt dearly, but had no intention of losing. How could she bolster his will to ensure the survival of their newly born dream? Even as this thought flashed through her mind, Vicki knew there were major problems on her side. Could she persuade her mother? Was she reading her father correctly? Feeling completely overwhelmed, she leaned forward and dropped her head into the palms of her hands. The crash from the afternoon's high was too much.

A-hong reached over and rubbed her back. "Don't worry, we'll get through this," he reassured her. "I'm just going to continue talking with my mother until she vents all her fears. She hasn't said one thing that I haven't been able to give a rational answer to. In the end, she'll relent. All mothers want their children to be happy, don't they?"

Vicki raised her head. She now understood how Sue felt just before Joe asked for her hand, exposed, emotionally naked before all creation. "Remember what I told you at Prince Albert's?" she snapped unintentionally. "She's a manipulative bitch only interested in what she wants."

A-hong chuckled wryly. "I remember. What if she wants you to be happy?"

She snorted at this. "That's not the impression she gave me. I wish I had Dad to talk to."

"Why? How do you think he would answer?"

"Sometimes I think he would agree other times I have these nagging doubts."

"We all have to make up our minds at some point to either live the life we choose or the one chosen for us, don't we. In traditional societies it was the life chosen, in modern times we should get to choose, no? Go with your feelings on this one, he wants you to be happy."

"I suppose. I'm definitely not letting my mother choose for me that's for damn sure," she stated before relaxing a little. "I think I'll go with the conveniently modern guy on this one."

"Conveniently modern?" he laughed in mock surprise. She joined him in his mirth.

Traffic slowed to a crawl. They eased up to a light and came to a stop as it turned red. The driver said something to A-hong in Taiwanese which brought a smile to his face. He replied in kind, but before the driver could continue the conversation a teenage boy speeding on a scooter attempted to turn in front of them. He wiped out, sliding to a stop alongside the cab ending with a shocked look on his face, but no apparent serious injuries other than a severely bruised ego. The driver opened his window, leaned out, and scolded the teenager as the light changed. He then accelerated and began a rant in Taiwanese obviously directed at the boy.

After a few blocks, he calmed down and drew in a deep breathe. A grin replaced his frown while he asked A-hong another question. Vicki sat quietly, resigned to being the obvious subject of two males without understanding a word they were saying. She felt an easy comfort with the idea that the driver felt a need to speak with and maybe even advise A-hong on matters pertaining to her. Of course, her assumption was based on the appearance it was a positive exchange. Hopefully, it was not too bawdy. A-hong chuckled at the driver's query before he replied. The response drew a short comment from the cabbie, who then chuckled to himself and fell silent. They pulled up to the hospital in short order where A-hong received one more bit of advice when he paid the fare. Vicki stepped out onto the sidewalk, determined to have her man reveal what all the chuckling was about. The cab pulled away, melding into the traffic flow as the couple walked toward the hospital entrance.

"That seemed like an interesting conversation," Vicki began.

"Yeah, nice guy," A-hong replied, dodging the subject.

"So, what were you two talking about?"

"Oh, he commented on the waywardness of today's youth," he stonewalled. "How they're so spoiled and so wild."

Vicki chuckled to herself for a moment then turned to him and smiled. "You're full of shit," she told him cheerfully.

His reaction was to burst out laughing. "Jersey girls are tough," he muttered while shaking his head. "So, yes there was another subject that came up, but you might find it embarrassing."

"Why, did you discuss sexual techniques or something?"

A-hong turned a delicious shade of red. "Vic, please, nothing like that ever came up. He was just wondering if we were a couple. Then he commented on how beautiful you were and asked if you spoke Mandarin."

"He didn't ask about Taiwanese?" she asked.

He chortled. "Well, that was his first question."

"So, you were conspiring the whole time," she accused.

"Conspiring?" he reacted. "I think you're getting a little carried away."

"Did he approve of your choice for companionship?" she pushed, enjoying the defensive responses she was getting. He was so lovable when caught in embarrassing circumstances.

"He did; said I was the luckiest man in the world," A-hong bragged. "And I agreed with him."

Now it was Vicki's turn to feel embarrassed, but also content and a little proud. They passed through the entrance, turned toward the elevators, and made their way to A-zou's room.

"Remember, we don't want to push them too far too fast," A-hong advised. "Let them adjust to the idea. They were the first ones to have it after all. Reassurance and comfort are what they need. So keep the emotions in check. The end game is to walk out of here today with their acquiescence, real approval can wait until all the pieces fall into place and that wouldn't be for a while."

"I'll try if you will," Vicki sighed. "Just make sure we keep eye contact so you can give me a boost if I need it."

"How does Joe put it?" A-hong tried to remember. "Sounds like a plan, right?"

Vicki shook her head yes. They both instinctively stopped just outside the room. After looking each other in the eye for strength they stepped in.

As soon as they passed through the doorway, Vicki had misgivings. The second bed in the room was empty. A-zou's roommate had been released. A level of controlling the drama was gone. She could only hope that the presence of the nurses on the floor would keep a lid on the proceedings. At least now everyone would have a seat. The curtain dividing the room was still drawn, so she could not see A-zou. Sue was sitting with her father along the wall at the foot of the bed. Mama, A-ma, and Mei-zhi *A-yi* came into view as they passed the curtain.

Mama was leaning over A-zou, trying to get her to drink, but A-zou was having none of it. As soon as she saw her great-grandchildren, the old woman brightened up, brimming over with excitement. Mei-zhi turned to see them then immediately turned away, refusing to acknowledge their presence. A-zou rattled off something which drew A-hong's mother out of her momentary self-imposed isolation. First she snapped at A-zou then she turned and fired a broadside at her son. A-hong let her finish and then countered in a calm voice. His mother turned away again.

"You see what you have caused," Mama scolded. Before Vicki could react, A-hong stepped in.

"*A-yi* I am the one who pursued her," he confessed. "She did all she could to dissuade me."

"You are a man," Mama laughed derisively. "What do men know about the ways of women?"

A-zou interjected herself and took control of the situation with one sentence. Vicki was amazed at what a little water and some rest could do. Her feisty great-grandmother had returned. A-hong stepped behind the curtain divider and quickly returned with two chairs. He and Vicki took up positions at the foot of the bed. When they were settled A-zou began to speak. A-hong took up his duties as translator, but Vicki was now only a spectator.

"When A-hui was born in America, I insisted on having the day and hour of her birth," she began. "The Americans are so good at that.

Babies are born in hospitals there and the doctors record the exact minute they begin to cry. As soon as I heard she was a girl, I felt it necessary to match her numbers and sign with A-hong's."

"Yes, these numbers are good. When matched with the year and the elements, all are very good," the fortune teller informed Chiu Bu. "These are a boy's?"

"No, no," Chiu Bu replied, having purposely withheld that bit of information so she could get a more accurate assessment. "These are my great-granddaughter's. She was born in America."

"Oh, a girl and an American," the fortune teller clucked. "Such a strong destiny. She may have a hard time finding a husband."

"Could you compare her numbers to these?" Chiu Bu asked.

The fortune teller looked over the numbers and information quietly at first. "Hmm, these are the numbers of a boy?"

"Yes."

"Then your great-granddaughter is very fortunate. The numbers and elements go together well. They will make a strong couple. Has this family approached you already? It appears that they may owe each other a debt from a previous life."

"The boy is my great-grandson," she smiled.

"Ah, such a strong family line you have produced," he laughed. "Will the Americans agree to such a marriage?"

"I think they will," Chiu Bu muttered. "They are not first cousins and as you said the signs say it is their destiny."

She then paid the man for his troubles and walked out thinking of how she could influence the situation to help these two souls repay their debt.

As A-hong finished his translation, Vicki sat quietly, flabbergasted at what she had heard. It was downright spooky. Twenty-three years before, her great-grandmother had decided the two of them were destined to be a couple. What had even put the thought into her head? She was not the only one with that question. A-ma jumped into the pause. "How did you know that?"

A-zou sat quietly for a moment, a forlorn look coming to her face. "When my son died at birth, I noted his numbers," she answered. "These were matched with Bong-chie's when she came into our home. I knew those numbers showed that a debt existed between the families."

"But Wei Shan-ji and Lin Jian joined the families," A-ma insisted.

"No they didn't. Their numbers weren't strong enough," A-zou informed them. "The debt would be paid in A-hong's generation. They are destined to bring happiness to both families as they join their lives."

Vicki could hold her questions in no longer. "My number?" she blurted out. "What numbers?"

A-hong asked A-zou. "They used a form of divination called *ba zi*, eight characters. The hour, day, month, and year each of us was born are used to determine our destiny. That was combined with the

Chinese astrological calendar to see if we were a good match. Seems we are."

Mama jumped in to throw a question at A-zou. "You consulted a fortune teller when A-hui was born?"

A-zou chuckled, obviously finding it surprising her granddaughter would ask such a question. "Of course I did, and when A-hong was born and when Shan-ji married. I knew my son's soul was restless and needed a home. It will finally find one with these two."

"How do you know?" Mei-zhi asked.

"I know because I know," she laughed. "It is their destiny. The only way they will be happy. The only way heaven will be content. You were not opposed when I pointed it out when they were children."

Mei-zhi sat quietly for a moment then muttered. "It was different then. Now I will be alone."

A-hong said something quietly to his mother, but this only caused her to turn away.

"Why resist what heaven ordained?" A-zou asked.

"Heaven ordained?" Mei-zhi snapped. "Heaven ordained that I be unhappy?"

"You have ordained that you will be unhappy," A-zou told her. "This is not 1920. They have not told you my story? It is I who was ordained to be unhappy until the two of them came. I will tell you this. If you do not accept them, they will be miserable and your life will be filled with regret until the day you die. Choosing poorly for your child never leaves you. I know that from experience." She glanced at A-ma after saying this.

Mei-zhi grew quiet, still visibly upset, but Vicki felt maybe something of what A-zou had said had reached her aunt. Looking at her mother, she knew it had not affected Mama's point of view.

"You are trying to abandon me," Mama bit in English.

It was just like her to remove everyone who would contest what she said from the conversation by speaking English, Vicki thought. It would be a matching of their wits, maybe with some help from A-hong and Sue. To her surprise, *Jiu-jiu* answered the accusation.

"*Mei-mei*, that is unfair. She does not want to abandon you. She wants to find happiness like all of us," he told her in Mandarin. "It is the happiness of your child that should most concern you. If she is not happy, you will not be happy."

What *Jiu-jiu* said pulled A-ma into the fray. "You have forgotten where you live?" A-ma reminded.

"Yes, and I remember why I live there," Mama cried before turning away.

Vicki saw Mama's defenses were weakening. The fear she was exhibiting somehow made her seem small and vulnerable. Vicki had never seen her mother like this, so human, so alone. There was no fire left in the two of them. This was a seminal moment for their relationship. Nothing would be the same after today. Either Mama would have to accept them as a couple or she would distance herself from her daughter. The very thought broke Vicki's heart, but the time had come for her to stand and be recognized as the arbiter of her own destiny. How to reason with a passionate woman already overcome with emotions?

"Mama, I'm not abandoning you," she began. "There is time to adjust. He has to finish his dissertation. I have to choose whether to continue my studies or work. We have to get used to being a couple. I have so many decisions to make no matter what happens. Your daughter has grown up, but you're still my mom. I can't trade you in for another model." She chuckled at the absurdity of her last sentence. Thankfully her mother joined her.

A-hong spoke to his mother quietly in Taiwanese. She responded in an accepting manner and then said something that made her son smile.

"She's trying to accept it," he told Vicki. "The last thing she said was we might just find out we don't really like each other."

"Highly unlikely," Mama added.

The small drama seemed to have played itself out with that. Acquiescence was the best they could do, but that was more than Vicki had thought would be accomplished. The only one who seemed unaffected by the sudden shift in generational relationships was A-zou. She sat contently in her bed looking very self-satisfied. When the room went quiet, she began to speak in her usual feisty manner.

"A-hui is here for a few more weeks," she reminded. "Let them get to know each other on a different level and we will see if heaven has really ordained this or it's just a silly old woman's dream."

Chapter Thirty-two

Vicki waited with her father outside the restrooms in the arrival hall of Chiang Kai-shek International Airport. She could not help but recall the magic of those three weeks in the summer when she had A-hong to herself. After staying at his uncle's, they had roamed the island looking for the locations of the tales A-zou and A-ma had told. Her family history was fleshed out beyond any reasonable expectation. Their relationship had grown just as quickly, although both were not the least bit surprised. A-zou had planned it out well, even if their mothers had gotten cold feet in the end. Vicki chose to accept the traditional view this once. It was a debt from a previous life.

The memories gave her the strength she would need by the end of this day. They were watching the carry-ons and Mama's purse while she went to the ladies' room. The pit stop gave the two a few minutes to talk without deferring to her mother. Ed Phaff waited patiently for his daughter to unload her concerns. They were standing along a wall away from the streams of people rushing to collect their luggage and go through customs. Vicki noted how different the air felt from the last time she was here. It was winter now. Although the air was still humid, it had lost its oppressive power. Now the weather would have a bone chilling dampness to it which reminded her of a rainy day in early spring back home. The dull hum of hundreds of people in transit would keep any conversation between father and daughter confidential.

"Mom thinks I shouldn't speak with Mei-zhi *A-yi*," she told him.

Ed Phaff laughed to himself. "I thought you said A-hong had brought his mother around to the idea."

"That's what he said, but now that we're here I'm having doubts," she confessed.

"You are you're mother's daughter," he sighed. "I think you're being overly pessimistic. Mei-zhi *A-yi* is nervous, but she's also thrilled. One of the biggest worries a Chinese mother has is her son marrying a woman she can't stand. You are a made to order bride. It wasn't that long ago she was conspiring to hook the two of you up."

She grew quiet after this, considering her father's reasoning. *A-yi* did come to the States for Joe and Sue's wedding. She had traveled alone because A-hong had to care for A-zou. It was disappointing that he had missed the wedding, but an unspoken benefit was his mother had gained the experience of traveling alone. That should have boosted her confidence and lessened the anxiety of her son settling in the States. But remembering the wedding only made her more anxious.

"She conspired before her husband died," she reminded him. "I think I have a right to be nervous. She didn't speak to me or even approach me at the wedding."

"A-hong has been speaking with her since then," he reassured her. "She's had time to adjust."

His reassurance rang hollow. It was easy for others to be confident everything would work out. It was her future on the line. Now that her feelings for A-hong were acknowledged, being separated from him was hard. There had been an almost physical ache inside all these months, even with the phone conversations. What if her aunt refused to budge? How open was A-hong to breaking with his mother until she relented to their relationship? So many questions and A-zou was no longer around to put the squash on her grandchildren's resistance. Did she have the reserve to ask her father about Mama's comments to him? Wei Jia-yi was as unpredictable as ever. What her mother told Vicki was not necessarily what she told her husband.

"Has Mom said anything to you about how she feels?"

"You haven't asked her?"

"Yes, but that doesn't mean she told me what she told you," Vicki sighed while keeping an eye on the ladies' room exit. A squabble over doubts and fears was to be avoided. They were here to say good-bye to A-zou, not to persuade the mothers into accepting what was now the inevitable.

"What your mother expressed to me was that she couldn't ask for a better son-in-law," her father told her, sticking to the party line. "I believe her when she says that, if for no other reason than it's true. She also was concerned with how often she will see you. When I pointed out that it would be an issue no matter who you married, she had a rather negative reaction and dropped the conversation. So, for what it's worth, she loves A-hong, but is nervous that you will follow her example and vanish from your mother's life."

His answer did not lessen her anxiety. Would Mama become an emotional wreck as soon as she saw *A*-yi and A-hong? At least they were taking the shuttle to the Grand Hotel. That would give time to recuperate from the flight. A little rest would go a long way to keeping a lid on things. It was five thirty in the morning. By the time they collected their luggage and passed through customs it would be anywhere from six thirty to seven o'clock. Mama had said a shuttle would leave at six forty-five. Hopefully, they would be on that one. Exhaustion should keep their conversation to a minimum giving less chance for Vicki to say something stupid. Mother and daughter were both upset about A-zou's passing. Poor Dad had been treading gingerly around his women's emotions for the past few days. No explosion yet, but they were just entering the most volatile period. Grief and exhaustion made for a witch's brew of suppressed feeling just waiting for an outlet. Mama came out of the exit doorway as Vicki finished this assessment. Their short interlude of calm was over. The general was back on the field.

Mama marched over. "What were you discussing?" she quizzed.

"The weather," Vicki lied. "When do you think we should pull out the jackets?"

"Oh, later, later, we have to get our luggage and get through customs," Mama stated the obvious.

Dad passed the purse to his wife. They each grabbed a handle to a carry-on and began the trek to baggage claim. All Vicki had gotten from the conversation was her father's opinion. He was an extreme optimist, a trait that would be expected of anyone married to Wei Jia-yi.

"When we get to luggage claim, Ed you stay up front by the carousel," Mama directed, beginning her usual orchestration.. "Vicki, you stay just behind him. I'll wait with the carry-ons. After he pulls the luggage out, you pass them back to me."

Nothing was left to chance or memory when they were in stressful situations such as collecting luggage. Every time Mama would assign roles to each of them. Vicki had asked her father once why he did not comment on this aspect of his wife's personality. His response was he knew that verbalizing her worries gave her comfort. After those years as a stewardess, she felt a certain degree of competency in this area. They reached baggage claim as the alarm went off announcing luggage was coming up. Red lights began spinning and the belt that carried the luggage started to move. Vicki could see the bags begin to climb out of the opening in the middle of the machine and slide onto the belt.

Since they had checked in early, their baggage would probably be one of the last out. She settled in for a long wait and took in her surroundings. The sign above this carousel announced that the pieces emerging from below were from their flight. The people standing around all looked familiar, confirming they were at the right location. The pieces being dropped onto the belt were an odd assortment. What was it about flights to Asia that produced such a strange array of baggage? Among the standard Samsonite type bag were strewn cardboard boxes, odd shaped packages, and heavy plastic bags tied tightly with thin nylon rope. Everyone waited vigilantly at the edge of the machine eying the bags moving past. When someone recognized what they had checked in, their arm would dart out much like a frog's tongue catching a passing insect. In one quick motion they would grab the handle of the piece and swing it up and out onto the floor next to them. All knew to give room to the person pulling the bag out. As a child the natural choreography of the situation had fascinated Vicki. Now it was just a given of modern life. The dance of luggage retrieval which was performed countless times every day at airports around the world. She found herself comforted by the familiarity of it, appreciating it at this moment because it occupied her mind, diverting it from her concerns.

"Ed, that's ours," Mama called. Her father quickly swung the piece Mama had pointed out. It looked like their wait would be shorter than Vicki had expected. Was that good or bad? Sighing, she realized that in the end it would make no difference. Easy or hard, their fate had been sealed. The outcome would not be affected by a few extra minutes waiting for luggage. She stepped up to her father, grabbed the piece from him, and dragged it back to Mama. In this assembly line fashion, they claimed what was theirs and began the walk to customs, each pulling a large luggage and a carry-on.

"You have the forms ready, Jia-yi?" Dad asked. Another given when they traveled as a family was the assignment of paperwork. When arriving in Taiwan, Mama took on the responsibility of customs forms. It was Dad's duty when they returned home. She wondered how Joe and Sue would divide up the chore. How about her and A-hong? It was one of the myriad tiny questions to be sorted out when they merged their lives. But that was for another time. Today was for sorting out the process that would lead to that merger and she was sure it would come to a head shortly.

As they approached customs, another question slapped her. Passengers were to divide themselves into those with foreign passports and those with Taiwanese passports. When the two of them traveled, they would have to go through customs separately. What of travel to other countries? Was he required to have a visa to enter European countries? An American passport did not need a visa to so many countries around the world which made travel so much more convenient. It was one of the reasons Mama had obtained her citizenship as soon as she could. Would A-hong do the same? They would have to settle in the States for that to happen. Had he spoken with his mother about it? It was another reason to be nervous about a possible confrontation between the generations.

They rolled up to the customs station as a family. While waiting it struck Vicki that it might be the last time with this categorization. If things worked out as she hoped, she would move on to the next stage of life and form her own family. Remembering the stories she had recorded over the summer, she appreciated how the world had changed for the better. The murmur of travelers waiting in queues behind yellow lines for the customs officers to wave them forward surrounded her. Mama and Dad were quiet as they inched toward the line and their turn. Vicki wished she could guess what was going through her mother's mind. Judging by mannerisms, she could tell Mama was deep in thought and nervous about something. That something certainly dealt with her daughter, but that daughter could not pin down where her mother stood and Mama had not shown any inclination to share.

When their turn to speak with customs arrived, Mama marched up to the window, dropped her passport, and began to speak in Taiwanese. The officer looked over at them, shook his head, and waved Mama through. Dad stepped up next and passed through after a quick review of his documents. The officer motioned for Vicki. He reviewed her passport, stamped it, handed it back, and then said he was sorry to hear of her loss. She thanked him and walked out, dragging her luggage and carry-on behind her. The family reunited in front of the door where the shuttle would pick them up. Dad nodded his head, pushed the door open, and stepped out of the customs area into the main terminal. After a few steps, he pulled up short. Standing just ahead of him was A-hong and his mother.

When Vicki saw A-hong her heart skipped a beat. This was totally unexpected. At no time in their conversations over the past week had he even hinted they would meet at the airport. Her aunt had a broad smile on her face, but tears in her eyes. His smile was just as broad. In his hands were two roses held tightly together at the base of their stems.

Mama pushed past her husband and walked up to her childhood friend. They embraced, laughed, and agreed to something Mama said. Vicki wanted to run up to A-hong, squeal, and jumped into his arms, but thought better of it. Instead she left her luggage with her father and walked up to him.

"What is holding the flowers together?" she asked coyly.

"A question," he smiled. "You know what it is. What is your answer Ms, Phaff?"

"A-zou said it was a debt from a previous life, right?"

"But isn't that traditional superstition?"

"We have to hold onto some traditions right?"

"Does that mean you won't answer unless I get on my knees?"

"No, the answer is yes Mr. Liu, providing you put a ring on my finger."

"You know where the ring is, don't you?"

Vicki held out her hand. As A-hong slid the ring onto her finger, she said a silent prayer to A-zou thanking her for this greatest gift. Hopefully, she would spend the rest of her life happily repaying the debt that brought them together.

www.ingramcontent.com/pod-product-compliance
Lightning Source LLC
Chambersburg PA
CBHW030031030726
47500CB00001B/47